Robyn Lee Burrows was born and raised in the north-western New South Wales township of Bourke, but has since settled in the Gold Coast hinterland. She is a Scorpio, born with the moon in Pisces, and describes herself as independent, emotional and creative. She is married with three sons, two of whom refuse to grow up and leave home, and custodian of two cats and a dog. In her meagre portion of spare time, she enjoys watching good movies, dining out and, naturally, reading. *Tea-tree Passage* is her fifth novel, and eighth book. To find out more about Robyn and her books, feel free to visit her website at www.robynleeburrows.com.

ALSO BY ROBYN LEE BURROWS

TEA-TREE PASSAGE

Robyn Lee Burrows

HarperCollins*Publishers*

HarperCollins_Publishers_

First published in Australia in 2001
by HarperCollins*Publishers* Pty Limited
ABN 36 009 913 517
A member of the HarperCollins*Publishers* (Australia) Pty Limited Group
www.harpercollins.com.au

HarperCollins_Publishers_
25 Ryde Road, Pymble, Sydney NSW 2073, Australia
31 View Road, Glenfield, Auckland 10, New Zealand
77–85 Fulham Palace Road, London W6 8JB, United Kingdom
Hazelton Lanes, 55 Avenue Road, Suite 2900, Toronto, Ontario, M5R 3L2
and 1995 Markham Road, Scarborough, Ontario, M1B 5M8, Canada
10 East 53rd Street, New York NY 10022, USA

National Library of Australia Cataloguing-in-publication data:

Burrows, Robyn, 1953– .
   Tea-tree passage.
   ISBN 0 7322 6880 X.
   I. Title.
A823.3

Cover illustration by Lloyd Foye
Designed by Darian Causby, HarperCollins Design Studio
Typeset in 10.5/13 Sabon by HarperCollins Design Studio
Printed and bound in Australia by Griffin Press on 80gsm Bulky Book Ivory

5 4 3 2 1   01 02 03 04

For Dale,
who comes to know my characters well,
and whose creativity and generosity of spirit
never ceases to amaze me

Coastal tea-tree *n.* otherwise known as *Leptospermum laevigatum*. Bushy trees growing to six metres. Found in sandy coastal areas along Australia's east coast. Salt-and-wind resistant. Used as windbreaks and also to stabilise sand movement. The bark is stringy, the grey-green foliage is fine and dense. White flowers — each containing five petals — appear in spring or early summer. The residue from the flower develops into a seed capsule after fertilisation. The botanical name — *Leptospermum* — is derived from the Greek *leptos*, meaning 'slender' and *sperma*, meaning 'seed'.

CONTENTS

PART ONE

Homecomings

Tea-tree Passage, Queensland

1919

CHAPTER 1

'Nina?'

The name wove towards her through the hot still air. To her right, the screen door wheezed open and she jerked to a halt, hands poised over the lump of dough she was kneading on the kitchen table. Confused, she stared in the direction of the voice.

Outlined within the framework, the shape dark against the glare, stood the figure of a man. He was tall and lean with square-set shoulders. The hat on his head was turned up at the brim. A slouch hat, Nina realised, suddenly aware of pale light glinting off the rising sun badge. A momentary bewilderment skimmed her awareness. A soldier? Here in Tea-tree Passage? The war was over, had been for ten long months.

The voice wove towards her again. Scarcely audible. Strangely familiar.

'Nina. I'm home.'

Frank! Oh, my God! It's Frank!

The realisation sifted oddly through her consciousness like leaves. Leaves the colour of mulberries. Wafting. Settling. Falling in layers upon the hard dry core of her. For one impossibly long moment she couldn't speak, couldn't move. Her legs were heavy, like lead. They refused to function and she simply halted, overwhelmed by the unexpected sight of him. Disjointed thoughts slid against her awareness. Why hadn't he written, let her know he was coming? She would have gladly gone into town and met him at the station, not let him come home like this.

Without thinking, her hands came up to straighten her hair. Then, remembering the flour, she let them flutter back to her side. Only seconds had passed since he'd said that first word, but it seemed like months, years. An eternity of time. And all the while he stood by the door watching her, waiting, as though unsure what to say himself.

'Frank,' she pronounced at last, her voice thick, as though from years of disuse. Then: *'Oh, Frank!'*

The shock had made her light-headed and she put out a hand to steady herself. The room spun. Tears blurred her vision, walls and floor merging for a moment into a smudged kaleidoscope of colour. She knew she should go to him, greet him in some as-yet unknown way, but the kitchen seemed miles wide, a vast expanse of table and chairs and linoleum separating them.

'I've missed you, Nina,' he said simply and, unbidden, the tears fell, tracking a course down her cheeks.

As though sensing her distress, he moved towards her with a purposeful stride. They came together beside the kitchen table, laughing, crying. Frank, this

4

stranger who was her husband, let the door slam shut with a loud bang and scooped her into his arms.

She was aware of inconsequential details: the rasp of his unshaven cheeks as his mouth moved over her own, the smell of tobacco, the stiffness of his khaki shirt — new, she realised with surprise — and a distant scream of gulls from the direction of the sea wall.

'Frank! I never thought —'

He pressed a finger momentarily to her lips and the words were lost. 'Hush. I'm here now. There's time enough for talk later.'

As his arms wrapped her in a tight embrace, a slow sigh escaped Nina's mouth. It was so long since she had been held. She swayed against him, savouring the moment. There had been times during the past years when she had wondered if she would ever see him again, would ever be enclosed in those same arms. So many men hadn't come home.

When at last she pulled away, Nina was dismayed to see her own floury handprints outlined against the khaki of Frank's coat. 'Oh, dear,' she pronounced as she tried to brush them away. 'Look what I've done.'

'Leave it,' he replied, grabbing her hands, holding her wrists to his mouth. 'I've been through worse.'

He stared at her with sudden intensity, an eager yet uncertain look, as he dipped his eyes and smiled. She met his gaze, studying that now-unfamiliar face — the smooth flat planes of his cheeks, aquiline nose, hooded eyes — and sensed a momentary shock. This was not the same Frank whose image had been captured on that single photograph she had treasured through those long years of separation. This Frank was older, war-weary. Small lines creased the corners of his eyes and mouth. A sprinkling of grey hairs lined his temple. There was a leanness to his face and a spareness to his body she had not remembered. And she saw, her attention drawn back to his eyes, a disconcerting emptiness she was at a loss to explain.

Yet again, time seemed suspended, caught between the various floundering layers of her own self. In her mind the differing separate images of him scattered on top of each other, causing her to draw her breath. Small unconnected fragments. Here an eye. There a nose, mouth. She sensed a wash of concern, almost maternal. A concern she might have lavished on her child, had there been one. Her mouth wavered into something she hoped resembled a smile.

Slowly Frank released one of her hands and moved his fingers down the curve of her cheek, all the while watching, watching. Their eyes were locked and she could not, for one awful moment, bear to look away. Perhaps she was dreaming. One blink, one glance elsewhere, might cause her to wake and the scene to unravel its threads about her.

His fingers were warm against her face and, unbidden, a memory shuddered through her. How many times had she prayed for this intimacy that had so long been denied? How many times, in the past four years, had she lain in bed at night, running her fingers over herself, imagining they were Frank's hands exploring her hot aching body? How many —

She stopped and snapped her head upwards, acknowledging the room and the man who evoked such familiarity. This was no dream. *Frank was home!*

The touching was like a spell, a familiar yet distant recollection, and her heart hammered away in her chest until she feared it likely to explode. Surely Frank could hear the pulse? His hand touched her breast, stroking and kneading at the nipple through the flimsy fabric of her dress. A slow heat built inside her, a giddying surge of desire that stirred in her belly and radiated outwards. *Four years*, she couldn't help thinking again. *It's been four years.*

His mouth trailed down, into that soft hollow at the base of her throat. Nina was aware, suddenly, of the ticking of the clock from the mantel over the stove. It sounded inordinately loud against the hushed stillness of the room. The clock, she thought, the idea random in her mind, was measuring out this homecoming, separating her thoughts, actions, into tiny compartments. *Tick! Tock! Tick! Tock!* Even the screech of the gulls had faded to some distant place, now unheard.

Frank's breath was warm on her skin. A sigh escaped his mouth, magnified unbearably. 'Christ, I've missed you! Missed *this*.'

He left no doubt as to the meaning of his words.

There was a sound behind them, a swish of skirt and a discreet cough. Face suddenly suffused with colour, Nina pulled away. Frank's mother stood in the doorway. 'You've come home,' she said, matter-of-factly.

'Mother.'

He went to her, giving her a quick hug and a respectful kiss on the cheek. Nina, watching, thought the older woman's body seemed stiff as she bent towards her son.

'You'll be wanting a cuppa, I expect,' Frank's mother went on, her voice flat and devoid of any emotion.

Nina glanced at her husband. *Something's wrong*, she thought, imagining her own reaction to a son's return after an absence of years. Had there been some family quarrel of which she was unaware?

Perhaps it is because of me?

The idea jangled back, taking her breath. She had always shared an uneasy alliance with Frank's parents since they'd taken her into their home after Frank joined up. 'So silly to keep a place going just for one,' Frank's mother had said, thrifty as usual, leaving her no valid option.

Nina closed her eyes and breathed deeply. When she opened them again, she could see the older woman had taken a pot from the cupboard and had begun, methodically, ladling in spoonfuls of tea. Her expression was stern, her mouth was pulled into a tight uncompromising line.

The kettle whistled on the stove, emitting a narrow swirl of steam. Behind his mother's back, Frank gave Nina an uncertain smile. He sat at the table, folding his long legs under the chair. His hands splayed out in front of him, bony, large-knuckled. The thought occurred to Nina that he looked uncomfortable there, out of place, as though he didn't belong.

Pushing back the thought, she took the cake tin from the pantry. There was, she knew, a sponge roll inside, made fresh the day before. Carefully she cut three slices, one larger than the other, and put them on separate plates. The biggest slice she placed before her husband.

We are strangers, she realised with certain clarity as she struggled to remember those first few weeks of married life before Frank had gone away to war. It had been a hasty marriage, too hasty, some had said. Nina knew they had waited, those long-ago critics, as the months passed, to see if she were carrying a child, a reason for such expedience. But they had been wrong.

She smiled to herself now, remembering, as Frank's mother slammed the pot of tea on the table, bringing her back to the present.

'You should have let us know you were coming. We would have gone into town and met the train.' His mother's words echoed Nina's previous thoughts. But, unlike her own, they were half-hearted, and had a recriminatory tone to them.

Nina poured Frank's tea. His fingers, as he took the cup from her, trembled slightly, and the cup rattled ominously against the saucer until he steadied it with his other hand.

'Where's Dad?' he asked, setting the saucer on the table.

Frank's mother inclined her head in the direction of the sea wall. 'Taken the boat out.'

'It's going along okay, then?'

'No use complaining.'

'Plenty of fish?'

'They're about,' she replied tersely.

The abrupt little phrases jerked at Nina. Perfunctory words. Mechanical replies. There was a heaviness about them, an inexplicable poundage, and she felt flattened by the weight. It seemed they were skirting some larger issue, mother and son, but the essence of it alluded her. She noted the small frown of confusion on her husband's brow and glanced sharply at her mother-in-law. *Leave him*, she wanted to say. *He has been through enough.*

But Frank's mother was staring through the screen door, towards the direction of the water. And when she said the words, they were so soft, so distant, that Nina wondered if she had imagined them.

'It's hard to think that Bill's not coming back.'

William, Frank's brother. Killed at Pozières in 1916. Bill, whose framed photographs clustered, shrine-like, on the top of the piano in the parlour. Bill as a baby in a white christening dress, then as a sturdy young man riding a horse, or on the deck of the boat. Bill looking rakish in khaki, his hat askew, smiling diffidently into the lens of the camera. Bill who had followed Frank to war, saying, despite his mother's protestations, 'I can't let my young brother upstage me, now can I?'

Bill — the favourite of the family.

Nina stared at Frank. His face was flushed and he blinked so rapidly that his eyelids seemed to be working overtime. Open. Shut. Open. Pale lashes fluttered against reddened cheeks. She fought back an impulse to lay a cool hand against them, to still the movement. Then her thoughts slammed to a halt, concentrating on one detail only.

It was at that precise moment that she knew. Knew what Frank's mother was thinking. Knew with shocking certainty the reason for the abruptness, the lack of warmth. Knew the God-awful truth. *The wrong son had returned.*

The realisation jolted her. She threw her head up, willing it not to be true. She felt a bubble of nausea growing, nibbling at her stomach, and a sense of shame that she was witness to all that had happened in that room during the past few minutes. Desperately she wanted to say something, wanted to scream at Frank's mother, to cry out at the injustice of it all. But she turned away, suddenly fearful. To voice her thoughts, she knew, would unleash and lay bare her dreadful knowledge.

I cannot say the words, she told herself. *Cannot! Cannot! Cannot!*

Instead, she ground her teeth against her tongue until she could taste blood, and the sharp sudden pain blotted out the need. Bending her head over the pot of tea, she arranged the remaining two cups and watched as the steaming liquid descended into pale china.

Frank will not suffer from this, she reassured herself. *He will not suffer.* Somehow she would take the remnants of their marriage and make them whole again. Together they'd build a new life, she and Frank, a safe haven. And, in time, there'd be children, children born of love and need and desire, not from any misdirected sense of duty or obligation. Children who would be *equally* loved.

She swallowed hard and raised her head, staring defiantly at Frank's mother. 'Here's to Frank's safe return,' she said, lifting her cup of tea towards her husband in salute.

After the banalities of tea and cake and halting forced conversation were dispensed with, Frank's mother made a great show of attending to the preparation of the bread, which Nina had long since abandoned. It was impossible, Nina thought, to set her mind to such a mundane task. There was a holiday feel to the air, a need to suspend those rigid timetables. Instead, she excused herself from the table and walked with her husband towards the sea wall.

There was no breeze, the air as lifeless and sluggish as before a storm. It was almost midday and the sun cast vertical shadows underneath the tea-trees that lined the track. To Nina, even the shadows seemed hot — dark steamy recesses below the delicate leaves. A small trickle of perspiration traversed the length of her spine, and she imagined it causing a wet discolouration on her loose shift, somewhere below her waistline. Frank held her hand and she felt his fingers warm against her own, which were inexplicably cold.

They passed the ramshackle buildings, fishermen's huts mostly, that constituted the small community that had sprung up, over the past fifty years or so, above the sea wall. Washing hung limply on clothes lines. The occasional dog ran, barking, from behind a front fence. The Melvilles, the Sharps and the O'Reillys had been there for years, almost as long as the Carmodys.

From the second last cottage came a surprised greeting. 'Blow me down! If it isn't young Frank Carmody!'

Mrs Melville teetered towards them down the front path on varicosed legs, beaming broadly. 'Your dad'll be pleased to see you back!' she exclaimed, holding Frank's hand for what seemed like a long time. 'He's been missing the help with the boat, what with you and Bill gone.'

Then her eyes clouded as she remembered Frank's brother, and her own boys. 'Ah, well,' she added. 'Lots of good families are missing sons.' And she turned away, overcome in some way by the remembrances.

They passed John and Maudie's cottage, which looked empty, the shutters like closed eyelids in a blank face. John was Frank's uncle, his father's brother. 'They're away on holidays,' Nina explained. 'Gone to the city.'

'To the city?' asked Frank with a grin. 'John hates it there.'

'It's been a good season on the boats and he promised Maudie a shopping trip to make up for all the time he's been at sea. They'll be back in a few days.'

'Broke as usual. I suppose nothing's changed there.'

Nina nodded. It was the same for most of the families at the Passage. Hard work. Hard lives. Money too easily spent. There seemed no need to save, to put something aside. Live for today, wasn't that what John often said?

The philosophy of the other inhabitants often seemed at odds with Frank's parents. To Nina, the elder Carmodys appeared frugal to the point of obsession. 'Waste not, want not,' was Frank's mother's favourite saying. And his father! Backbreaking hours spent mending the nets, hunched over the continual holes and rips in the rotten rope, whereas the only place the wretched thing was fit for was the fire.

At the water's edge, shielding her eyes with one hand, Nina scanned the rocky promontory that constituted the sea wall. A trawler worked its way towards them, a bright dab of red against the blue water. It was the *Sea-spray* and, even from this distance, she could make out the figure of Frank's father at the wheel, guiding the boat homewards.

At last the boat docked alongside the pier. Frank leapt onto the deck and threw out the mooring rope, looping it over the bollard. The action seemed to come naturally, Nina thought, watching as the cable played out, coiling through the heat-heavy air. She thought also that she would always remember that moment, that those images would somehow stay stamped indelibly on her mind. Frank's hands. The sound of the boat's wash against the paint-peeling wharf. The raw salt smell of the sea.

Deftly Frank wound the rope in and the boat drifted sideways, timber hull grinding. He disappeared into the cabin to greet his father and, suddenly, Nina felt loath to follow.

By the time they returned to the house, Frank's father in tow, the kitchen had been tidied and the table cleared. The aroma of baking met them.

'Lunch'll be a while,' said Frank's mother. 'The bread's not done.'

It was a barely disguised rebuke but Nina didn't care. Frank was home. The days to be spent in his parents' house were finite. Soon they'd have their own place. A neat little cottage in town, perhaps. In time things would settle, she reassured herself. Bill's death, Frank's return — all relegated to their proper perspective.

It was late, after ten o'clock that night, before Nina and Frank finally stole away. Bidding his parents goodnight, they walked arm-in-arm along the hallway to their room. It was small, the room, just large enough for the double bed, lowboy and dresser. A cane chair sat under the window. Frank's unopened suitcase stood alongside.

Earlier, while turning down the blanket, Nina had taken a pale pink nightgown from the bottom drawer of the dresser. It was draped across the bed and, as she went to retrieve it, Frank took it from her and whispered, 'You won't need that.'

She stared at the gossamer fabric held loosely in his large hands, the memory catching her unawares. She had worn it on their wedding night, on that long-ago evening when she had given herself to him for the first time. In her mind's eye she saw it all now, images wavering before her like one of the black-and-white movies they showed in the theatre in town.

Frank turned down the lamp until the flame flickered and died, and the room was enveloped in sudden darkness. Was it now or then? Nina asked herself, momentarily confused, unable to differentiate between the past and the present. It was as though that long-ago scene was replaying itself, and she felt disconnected, merely a tangled compilation of her own fragmented parts. Was she Nina the daughter, the child, or Nina the lover, the wife? But her parents had been dead for years and, along with Frank's absence, it was a long time since she had been any of these — child or lover.

Her eyes adjusted to the darkness and, in the pale light from a crescent moon, she made out the vague shapes of the furniture. Frank's fingers fumbled at her buttons and a sense of deja vu swamped her. She had been there before in that same room with the same man, doing these same things. Nothing had changed. The four years, between Frank's leaving and return, telescoped into insignificance, a mere eye blink. And perhaps, she thought, those lost years amounted to, in relation to the rest of her life, a mere hiccup in her existence.

Impatiently Frank pulled at Nina's clothes and his breath was warm against her ear. But the walls were paper-thin and she heard Frank's father mutter something indecipherable in the next room, and her mind slid sideways to the image of his parents readying themselves for bed.

Brassiere. Knickers. As Frank tossed the last of her clothing on the floor, he began tugging at his belt, his trousers. The springs creaked alarmingly as he pulled her onto the bed. Nina held her breath and waited for some sign, some noise from the older couple. She imagined them, Frank's parents, listening for illicit sounds, ears pressed to the wall, and stifled a laugh.

Frank's mouth covered her own with warm wet kisses but her mind was elsewhere, in that adjoining room. His hands groped insistently at the mass of dark hair below her belly. Fingers probed, kneading the skin. He levered her legs apart with his knee and his hardness pressed against her, insistently, until her body yielded. In response to the momentary pain, she stifled a sob.

Frank's hand clamped firm against her mouth.

'Sshh,' he said as he shuddered into her.

Pale moonlight bathed the room. Nina lay on her side, head propped in the palm of one hand and watched her husband. By the steady rhythm of his breathing and the regular rise and fall of his chest, she knew he slept. Yet that same sleep eluded her.

Events and images of the day drifted, intertwined and blurred in her tired mind. Her husband's unexpected arrival. Her own floury handprints on his uniform. Frank's mouth against her wrist, lips resting against that pale blue-veined skin. But layered over all that was the memory of Frank's mother staring through the screen door, towards the direction of the water.

It's hard to think that Bill's not coming back.

Restless thoughts projected themselves into the vague and formless future of her imagination. What would become of them, she and this stranger who was her husband? After all that had happened — the separation and those long, long years of war — how could they simply pick up their lives and continue? Her own existence had altered, she knew, realigned itself, shifted in some intricate way since she and Frank were last together. No longer was she emotionally reliant on anyone except herself. She had become self-contained; already she sensed that. So what was her position, her importance, in their relationship?

The questions remained unanswered, churning round and round like some out-of-control carousel until, eventually, they comprised the substance of an equally vague and formless dream.

Some time during the night, Nina woke to his cries. They were shrill and desperate, like an animal cornered. Instinctively her own heart beat a terrified tattoo in her chest.

'Hush,' she soothed, realising the cause to be nothing more than some bad dream. 'Just a silly nightmare. You're safe here.'

'Yes,' he replied, his voice tremulous and his breathing laboured. 'It was just a dream.'

A grumble of annoyance came from the room next door. Frank's body was wracked by an uncontrollable shaking, though it wasn't cold, and Nina folded her arms around him, hugging his bony chest. She stroked one finger along the ridge of his shoulder, tracing the outline of the clenched muscle.

'Hush,' she whispered again, clutching him tight. He was like a child, she thought, some part of him lost to her, lost perhaps even to himself. Tenderly she clasped his head against her breast until his breathing slowed and he relaxed once more.

CHAPTER 2

Weeks passed. Spring became summer. Christmas came and went. Suddenly it was a new year: 1920. Some days Nina found it hard to imagine life was ever different, and Frank's years away at war became a memory, nothing more. There were times when she could almost believe he had never been away at all, so unobtrusively had he slotted back into their lives.

In the house in Tea-tree Passage, she found the chores interminable. Scouring, baking, washing and ironing: the tasks ground endlessly. Stoically she bore Frank's mother's silent antagonism until she wondered if she might go mad with the strain of it. She felt smothered within those walls, like a guest, and an unwelcome one at that.

Of Frank, she saw little. He was gone at dawn with his father, down the front steps into the sunshine, en route to the collection of ramshackle jetties opposite the sea wall where the *Sea-spray* bobbed on the tide. Together the men took the boat past Turtle Island and the furthest visible line of breakers, beyond Nina's vision. They were endlessly busy, the two men. Fishing. Mending nets. Scrubbing the salt from the deck. Every day Frank came home to her, stinking of raw fish. She wrinkled her nose at him, shooing him to the bath.

Occasionally she walked down to the wharf and watched as they loaded the catch into boxes which, in turn, were stacked onto the back of the old lorry, to be taken to the Ice Works in town. They were shiny and silver, the fish, scales gleaming in that late afternoon light.

Sometimes, after the fish were unloaded, Frank and his father went to the pub in town. From the verandah Nina watched them leave, jolting down the track in the lorry. She stood, almost invisible in the shadows of a tumbling bougainvillea and wished she could accompany them, to escape the awful oppression of the house. 'Come with us,' she imagined her husband saying, holding the door of the truck open for her. But the offer was never made.

'Women don't go to pubs!' Frank declared, scandalised, when she finally suggested it.

'Yes they do! Maudie says there's a special lounge for the ladies.'

'As if Uncle John'd let Maudie in there! Pubs are for blokes, not sheilas.'

'Some men like to spend time with their wives,' retorted Nina reproachfully. 'A picnic on the weekend or the pictures in town would be nice.'

But Frank wouldn't hear of it. He was working seven days a week, saving hard, putting every spare penny in the bank. 'It's for our own place,' he assured her. 'Someday you'll thank me.'

So, except for those few night-time hours, with just the two of them sharing that squeaking, lumpy bed, she scarcely saw her husband. And when she did, he plied her with questions she had no answers to.

'Did you miss me while I was away?'

Had she? They had had so little time together after their marriage. No time to adapt to routines and habits. No time to savour that new familiarity.

'Yes,' she said, knowing that was the expected reply.

'What did you miss the most?'

'Little things,' she responded, after some consideration.

'Such as?'

'Oh, you know. Someone to curl up against at night. Kisses. Cuddles.'

'And sex? Did you miss the sex?'

Her thoughts drifted back to those first weeks of married life. Their lovemaking had been hurried and perfunctory, not what she had expected at all. No tenderness. No intimacy. Frank, she knew, had been as inexperienced as she. And each time she'd been left with a feeling that there was more to it all, that somehow she had been short-changed. And now, after four years, nothing had altered.

Resignedly. 'Yes. I missed the sex.'

Would God punish her for lying? she wondered.

He sighed and rolled towards her, kissing her long and hard. His mouth bruised hers. His tongue —

warm darting flesh that probed her teeth — reminded her of the fish he tipped from the nets each day and she suppressed a shudder.

'Do you love me?' he asked later, lying back and lighting a cigarette. In the flare from the match, his face seemed strained and exhausted. She waited a moment, perhaps too long, before replying.

'Of course I do. I married you, didn't I?'

The tip of the cigarette glowed red in the dark. 'You never tell me.'

It was an accusation of sorts. *I love you.* She knew how desperately he needed to hear those words, but something stopped her, and they choked in her throat.

Do I love him? she questioned herself repeatedly as she went about her chores. And what was love, anyway? Dependence? Servitude? Subservience? She saw all those traits in herself and despised her own compliance. But it was easier this way, living in Frank's parents' house. Easier to give in than argue. Time enough later to make a stand for herself, when they had their own place. If only she was more needing of him.

Somehow it had become a ritual: Nina walking down to the sea wall late each afternoon, waiting for the *Sea-spray* to dock. She watched her husband standing against the stern of the boat, holding the rope. Sandy hair flopped across his forehead as he grinned at her, dipping his head in acknowledgement of her presence. Why couldn't she run to him? she wondered, throw her arms around his neck and whisper those words he wanted to hear? What was stopping her? The presence of Frank's father? Those four years causing a barrier between them? Or did she truly not love him?

Why had she married him, then? Was it because of the war, those unreal heady days when decisions were based on emotion, not logic? Was it the fact that she had been almost twenty-six, four years older than Frank — an old maid with no immediate prospects? Had she rushed, accepting Frank's stammered proposal because she believed life had nothing better to offer?

Frank's parents had tried to dissuade them. 'Wait until the war's over,' they had urged, shaking their heads. 'There's no hurry.'

She had overheard Frank's father whisper later, as she left the room. 'You haven't got her up the duff, have you, you silly bastard?'

At times she wondered if she should simply walk away, leave herself and Frank both free to find someone more suited. Then she imagined the shame her desertion would cause, the reaction of Frank's parents and, somehow, it seemed easier to stay.

Unlike Nina, Frank loved to stroke, to feel. He was always running a hand along her arm, fingers through her hair. Mostly she didn't mind, but there were times when she found his touch unbearable and she pulled away, feigning some task, some preoccupation that demanded her attention. Perhaps, she considered, she had been too long without him. The need had gone, sunken into the shrivelled heart of her.

She had become, she knew, a master of deception. Her manner was always purposefully brisk, her voice cheerful. She tried, for Frank's sake, to ease the constant tension in the house. 'Good morning,' she announced in her brightest tone as the others filed into the cramped kitchen for breakfast.

If Frank was aware of the strain, the constant anxiety, he didn't say.

Eventually she tackled him on the subject of their own home. 'A little place in town,' she suggested. 'Nothing flash.'

'Soon. Soon,' he placated. 'Just another few months and I'll have enough saved for a deposit.'

'There's the money from Pa's place,' Nina reminded him. Her father had died twelve months before the start of the war. After Frank went away and she'd moved in with his parents, she had sold her father's small cottage and put the proceeds in the bank.

But Frank was strangely reluctant, and there was a hint of irritation in his reply. 'No. That's your money. Just be patient, Nina. I'm doing the best I can.'

At odd moments, labouring over some menial task, she remembered the day of Frank's arrival and the outline of her own floury handprints on his khaki coat. 'Leave it,' he'd replied when she'd tried to brush them away. 'I've been through worse.'

I've been through worse.

The words chugged laboriously through her awareness, refusing to leave, bitter and brutal. She had seen the photographs, of course, in the daily newspapers. Horses pulling carts through the infernal mud; the shell-like remains of the buildings at Ypres, Mons and Amiens. Sometimes Nina could almost imagine she had been there, she who had never lived anywhere but Tea-tree Passage.

I've been through worse. A collection of words that had no precise meaning. Frank had been *there*. Frank, who had a tic that worked endlessly at his temple, had seen first hand the mud. Frank, whose smile froze when she mentioned those faraway names, had walked amongst the ruins. What *had* he been through?

Sometimes, during those early days after his return, she ventured a few questions. But Frank told her nothing.

'What was it like? How did you cope?'

Tersely. 'Leave it, Nina!'

'But I *want* to know.'

'*I* don't want to remember.'

He shied away from the words, silencing her questions with his mouth.

'Sshh,' he whispered. 'Don't let's talk about it. It's gone. All in the past. The future, that's what's important now. You and me.'

Frank remembered the first night he and Nina had shared the small cottage that had belonged to Nina's father. The wedding had gone smoothly — a dozen or so guests at the tiny church, followed by a slap-up tea at the hotel in town. A few friends had been present, his mother and father. And, of course, his brother, Bill.

Nothing fancy, the service. Just a simple exchange of vows. 'Do you promise to love, honour and obey ...'

He remembered fragments. Whispered replies. Nina's tremulous smile. His mother sniffing into one of her lace handkerchiefs.

He remembered them both coming home later from the pub, a few beers under his belt. Nina had lit the fire and together they'd opened the wedding presents. A set of shiny new saucepans from John and Maudie. A silver photo frame from Bill. From his parents: a substantial cheque.

He remembered the smoke, unnoticed at first, billowing down from the chimney into the room.

'What the —!'

Remembered pushing Nina towards the door, hand over her mouth, and their frenzied rush outside, coughing and spluttering.

'Surprise! Surprise!'

Looking up, holding the lamp towards the roof, he'd seen them there. His brother Bill, Jimmy and Paddy Melville, and the wet hessian bag over the chimney.

The others had stepped out from the dark. Wives. Girlfriends. Banging on all sorts of pans, pots and kettles imaginable.

Bill, clambering from the roof, had slapped him heartily on the back. 'Come on, old chap. You didn't think you were going to escape a tin-kettling on your wedding night, did you?'

They'd crammed inside the small cottage, perching on the settee, windowsills, the floor. A large table had materialised, loaded with food. Paddy had produced an accordion while Jimmy sang.

I've got the time —
I've got the place —
Will someone kindly introduce me to the girl.

Even now, years later, Frank could still see shreds of that night with perfect clarity, could still hear the songs.

Oh! Mr Porter
A Little of What You Fancy Does You Good

'You know what I fancy,' he'd whispered in Nina's ear.

Nina laughing, looking beautiful in the yellow light of the lamp. He'd wanted to kiss her, right there and then, but someone — was it Jimmy? — had whisked her away and he'd watched them dancing instead, marvelling as her feet followed the steady rhythm and her body swayed to the music.

He remembered Nina leading him to the tiny bedroom after their visitors had gone, blushing shyly, stepping out of her clothes, tantalising him by that slow striptease. He'd stood, scarcely able to breathe, watching her, the desire a sudden unbearable ache in his groin. Nina undoing the buttons on his fly, her mouth brushing his skin, bringing him to almost immediate release.

He shook his head, believing those first weeks before he went away as one of the happiest periods of his life.

But it was all gone now, that bright young future left behind in the muck and monstrosity of the past four years. Bill dead at Pozières. Paddy at Mons. Jimmy in rehabilitation in the city, trying to live without the use of one of his legs. And the girls? Gone to the city mostly, trying to get on with their lives.

There were times when his entire existence seemed unreal, out of kilter. Days were disjointed, broken into fragments by the memories that surfaced at unexpected moments. The dead walked nightly through his dreams.

Faceless night-time soldiers.

He heard the tramp of their feet first, a distant *thump, thump, thump*. Then, through the mist, he saw the men approach, coming towards him from the gloom. *Thump. Thump. Thump*. Their boots echoed against the chalky substance of his sleep, throwing up puffs of white dust. Dust as white as bloodless faces. On and on they marched, night after night, a never-ending parade.

There were hollows where eyes and mouths should be. No lips to cry out in pain. No sight to witness the horror. He scanned their faces. They all stared back at him, and each one was Bill.

'NO! NO! NO!'

'Sshh! It's all right. Just a dream. Just a dream.'

Eventually Nina's whispered words brought him back to wakefulness. His bedclothes were awash with perspiration. His heart hammered uncontrollably in his chest. He felt an urge to flee, to run and never stop, from all that was safe and familiar.

Something touched his face and he thrust his head away, peering through the dark. But it was simply Nina, running a finger lightly along his brow.

Soothing.

Soothing.

Pushing those images back into his subconscious.

*   *   *

The thought of Nina, the promise of an eventual homecoming, had kept Frank going through those long years in the trenches in France. He had loved her then, and loved her now. Yet, as he resumed his former life, he realised how little they shared, how vastly different his expectations were from hers. They were almost like strangers, his own war experiences and their lack of common ground a dividing wedge.

To give her credit, she tried to understand, wanted Frank to share those terrible years.

'Perhaps if you talked about it,' she ventured after one particularly bad nightmare.

'No! Not now! Not ever! For God's sake, leave it, Nina!'

Calmly. 'Please don't yell. It's the middle of the night. You'll wake your parents.'

'I don't care!'

The thought of reliving it all terrified him. What if he broke down? What if he cried? Somehow he couldn't bear the possibility of Nina seeing him like that, losing control, acting like a child.

Abruptly she sat up in bed and faced the window. Frank saw the faint outline of her neck and shoulders silhouetted against the night sky. Her voice, when it came, was muffled. 'There's no need to be so god-damned self-sacrificing.'

'*Self-sacrificing*! What's that supposed to mean?'

'I only want to help.'

'I spend all my waking hours trying not to think about the war, and all you want me to do is rehash every last gory bloody detail. What do you want me to tell you? How I watched my best mate's blood drain out of him for four hours on a summer's morning in a field near St Quentin? Or how the ground shudders when a bomb hits the trench and the dirt explodes over you, finding its way into your eyes and nose and mouth, until you think you'll never be able to breathe again? Or what it's like when you're so bloody scared that you shit yourself, like a baby?'

He had tried to shock her, to make her back off, and was immediately ashamed. She hadn't deserved that. She lay back down on the bed, her back to him, not speaking.

'I'm sorry, love,' he offered after a while, conscience-stricken, unable to bear the silence. 'I shouldn't have said what I did.'

'No. You're right,' she replied eventually. 'You're perfectly right. Telling me isn't going to help. I'm sorry I asked.'

How could he explain to Nina why he couldn't discuss those wasted, wasted years? What words could he use to describe the horror? The details themselves were too shocking, too raw. Even the memories disgusted him, and he felt tainted by their immediacy. Besides, more importantly, her lack of involvement, her not knowing, set her apart from it all. She was a safe haven, an escape from those jumbled recollections that tracked through his mind.

He stifled a sigh and reached for her hand. 'Please, Nina. Don't let's argue. It's not important.'

It was a peace offering, of sorts.

* * *

Jimmy came home for a visit. From the deck of the *Sea-spray*, Frank watched old Mrs Melville push her son down to the wharves in the wheelchair, and felt that same old churning in his gut. In a few minutes, when he had composed himself, he'd go over and say hello, but part of him wanted to run from any meeting.

'Hi, Jimbo,' he said instead, clasping his old mate's hand. 'How's it going?'

'Fine, fine,' answered Jimmy, as Frank averted his eyes from the knotted trouser leg that concealed the stump of what was once Jimmy's lower leg. 'And you?'

'Fine,' echoed Frank. 'No complaints.'

Lies. All of it. But what else could he say?

It's bloody horrible, mate.

I hate it here. I hate my life.

Thank God for Nina.

The words pranced and died, unspoken. The two men stared at each other. It seemed they, too, had no common ground, he and his mate Jimmy who had danced with Nina on that long-ago wedding night.

Unbidden, the words crowded into his head.

I've got the time —
I've got the place —
Will someone kindly introduce me to the girl.

What girl would ever want Jimmy now?

And why had he, Frank, survived physically intact when so many others hadn't?

CHAPTER 3

Frank's mother constantly dusted and rearranged the collection of photographs on the piano in the parlour. Frank often found her there, frame in hand, staring at the sepia image of her eldest son. He found it ghoulish, morbid, that pathetic innate memorial.

'Mum,' he said, touching her on the hand. 'Are you all right?'

But she turned from him, not speaking, and walked from the room.

He felt shut out at every turn: Nina, his parents. The minutiae of daily life at Tea-tree Passage had become a leaden weight. How could he ever live such an ordinary life after such an extraordinary experience?

Every morning he kissed Nina goodbye and walked through the front door with his father, heading along the track that led to the sea wall. Birds sang. The tea-trees that lined the track sighed in the breeze. Even at that early hour he felt the heat from the sun on his back.

Silently he counted the hours he spent on the boat. Counted the hours and days and, eventually, the weeks. Wasted seconds and minutes frittered away on that glassy sea.

Scant conversation flowed from the old man, as though it were an effort to speak. Frank hated the prolonged silences — which made him feel small and insignificant — and the condescending way his father allowed him to attend to the menial tasks: pulling in the nets, slapping the fish into the boxes ready for the trip into town. He detested the smell of them, that raw briny stink, and the way the boat bobbed up and down on the occasional swell until he became quite nauseous.

Then there were the constant references to Bill, the old man's eyes growing watery as the discussion wore on.

'He was a good lad, Bill.'

And I wasn't?

'Yes, Dad.'

'Good fisherman, Bill.'

And I'm not?

'Yep. He was a good fisherman.'

'Did what he was told.'

And I don't?

The mental replies wearied him, wore him down.

Contrary to what Nina thought, he seldom went to the pub in town. In his spare time, after dropping the cases of fish at the Ice Works, he wandered the streets instead. Soon he knew every vacant block of land. Knew their size and shape, their availability, their price. *It's a choice bit of land, that one. But Old Smith won't let it go under three hundred.*

Three hundred pounds! How could he ever afford that?

Then. 'There's scarcely any building supplies since the war,' the builders all said.

'There are still shortages. Stay where you are.'

'At least you've a roof over your head.'

But Frank hated living in that rambling house at Tea-tree Passage, and the idea of remaining in that tightly-knit community depressed him in some inexplicable way. The house hemmed him in, with its photographic shrine and reminders of his boyhood. He knew his parents watched him, sensed that his performances as a man and as a husband were being measured and weighed, and were somehow found to be lacking. In his parent's house, he was still the child.

He tried to talk to his father about those war years. Man to man. No holds barred. Needed to tell *someone*.

But his father cut him off. 'Best forgotten, all that,' the old man replied gruffly.

Frank halted, staring at his father. 'Yes, well you're probably right. Best forgotten, as they say.'

He knew, if he closed his eyes, he would see it all again. Images of mud and death. Jimmy in the wheelchair on the wharf. The photographs of his own brother arranged in a semi-circle on the polished piano.

Even before she went to the doctor, Nina suspected she was pregnant. For the past week she'd barely been able to drag herself out of bed. Her stomach heaved at the sight of food and her breakfast had disgorged itself for the last three mornings in a row. Of her monthlies, due weeks ago, there had been no sign.

She caught a glimpse of herself in the mirror. A pale face stared back, dark hair lank, smudged circles under the eyes. Was this how it was going to be? she wondered. She had no-one to confide in. If her mother had been alive, perhaps she could have ventured a few questions. Frank's mother — no, that was unthinkable. Besides, she felt embarrassed by their very nature.

Finally it was Frank's Aunt Maudie who found her sitting on the wharf, legs dangling in the water, waiting for the *Sea-spray* to dock.

'Bloody hot today!'

Maudie lowered herself down beside Nina. She was a big woman — *bloody fat old cow,* Frank's father called her, out of earshot — and in her late forties, Nina supposed. Although she'd been married to John Carmody for over twenty years, there were no children. 'Some problem with me innards,' she had overheard Maudie once say.

'Yes.'

Nina pushed a damp strand of hair from her face and glanced at Frank's aunt. The older woman's face was flushed from her noonday walk from the house, her voice breathless.

'Too hot to be sitting here in the sun,' she gasped, fanning her face with her hand.

'Yes,' said Nina again. Words seemed to have deserted her, her mind sucked dry from the heat of the day.

'I suppose it's been lovely having Frank home.

Take a bit of getting used to, having a man about the place again, if you know what I mean.'

She had scarcely seen Maudie since Frank's return. The two families never socialised, so it was during unplanned meetings like this that Nina had come to know a little of Frank's aunt.

Maudie gave a hearty chuckle and Nina sensed her cheeks colour. Maudie wasn't one to beat around the bush. 'No flies on Maudie,' was the usual saying around Tea-tree Passage.

'Anyway, what's up, dearie? You look a sight, if you don't mind me saying so.'

Nina had to tell someone. As the words formed on her tongue, she imagined herself poised on the brink of something monumental, though the exact nature of it alluded her.

'I think I'm pregnant.'

Maudie clapped her hands. It had been a long time since a baby had been born at the Passage. 'So, what does Frank think then?'

Nina shook her head. 'I haven't told him.'

Maudie gave her a hard searching look. 'You should, you know, before you tell anyone else. He has a right.'

'And what about me? I have rights, too.'

'Don't you want this baby?'

Despite her best intentions, Nina's eyes flooded with tears. Angrily she wiped them from her cheek. 'Of course I want my child! It's just ...'

Words failed her. How could she tell Maudie? Bringing up a baby in that dismal house — what kind of a future was that?

Maudie passed her a clean handkerchief. 'No use crying about it, love.' She nodded her head in the direction of Frank's parents' house. 'Just get you and Frank out of there, hey? That's no place to raise a child. A child needs a happy home.'

With a cheerio, Maudie hauled herself to her feet and waddled back up the path to her own cottage. Nina watched her go with a mixture of relief and regret. Relief for the way in which the conversation was cut short; who knows what Frank's aunt might have gone on with. And regret that, of all those who knew her, Maudie was the only one who understood.

The following afternoon she asked Frank to take her to town. Lying on the examination table in the doctor's surgery as he prodded and probed, Nina remembered the day her husband had left for war. After she had stood at the railway station and watched him disappear into that surging sea of khaki, there had been a few weeks of anticipation when she'd hoped that the animal-like mating, that hot puff of sweaty bodies and grappling limbs, might have led to a baby, something to keep her mind centred on the fact that she was a married woman. But there'd been nothing, except for that regular bloodied discharge that had sent her weeping into her pillow.

Now, on the footpath in front of Mulligan's Drapers, she told Frank about the baby. He was silent for a while.

'Are you angry?' she asked at last.

'No.'

'Well? Aren't you going to say something?' Disappointment tracked a bitter course. At least he could pretend to be glad.

His face broke into a sudden smile. 'What do you want me to say? That I'm pleased, ecstatic? That I think you'll make the best mother who ever lived? Anything else?'

He picked her up and swung her round. 'Stop it, Frank! Put me down!' she laughed. Then. 'People are *watching.*'

'I don't care. Let them.'

Somehow he couldn't share the news, couldn't bear to see the expression on his parents' faces. The baby was his secret, his and Nina's.

The thought of it chugged in his mind during all those repetitive tasks. In his imagination he saw them — he, Nina and that faceless nameless child — as a family, in a snug home far away from this place.

As the days passed, the need to escape became stronger. He might take Nina to the city, he thought, where they knew no-one, and they could lose themselves in the anonymity, in the crush and crowd. Their world would encompass only each other and their unborn child. No disapproving faces. No need to conform. In the city he, Frank, could finally be himself. Not his parents' son. Not Bill's younger brother. But *himself.* Frank Carmody. Husband of Nina.

It was in this frame of mind that he saw the bodies on the strip of sand below as the *Sea-spray* docked. The men wore Australian uniforms. Several, he knew instinctively, were dead, but one man sat, stunned, on the sand. A German soldier crouched, rifle poised, ready to fire.

'No!' cried Frank. Without thinking he leapt from the deck of the boat, his legs taking the weight of his body as he landed on the sand, running, tripping, towards the men.

He lunged forward, scrambling towards the gun. As he went, the thought occurred to him: why hadn't the German moved? Surely he could see him coming? Then another thought. Perhaps it was a set-up.

He crouched low, blinking, and the scene disintegrated into sharp teasing fragments. The men faded out of focus. The German was nothing but a rock on the beach and the stunned man, a lump of driftwood.

'What's up, Frank?'

He stared towards the deck of the boat, into his father's face. There were lines of puzzlement on the old man's brow.

'Nothing.'

'Something's wrong. A man doesn't sit like that on the sand. A man not in his right mind anyhow.'

Frank stretched his leg, then slowly clambered to his feet. It was not the first time this had happened, but it was the only time his father had been a witness. He sensed a little-boy shame that he should be seen like this, caught out by some malfunction of his mind.

A pain began in his chest, down low, and he had an urgent need to urinate. He felt the blood squeezing, pressing through his veins. An anger consumed him and the words spilled from his mouth, uncontrollable and long overdue. 'Yair, Frank's a bloody loony, right?'

His father turned away.

Frank sprinted along the wharf and clambered down the rickety stairs onto the deck of the boat. He grabbed his retreating father by the shirt. 'That's what you think, isn't it? That I'm fucking mad?'

'Don't be ridiculous!'

'*Ridiculous*! I see the way you look at me. Like I'm a moron. I'm sorry. I'm not Bill.'

'You're not half the man Bill was.'

Frank slammed to a halt and stared at his father. The words wound sluggishly through his mind, fighting to be understood. '*What did you say?*'

'Just leave it.'

He contemplated the words for a moment, then said, 'We're leaving, Nina and I. Going to the city.'

'You can't. I need you here.'

'I have to go, make my own way.'

'I forbid it!'

Frank shook his head, unable for a moment to speak.

His father faced him, furious, hands on hips. 'If you go, who'll take over the business?'

They had come, Frank knew, to the crux of the matter. The emotions of the past months were about to be exposed. Sensibilities and passions were about to be laid bare. Whatever words were said, they could never be retracted.

'Does it really matter?'

'Well, Bill's gone,' the older man replied bitterly,

'and you're a bloody disappointment. I lost my best son in the war. All I'm left with is the dregs, and even the dregs are leaving.'

His father raised his hand and tried to strike Frank, but he grabbed the old man's wrist and held the hand away. His father was frail now, and Frank could easily snap the thin bones.

He stood for what seemed like an eternity, staring into his father's eyes. They were dark, those eyes, dangerous, full of bitterness and hate. The old man's mouth twisted into a vicious smirk, as though he knew something Frank didn't. 'You don't know nothing, Frank,' he said.

Sinking the knife in a little further, Frank thought. His father's words spun and tumbled, scarcely heard, mixed with the sound of the sea. They droned on and on, monotonous, and he closed his mind to them. All he heard was the one sentence, previously spoken.

I lost my best son in the war!

The words slapped at his consciousness, demanding attention, but he was tired. The antagonism rose towards him in waves, suffocating, and he turned to see his mother standing on the wharf, a hand to her breast.

'Frank.'

She mouthed the word, inaudible over the slap of the water, and he saw her lips moving.

Disgusted, he thrust his father's hand away. The scene whirled around him, swaying alarmingly. Perhaps he might fall, he thought, closing his eyes for a moment. Then his feet took him across the deck and up the stairs with purposeful strides, past his mother who stood motionless on the bleached planks.

'Frank!'

He heard her now, that shrill animal-like keen, heard the low sob to her voice. But he kept on, stumbling past the fishermen's huts, the straggly line of tea-trees. The heat seared his back through the thin shirt. 'Nina!' he yelled when he was in earshot of the house. '*Nina!*'

He watched as she came to the door, a frown on her face as he staggered past her into the cool confines of his parents' home. And the ragged wheeze he heard, the noise that had accompanied him from the wharf, he realised, was coming from his own mouth.

PART TWO

Adrift on a Wine-dark Sea

Sydney

1920

CHAPTER 4

Nina understood nothing except Frank's need to escape, and her own urge to flee from that dismal house. The events that followed blurred into each other: the hasty packing of bags, Frank pushing her out the front door, his mother's anguished cry. Somehow they were stumbling along the track towards town, the suitcases a dead weight. After what seemed like an eternity, but was probably only minutes, old Jack Sharp stopped in his motor car and offered them a lift.

Something dreadful had happened, she knew that much. Yet Frank was not forthcoming with an explanation and, with the firm set of his mouth and Mister Sharp's presence behind the wheel of the car, she was reluctant to ask.

'This'll do,' Frank said brusquely as the railway station came into sight on the edge of town. The car stopped with a swirl of dust and he hoisted the cases onto the ground.

'Frank,' she finally ventured as they waited on the

platform. The afternoon train was due and groups of travellers milled along its length. 'Where are we going?'

Frank tapped his foot impatiently. 'To the city.'

'Brisbane?'

'No.' Staccato syllables. Curt. 'Further.'

The tone of his voice discouraged conversation. She fought back a surge of disappointment and said nothing, watching instead down the empty length of track. The least he could do, she considered, was tell her his plans. She was, after all, a not-unwilling companion.

The train came hissing into the station, and the next few minutes were taken up with finding a compartment with empty seats, and with stowing bags. There was an awkwardness between them: Nina not knowing the words to say and Frank obviously not knowing *how* to say them. He refused to meet her gaze, busying himself instead with unstrapping the tartan rug from one of the cases and laying it over her lap.

The train wheezed from the platform and gathered speed. A dog ran alongside. Behind the closed window, Nina saw its mouth moving and imagined the excited barking. *Clickety-clack. Clickety-clack.* The wheels beat a steady rhythm that somehow soothed, compensating for Frank's silence. The carriage rocked, swaying over the points.

They travelled south, staring from the windows of the second-class compartment. It began to rain. A soft mist covered the countryside, reducing the scene to a uniform grey. Grey skies. Grey trees.

Grey muddy rivulets coursing down grey slopes. Small towns came and went, each one blurring into the next.

'You have to tell me what happened,' she said at last. 'I need to know.'

Frank closed his eyes and laid the back of his head against the leather upholstery. His voice, when it came, was a hoarse whisper. 'Don't, Nina.'

'Frank, please! I can't help if you won't tell me.'

His eyes shot open: dark orbs in a chalk white face. 'Second best! That's what I am!'

The words exploded into the space between them. 'No!' she denied hotly. 'That's not true.'

'It's what *they* think!'

On a deep breath he recounted the scene on the boat. Nina listened to the faltering, halting phrases, the poisonous words, watching her husband's face. His brow was creased with fine lines Nina had never noticed before. His expression was a mask of anguish, as though the innermost part of him was struggling to deal with the events of the past day.

'You know what this is all about?' he demanded, when he had finished relating the scene. 'Do you bloody well *know*?'

'What, Frank?' she asked warily.

'They blame me for Bill's death! They blame me as much as if I'd got a gun and shot him myself!'

'No.'

Why was she denying the fact? She'd known it for months, since that day of Frank's return. Yet to agree with him …

'I was the first to enlist,' he went on, as though she hadn't spoken, 'then Bill joined up, too. "I can't let my young brother upstage me," he said.'

'Frank, that was five years ago.'

'So my father reminded me,' he replied bitterly.

'This'll pass. In time they'll realise how wrong they are.'

Frank stared directly ahead. 'I have no parents,' he intoned. 'I have no family. I have no home. All I have is you, Nina.'

She couldn't bear his misery. Tentatively she reached out and took his hand, offering him a wan smile. 'Everything will be all right, Frank. I know it will.'

'Nina,' he said after a while. 'You do understand?'

She nodded and bit her lip, not trusting herself to speak, staring hard at the grey landscape. Tears threatened momentarily and she blinked them away. *Silly! Silly!* She chided herself. *You wanted to leave, too. This is an adventure. You and Frank going to the city.* Then a little voice of doubt surfaced. *Where will you live? What will Frank do? He only knows how to be a fisherman. The money will only hold out for so long.*

She thought of her bankbook stowed safely in her handbag. Over one hundred pounds there. Money from the sale of her father's house. Added to the sum she knew Frank had saved, it would tide them over for a while.

'Nina?'

She turned to face him. 'Yes, Frank.'

'I couldn't stay. Not after what happened. I'm sorry.'

'You don't have to be sorry.'

'No.'

She glanced down at her hands, wound tightly together on her lap. 'Where will we go?'

His expression was one of determination. 'As far away from Tea-tree Passage as possible.'

Katmandu? Timbuktu? Malacca? The names, distant and exotic, slid into her awareness. *I'm leaving all that's safe and familiar*, she thought and felt a momentary panic.

Frank touched her shoulder lightly. 'Sydney,' he added, as though sensing her alarm. 'That's far enough.'

Snapshots. Scenes printed indelibly into her memory. Miles and miles of bush, broken by periodic halts at tiny railway sidings. Occasional passengers huddled, waiting in the rain. Workmen unloaded supplies. Nina tried to sleep, but could not. Constant nausea plagued her, reminding her of the child that grew inside. Her thoughts were full of what had happened, and Frank's faltering explanation.

I lost my best son in the war.

How could a father say that to a son?

How? How? How?

Night came. Cinders from the engine flared into the blackness like frantic fireflies, flickered then died. Years later, a few memories would stand out for Nina: rattling through darkened towns, bells clamouring on crossings; yellow gas lamps casting elongated shadows along chilly platforms; a mug of steaming coffee and a cold pie in a railway cafeteria at midnight. Throwing up in the swaying lavatory at the end of the carriage corridor.

She suffered through a day and night of stop-start jerking, followed by a two-hour delay in Brisbane. Then the train headed south again, inland at first, through rolling hills and valleys. Bush gave way to occasional towns as they swayed over bridges, water foaming underneath. Other trains passed in a blur. Then row upon row of dark brick houses lined the tracks. Factories. City platforms.

CHAPTER 5

Central Station. Nina had never seen such a hive of activity. In the domed concourse, pigeons fluttered high overhead as passengers bustled past, loaded with suitcases. Other travellers stood under the huge indicator boards, searching for the correct platform. As Frank steered them through the thronging crowds, it seemed her body was still rocking with the movement of the train.

Labouring under the weight of the luggage, they stumbled through the station entrance into late-afternoon sunlight. Nina blinked in the glare. Cars and trams trundled past. Buildings towered, several storeys high. From the Tooheys Brewery opposite came the sickly sweet smell of hops and beer.

'Come on,' ordered Frank, grabbing her elbow with his free hand and steering her towards the road. 'Let's find somewhere to camp for a few days till we get our bearings.'

They found a boarding house in a laneway off Albion Street. Two shillings a night. Extra for the gas. 'We won't be here long,' Frank assured her as Nina inspected the mildewy walls and stained bedspread. 'Tomorrow I'll get us a decent place.'

Famous last words, she thought later. Accommodation, it seemed, was scarce. Every morning Frank bought a newspaper, sifting through the TO LET columns. But there were, he soon discovered, queues waiting for every vacancy.

'Terrible shortage after the war,' explained one agent. 'Nothing's been built for years. Now all the blokes are back from overseas, getting married and having kids. There's nowhere for them to go.'

'And we're no different,' Frank told Nina grimly.

After three weeks of searching, a time when Nina despaired of ever finding something suitable, they chanced upon a flat in Surry Hills. It was only small — two rooms on the third floor and a share bathroom down the hall — but at least it was theirs.

Frank found a job in a factory. The hours were long and the pay abysmal but, for the first time in a long while, he seemed happy. He arrived home each night full of plans and ideas. Nina, lumbering around the flat as her pregnancy advanced, gave them scant attention. Frank's schemes, she soon discovered, were short-lived and apt to change with the wind.

She supposed she was content. Away from Frank's parents, their marriage had finally assumed some sense of normalcy. No more pretending. No more forced cheerfulness. There were days when she could scarcely remember what it had been like in that house at the Passage, the memories crammed into some corner of her subconscious, needing to be forgotten.

As she padded around the rooms, making the bed or tidying their few possessions, her own thoughts were consumed by the child. The first tentative movements she likened to butterfly wings. Tiny fluttering motions, barely felt, caused her to halt whatever she was doing. *My child*, she thought, breathless with wonder. *Frank and I created this.*

But there were times, during Frank's daily absences, when the anticipation of the child was not enough. Nina was in a city where she knew no-one, and she craved company other than her own. She needed someone, another woman, to exchange the daily chitchat that Frank seemed to dismiss as 'women's stuff'. Apart from a few schoolmates in town, she hadn't had any friends her own age at the Passage either, she acknowledged, but at least there had been company: Frank's mother, Maudie's impromptu chats on the wharf, old Mrs Melville's cheery wave.

At varying times during the day, she stood at one of the grimy windows, staring into the laneway below, a sense of loneliness consuming her. Hawkers' carts came and went, the horses' hooves sounding a satisfying clip-clop on the paved surface. There were cries of the vendors in the nearby streets, the rattle and clank of the trams, and the occasional train whistle.

It was during those daylight hours, when the chores had been completed, that the walls confined her in that tiny flat. She thought longingly of the streets beyond, of losing herself amongst the rush and bustle of the city. One day she took the key and walked out the door. 'I won't go far,' she told herself. 'Just around the block.'

She stopped at the fruit shop at the end of the street and hesitated over a tray of grapes. The owner's wife came out through the curtain that divided the front of the shop from the rear. She was a big woman, with a dark-haired child clinging to her skirt. 'I'm Maria,' she introduced herself in a heavily accented voice. 'Haven't seen you in here before. Live around here?'

Nina pointed along the road, towards the block of flats. 'Up there.'

'When's your baby due?'

'Not for another four months. Christmas,' replied Nina, placing her hand on her stomach, feeling a frisson of pleasure that someone had noticed. It made her feel almost one of *them*, a prospective member of that enigmatic enclave of women who had experienced the intricacies of childbirth.

She bought half a pound of grapes and two shiny green apples, and went back to the flat, singing.

During the following weeks, Nina began venturing further. There was, she soon discovered, a seemingly limitless number of shops only a tram ride away. Small cramped stores housed all manner of bric-a-brac, wares spilling in a riot of colour onto the footpaths. Larger department stores, several storeys high, sold everything from imported foodstuffs to clothing and furniture. Her favourite was Anthony Hordern's, whose windows displayed a mind-whirling array of household goods. Nina strolled along the aisles, looking, wishing over cane perambulators and white wooden cots. In the fabric department she bought yards of batiste and lawn, cutting and sewing, making impossibly small garments.

Every Friday she searched the markets near the railway goods yards west of George Street. There were boxes of strange-looking exotic fruit — persimmons and lychees, dark red cherries and rough-skinned coconuts. She paused over them, settling instead for the bananas and oranges she knew Frank liked, lugging home the bags of vegetables and fruit, stretching Frank's wage as far as she could.

Sunday was Frank's day with Nina, *their* day, to spend however they liked. Invariably they rose late — well, late compared to Frank's usual pre-dawn weekday struggle from the sheets — and Nina cooked breakfast fit for a king. Bacon. Eggs. Tomatoes. Two slices of toast and a pot of tea. They ate together, perched at the table near the window in the kitchen, spearing long fingers of toast into runny part-boiled eggs.

They were like children, he thought, watching as she flicked a strand of dark hair back from her face and smiled at him.

'If you smile in the morning, you'll smile until night.' His voice was a rich baritone as he sang the first words to the popular song.

'Smile at the world and —' Nina joined in. They both laughed and he felt an ache of tenderness towards her. Nina: his wife, mother of his unborn child.

It was times like these when he felt he knew her best, when he saw Nina as she had been before the war. Capricious. Spontaneous. A memory surfaced. Nina marching away from him, swinging her hips. 'I won't marry you, Frank Carmody, unless you get down on one knee and propose properly.'

And he had. Made a fool of himself in her father's parlour, kneeling on the worn carpet. Afterwards she had kissed him on the settee and he had felt the press of her breasts against his chest, setting his senses on fire.

That moment had promised so many things. Sharing. Secrets. A lifetime together. Her hand on his groin. Himself arching towards her, saying, 'For God's sake, Nina!'

Even then she had made him wait until the ring was firmly on her finger. Tease. He turned towards her now, remembering, thinking that nothing much had changed, after all.

What had happened between that moment and this? All those intervening seconds, minutes and hours since they had become husband and wife, lost in vague and formless yesterdays, never to be regained. Why did he feel they were now moving in opposite directions? He'd felt her drawing away from him lately, the child a barrier between them.

Frank. Nina. And now a baby.

He found himself both fascinated and repelled by her changing body. Sometimes he caught himself watching as she dressed for bed, amazed at the way her belly pushed out with the shape of it. He watched, too, as she unconsciously brought her hand there, to that pale blue-veined mound, running fingers lightly over the skin. Stroking. Kneading. Placating. And he found himself waking in the middle of the night, with his hand cradling that same mound. However, for some unknown reason, he could not bring himself to make love to her. The need was there, but not the mechanics.

Nina didn't seem to worry. She was self-absorbed these days, planning womanly things that he felt distanced from. He knew he was seeing another aspect of her, a preoccupied maternal side.

He tried to involve himself with her pregnancy, to ask lots of questions and sound interested, though he was so bone-weary from the long hours at work that he scarcely had enough energy to eat dinner when he arrived home. At times, while she stood at the stove stirring the contents of some saucepan, he would come up behind her and run his palms along the side of her stomach.

Touching, feeling the shape of the child. It was, he supposed, his way of involving himself in something he saw as a feminine process, something which he was not a part of. But she seemed to shy away from his touch. It was as though the child were hers alone, as though he had had nothing to do with its conception. *Include me*, he wanted to say. *I am part of all this*. But the words died in his throat, unuttered.

He found himself referring to the child as Nina's baby. Son or daughter? he wondered. Either way, it didn't matter. There was nothing for a son to inherit. A run-down rented apartment in the city and a few pounds in the bank. But it was a start. Eventually he'd buy them a nice place. A cottage. Two bedrooms: one for himself and Nina and one for the child.

He could see it now. Picket fence. Smoke curling from the chimney. Nina playing on the lawn with the baby. In time there'd be more children: a new generation of Carmodys continuing on into perpetuity. Making his own family out of the ashes of the old. Proving himself. But to whom? Nina? The parents he never saw, never contacted?

I am a man.

My wife is with child.

Whatever happened in the past, I can leave behind.

On those lazy winter Sundays, when the heat from the sun scarcely seemed to warm them and drifts of red-gold leaves lay on the footpaths, they strolled around the inner-city streets or took a tram ride to Hyde Park, where Nina loved to feed the pigeons. At other times they wandered through the older established suburbs. There were lovely brick homes with gabled roofs and rambling gardens. Children played near shady trees while groups of women sat under trellised verandahs. From the footpath Frank could hear the muted *clink-clink* of teacups.

The images sustained him through the ensuing weeks: Nina, coat pulled tight across her belly, laughing as she stepped from the tram, her cheeks pink against the wind. Nina peering over fences, exclaiming over neat hedges and flowerbeds. Nina pulling him towards the swings in a nearby park, saying, 'Come on, Frank! Push me to the sky!'

Seeing her like that, he wanted to take her in his arms and bury his face in her hair, wanted to hold her and never release her. But she was already running from him, across the lawn, and he sensed that it was already too late, that at some undefined moment in the past, he'd already let her go.

Later, trudging tiredly back to the tramline, they stopped in front of a fine Edwardian-styled home. An avenue of pines lined the sweeping drive. Several automobiles were parked at the front door.

'Isn't it beautiful?' said Nina wistfully, pausing beside the wrought-iron gates.

'One day I'll buy you a place like this.'

She laughed and placed a hand on her belly, feeling the swell of the child. 'Big dreams, Frank.'

'No use dreaming small.'

She took his hand and he felt the warmth from her fingers. 'You'd need a small army just to maintain this place. Gardener. Housekeeper. Imagine mowing all that lawn!'

A toot behind them made them jump as an automobile screeched past them, along the driveway. The man behind the wheel was wearing a straw boater. His companion, a young woman with short blonde hair, was laughing at something the man had said.

Nina stared wistfully after them. 'Just a small place would be fine, Frank. Do you think we have enough saved now?'

Frank shook his head and steered her along the footpath, away from the house. 'Enough for a flat in the city.'

'Well …' She stopped and looked at him questioningly. 'What are we waiting for?'

'Because I want better than that for us, Nina. A *nice* home, not some squalid dump where the children have to play in the streets. I want a car. Expensive furniture. Best schools for our children. That's why I'm working the hard slog, the long hours. One day we'll have something, anything, more than we have now.'

Away from Tea-tree Passage, Frank's nightmares had lessened, though not stopped. One dream in particular surfaced regularly, bringing him eventually to unexpected wakefulness, his heart hammering and his skin crawling.

They are moving up to the front line near Pozières, marching two abreast along a muddy lane, past sodden fields and shell holes brimming with water. To the left, the skeletal remains of an avenue of poplars reach bare branches towards a grey sky. Marching. On and on. One foot after the other, boots rubbing a blister on his heel.

Suddenly, without warning, a shell bursts, mere yards ahead. The world rocks around him, grit and dirt pressing into his mouth, his nose. He hunkers against the ground, holding his head against his knees, arms binding his legs. The muscles in his leg ache. His head throbs with the noise.

Finally, when the dust clears, he can see one of his own men lying in a pool of blood. He knows, even before he reaches the spot, that the man is Bill. Bill lying face down, his body twisted unnaturally, the legs of his trousers shredded at the place where one knee should have been.

He sinks down beside his brother, shaking, pummelling the body. 'Bill? For Christ's sake, man! Get up!'

Someone pulls him away.

'It's no good, mate. He's dead.'

'No!'

A sound, a terrible wrenching cry, comes from his mouth and he is powerless to stop it. On and on it goes, echoing shrilly.

'Frank!'

Someone is prodding him. There are hands on his shoulder. *Go away!* he wants to yell. *Leave me be!*

But the hands and the voice keep on.

'Frank! Wake up!'

He stumbled into consciousness, hardly able to draw breath. Nina leant over him, her hands firm against his chest. He took a lungful of air, felt it pushing, squeezing through his veins.

He played down the nightmares, telling Nina, 'All the blokes get them. There are some things about the war you just can't forget.'

'Perhaps you should see a doctor?'

'A shrink, don't you mean?' he asked bitterly, remembering that last conversation on the boat with his father. 'I suppose you think I'm mad, too!'

'Please, Frank.'

She had that infuriating way of looking at him, patiently, as though he were a wayward schoolboy rebelling against a perfectly reasonable suggestion.

The constant headaches, though, proved annoying. A gnawing pain seemed to be intermittently there, across his forehead. It came and went at odd times, surfacing unexpectedly. In his work bag, away from Nina's prying eyes, he kept a supply of powders.

Towards the middle of spring, he took Nina on a ferry ride to the beach. Though the sun was warm, a cool wind still blew across the sand. Children frolicked at the water's edge while mothers hovered anxiously. A few men clad in neck-to-knee bathers braved the waves further out.

We'll be like that next year, he thought, watching a small child with a spade, digging happily in the sand. A family.

He tried to picture them there — he, Nina and the child — and failed. He could never be like those men who swam the waves so carefree. His mind was too burdened, his thoughts too preoccupied. Nightmares. Headaches. Bill. His parents. All conspiring to make him feel less than all this. How could he ever feel *normal* again?

And Nina? He glanced down the beach towards her. She had wandered further than he realised, a lonely figure on the sand. She held her shoes in her hand while the wind blew her dress about her legs, whipped her hair into a wild dark mass. She moved slowly, as though walking was an effort. And he supposed it was in a way, her body weighted heavily with the child. Feet trailing through the water. Hand shielding her eyes from the sun. Staring at a hazy horizon.

What was in store for them? Certainly he had dreams, but were they just that, an illusion?

Slowly he walked towards her, away from the laughter of the children, dragging his feet through the sand, feeling the gritty grains between his toes. 'Nina?' he called, and she turned towards the sound.

As they came together, there on that lonely stretch of beach on that late October afternoon, their shadows loomed, looking weird and deformed, towards the incoming tide.

CHAPTER 6

One evening in early November, Frank came waltzing through the door, carrying a bunch of flowers. Nina looked up in surprise from the book she was reading.

'For you,' he said, depositing them in her lap and awarding her a grin.

'Why are you smiling like that?'

'Me? Smiling?'

'Yes, smiling like a gob-smacked fool. Tell me what's up, Frank Carmody. You know I can't bear a mystery.'

He sank down on the settee beside her. 'You know the hours are pretty long at the factory, and the pay's lousy.'

'Yes.'

'Well, I've been thinking we might start our own business.'

She looked down at the flowers. Daisies and roses. Lilies. Baby's breath. They must have cost a small fortune. The lilies — white trumpet-shaped blooms — had a sprinkling of yellow pollen on the petals. A faint subtle perfume rose up to meet her.

Carefully. 'What sort of business?'

The words came tumbling out, tripping over each other in their haste to be heard. 'I met a chap in the pub and we got talking. He knows where there's an old terrace house going for a song. It needs a bit of work but, between us, we'd manage. We'd be able to get four flats out of it.'

'House renovations?' she asked incredulously. What did Frank know about building? He was a fisherman, after all.

'George is a carpenter —'

'George?'

Patiently. 'The man I met in the pub.'

'And he wants you, Frank Carmody, who has never built so much as a chookhouse in his life, to go into partnership with him?'

'I'm not that bloody *useless*, Nina.'

'Frank, it's just that —'

But he went on as though she hadn't spoken. 'George hasn't enough capital. He's got his own place, a few suburbs over. Says he could raise some of the money on that. But he needs double. That's where we come in.'

She understood, finally, the thrust of the conversation. Frank wanted to take the precious pounds they had saved towards a home and give them to a stranger for some ludicrous business proposition.

'There'd be four flats,' he repeated, continuing on regardless, as though anticipating her objection. 'Two each. I thought when the job was finished we could move into one. At least we'd have our own place.'

She shook her head and rose from the settee, heading towards the kitchen. 'I don't know, Frank. It seems too risky. You don't even know this chap.'

His voice floated after her. 'You have to take a chance sometime. That's what life's all about. Look at us! Coming to the city: that was a risk.'

'That was different and you know it.'

'Nina.' Suddenly he was beside her, his hands on her shoulders. She could almost feel the excitement, the eagerness, flowing from him. 'It's a chance to do something other than grind away in that lousy factory for the rest of my life, don't you see? And besides, what's the *risk*? You read the newspapers. There are families out there desperate for somewhere to live. Look at the trouble we had getting this place.'

Nina bit her lip and thought hard. What Frank said was true: accommodation *was* scarce.

'This sort of opportunity doesn't come every day,' Frank added in a low voice, as though sensing her hesitation. 'If we're not quick about it, George reckons we'll miss out altogether.'

What if Frank were right? What if they could make money, good money, from renovating a run-down building? She could feel herself wavering, torn between caution and a sense of recklessness.

'I'd want to meet this George first,' she conceded, hands on hips.

A grin creased his face. He leaned forward and kissed her firmly on the lips. 'That's my girl! George is having a party on Saturday night. Few drinks, that sort of thing. We're invited.'

Nina could already hear the music as they walked along the footpath towards George's house. Jazz, with a beat to set your feet dancing. Scratchy, tinny, the words jostled along the pavement towards them.

It was a worker's cottage, small, with a neat lawn and garden behind a white fence. Several automobiles were parked haphazardly by the kerb. A yellow glow spilled from the uncurtained windows and figures moved across the light. Someone was dancing, arms swinging. Frank pushed open the front door of the cottage to a babble of voices and the clink of glasses.

'Frank! Glad you could make it!'

A short thickset man materialised out of the crowd and came towards them, extending his hand to Nina. 'I'm George. And you must be Frank's wife.'

'Nina,' she said, feeling the firm grasp of his handshake.

'Frank, why don't you get Nina a drink?' He waved towards an adjoining room. 'Bar's in there. I'll just find Mim.'

George's wife Miriam was petite and dark. And oh-so-very modern. Her hair was bobbed, quite short, Nina noticed, and she wore a yellow sleeveless dress that fell in a straight line to just below her knees.

'Hello,' she smiled, surprising Nina by kissing her on the cheek, as though they were old friends. 'I'm Miriam. Call me Mim. Everybody does.'

'Hello, Mim,' replied Nina shyly, momentarily lost for words.

Mim stood for a second, glass in hand, staring at Nina's stomach. 'George said you were having a baby. When's it due?'

'About six weeks.'

'How very brave.'

'Brave? What's to be brave about?'

Mim flapped her hands, almost spilling her drink in the process. 'All that pain, darling. Too horrid for words, wouldn't you agree?'

'It's not something I —'

Mim cut her off. 'Then there's the crying and teething. Staying up till all hours at night.' She stopped and gave a brittle laugh. 'Well, it is all right to stay up till all hours, but only when you're having *fun*.'

Mim obviously wasn't keen on babies. 'You have a lovely house,' observed Nina, changing the subject.

'Too damn small to hold a decent party, if you ask me. But it's been in the family for ages. George inherited it when his mother died. Would you like to look through?'

Nina, out of politeness, glanced through the house while Mim went off to the bar to replenish her drink. The rooms were tiny, made smaller by the dark timber furniture. In the dining room, on the sideboard, she paused in front of a cluster of family photographs. One in particular caught her attention. A woman in a white dress, sunhat on her head. She picked it up.

'That was George's mother,' said Mim, coming up behind.

Nina replaced the frame on the sideboard. 'She was a very beautiful woman.'

Mim handed Nina a drink. 'Here. Might as well get sloshed. Everyone else is.'

Nina took a sip. The liquid slid to the back of her throat, burned for a moment as she fought back an urge to cough. 'What is it?'

'Martini. Too divine for words, don't you think?'

'Too divine,' murmured Nina in agreement.

'So, do you miss your family now that you're living in the city?'

'I don't have any,' replied Nina, embarrassed by the familiar tone of the conversation. She barely knew this woman, Mim, yet she was asking all sorts of personal questions.

Mim shot her a questioning look. 'None?'

'My parents are both dead, and I was an only child.'

'And Frank?'

Nina closed her mouth abruptly, remembering that last day at Tea-tree Passage. The air lodged in her throat and, for a moment, she couldn't breathe. She shook her head, willing the memories away. 'Frank's only brother was killed in the war.'

Bill.

Silver frames on the piano.

Frank telling her: *I lost my best son in the war.*

How could she ever forgive them?

'And his parents?'

'Dead, too.'

She closed her eyes and the lie echoed through her consciousness.

But Mim was dancing away, swinging her hips to the beat of the music, beckoning Nina to follow. 'You're so lucky! Family! They drive you mad sometimes. Always turning up on your doorstep, wanting this, wanting that.'

Nina walked back into the main room where the party was in full swing. As they reached the doorway, Mim stopped and pointed towards Frank.

'You know,' she said, taking a long sip of her drink and staring at Nina over the rim of her glass, 'I think your husband's quite the most handsome man here tonight.'

'Frank?'

Surprised, she glanced through the crowd, seeking him out. He was standing by the window, engaged in an earnest conversation with a man wearing a pink shirt and green pinstriped trousers. Frank handsome? She hadn't considered that before. To her he was ... well, just Frank. Awkward bumbling Frank with big knuckled hands and —

She stopped, from that distance trying to picture him as he might appear through another's eyes. In an odd sort of way, she supposed he *was* good looking. Tall. Shock of sandy hair. Square jaw. The man in the pink shirt had obviously said something funny and Frank reacted. It was as though she was seeing him smile for the first time.

'Yes,' she said happily. 'I suppose he is.'

George came bustling up, taking Nina's arm and steering her away. 'I've just been telling Frank what a wonderful start this new business is going to be, for both of us. And I have to tell you, it's great you agreed to go along with it, too.'

She had? Nothing had been decided between her and Frank, as far as she was aware. That was what this evening was all about: getting to know George and Mim.

They had come to a halt in front of a window. George leaned forward, bringing his face into alignment with her own. 'Not that we blokes would let such a minor thing as an uncooperative wife stand in our way. Not when there's money involved.'

She knew with awful certainty that the decision had already been made. Frank had sanctioned this business arrangement before he had even discussed it with her. The finances had been promised, the deal probably sealed with a handshake over an after-work beer. Coming here tonight had merely been a formality, an act to appease her own concerns.

Anger flared inside her and she clenched her fists, unaware for a moment of her nails digging into the palm of her hand. How dare Frank? Wasn't their marriage a partnership, too?

Obviously not.

She returned George's stare. 'I can only hope,' she said, keeping her voice as even as her shaking hands would allow, 'that you both know what you're getting yourself into.'

It was late when the party ended and the trams had stopped running. 'Never mind,' said Frank, taking Nina's hand as they picked their way along dark footpaths. 'We're only a suburb away. Eight or nine blocks. The exercise will do us good.'

Nina felt little like walking. She was exhausted and the baby had kicked all night. Bed would have been welcomed hours ago but she had soldiered on, knowing Frank was enjoying himself.

'Great party,' enthused Frank as they passed a row of shops. A cat was scavenging in one of the rubbish bins. It ran at their approach, scattering refuse as it went. 'Did you enjoy yourself?'

'Yes, Frank.'

She could barely bring herself to talk to him, so intense was her anger. It surged, white hot, about her, churning away relentlessly. Scenes from the evening flickered and died. Mim watching Frank. *Your husband's quite the most handsome man here tonight.* George steering her across the crowded room. *Not that we blokes would let such a minor thing as an uncooperative wife stand in our way.*

But Frank seemed not to notice. 'They're a great couple, George and Mim.'

Were they? She hardly knew them well enough to tell. George: overweight and overbearing. Elusive fun-loving Mim who had a way, Nina thought, intentional or not, of making her seem small and inferior. As though Nina's own needs were too insignificant, too unimportant to be considered. She remembered Mim staring at the bulge that was Nina's baby. *All that pain, darling. Too horrid for words.*

The world, Nina had decided, as far as Mim was concerned, revolved around her, and her alone.

Uncooperative wife? Even now, hours later, George's words rankled. Was that how Frank saw her? Was that why he had gone behind her back, promising the money before talking it through fully with her? Like George, had he thought she might prove to be an obstacle to their scheme?

Say nothing! she told herself, willing her feet forward. No use causing a scene, neither about Frank's new-found friends nor his lack of concern for her own importance in their marriage. What was done, was done. The money had obviously been promised.

Please God, she thought as she climbed into bed later, let this not be a disaster.

CHAPTER 7

It was hot, so hot. Nina sat at the table wrapping presents, the windows flung wide open to catch any passing breeze. Occasionally she stopped and wiped the perspiration from her face with one of Frank's handkerchiefs.

It was mid-December, two weeks before Christmas. Fourteen days until the baby was due, although everyone said that babies, especially the first time, always arrived late. So when the pains had begun after breakfast, she had dismissed them.

'It's too early,' she said to Frank, shooing him out the door. He and George had organised a meeting with the bank manager. 'I'm sure it's just a false alarm. I'll be all right.'

Mim called in mid-morning, accepting a cup of tea and several of Nina's home-made biscuits. 'Just popped in to see how you're getting on,' she said, grimacing at the tea. 'Too bloody hot for this, though,' she added, settling back in the chair. 'A nice cold martini, that's what I fancy.'

Privately Nina thought Mim drank far too much. She and Frank had been invited to George and Mim's home several times in the past few weeks — Nina attending more out of politeness than desire — and it seemed as though the woman was never without a glass of some alcoholic beverage or other in her hand.

Stiffly. 'I'm sorry but there's nothing else I can offer —'

Mim cut her off with a scratchy laugh. 'Really, Nina! You're far too sensitive. I wasn't criticising.'

Was she? Sensitive? Some days she felt she hardly knew herself any more. Her body had become a lumbering cumbersome incubator. And where Frank was concerned, as he sat each night at the table poring over plans and lists of repair costs, it seemed she hardly existed.

'Oh, don't bother about me, Nina,' Mim went on, breaking her thoughts. 'George says I drink far too much.' She regarded Nina lazily. 'What do you think?'

A pain wound itself low in her belly and Nina closed her eyes against the force of it. What to say? She didn't want to alienate the woman. After all, their husbands were about to become business partners. No, she considered firmly. Mim wouldn't draw her on that one. 'I think I could do with one of those ice cold martinis right now,' she smiled.

'Ah, Nina. Ever the diplomat.' Then. 'Are you all right?'

'Just a pain.'

'The baby's not coming?' Mim looked alarmed.

Nina shook her head. 'The doctor says it's not due for a fortnight.'

'And babies keep regular timetables?' Mim rose from her seat. 'I could find Frank, if you like.'

'No. Don't bother him. I'm sure it's nothing.'

'Well, as long as you're fine, I'll be off. Don't forget the party on Saturday night.'

And Mim was gone in a flurry of perfume and swirling skirts.

As the hands of the clock moved steadily towards noon and the mercury in the thermometer on the kitchen wall crept higher, Nina realised she had been mistaken. The pains were more regular now, insistent, with a sharp edge to them. Several times she was forced to sit on the settee, clenching her hands into tight fists until the agony passed.

What should she do? Wait for Frank or make her way to the hospital alone? There was no way of knowing how long he'd be. Finally, in desperation, she took the small suitcase — packed weeks earlier — and let herself out the front door of the flat.

Mim waited outside the bank. After a few minutes the two men descended the stairs into the sunshine and she hurried along the footpath towards them.

'George! Frank! How did it go?'

They turned towards her, smiling. George caught her up in an embrace, swinging her around. 'We got the money, honey! What do you think about that?'

'I think we should celebrate.'

George let her slide from his arms. 'That's my girl. And we will. Tonight.'

Mim pouted. It was a gesture that usually won George over. 'But I want to celebrate *now*. Come on, darling. Don't be a spoilsport.'

George glanced up towards the clock tower. 'Love to, but I've got an appointment. Why don't you ask Frank? He's at a loose end for the rest of the day.'

'Well, I should be getting home. Nina —'

'Nina's fine,' broke in Mim, taking Frank's arm and offering him a smile. 'I called in earlier for a cuppa and she was busy wrapping Christmas gifts. Come on, Frank. Just one little drink.'

She set her mouth just so, that come-hither look she had perfected standing in front of the bathroom mirror, daring him to refuse.

'Go on, Frank,' urged George, digging in his pocket for loose change. 'Here's a few bob. The first drinks are on me.'

The lights in the flat were off when Frank arrived home. Nina had obviously gone to bed. She would be angry with him, he knew. Missing tea. Coming home late and stinking of gin. But it had been a monumental day, in more ways than one.

He stood in the doorway, wondering if he should simply bunk down in the living room and not wake her. She had been sleeping badly of late and he didn't need an argument at this time of night.

Carefully, trying not to make any noise that might wake her, he groped his way across the room, easing himself onto the settee. Curling into a ball, he slept until the first bright rays of sun warmed the room.

CHAPTER 8

Frank arrived the following morning, clutching the note Nina had left on the table and full of apologies. He stood at the doorway to the room, watching her perched high in the bed.

'I'm sorry, Nina,' he began. 'I didn't know, didn't realise until ...' He held the note forward. 'Mim said you were all right,' he added lamely.

'Don't you want to know about the baby?' Nina asked crisply, as though the mere mention of Mim's name grated on her.

'The baby?'

'A girl.'

Frank made his way down the corridor for his obligatory visit to the nursery. He watched the nurse push a crib towards the large window. Grudgingly she folded down the pink blanket and he could see a small fist, fingers uncurling against the sudden exposure to air. Red wrinkled face, thatch of dark hair: he stood, hands pressed flat against the glass and stared in wonder at this tiny life he and Nina had created.

He would have liked to hold the child, feel the weight, the substance of her. Would have liked to touch his own rough finger to hers. But her tiny mouth puckered, and the nurse swiftly pulled the blanket back into position and wheeled the crib away, leaving him standing staring into the nursery and the rows of sleeping babies.

He felt empty inside, superfluous. The part he had played in all this had been so small, so insignificant. It was Nina who had carried the child, felt the first movements. It was Nina who had pushed the child from her body, watched as their daughter had taken her first breath and cried for the first time. And here he was, hours later, so far removed from all that had happened that the only view of her was through a plate-glass window.

'She's very small,' he said when he returned, looking concerned.

'Six pounds, four ounces,' replied Nina proudly. 'Matron says she's a good size, seeing she came early.'

'Her face's all red and screwed up.'

'Frank!' reprimanded Nina, indignant that he could possibly think otherwise. 'I think she's beautiful.'

Tactfully Frank changed the course of the conversation. 'Of course she is. Just like her mother. What do you want to call her?'

They had discussed names over the past few months. Nina thought for a moment. 'Claire,' she said at last. 'I think I'd like to call her Claire.'

*　*　*

Trams trundled past, heading in the same direction, but Frank ignored them, preferring instead to walk as he headed back to the flat. Two blocks from the hospital, he stopped outside a florist's window, admiring the display. Selecting a dozen long-stemmed red roses, he ordered them sent to Nina's room. Then, from the confectioners next door, he selected several boxes of chocolates. He would surprise Nina with them when he went back to visit that evening.

Seeing his wife sitting in that hospital bed, her face pale, his guilt had known no bounds. Somehow he had to make it up to her: his late arrival after his daughter's birth and what Nina perceived as his seeming lack of concern.

Blast Mim! It was all her fault.

In that darkened bar on Lower George Street the previous afternoon, one drink had led to two, then three. The alcohol had loosened her tongue and Mim had been talkative, telling him things, personal details, about her own marriage that he was reluctant to hear. George was his mate, after all, and he felt some allegiance to the man. More so, when he'd walked Mim home later that evening and she'd reached up and kissed him.

He'd been so surprised, so startled that, for a moment he'd simply stood there, feeling her lips on his. Her tongue had urgently probed his mouth. Her body had pressed suggestively against his own. The invitation had been obvious and, for one long moment, he had been tempted. Then he'd remembered George, his mate, waiting in the nearby house and had pulled away. Shocked.

'Mim!'

She'd laughed, swaying against him as she withdrew a packet of cigarettes from her bag. Capstans, Frank had noted earlier. 'Now I suppose you're angry with me?'

Angry? No. Certainly appalled. Confused. Stunned. Not to mention frightened by his own immediate response. He had leaned forward and struck a match for her. The flame had flared and he'd seen her questioning upturned face in its glow as she bent forward to light the cigarette.

'No. Not angry.'

She'd taken a long draw on the Capstan then leant back, rocking unsteadily on her heels. 'I've embarrassed you, then?'

'Why would you say that?'

'Because.'

He'd given a shaky laugh. 'Don't be silly.'

'I know you wanted to.'

'What?'

Word games, that was what she was playing. Teasing him. Seducing him with her mouth. It seemed he couldn't take his eyes from those red-painted lips as they closed around the cigarette.

'You wanted to fuck me, Frank!'

The force of the word struck him and he'd stepped back. 'Mim!' he'd said again, stunned.

'Don't tell me it isn't true.'

He'd been silent for a moment. Thinking. What *could* he say? Of course it was the truth. She was young and pretty, and very desirable. She was also George's wife.

'I hate lies, Frank,' she'd prompted.

Tactful. Tread softly. 'In another life I might have been tempted, but there's George and Nina —'

Vehemently. 'George wouldn't care!'

'Of course he would. George loves you.'

Did he? Frank hadn't known. But he had to diffuse the situation somehow.

'George and I have —' Mim had paused, staring at the cigarette for a moment, as though selecting the right word. '—an arrangement, if you like. He has other ... lovers.'

'Don't you mind?'

'Do I have a choice?'

'Yes.'

Her laugh had sounded forced. 'I'm not talking about *women*, Frank.'

'Oh!' He hadn't expected that.

'I knew all the time. He was honest about it when I first met him. Upfront.'

'So why —'

'Why did I marry him? Simple. I thought I could change him.'

'But you couldn't?'

'Of course not. It's not something you can *cure*; I know that now. So, you see,' she had continued bitterly, her voice strained, 'it's all a bit of a sham, really: our marriage, sharing a bed. Oh, don't get me wrong. George is good fun, and we have a great life together. There's just no sex.'

'I don't know what to say. I never guessed, never suspected.'

'George and I play a well-rehearsed charade. Cloak of respectability, and all that. No-one knows.'

'I can see that.'

'But underneath I'm a normal healthy woman. I have needs and desires.'

He'd been silent for a moment, trying to muster non-existent words.

'So this business that you and George are starting. I'm counting on it to do well,' Mim continued.

'We're all hoping for that!'

'You don't understand. There has to be some sort of compensation, doesn't there? Money. Social standing. Otherwise there'd be no point in going on.'

'I suppose not.'

She drew furiously on the cigarette, then looked thoughtful for a moment. 'I must be drunk. There's no way I'd be telling you this if not. How many martinis did I have, do you remember? George always says I drink too much.'

'I lost count,' he'd admitted sheepishly.

'About what happened before. You won't say anything to Nina? It was just a harmless bit of fun.' She had stared at him, hard, as though daring him to say otherwise.

'Of course not. We'll forget this ever happened.'

Silently Mim had flicked what was left of the cigarette into the gutter, where it had glowed, the tip red in the dark. She had brought her hand to her mouth and her eyes seemed to glitter. Tears? he'd thought, surprised.

'I think I'd better take you home.'

She had said nothing for the remainder of the walk, folding her arms across her chest, creating a barrier between them. He hadn't known what to say, so he, too, was silent. At the front gate she had paused, her hand on the palings. 'I'm not sorry for what I did or said,' she had whispered. Then she had turned, purposefully, and walked inside.

Frank had stood for a long time outside the house. A warm breeze rustled in the trees overhead and, from somewhere inside the house, a gramophone started up, playing scratchy music.

I've got the time —
I've got the place —
Will someone kindly introduce me to the girl.

A picture of Jimmy Melville had flashed across his consciousness. Jimmy sitting in the wheelchair, one trouser leg knotted at the knee. Bill and Paddy, both dead. Thousands of others, too. What was luckier? he had thought. Being killed in some French field, or being suffocated slowly by the memories?

Unconsciously he had brought a hand to his groin and was surprised by the bulk of hardness there. *Christ!* he'd thought, hating himself, despising his own reaction to Mim's fleeting proposition. Nina and the baby. His own inability to touch her while she was pregnant. It was all too much.

Now, standing at the confectioner's counter, boxes of chocolates in his hand, he sensed that the events of the previous afternoon had been contrived. Mim's appearance outside the bank. 'Let's celebrate,' she'd said, knowing full well that George had other pressing matters to attend to. The drinks, paid for by George's money, loosening tongues and inhibitions.

You wanted to fuck me, Frank.

Mim's words jarred at him, and he felt a slow flush spread along his brow.

'That the lot, mate?' asked the confectioner, taking the boxes of chocolates from Frank's hands and wrapping them.

Frank nodded numbly. If he answered, he was sure his voice would be nothing but a whisper.

That night, the dream came again. He was awake, or so he thought, when he heard the tramp of feet. *Thump, thump, thump.* His heart quickened. His ears strained for other noises. Screaming. The thud of gunfire. But, apart from the sound of boots striking the chalky earth, there was only silence.

He peered through the gloom, seeing the dusty figures approach. Slouch hats. Khaki puttees. Bloodless faces staring straight ahead, not seeing him. Am I invisible? he wondered. Perhaps these men are real and I'm dead?

The features were familiar on the man passing him now.

'Bill?'

Tentatively Frank reached out a hand, clutching at his brother's arm. His fingers immersed themselves into putrid flesh. Maggots wriggled on the sleeve, plopping noiselessly to the ground. A stench, like no other he had encountered before, rose up to meet him, permeating his nostrils.

'NO! NO! NO!'

A foul liquid filled his mouth. He gagged, leaning forward, spewing a mixture of fear and remorse — remnants of his previous evening with Mim.

The room was gloomy, lit only by a faint glow from the streetlights below. 'Nina!' he cried, frantically searching the bed with his hand and encountering only emptiness.

'NINA!'

Where was she? He needed her. Had she gone, too, like everyone else important in his life?

Then he remembered. Nina was in the hospital. He had visited her there. She'd had the baby. A daughter. Claire.

Relieved, his head sank back against the pillow, which was damp from perspiration. His heart pounded. A pain had begun in his chest, a tight band, near the place where he imagined his heart to be. Perhaps I'm dying, he thought, momentarily alarmed.

In his mind's eye, he imagined her there, his wife.

'It's all right. Just a dream. Just a dream,' she'd say.

Whispered words. Nina running a finger down his cheek. Soothing. Soothing. Stroking away the horror.

When he woke, it was morning. The sun shone. Outside, the traffic rumbled. It was almost Christmas. A new year.

His thoughts turned to George and Mim, and their sham of a marriage.

George has other lovers.

I'm not talking about women, Frank.
You wanted to fuck me.

Had he? Of course not. And neither had Mim. It was simply the grog talking. All he had to do was make sure he never placed himself in that same situation again.

He thought of those last awful days at Tea-tree Passage, and the new existence he and Nina now shared. This tiny flat. Pinning his hopes on the building venture with George.

George! Remembered Mim's revelations again. He never would have guessed!

Lastly he thought of his daughter. Claire. Puckered face and mop of dark hair. Hand curling, fingers splaying out.

Perfect.

Perfect.

Nothing mattered, he considered drowsily, watching the curtains move sluggishly in the early morning breeze.

Nothing mattered.

Except Nina and the child.

CHAPTER 9

Claire Elizabeth Carmody.

Nina doodled the name on spare pieces of paper, watching the flow of words, the rise and fall of the letters. There was a rhythm to the names, a cadence that she found soothing. 'Claire,' she whispered, basking in the sound of it, as she held her daughter to her breast, and the baby stared up at her with age-old eyes.

The child consumed and delighted her and there seemed to be time for little else. Hours that once dragged now passed miraculously, one day gliding into the next, so that she was surprised how quickly the weekends seemed to flow into each other and the weeks became a busy blur.

During those first few months she came to the crib at odd times, watching her daughter as she slept. She stood, mesmerised by dark eyelashes fluttering against porcelain skin and the rise and fall of that tiny chest. She was like a miracle, Nina thought, evolving from what seemed like nothing into this living breathing person. Part of her, part of Frank. A blend of them both.

Then, guilty because the housework had fallen behind, she hurried around the flat while the baby slept, tidying this, cleaning that. And by the time Frank came home, late and ready for his supper, she had a hot meal waiting, though she was exhausted and desperate for sleep.

She wrote to Frank's mother and father, telling them they were grandparents. There had been no contact with the older couple since Nina and Frank's hasty departure from Tea-tree Passage, but she felt they had a right to know. However the letter came back, weeks later, unopened, bearing the words, *Return to sender*.

Despite all that, Nina felt a sense of contentment. Her role seemed complete. Mother. Wife. Though it was lucky, she thought sometimes, that she had Claire to remind herself of her husband, as she saw so little of Frank. With the renovations of the flats well underway, he was often home late, picking tiredly at his tea before collapsing into bed. Each morning he was gone before sunrise.

Mim came to visit unexpectedly, looking fashionable in a lemon hip-waisted dress and leaving a waft of Muhlen's Oriviola perfume in her wake. Nina, still carrying a little excess weight since Claire's birth and wearing an old housecoat, felt dowdy by comparison. And the flat, she thought, glancing around in dismay at the pile of unfolded nappies and baby paraphernalia, seemed more a shrine to motherhood compared to Mim's immaculately neat home.

'Sorry about the mess,' she apologised, scooping up the remnants of Claire's bath-time towels and soap. 'She's such a little scrap but she seems to take up all my time.'

Mim waved her hand dismissively. 'You poor dear. So tied down here. Don't you just *hate* it?'

'No,' replied Nina firmly, handing Claire, freshly washed and dressed, to Mim. 'And if you're going to come here spouting the disadvantages of motherhood, you can experience some of them first hand. I've just fed her and she'll have a bit of wind. Hold her, just so, and rub her back.'

Mim sat on the chair holding the baby, looking most awkward, while Nina proceeded to assemble the necessities for morning tea. Obligingly Claire burped, and Mim promptly handed her back when Nina returned with the teapot and a plate of biscuits. 'She's so little,' she protested. 'If I dropped her, I'd never forgive myself.'

It was like that with Mim, Nina thought and, try as she might, she found it a burden being with her. Mim was a complex character, running hot one minute then cold the next, and Nina was unable to pinpoint her exact feelings towards the woman. At times she found her selfish, full of her own concerns, and rarely felt comfortable in her company.

Yet, on the other hand, Mim had made several attempts to include Nina in her own circle of friends. There had been invitations to various events during the day, which she had attended out of loneliness and boredom. Mim's group were mostly arty bohemian types: Henry the writer, Peter the artist and Zoe who did crafty things with shells and pieces of driftwood.

Mim, she thought privately, was everything that she, Nina, was not. She was younger. She had family, a nice home, and George didn't seem to suffer from any of the post-war problems that Frank had. There appeared to be plenty of money — so why had George needed a financial partner? — and the couple were always throwing lavish impromptu parties.

Yet despite Mim's efforts to include her, there was something blocking their possible friendship, and Nina felt awkward and out of place around the younger woman. Thankfully, since Claire's birth, the invitations had dwindled.

She tried to discuss the problem with Frank, but he was defensive, touchy, where George and Mim were concerned.

'Mim's a free spirit,' Frank countered. 'You could learn a lot from her.'

'Such as?'

'For a start, she could teach you to lighten up a bit.'

'Lighten up! What's that supposed to mean?'

'Sometimes you're so serious. Mim now, she knows how to have fun.'

'So I'm old and staid, is that what you're saying?'

'Don't take it personally. I'm only trying to help.'

They argued on and on in the same vein, until Claire, disturbed by the voices, woke.

'Now look what you've done!' chided Nina.

'You were arguing, too.'

She took Claire from her crib and unbuttoned her blouse. *Lighten up!* she thought as the baby nuzzled her breast. *Sometimes you're so serious!*

Frank's words stung. Was that how he saw her, a frumpy old thing? It was all very well for Mim to act like she hadn't a care in the world, but she and George didn't have a family to support.

Frank, as usual, had the last say. 'Good God, Nina! For the sake of the business, can't you just try to get on with her?'

The altercation simmered between them for days, unspoken words creating an almost-palpable tension. Nina busied herself with the child, ignoring Frank who seemed moody and preoccupied. He was tired, she knew, and likely to flare up at the smallest thing. He and George were working to a deadline with the renovations. Costs had gone over the allocation and money was short. She, herself, was on a strict budget.

In the end she capitulated, just to restore peace to their small household. Frank was right, she conceded grudgingly. For his sake she'd smile and be polite, say all the right words. And maybe, in time, the suspicion that there was more to Mim than was first apparent would disappear.

Frank felt at home there, in that bustling scurrying city with its narrow alleyways and back lanes. Life ran at breakneck speed, not slow as at Tea-tree Passage. There was always something to see and do, and he could easily lose himself in the anonymity of the crowds.

There were times when his thoughts returned to

that place where he had grown up, and from which he had fled a year earlier. The old wharf. Watching the *Sea-spray* as she came across the bar. Mrs Melville padding out to the dirt pathway as he passed, waving cheerily. He wondered fleetingly about John and Maudie. Were they well? Had they had a good season on the boats?

He thought about his parents, particularly his father, and those same old words crowded his mind, blocking further reflections:

'You're not half the man Bill was.'
'. . . you're a bloody disappointment.'
'I lost my best son in the war.'

Then he'd clamp off the memory of those words, halting them with some distraction or other, willing them gone. What was done, was done, and there was no going back. Tea-tree Passage and everything associated with it belonged in the past. Their own future — his, Nina's and the child's — was in this city, not in some lethargic backwater.

He and George were spending every available minute at the flats. The renovations were running behind schedule and they were working long hours, trying to catch up. There had been some unexpected hiccups — one of the floors had been riddled with dry rot and had to be replaced, and several plumbing pipes had corroded away to almost nothing. New baths. Indoor flushing toilets. Freshly painted walls. Trucks delivered still-hard-to-get supplies. Slowly the project was taking shape.

Replastering, painting, sanding: he found he adapted readily to these new skills and he enjoyed the work. It distracted him, kept his thoughts on an even keel. Some days the war years receded altogether, blotted out by the urgency of the present. Some nights he was too tired to dream.

Try as he might, he found it hard to forget the scene with Mim, months earlier. She was always there, at some party or meeting, hovering on the periphery of his consciousness like a bright bird. Unconventional daring Mim. Truthfully, he didn't find her physically attractive. She was thin, too much so perhaps, and had her hair cut into an unfeminine fashionable bob. Her hemlines were shorter than those of any other woman he knew, her breasts flattened by the tight fabric. But there was something about her, some inexplicable vivacity that fascinated him. At parties she seemed to always corner him in some dark quiet place — or was that only his imagination? — laying a hand on his arm, asking advice about some trivial matter.

'George says we should paper the bathroom. What do you think?' she asked.

He shrugged and sipped his drink, uncertain what to say next, trying not to look at her mouth or let his gaze slide to her breasts. 'I don't know, Mim. Whatever appeals to you.'

'You appeal to me.'

'Sshh!' He looked wildly around. Had anyone heard? Where was Nina? 'For God's sake, Mim!'

'It's all right. I checked first.'

She moved forward, pressing her body against his until he could smell her fragrance. Casually she brushed her hand against his crotch. 'I need you, Frank.'

'Don't do this, Mim.'

'Don't do what?' And she smiled at him, slow and teasing, before walking away, leaving him with an overwhelming ache in his groin.

George was his usual effusive self, and Frank found it difficult to think of him in *that* way. Was it true? he wondered. Surely Mim wouldn't fabricate something so ... He searched his mind for words. Obscene? Smutty? So blatantly unimaginable. But whatever Mim was, he didn't think she'd stoop to lying.

He caught himself watching George at the various social events they attended. He seemed always surrounded by clusters of women, yet Frank noticed a disinterest there, a complacent acceptance.

Days, weeks and months blurred into one another, none standing out as distinct and separate from the rest. He measured the passing time by his daughter's first smile, her initial clumsy attempts to roll over. Claire: tiny dark-haired scrap. By the time he arrived home each night, he could hardly stand for exhaustion and she was usually in bed. While Nina reheated his supper, he stood by the crib staring at her pale skin, her small upturned nose, the mouth that puckered in sleep. As he watched, a feeling of love welled up inside him, accompanied by a sensation akin to grief. She was his daughter, yet she seemed like a stranger.

Sometimes he found himself referring to Claire as Nina's baby, checking himself too late. If only I had more time, he thought. More time for Nina. More time for Claire. I'm her father, yet she scarcely knows me.

At night he lay awake, listening. Was he hoping she'd wake? he wondered, anxious to hold her. At the sound of the first whimpering, he lifted the child from the makeshift crib he had built, months earlier.

'Sshh,' he soothed.

But it was Nina she wanted, her mother. Carefully he brought the baby to the bed and lightly touched Nina's arm. She stirred, her movements heavy with sleep. Wordlessly he handed her the child.

It was at times like these he felt superfluous, shut out. He saw Nina's face, dark and mysterious in the lamplight, all hollows and ridges as she held the child to her breast. He watched Claire's mouth moving furiously against that brown nipple — a most intimate action — and her tiny hand curling and uncurling against Nina's skin, but he was not part of it.

Nina was growing away from him, he knew that, and he was powerless to stop her. She was absorbed with the baby; he worked such long hours that they seldom saw each other. We're like ships that pass in the night, he thought, remembering those times when it had just been the two of them alone in the city.

Nina said nothing. She was like that. Silent. Holding it all in. 'I'm sorry we're spending so little time together,' he told her. 'Things will change soon. The renovations are nearly done.'

But what would he do then? He loved the work, enjoyed watching it all come together like a giant jigsaw puzzle. Rooms becoming livable again. Beauty rising from what had once been sheer ugliness.

He took her to the flats, showing her the largest one on the top floor. Two bedrooms. New kitchen. Bathroom with gleaming white fixtures. There was a balcony which had a fine view to the distant hills, and a living room with a black pressed-metal fireplace.

'This one will be ours,' he said, watching as she prowled the rooms while Claire slept in her pram.

She paused in front of the fireplace, running her hand along the polished mantelpiece. 'This is beautiful.'

'It's mahogany. George managed to find it. Despite all the shortages, you can still put your hands on the right materials if you know where to look.'

'I can see us here in winter, in front of the fire.'

He moved forward, wrapping his arms about her, and she raised her face to his. The years slid away, dissolving into a blur of memories. He saw her as she was then, on that first night of their marriage. Smiling, her face radiant in the yellow lamplight. Jimmy. Paddy. Bill. Their girlfriends. Sound of accordion. Happy, happy time.

Of that laughing group, only he and Nina were left. The girls were gone, dispersed like the wind. Paddy was dead. Bill too. And Jimmy . . .

'Nina?' He had to make it right, repair whatever damage had been done to their relationship during those intervening years.

Downstairs, he could hear the workmen's hammers. She glanced towards the sound, and laughed. 'Should we?'

'You want to, don't you?'

'Yes.'

He locked the door and took her in his arms, gently, tracing the outline of her cheeks, her mouth, with his lips.

Claire was seven months old when Nina discovered she was pregnant again.

'I know this isn't a good time,' she told Frank, biting her lower lip. 'But the doctor says I'm already three months gone.'

One of Mim's friends had told her there was no way she could fall pregnant while she was breastfeeding. So much for that good advice, she thought now, facing Frank.

'So, we plan our children for the good times?' he asked. 'What will be, will be. If you're happy, then I'm happy.'

'Are you sure?' she asked, looking doubtful.

'We always said we wanted lots of kids. Besides, this one might be a boy. Carmody & Son. I can just see it now.'

'Oh, silly.' She gave him a playful punch, then looked serious. 'You're working too hard. Look at you. Face grey. You should slow down more.'

'Soon. Soon.'

'That's what you said last month. And the month before.'

'It's for us, our future. There are years ahead to slow down.'

Promises, assurances: she was forced to be content with them. Frank's continuing absence, the feeling that she was bringing up Claire all by herself. Morning sickness that seemed to last all day. The one thing that kept her going was the thought of the new flat, almost completed. They'd be able to move in before this new baby was born, taking them from the cramped quarters of their present home.

A few days before the completion of the renovations, George asked Frank to meet him at the pub. 'There's someone I think you should see,' he said, when pressed for a reason.

The man was an agent. He had a client wanting to purchase a block of inner-city flats. The building was to be rented, so condition was important. Frank and George's building was perfect. Would they consider selling?

'Think about it,' George cautioned later, after the man had gone. 'We can turn this place over and sink our capital into something bigger. The sky's the limit and that's where we should be aiming. Upwards.'

'But I promised Nina one of the flats.'

'There'll be others. I already know of a little place ...'

Frank tossed and turned all night, unable to sleep. He thought of Nina running her hand across the mantelpiece. 'This is beautiful,' she'd said. And so it was. He remembered making love to her there, Claire asleep in her pram and the dust motes dancing in the shaft of sunlight that had fallen on the carpet next to them. He remembered, also, Nina chasing them with her hand, and those minute particles sliding away, always out of reach.

That was what life was about, he thought, despondent. Happiness. Always elusive, waiting beyond his grasp. And what was happiness, anyway? Doing what you enjoyed most? Having the love of a woman, the innocent adoration of a child? What a damnable position he was in! George wanted to sell, but he knew Nina wouldn't. So whom should he please?

By morning he had made his decision. George was right. There would be other places. Bigger. More modern. Nina deserved the best. She'd just have to wait until it came along, that was all.

Frank went to see the agent. He named a price, far in excess of their costs. A few days later, the offer was accepted.

Nina was very quiet when he told her, and he could see the disappointment in her face. Instantly he hated himself. He had made promises that he had not kept. All she had wanted was that lousy flat, some place to call home.

'That's wonderful news, Frank,' she said and turned away.

'Hey,' he said, taking her arm and drawing her towards him. 'I know you had your heart set on the place, but this makes better financial sense. We've covered wages and there's a tidy profit in the bank.'

'I'm happy,' she replied in a wooden voice. 'I'm happy, Frank.'

'There'll be another place for us. Something better.'

But he could see from her expression that she would not be immediately placated.

* * *

Nina's disappointment was palpable and lasted for weeks. The thought of someone else, someone other than herself, living in those beautiful rooms made her feel wretched.

'He promised,' she told Mim.

But Mim's mind was on the profit they'd made and she was already planning a party to celebrate. 'Something else will come along,' she replied blithely. 'Now, do you think I should have vodka, or just stick with the gin and scotch?'

A week later Frank arrived home early. He was obviously in a good mood. 'Come on,' he said, laughing. 'Get Claire ready. We're going out.'

'We are? Where?'

'There's something I want to show you. Well, two things, really.'

She came downstairs onto the street, Claire on her hip. Frank was waiting on the footpath, holding open the door of a shiny red automobile. She stood, open-mouthed, staring at him. 'Frank?'

'Well, come on. Can't stand around here all day. There's people to meet, places to go?' Then. 'Do you like it?'

'This is ours?' she asked incredulously as he helped her into the front seat.

'Things are on the up and up for us, Nina. As George says, the sky's the limit.'

They bowled along the city streets, Nina aware of the admiring glances towards the car. Claire sat on her lap, her nose pressed flat against the window. Frank's driving seemed purposeful and not lacking direction. He was obviously not taking them on a leisurely outing.

The central city became suburbs and they passed through new estates. It seemed to Nina that houses were going up everywhere, the skeletal frames rising out of the ground like the proverbial phoenix. Lorries rumbled by, carrying loads of timber, corrugated iron and bricks. Workmen hurried.

'Where are we going?' she asked, as suburban streets gave way to farms.

'Just wait,' Frank said, smiling mysteriously. 'All will be revealed in due course.'

With a flourish, he brought the car to a halt next to an old farmhouse. He helped them from the front seat and together they walked to the fence that separated the property from the road. Frank leant against it, surveying the land that rose and fell, stretching as far as the eye could see. Yellow wildflowers danced in the breeze, faces bobbing up and down. To the far left, several calves lay in the shade of a clump of trees.

'This is our next venture.'

Mystified she turned to look at him, shading the sun from her eyes with her hand. Frank was talking in riddles and she was supposed to understand? Was he planning on taking up farming?

'It's a cow paddock.'

'Not for long.'

'You're going to build houses here?'

'Yep.'

She shook her head in disbelief. 'It's so far out, and there's nothing for miles. Who'd want to live here? It'd take forever to get into the city for shopping.'

'Progress, Nina. This is the way of the future. Self-sufficient suburbs with their own shopping centres.'

'Shopping centres? *Out here*?'

'The land's going for a song, and we'd be mad not to take the opportunity. It means investing all the profit from the flats, and the bank has offered to lend us the balance. Twelve months and you won't know this place. Roads. Fences. We're planning on building the houses ourselves, selling them as a complete lot.'

She tried to match his enthusiasm, tried to envisage the houses and roads, the shopping centre. 'That's very ambitious. Don't you think you're trying to get too big too quickly?'

'Don't be a wet blanket! You've got to aim high, Nina, have big goals. The little ones aren't worth fighting for, I reckon.'

'Goals,' she said lightly, thinking about the flat Frank had promised, then taken away.

He took her hand, bringing it to his mouth. 'Look, I know this is difficult. We never see each other, and there's going to be a new baby. But hard work never killed a man, and this is for us, our future.'

The baby inside her kicked, and Claire wriggled in her arms. Suddenly it all seemed too much to think about, too overwhelming. She herself needed smaller boundaries. Home. Children. She was content with that.

CHAPTER 10

She named the baby Joseph Francis Carmody, but mostly everyone called him Joe. He arrived a week late, long and lean, with a crop of dark hair like Claire. Thankfully he was a placid child, happy to lie in his crib for hours, watching the movement of light on the ceiling or reaching fingers towards the butterfly mobile Nina had made from a few scraps of bright paper and string.

Claire adored her little brother. She had not long celebrated her first birthday and was tottering around the flat on unsteady legs. Under supervision, Nina let her hold Joe, sitting both her children on her knee.

'Bubby, bubby,' chirped Claire, kissing him ardently on the cheek at every available opportunity.

Space was at a premium in their tiny cramped quarters, so Frank took a lease on a new flat. It was in the same building but on a higher floor, larger, with two good-sized bedrooms and a small balcony that Nina was apprehensive about letting Claire have access to, in case she climbed the railing and fell.

One more set of stairs to lug two babies and a pram. Obviously Frank hadn't considered that, she thought, as she manoeuvred them all down to the street that first time. Claire wriggled on her hip while Joe slept in the other arm. Nina bit her lip, worried that she might miss her footing, slip, and send them all toppling down the stairwell.

It was a marathon effort just to reach the footpath. She stood there, catching her breath before moving on. The worst of the hot weather had gone. A cool breeze blew through the city streets and she pulled the blanket tighter over the sleeping baby. Claire toddled alongside for a few minutes then demanded to be picked up. Nina struggled along, pushing the pram with one hand.

Their new afternoon routine included a visit to the local park. The small square of land was sandwiched between two tall buildings. There were seats and slippery dips, swings and a seesaw, but little sunlight. Claire enjoyed the company of the other children, playing happily in the sandpit while Nina watched.

There were other mothers pushing prams, gathering around the swings, laughing and talking. To Nina it seemed she was on the sidelines, looking on. Part of the overall scene, yet not partaking in it at all. One of the women had stopped once, chatted about some inconsequential thing, and she had been all tongue-tied, unable to say much except mumble a few replies. Then the woman had excused herself politely and joined the others.

'I'm a solitary person,' Nina told herself firmly. 'I enjoy my own company.'

Yet she knew that wasn't true. She craved friendship, needed the closeness the other women shared.

So what was stopping her from joining them? Nina didn't know. Shyness? Her own stupid sense of not belonging? How could she walk up to a stranger and start a conversation? What could she possibly say to these women who smiled and gossiped so easily? She herself lacked those skills. Unlike Mim, she thought enviously. Mim would have known exactly what to say — some amusing anecdote or a witty introduction.

Then she wondered why she had thought of Mim, who would no more go to a children's playground than fly? Because, she told herself, that of all the people in this sprawling busy city, Mim was the only one who had made any effort.

Since the birth of the children, she had felt herself caught in that narrow tract of time and place. Disjointed. Adrift. Without purpose. The flat, the corner shops, the park, had become the boundaries to her world.

'You're becoming boringly prosaic,' Mim had said only a week earlier, when Nina had refused yet another invitation to join her for a mid-morning get-together.

'I am not,' Nina had denied hotly. 'I'm busy with the children, that's all. We have a routine.'

'Oh, routines, *routines*,' mimicked Mim. 'Joe sleeps all day whether you're home or not, and

Claire's old enough to enjoy a change from the predictable.'

Later, thinking about it, she had taken out the accusation, examined it, and knew that Mim was right. That's me, she thought. Dull, unimaginative Nina. What on earth does Frank see in me? Frank, who took risks that she herself would not. Frank, who was not afraid to have goals. It seemed the more he ventured forward, the further she retreated, hiding behind her family and making excuses.

Only the previous week she had taken the children into the city centre, walking through the huge arcades. The domed roofs had stretched high above, pigeons fluttering against the glass. Trapped, she thought, like herself. Caught up in that thronging surging mass, she had felt out of her depth, as though the crowds might swallow her.

No-one knows me, she thought. No-one knows *me*. Neither my past nor my present. And as for the future . . .

Now, sitting on that hard bench in the park, she glanced at her children with a fierce maternal pride. Joe sleeping in his pram, Claire chasing the pigeons across the shadowy expanse of grass: her whole existence seemed caught up in them, bound by them. What if something happened? she thought, unable to imagine her life without them.

Abruptly she called Claire, tucked the blanket tighter around the sleeping baby, and made her way back to the warmth and safety of the flat.

*   *   *

Nina stood in front of the mirror, naked, turning this way and that. It was only six months since Joe's birth yet, as she peered at her reflection, there was certainly no evidence remaining. Trim hips. Flat stomach. In fact, she thought, she had even lost weight.

Frank came into the room, fresh from his bath. She watched him in the mirror as he came up behind her, bringing his hands up, cupping her breasts. They were large hands, the fingers calloused, yet surprisingly gentle. And despite all that had happened, the distance she sensed growing between them, he still had that same exhilarating effect on her.

'You're beautiful,' he said now, bending, nuzzling at the skin on her neck, little nips of pleasure that sent a surge of warmth between her thighs.

'Not now, Frank. Mim's party —' she began, instantly regretting the words. What had she promised herself, after that day in the park months earlier? I will *not* be predictable. I will be innovative and resourceful and clever. I will be more like Mim.

Mim would have turned in her husband's arms, Nina knew. Turned and embraced the moment. And she, Nina, should do the same. Besides, there would be no interruptions. The children were staying with a neighbour, and she and Frank had the flat to themselves.

Frank was kneading her nipple now, slowly, between thumb and forefinger. Let it flow, said a small voice inside her head. What does it matter if you're late?

'It doesn't matter if we're late,' said Frank, his words mirroring her thoughts as he brought his hand down across her belly. 'How often do I have you totally to myself? In fact, given the right encouragement, I could be tempted to stay here all night.'

No matter how good the sex was, how stimulating, she always felt some relief when it was over. 'I love you, Nina,' he said later as they lay on the bed, sheets rumpled.

And he did. She knew that. But it was a smothering all-or-nothing kind of love, one she could not reciprocate.

She slid from the bed, pulling a Capstan Oval-heavyweight from the cigarette case on the dresser. Smoking was a habit newly acquired, and she found it soothing. It calms me, she told herself. Cigarette in hand, she padded around the room, gathering the necessities for the evening. Brassiere. Knickers. A small black clutch purse.

'What do you think?' she asked Frank, holding forward a red dress.

'I think I'd prefer it if you didn't smoke. It's very masculine, Nina.'

'This one or the blue?' she asked, ignoring the comment.

'Neither.'

She swung around, stared at him hard and took a long draw on the cigarette. 'It's a little difficult trying to make a silk purse out of a sow's ear on a budget, Frank. We can just forget the evening, if you'd prefer.'

'What I'd prefer is that you go back to looking like yourself.'

'Myself!'

'Look at you! Skirts up to your knees! Breasts squashed under those unflattering dresses. Hair cut so short that from the back I'd almost think you were a bloke —'

Indignantly she replied, 'I do *not* look like a bloke!'

'You look like a replica of Mim. What about a bit of cleavage? You have nice breasts. Why not show them off?'

'*Frank!*'

'For God's sake, Nina. I want you to look like a woman, not a boy.'

Tears stung her eyes and she turned from him, blinking them away. She would not let him see her cry. She took one of her old gowns from the wardrobe. It was plain, pale blue with a low neckline that would show off her *cleavage* just fine, she thought savagely.

As she pulled on stockings, rouged her cheeks and dabbed scent on her wrists, her thoughts tumbled angrily. No matter how hard she tried to please Frank, it seemed there was always something wrong, some fault to be found. And how was it that their relationship could change so quickly, from that loving sexual ambience to these bitter criticisms?

At the party she smiled and said all the right words, like a dutiful wife. And as she sipped George's martinis — far too quickly — she saw Mim's writer friend Henry staring unashamedly at her breasts. I hope you're *satisfied* now, Frank! she thought savagely. Later, dancing the Charleston on the back lawn to the sound of those scratchy tunes, she kicked her shoes off, feeling the dew-damp grass under her toes.

She glanced towards the house and felt a surge of resentment. Frank stood in the open doorway, glass in hand, staring at Mim. What was it about her? Nina wondered. Style? Personality? That sort of bohemian nonchalance that men find attractive?

Frank's gaze swivelled and caught hers. He put his drink on the window ledge and came towards her, across the wet grass. Firmly he caught her within his grasp, holding her hand a little too tightly. 'This dance is mine,' he said roughly.

She heard the music and saw the other guests mouth words that she couldn't hear. Frank's strong heart beat next to hers. His arms encompassed her. The caress of his skin against her bare shoulders felt strange and unreal — the touch of a stranger.

CHAPTER 11

Lydia was born the following April. Whereas Claire and Joe had been placid dark-haired babies, his new daughter was fair and restless, needing constant attention. The pregnancy had been difficult, Frank knew, made worse by the demands of two small children and, during those long hot summer months, Nina had struggled just to keep pace with the household chores.

'No more,' she told him the day they brought the baby home. 'I'm thirty-four years old and I've had enough. Three children in three years. It seems I spend all my life being pregnant.'

She appeared to go out of her way to avoid him, coming to bed long after he had gone to sleep or pleading some feminine ailment. On the rare occasions when they did have sex, it was half-hearted and mechanical, and he knew she received no pleasure from the act. It was, he sensed, a token effort to satisfy his own urges.

The year was 1923. Stanley Bruce was the new

Prime Minister. The words to the song 'The Road to Gundagai' were on everyone's lips. In the suburbs, new subdivisions reached out like insidious tendrils, roads and houses snaking across hills and valleys, red roofs mushrooming like blooming algae.

There were days when he could scarcely believe how successful the business had become in the last three years. No longer did they have to scrimp and save, though most of the profits were ploughed back. 'Expansion' was George's motto.

And successful it was. The cartage expenses for bringing in supplies had been horrendous, so six months earlier they had started their own carrying company. First, one truck, then two, and so on, until they had to set up an office and a yard for the vehicles, employ a secretary, drivers and a storeman.

The success had come at a price, though. Increasingly Frank found himself retreating further into the business, staying even later than before. Work was constantly piling up and weekends were often spent at the office, preparing quotations, writing cheques and organising repairs.

It was a perfect make-believe world, where the only constant event was work. Living on borrowed money, unseen profits from the housing estate sales being invested back into more land, more houses: he spent every waking hour thinking about finances and proceeds and assets.

The headaches had returned. They were slight at first, a discomfort that came and went, scarcely registering. He'd sit at his desk and unconsciously massage his temple, as though pressing the pain into some distant place. But, as time went on, they became stronger, more debilitating, reducing him to constant agony.

He took painkillers, little sachets of pink powder washed down by a glass of scotch. At times he wasn't certain what had the most effect, the aspirin or the grog. So he increased the scotch, and it deadened the pain in every way.

The business side of his life was booming yet his personal life lay in ruins. They were still living in that same two-bedroom flat they'd moved to when Joe was born. He'd offered Nina a new home in the latest estate, but she had baulked at that, preferring to stay where she was.

'Live out there in that remodelled cow paddock? Thanks, Frank, but I'd feel so out of it all, so far away.'

She wanted an established place, closer in, though God only knew when he'd get time to look for one.

His wife and children wafted in and out of his daily existence, like phantoms, scarcely seen. I must try harder, he thought, make time for them, too. Balance everything more evenly. Next week, when things slow down, we'll spend some time together. However, by the following week, a whole new set of problems had surfaced and his plans were put on hold.

'I'm doing it all for them,' he told himself repeatedly.

Yet he knew that was only partly true. He was doing it for himself also. Proving something. Making a statement. I, too, can be successful, make a go of it. *I am not second-rate. I am as good as Bill.*

Despite the car, there were days when he chose to walk to the constant inner-city meetings. Increased loans, relaxations on building codes, deferment of accounts: the banks, local councils and regular suppliers all had to be indulged and placated.

George usually let Frank handle the negotiations. 'You're better at it than me,' he declared. 'I'm too blunt. Say what I feel. My mouth sometimes gets me into more trouble than it's worth.'

It was a cool winter's day, all sunshine and scudding clouds, and a cool salty wind blowing up from the harbour as Frank let himself out the front lobby of the flats at eight o'clock. First on the schedule was a meeting with the bank manager, then he'd cab it to the office.

The meeting wasn't until eleven o'clock. Three hours to kill. One hundred and eighty minutes. It had seemed silly to leave so early, but he'd had to escape the confines of those rooms. Claire and Joe were squabbling over a basket of toys, and Lydia had been screaming for a feed. The first faint signs of a headache were niggling.

He strode along the winding streets that led down to the Quay. Everything seemed damp and he pulled his coat tighter. Shopkeepers were hosing down footpaths in preparation for their daily trade. Others were stacking their wares beside doorways, baskets of goods spilling out onto the pavement. The aroma of freshly baked bread wafting from a nearby bakery reminded him he hadn't eaten that morning.

He wandered into a pub. It was a few minutes after opening time, yet already several men breasted the bar. They were older bearded men mostly, wearing tattered clothes. Poor sods, he thought, scanning their blank faces. Nowhere to go and scant money either. What they did have was frittered away in places like this. Still, that wasn't his problem. There was no way he'd let himself get like these men. Hard work, that was the answer to the future. Wasn't his own life proving that?

He'd have a pie, and a drink to wash down the painkiller. Then maybe he'd take himself on a ferry ride to clear the cobwebs from his brain and fill in time.

Munching on the pie, Frank let his thoughts wander back to those early days of their arrival in the city. It had been just himself and Nina then, no children, working hard at the factory. And for what? Little pay and long hours. Well, he worked more hours now, as Nina constantly reminded him, but at least there was something to show for his trouble.

That first tiny flat: how happy he and Nina had been then! Wandering about the suburbs on his days off. Planning. Dreaming. Nina, pregnant with Claire, sitting on the swing in that park, face pink from running. *Come on, Frank! Push me to the sky!*

Frank downed the last of the drink and slid the empty glass back across the counter. 'I'll have another, thanks,' he told the barman.

Sipping the cold liquid, he let his thoughts drift along. Claire's birth. Joe's. Bringing Lydia home from the hospital, only months earlier. Momentous occasions in any man's life. But Nina had closed herself off to him. *No more, Frank. It seems I spend all my life being pregnant.*

He thought back to the flat that same morning. Lydia screaming. Claire and Joe fighting. Nina sitting on the settee, unbuttoning her blouse, proffering her cheek to him as he left. What was wrong with kissing him on the mouth, for God's sake? She'd been more intent on pacifying the baby than even noticing him.

Was love calculable? It had a beginning so, in theory, it must have an end. And if so, how did one determine at what point one's emotions were at in a relationship, at any given time?

But, he told himself, Nina loved. God how she *loved*. Only the object of her emotions was no longer himself. So when, at what precise moment, had her love transferred through to her children, leaving him adrift on that cold and wine-dark sea? *When*?

There's no room for me, he thought bitterly.

He had another pie and drink, then looked at his watch. If he planned to take the promised ferry ride, then he'd have to leave. But he was reluctant — too mentally exhausted and too damn miserable — to drag himself from his seat.

His thoughts turned to Mim, as he found them doing all too frequently these days. Tiny mysterious Mim, waiting in the wings like some despondent butterfly. Why did she persist? And why him? Surely she could have almost any man. Except George, he considered wryly. Was it some form of payback, or was it simply that he was handy, and she could sense his own unhappiness?

Questions, questions, questions. Yet he had no ready answers.

'Come up to my room,' she'd whispered to him at a party only the previous week. 'I can teach you things.'

She'd been drunk. Again. Swaying against him, seducing him with words and the caress of a hand, unseen by anyone but himself. There had been a momentary searing of heat where her skin had touched his and, for one long insane moment, he'd been tempted to kiss her, right there and then, careless of who saw. Wanted to put his mouth on hers, to feel her teeth with his tongue. Wanted to trace the outline of those flattened little-girl breasts. But he'd regained his senses and laughed at her, pushing her playfully away. 'Go on with you,' he'd said, trying to diffuse the situation. 'You'd regret it in the morning.'

'I would not.'

She'd turned her back and walked away from him, unsteadily, head held high. That was the thing about Mim. She had dignity, a sense of style and class. And he'd watched, feeling a combination of amusement and irrational jealousy as she had draped herself over her friend Henry the writer, turning to stare back at Frank, expressionless, with those grey soulful eyes.

A sense of propriety, a feeling of wrongness about the whole thing had held him back. No, he'd thought savagely, glancing away, trying to seek out the familiar and comforting form of Nina in the crowd. There was no way he'd be tempted. He'd acted out of respect — respect for George and his own wife, though in truth, if he were honest with himself,

George probably couldn't have cared less, and Nina scarcely wanted anything to do with him in *that way*, these days.

But now, he thought, taking a long swig of his drink, maybe he should have taken her up on the offer.

The pain in his head had begun, an insidious throb; he had to be rid of it before the meeting at the bank. No use trying to make important decisions like that. He glanced up at the clock, but the hands were a blur. He refocused his eyes, staring hard. Ten o'clock. Another hour. Plenty of time.

He took a small sachet of powder from his pocket, carefully opened it and placed the contents on his tongue. It tasted bitter, a mixture of despair and doubt, and he followed it with a long swig of scotch.

'Don't you think you've had enough?' asked the barman.

'Just one more. Come on.'

Someone else's voice came from his mouth. Slurred. Syllables running together, scarcely making sense. He shook his head and the pain throbbed. The wretched powder wasn't working.

Later, when he thought about it, he didn't remember the cab ride to the office. The first thing he was aware of was George shaking him awake on the settee in his room. George was angry, he saw, a line of red slashing his cheeks.

'Where have you been?'

'Wwh-a-a-t?' George's face faded in and out of Frank's awareness. He felt groggy and wanted to return to that blissful sleep.

'The meeting at the bank. You were supposed to be there at eleven. Now the manager's pissed off, and we'll have to go crawling to get the new loan.'

Frank struggled into a sitting position, running a hand across his forehead, trying to remember. And when he did, he experienced that awful sense of failure. The bank. The planned meeting. Oh, Christ! He'd really stuffed things up this time.

He took a day off work, a Friday, hoping to restore some sense of balance to his life. 'Get dressed,' he said to Nina, who was busy clearing the breakfast mess from the benches. 'I'm taking you shopping.'

'I don't need anything,' she replied.

She was like that, never wanting things for herself.

'No,' he insisted quietly, noting the old housecoat she wore. 'I want to buy you clothes.'

'I have enough clothes. It's not necessary.'

'I want to do this. I took a day off work especially. Humour me, please.'

'You could spend the day with the children, instead. They scarcely know you.'

The words were said with a smile, but there was an underlying coldness to her eyes that he had never seen before. He blinked and took one step backwards, unsure of what to say next. What had he thought? That all the built-up indifference, the problems of the past few years, could be wiped out by one shopping expedition?

Yet he had offered and wanted to go through with it.

'Nina. I'm proud of you. When I take you out, I want other men's heads to turn.'

She blushed, a slow flushing of her cheeks. 'Really, Frank, you say the strangest things.'

In the end, to please him, she ordered two suits, one beige, the other navy, and a taffeta gown. It was emerald green and matched, so Frank said, the colour of her eyes.

The children had been well-behaved, Lydia sleeping in her pram and Claire and Joe sitting demurely on a chair outside the changing room. And afterwards, instead of going directly home, Frank headed the car in the direction of Circular Quay, where they sat on a bench on the foreshore and ate fish and chips, watching the ferries as they plied their way across the choppy water.

It was a lazy languid day, reminiscent of those old times before the children had arrived, before Frank had met George. A wintry sun tried desperately to pour its warmth on them. A cold breeze blew from the water. Yet, for a while, Nina felt none of it, seeing instead the Carmody family picnicking, as all families should. Saw herself and Frank, husband and wife, and thought fleetingly that perhaps all could be restored.

There were several letters lying in the letterbox when they returned to the flat. Frank collected them, spreading them out for inspection on the dining table. One in particular had the original address partly scratched out, with the words, Return to sender, written across it in a thick scrawl.

121

Oh, God, she thought, turning away. Of all the days for Frank to be home!

She had been writing regularly to Frank's parents, telling them about his success, the children. By detailing their life in minutiae, she had hoped to raise some spark of interest. But this letter, like all the others, had come back unopened.

Frank picked up the envelope. 'What's this?'

The day, this magical wonderful day was, she knew, about to be ruined. 'It's a letter.'

He stared at it for what seemed like a long while. 'To my parents?'

He threw it on the table and stood, looking at her. His face was a mask, unreadable. Words failed her — what to say, anyway? — so she nodded numbly.

'How long has this been going on?'

She couldn't lie. 'Three years. Since Claire was born.'

But it was as though he hadn't heard. His voice was cold and sharp, like a knife, cutting through to the very core of her. 'We had a deal, Nina, to leave all that behind when we came here.'

'We have. But they should at least know where we are.'

'I don't want them to know!'

'You should be proud of your successes, Frank.'

'I am, but it's nothing to do with them.'

'Well, you needn't worry. The letters always come back like this. No-one reads them.'

'I want you to stop.'

'No!'

He stared at her. She could tell he was angry by the way his skin seemed to pull tight across his face.

'What did you say?'

The words were slow and measured, each one spat out singly so they could not be misunderstood. He raised his hand, bringing it across her cheek in a stinging slap. Her head slammed backwards and she brought her own hand to the place, holding it there as though trying to contain the hurt.

Tears filled her eyes but she held them in. *Please don't let him see me cry.* Anger and shock coursed through her. How dare he!

'Don't you ever, *ever* do that again, Frank Carmody!'

'Mummy? Are you all right?'

Little piping voice. She turned, horrified, toward the sound. Claire and Joe were standing round-eyed in the doorway. How much had they seen and heard?

'Mummy,' said Claire again, taking a step forward.

She ushered them before her, into the bedroom, and firmly shut the door. It was hard to breathe; the air lodged somewhere in her throat was like a huge lump. 'It's all right,' she soothed. 'Come on. On the bed. Let's take a nap.'

She lay with the children, listening to the pounding of her own heart. Her cheek still stung. Claire held her hand tight, chubby fingers grasping her own.

The front door slammed. Frank had obviously left. After a while she eased herself from the bed. The children stirred, but did not wake.

Mechanically she took the clothes Frank had bought earlier in the day and laid them on the bottom of the bed; then she stood back and surveyed them. They were his choice, really, not hers. He was still trying to mould her, after all these years of marriage, into someone other than herself. Where would she wear these classic, expensive garments? Her life scarcely ventured further than her house, and she had accepted them only to keep the peace.

Gradually she let her thoughts slide back to that scene at the dining table. Frank was right, she thought. She shouldn't have written to his parents. Frank's life, and hers, was none of their business.

He hit me and I deserved it.

The thought slammed at her awareness, shocking her. Somehow she'd try to be a better wife. Love, honour and obey: wasn't that what she had promised all those years ago? What had happened since? What had brought them to this?

She sighed, not knowing, wrapped the dresses back in the layers of tissue paper and stored the box in the bottom of her wardrobe.

Frank stormed from the flat, slamming the door hard behind him. Down the stairs he went, taking two at a time until he reached the footpath. Confused, he stumbled directionless until his back encountered the front wall of the building, and he sagged against it, his breath coming in short sweeps.

He'd hit her! Oh, Lord, he'd *hit* her!

The sight of her seemed burnt into his soul. Nina holding a hand to her cheek, a red ugly welt appearing beneath the span of her fingers. Her eyes: hollow and dark and brimming with unshed tears. The children waiting in the doorway, bewildered expressions on their faces. What had he done?

Then the anger swept through him again. How dare she go behind his back, contacting his parents! They'd had an agreement and she'd broken it, let him down. He'd trusted her and she'd betrayed him.

He swung himself into the car, started it with a series of loud revs and pulled away from the curb. He had no destination in mind, merely a need to distance himself from her. He'd drive for a few hours, or maybe visit someone, calm himself down before returning home.

Somehow he found himself outside Mim and George's house. The place looked shut up, the curtains drawn and windows locked, and he knew, even before he knocked on the front door, that no-one was home.

Shit!

He sat in the car for a few minutes, waiting. Then, with no sign of either of them in sight, he roared off in the direction of the pub.

He was driving past the shops when he saw Mim. She was tottering along the footpath, carrying an armful of packages. He pulled alongside her and clambered out.

'Want a lift?'

Relief flooded her face. 'Frank! Thank goodness. I've been trying to get a taxi for at least half an hour.'

He took the parcels and tossed them on the back seat. As he drove away, she gave him a puzzled sideways look. 'What's wrong?'

'Nothing!'

'Well, something's certainly bothering you. You're in a foul mood.'

'It's Nina, if you must know,' he blurted. 'All a bloke asks for is a bit of honesty and respect.'

'You've had an argument?'

He nodded, not trusting himself to speak. He couldn't tell her, couldn't say the words: *I hit my wife*.

Frank carried the parcels into the small cottage while Mim threw open the windows, letting the mid-afternoon sunlight flood in. Her voice floated through the rooms as she went, chattering about something inconsequential.

Carefully, suddenly aware they were alone for the first time, he asked, 'Where's George?'

'He left at lunchtime. Gone away for the weekend.'

'Oh.'

'With one of his *friends*,' she said, coming back into the room.

There was a terrible emphasis on the word and, for a moment, she looked so vulnerable, that he almost went to her, wanting to protect her against the pain.

But Mim was dancing away, her face composed once more. 'Have you had lunch? I know it's getting late, but I'm starving. Let me make you something.'

'It's not necessary.' He looked down at his hands, surprised to find them shaking. 'I should really be going.' Back to Nina. Apologise. Something.

'Nonsense. A man has to eat.'

She turned the radio on. The announcer was introducing a song. The melody reached out towards him, wearing him down.

Mim seemed not to notice. She was busy pouring him a drink. Scotch. Just how he liked it. He sat back in the chair and closed his eyes. There was a warmth in the room that didn't come from the sun, a cheerfulness that soothed him. The argument with Nina receded, pushed to the periphery of his consciousness by a delicious aroma.

'What are you making?'

'It's a surprise. You'll have to wait.' She took a bottle of wine from the shelf above the bench and passed it to him, along with two glasses. 'Here. Make yourself useful and open this.'

'Not for me. I never drink red wine.'

'Why not?'

He shrugged. 'I don't know. I just don't, that's all.'

'Rubbish. Go on, taste it.'

He raised the glass to his lips and took a tentative mouthful.

'So?'

'It's okay.'

'Men! You're so predictable.'

Affronted. 'We are not.'

She gave a laugh and stopped behind the chair, massaging her fingers lightly across his shoulders. 'It's okay to try new things, you know. Nothing like getting rid of the boredom in your life.'

Her mouth came down, lips brushing along the length of his neck. Then, before he had time to register what had happened, she had moved back to the stove.

He knew she was teasing him. Teasing with words and music, and an aroma that made his mouth water. Teasing him with the softest of touches, barely felt. He glanced across at her and she smiled. 'Relax, Frank.' Then she was placing plates of steaming food on the table.

'What is it?'

'Pasta.'

He made to push the plate away. 'Come on, Mim. That's wog stuff. Nina made it once. I wouldn't touch it.'

She stalled him, placing one hand over his. 'Try it.'

He sat there, looking at her hand. Fragile. Tiny bones, like a bird.

'*Try it*, Frank.'

The words seemed an invitation, a plea that had nothing to do with food. He turned her hand over, placing his mouth against the inside of her wrist, and she made a small sound, somewhere between a sigh and a moan.

'Don't tease me, Frank.'

'I'm not.'

She stared at him and he held her gaze, then somehow she had slid from her chair onto his lap, kissing him, flicking her tongue past his lips.

The rest, he thought, was inevitable. Even if he'd wanted to refuse, they had already gone too far to consider turning back. He groaned, sensing his own erection, and she pulled him to a standing position. He heard the click of her shoes on the timber floor and felt the pressure of her fingers on his arm as she propelled him along the hallway towards the room she and George never shared.

The canopied bed was draped with filmy fabric. Aladdin's forbidden cave, he thought, surprised, noting the silk sheets neatly turned back. Impatiently he tugged at his own clothes, hers.

'Slowly. Slowly,' she cautioned, stalling him, stepping out of her knickers and folding them across the chair.

Chest rising and falling, as though she found it difficult to draw breath, she stood before him, waiting. And when his hands cupped her naked breasts, her nipples were hard, like tiny stones. She knelt, fingers, mouth, moving down, exploring his hardness. Caressing. Little flicking movements. Bringing him almost to release. Oh, God. Not yet! Not yet!

'I want to remember you,' she said. 'Every detail.'

'Sshh. Don't talk.'

He pulled her upwards, back into alignment with his own body, and kissed away the words. There was a distinct sensation of falling though space and time — would they ever land? But they must have, he thought, her body pliable and responsive beneath his. Finally, hands guiding him impatiently. Every sense singing.

'I can make you happy.'

Had he said the words, or Mim? He didn't know.

Instead she arched upwards with frantic movements, her hands on his buttocks, drawing him deeper. 'Now, Frank! *Now!*'

It was light when he woke, pale rays sliding past the drawn curtains. He rolled over and reached for Mim, but his arm encountered only emptiness. Where was she?

A clatter of crockery drew him along the hallway to the kitchen, where he found her making up a breakfast tray.

'Good morning.'

She came to him, kissing him firmly on the mouth. 'It's a *lovely* morning. The sun is shining. The birds are singing.'

'Are they?' he smiled. 'I hadn't noticed.'

She looked momentarily serious. 'Before you say anything, I have no regrets about last night.'

'No.'

'Do you?'

He shook his head. 'It's our secret, darling Mim.'

They sat on the back verandah in the sunshine. Mim had prepared little moon-shaped croissants — served with a selection of jams — and milk coffee in tiny cups. He studied her as she ate. The satin robe she wore fell open at the neckline as she leant forward, revealing small white breasts — breasts he had trailed his mouth and fingers over the previous night.

The thought of it made him harden again with desire. 'Mim,' he said, his voice hoarse.

Wordlessly she rose and took his hand, leading him back to the bedroom.

Mid-morning, Frank showered and drove home. He took the longest route, delaying his arrival and the questions that would inevitably follow.

What would he say? A dozen excuses ran through his mind, each one sounding unlikely. I fell asleep at the office. I slept in the car. Perhaps, he thought recklessly, he might tell Nina the truth, shock her, draw her out of her complacency.

I fucked her. Your friend. Mim. We tasted each other's bodies. We lay there all night in each other's arms. And in the morning we did it all again.

But it was fanciful thinking. Wild and reckless. He could never say those words, could never bear the hurt in her eyes.

'Frank,' Nina acknowledged him in the hallway.

'I'm sorry I hit you,' he replied, eyes lowered, unable to meet her gaze.

But she had moved on, busying herself with some task, and he stood there, feeling abandoned, not knowing what to do next or whether she had even heard his words.

Day after day he waited, certain she was playing some game. He wanted to shake her, pose his own questions: *Don't you want to know? Aren't you in the least bit curious where I was?*

But she was seemingly indifferent to his night-time absence. No accusations. No mention of it at all.

Just silent reproach.

PART THREE

Drowning Slowly

Sydney

1928

CHAPTER 12

It was late Spring. Work had begun on the new bridge linking both sides of the city harbour, and the first section of the underground railway had opened two years before. Loan money, at a high rate of interest, poured in from England to finance the work. Meanwhile, Nina could scarcely contain her excitement. After years of searching, she had finally found a house the Carmody family could call home.

Actually, she had found it years earlier, on one of those lazy exploring Sundays she had spent with Frank in one of the older established suburbs, before the birth of Claire. It was the Edwardian-styled home with the avenue of pines lining the sweeping drive, the one she and Frank had stopped in front of, admiring the fine lines of the building and the wrought-iron gates.

One day I'll buy you a place like this.

Big dreams, Frank.

No use dreaming small.

No way, she had thought then. There's no way we could ever afford a place like this. But the business had thrived and expanded. Money wasn't an issue any more, and Frank had been at her for years to find a house to call their own. She had looked and looked, driving the local agents crazy when all their offerings had failed to meet her expectations. But she had been patient. Something would come up and she'd know, the minute she stepped inside the front door, that it was the one.

The discovery had been accidental. She and Mim had been driving past, looking for a new shop that had opened nearby, when she saw the sign.

'Stop! Stop the car!' she had screamed, and Mim had slammed on the brakes, almost sending her into the windscreen.

'What's wrong?' Mim's hands gripped the wheel, knuckles white.

Nina pointed over her shoulder. 'I'm going to buy that house.'

'Don't be crazy. You don't even know what it's like inside.' Mim looked doubtful. 'Besides, it'd cost a small fortune in this suburb.'

But Nina was undaunted. She telephoned the agent listed on the sign and arranged an inspection.

'It's a bit run-down,' the man cautioned. 'No-one's lived there for years.'

'I don't mind,' replied Nina happily.

It was a sunny spring Saturday when Nina, Frank and the children went to the house for the first time. Frank was all for leaving the children at home, in the care of a babysitter, but Nina wouldn't hear of it.

'No. This will be their home, too. They should have some say in it.'

'I haven't bought it yet,' warned Frank.

'I just know we'll love it,' she continued earnestly, mentally blocking out his caution. 'It's a good solid home, close to the city, in an established neighbourhood. And it has character, Frank, not like those little boxes you and George build.'

'Don't forget it's those little boxes that have gotten us where we are today!'

'You know what I mean.'

Nina asked Frank to park the car on the street, and they walked down the long approach to the house. She wanted to savour the moment, feel the ambience of the surrounds. Above the topmost branches of the pines, the gabled roof bobbed in and out of view, second-floor windows glistening in the sun. Beds of agapanthus bordered the driveway, purple heads nodding against a backdrop of dark vegetation. From underneath the lilies came the sweet odour of rotting leaves.

It smelt, Nina thought, of solidity and comfort.

She loved the house, despite its shabby elegance and air of neglect, as she had known she would. The spacious rooms melded and flowed into each other. Light poured through the tall windows. Tiny specks of dust danced in its brilliance, hovering over the covers that shrouded the few abandoned pieces of furniture, and the huge kitchen echoed with their voices.

Opening a glass doorway, Nina stepped onto the wide sandstone terrace that ran the length of the rear of the house. Across the harbour, the city skyline appeared to rise out of the water. She stood, speechless for a moment, watching the small boats bobbing about on the tide in the small bay below. 'Look at the view!' she exclaimed. 'We can sit out here and have breakfast!'

Frank was not so enthusiastic. 'Christ, Nina! This place's a dinosaur! It needs work, not to mention money.'

'But it's selling at the right price.'

It was, Nina thought, a family home, a place where her children could bring their own offspring in years to come. She imagined herself presiding over them at the dining table — children and grandchildren bringing laughter to her life.

The children came running up from the water's edge, across the wide expanse of lawn. Claire: almost eight, gangly and long-legged. Joe: a year younger, dark eyes gleaming with excitement. Lydia trailing along behind, fastening a flower into her blonde plait.

She turned to Frank. 'See, the children love it. It'd be so good for them.'

'Maybe.'

Joe threw himself down on the terrace. 'Hey, Dad! There's a jetty down there and the water's so clear you can see the bottom. There are fish! Hundreds of them. Do you think we could go fishing?'

'And there's a lovely garden!' broke in Claire. 'And a bench and a table. I could draw and paint down there.'

'What about you, darling?' Nina asked Lydia, pulling her younger daughter close. 'What do you think?'

'Can I have the biggest bedroom?'

'Forget it, Nina,' said Frank later, back at the flat as they sat at the dining table over a pot of tea. 'The bathrooms are antiquated and the kitchen needs replacing. Every room needs a paint job. It'll take months of work.'

'I don't mind.'

'And the cost! Let's look at something smaller, with less upkeep.'

'It'll give me something to do,' she replied stubbornly. She had made her mind up. She wanted that house, no matter what Frank thought.

For the life of him, Frank couldn't understand Nina's obsession with the house. Sure, it was in a good location and the views were superb. But the work involved! He didn't have the time or the inclination.

It hung between them for days, a dividing wedge. Nina was tight-lipped. Her eyes were wide and dark in her face. Please Frank, they seemed to say. The children were full of talk of the place. Joe chattered on and on about fishing. Claire and Lydia were excited about the possibility of having their very own room, not having to share. It seemed he was the only one who had raised no enthusiasm.

The following Saturday he went back, alone, except for the agent. No children. No Nina. Nothing to distract him.

He wandered through the huge living room, past the few pieces of furniture covered in dust sheets, his footfalls echoing hollowly. His gaze lingered on the perfect ornate cornices and ceilings, the huge fireplace. He touched his hand to one of the curtains and it powdered between his fingers. Furniture and furnishings would be expensive.

Stepping over the remnants of newspapers and mice droppings on the floor, he surveyed the kitchen. It would, as he had told Nina the previous week, have to be replaced. It was too old-fashioned, too unwieldy, with the huge wood stove and big pantry. But somehow he could picture her there, busying herself at the long bench that overlooked the water.

In the past they had done so little entertaining. With this place they could have a few decent dinner parties, invite clients around. Old McBeath, the bank manager, for instance — he'd like to impress him. And Mim and George.

Especially Mim.

Rubbing his fist across the grimy window pane, Frank let his gaze travel along the lawns and gardens. He could picture garages where the old stables now stood. Three acres of land! They'd never need all that. He would sell some off, the bottom section, keeping the narrow bit that ran down to the jetty. Perhaps he would buy a boat.

He walked back through the empty rooms, trying to imagine them living there. There was, he had to admit, a certain prestige to the suburb. And despite the neglect, there was an understated elegance about the house. When restored, it would be worth several times more than the asking price. Nina had taste. Perhaps she could make something of the place. And didn't she deserve something nice, after all these years living in that cramped flat, never complaining?

He had, he realised with a start, come round to her way of thinking.

He walked outside, into the sunshine. The agent was leaning against the car, newspaper open on the bonnet. At Frank's approach, he folded it and tucked it under his arm.

'I'll take the house,' said Frank brusquely, offering a price far less than the owners were asking.

'It's worth more. A place like this, you'd never replace it —'

'It's a liability.'

'Your wife liked it.'

'She's not aware of the cost of repairs,' he replied darkly.

Back at the real estate agency, a deal was negotiated with the owners over the telephone. It was a fair price, Frank thought as he wrote a cheque for the deposit. A fair price for a fair house.

On the way home he stopped at Mim's. She met him at the front door and drew him impatiently into the hallway. 'Thank God you're here. I've been waiting ages,' she said breathlessly between kisses.

'Where's George?'

'At the office. We've an hour, at least.'

Hand on his crotch. Rubbing. That familiar surge of need. 'Mim, there's something —'

'Sshh. Don't talk. Just fuck me, Frank.'

The affair was years old, yet she was insatiable. Several times a week, she rang him at the office. 'George's out,' she'd say. Or, 'Meet me at the Metropole,' where they had a favourite room on the fourth floor. And dutifully he'd drop whatever he was doing and run to her, his own needs matching hers.

Once she'd come to his office, marched past his surprised secretary and locked the door behind her. And he'd screwed her right there on the desk, amongst the papers and pens, in broad daylight, with the blinds not even drawn, at every thrust expecting a knock on the door or the phone to ring.

She was unpredictable and uninhibited, not caring what she said or did during those stolen hours. Sex for Mim was not a self-sacrificing act, but one of fulfilling pleasure. Satisfying herself. Exhilarating him in a way Nina never had.

There was a certain element of danger about the liaison, which he enjoyed. Clandestine meetings. Hurried furtive phone calls. ('Who was that, Frank?' 'No one you'd know, Nina. One of the suppliers.') Sitting in a darkened corner of a restaurant, Mim's hand on his leg under the tablecloth. Showering himself in strange hotel bathrooms before returning home.

Yet there were times when he hated himself, despised his deceit. Nina deserved better, not this adulterous betrayal. He had taken their marriage vows and made a mockery of them. Perhaps if he'd tried harder at home ...

At regular intervals he decided to end the affair. Though it had gone undetected for so long, ultimately his luck would run out. What if Nina found out? George? Despite the man's alternative sexual preferences, Frank suspected Mim's husband would not condone the relationship. And Nina? She was asexual these days, needing no-one except the children. Her social outings were few and conducted, he suspected, only to please him. Though she and Frank seldom shared the same bed, the exposure of the affair would be the ultimate betrayal. Too raw, too close to home.

Good intentions. But he had only to see Mim again, to feel her skin beneath his hands, to know he could never leave her. She excited him, made every day worth living. From the moment they parted, he counted the minutes, hours and days until their next rendezvous. Counted and waited. Impatient.

Now, satisfied, she slid naked from the bed and lit a cigarette, then sat on the window ledge, the shape of her body outlined against the filmy curtain.

'Did you see the house?'

'Yes.'

'And?'

'I bought it, though God only knows why.'

She took a long draw on the cigarette. The habit annoyed him, though he had long since learned to say nothing.

'But Nina loves it.'

'Yes. Nina has her heart set on it,' he agreed.

'And *you* couldn't say no?'

He flung his hand out, suddenly annoyed, indicating the room. 'She deserves something — for all *this*.'

'Don't, Frank. Don't make this out to be some sordid little affair —'

'I'm not damn-well making it out to be anything! Leave it, Mim!'

'So you're buying the house with guilt money.'

'Stop it!'

She came across the room, battering her fists against his chest. 'Damn you, Frank! Damn your bloody hypocrisy. Can't you just say what you feel?'

'I love you, Mim.'

'*Love!*' she mimicked. Then, sadly, 'Oh, Frank.'

He found Nina at the stove, the aroma of something delicious wafting through the flat. Coming up behind her, he sat the receipt for the house deposit on the bench.

'What is it?' she asked, putting the spoon down from the saucepan she had been stirring.

'A surprise.'

As her eyes scanned the paperwork, her mouth widened into a smile. 'You bought the house! Oh, Frank! Thank you! Thank you!'

Instantly her arms were around him, and he could feel the salty wetness of her tears on his cheek.

CHAPTER 13

Christmas came, their first in the new house. Frank brought home a pine tree that reached almost to the ceiling, and they decorated it together, the five of them. The room echoed to the delighted squeals of the children and, for a while, it almost seemed like old times. Until Mim and George dropped by.

Frank had asked them for dinner. George — blustery and noisy, as usual — knocked once on the front door. Nina went to answer the knock but George had already let himself in, booming his hellos, Mim striding along behind. It was a habit Nina had thought, over the years, that she might have become accustomed to, but had not. Frank's business partner, it seemed, felt quite at home in the Carmody household and felt no need of any invitation.

'George, Mim,' Nina said, biting back a rebuke, 'how nice. Why don't you come *in*?'

While the two men went onto the terrace with a beer, Mim prowled about the house, poking her head into every nook and cranny. 'Why you'd want to live in a mausoleum like this is beyond me,' she said, when she had finished her inspection of the lower floor.

'I like this house,' Nina replied stubbornly.

Mim pointed to the stairway. 'What's up there?'

'Bedrooms.'

'Come on. Show me.'

And Mim was bounding up the stairs, heedless of whether Nina followed her or not.

She counted the rooms as she went. 'Pure hedonism, darling. You'd need another dozen kids just to fill this place.' She stepped into the master bedroom and perched herself on one of the beds. 'Singles! You and Frank not sleeping together?'

'It's more comfortable this way,' explained Nina, sensing her cheeks colour.

'What does Frank think about that?'

'I don't think he cares one way or the other. He hasn't come near me for months, not in *that* way,' she said with a rush, instantly regretting her words.

Mim gave her a long look. 'Do you think there's someone else?'

'Another woman?'

Mim smiled and shrugged. 'It's possible.'

'Not Frank!'

'Well, men do have urges.'

'When would he find the time? He's always working.'

'You're right,' agreed Mim, clambering off the bed and making her way downstairs again. 'You're perfectly right.' Then, changing the subject: 'Frank could have built you a lovely new home for much less than the cost of this.'

Nina came to a halt on the stairs, her fingers clenched around the handrail. 'How do you know what we paid for the house?'

'Well — I don't.' Mim looked flustered. 'But I do know what places like this are worth.'

It struck her then that Mim was jealous. Jealous of the house. Jealous, perhaps, of the children. Was she jealous of Frank, too? 'It'll all look different in a few months,' she said, changing the subject. 'We're starting the renovations right after New Year.'

'How boring, darling. Remind me to stay away.'

Nina laughed and took Mim's arm, leading her onto the terrace, where they joined the men. 'The one thing Frank couldn't build, though, is this view. Isn't it wonderful?'

Single beds! she thought later, annoyed. What business was it of Mim's, anyway?

They lived among the mess and noise for months, and Nina loved every minute of it. Enjoyed the bustle, the activity. Enjoyed seeing what was faded and tattered bloom again. Frank hired a decorator to help and she was glad of the man's experience. He knew just where to find the right rug or vase, knew the best furniture shops.

She wanted something airy and welcoming in the living areas, something comfortable. So she settled for pale cream walls and carpets, and big chintz sofas covered with cabbage roses fabric, rich and dark. There were low timber tables and vases of fresh flowers everywhere. At night, light glowed softly from the wall lamps.

The new kitchen was a modern marvel, with its electric refrigerator and stove. And the bathrooms were sheer elegance, with their gleaming tiles and hot and cold running water, not to mention the indoor lavatories.

The house was finished by mid-April, and Frank insisted on employing a housekeeper and a gardener.

'I don't need anyone,' argued Nina. It would be strange, she thought, to have other people working permanently in her home. Strange, too, to have another woman in her kitchen.

'This place is far too big for one person to manage,' Frank countered. 'I've been asking around. Mim knows of a couple who might be suitable.'

Mim! she thought, annoyed. Couldn't Frank even let her choose her own staff without Mim's interference?

Olive and Jack Buchanan turned out to be an amiable couple in their fifties. They slotted inconspicuously into the Carmodys' lives and home. Frank had built the promised garages where the old stable had once stood, adding living quarters for the couple to one side. Jack set to in the garden, turning the jungle into a manicured delight, setting out a new vegetable garden and small orchard behind the house.

The night of the housewarming party arrived. Weeks of preparation had gone into the event and Frank had invited, or so Nina thought, half of Sydney. Invitations had gone out, acceptances received. Caterers had been called in, waiters and barmen.

Lydia came wandering into the kitchen where last-minute preparations were underway. Nina glanced at the clock. 'Run upstairs and change, darling. Everyone will be here soon.'

'Who's coming?'

Nina named a dozen people whom Lydia already knew, finishing with Mim and George.

Lydia wrinkled her six-year-old nose at her mother. 'Well, I don't know why we have to have dinner with *them*. Mim talks too much when she's had a few drinks, and George has an awful laugh.'

'Lydia!'

Nina pretended shock, secretly suppressing a smile. Lydia, despite her youth, was uncannily observant. Mim did prattle on and George, after a few gins, had a dreadful braying laugh that was reminiscent of a donkey.

Sometimes she wondered why they saw so much of the couple. Certainly, Frank and George were business partners, but that was where the link ended. On the surface they had nothing else in common. No two couples, she conceded, could be more unalike.

While waiting for the guests to arrive, she wandered around the rooms, straightening a cushion here, a rug there. How far we've come, she thought, her mind skimming back to those early days in Teatree Passage. Frank's parents. John and Maudie. Oh, if they could see us now! Our lovely, lovely house. Frank's business. The children. Then she whispered to herself, 'Oh, foolish pride!'

Echoing down the years, she could almost hear her father's rebuke. 'Pride cometh before a fall, Nina.

Always remember that!' But what could happen now? Life had turned full circle for them. Nothing could ever alter that.

Yes, tonight she was proud. Proud of the way the business had grown. Proud of her children, her beautiful home. Tonight she could almost forget all the things that weren't right. Frank's drinking. Their own sterile relationship.

Do you think there's someone else?

Mim's words knocked insistently. Did she? Nina didn't know. At the time she had been quick to come to Frank's defence but now, the intimation having had time to settle, she wasn't so certain.

No, she considered, resolutely suppressing the idea. Tonight was hers, the celebration of her own achievements with the house, and she'd not let Mim's mischievous suggestion spoil the evening.

As the days and months passed, Claire scarcely thought about the time before they'd moved to the new house. She loved her present surroundings, the spaciousness of the house and the way it sprawled across the land, long and low. Loved the sweep of lawn leading down to the water, the view of the harbour which she tried to capture on sheets of paper. Blue of sky and water. White of jetty. Slash of red and yellow — sails of the boats that bobbed on the harbour's choppy expanse.

They seemed amateurish, the sketches. Malformed. Disconnected. So she studied art books, part of the collection her father had ordered to fill the shelves of the downstairs library, analysing form and structure, seeing angles and distance and perspective through fresh eyes.

It was a new world, with new experiences, and she was eager to know more.

Some days she waited until her mother left the house about mid-morning, then ran to her parents' room on the top floor. It was quiet in there, dim, the curtains pulled against the light. Reaching on tiptoes, she took the box from the top shelf of the cupboard.

She had first seen it months earlier, while helping her mother unpack their belongings in the new house. 'What's this?' she had asked, curiosity aroused, but Mummy had whisked it away, saying, 'Nothing you need worry about.'

Now, alone in the house except for Mrs Buchanan, who was busy making scones in the kitchen, she spread the contents on her mother's bed.

The photographs were mostly of two sets of couples. Her grandparents? Only last week Mummy had explained that her parents had died before she, Claire, had been born. 'But Daddy's parents? Where are they?' she had asked.

Mummy had gone strangely quiet, just for a moment, then said, 'They live at a place called Tea-tree Passage.'

'Will we ever go there and meet them?'

Her mother had shrugged. 'Who knows? Maybe one day.'

Claire's friends all had grandparents who came on Christmases and birthdays, bringing armloads of presents. But their family had no-one. No cousins. No aunts and uncles. Except for Uncle George and

Aunty Mim, who didn't really count, as they were no blood relation at all.

Now, puzzled, she turned the photographs over, but there were no notations on the back. Simply the name of the photographer and the words Tea-tree Passage.

There. That name again. *Tea-tree Passage*. She had tried to find it in her atlas at school, but there was nothing that remotely resembled the words. Then she had asked her teacher, who had never heard of it, either. Maybe it was a tiny place, not worth a mention, she had suggested.

At the bottom of the box lay a photograph of a man wearing a soldier's uniform. At least a name had been scratched on the cardboard backing, and dates: William Carmody. 1891–1916.

Carmody. Her own name. Her father's brother, she realised, remembering her mother had once told her about Uncle Bill who had died in the war. Soberly she studied the face. Sandy curling hair and a smile that crinkled the corners of his mouth. He bore a resemblance to her father, although he looked much younger.

As she sat on the bed, her gaze slid to the photograph on the dresser. It was of the five of them — her parents, Joe and Lydia, herself — taken in the refurbished drawing room. Her father, she noted, had a frown on his forehead that even the photographer, with his friendly jokes, had been unable to dispel.

He *had* been looking worried lately — not that Claire saw much of him. Most of his waking hours were spent at the office, or on one of the large building sites. He had taken her there once, to the office, but the whole thing had been a blur and she hadn't really been interested. Now he mostly took Joe.

When he was home, he spent hours in his study poring over the *Sydney Morning Herald* or *Sun* newspapers that bore headlines such as 'World Prices for Wool and Wheat Collapse' or 'Shearers Threaten Strike'. At odd times he'd shake his head and, when Claire asked him what was wrong, he'd go on and on about the state of the economy.

It was true, Claire knew. Prices were all over the place, up and down, and some were feeling the pinch. Several of the girls at the exclusive school she attended had already been withdrawn by their parents. On a recent occasion, she and Mummy had attended the ballet at the Elizabethan Theatre in Newtown. After the show, there had been dozens of cabs waiting at the rank and they'd had their choice of vehicle. The taxi rate had been lower than usual, and Mummy had tipped the man generously.

'No-one rides any more,' the driver had grumbled. 'They all walk. We've got families to feed. Everyone's tightening up.'

'Yes,' Mummy had agreed. 'It's been a disastrous season. Last week we went to see Al Jolson in *The Jazz Singer*, and the theatre was half-empty.'

'We'll be fine,' Daddy had told Claire later when she voiced her concerns. 'People still need places to live, whatever the state of the economy, so we'll keep building houses. Anyway,' he went on, ruffling her hair, 'you're much too young to be bothered by such things.'

Too many problems. Too few solutions. Some days she felt as though the weight of the world rested on her shoulders. And, despite his protestations, she could see the worry etched on her father's face. Was that why he drank so much? she wondered, remembering the previous evening.

He had arrived home late, well after Mrs Buchanan had cleared the dinner plates away and retired to her own quarters. His voice had been slurred, his step unsteady. 'Where's dinner?' he had yelled, letting himself in the front door with a loud stamping of feet.

'Go and see to your father,' Mummy had whispered, pushing Claire towards the hallway. 'I'm tired and I have a headache. There's a plate of food left warming in the oven.'

And she'd shooed the other two children up the stairs, letting Claire deal with her drunk and fractious father.

She had stood in the hallway, watching with a mixture of resentment and despair as Daddy fumbled with his shoelaces, part of her wanting to help him, the other part repulsed by his bumbling movements. He had refused the plate of food in the oven, so she had made him a sandwich instead and tucked him up on the couch, watching from the shadows as he fell asleep.

Claire, the good girl. Claire, the daughter who makes everything right.

Remembering, she sighed and laid back against the pillow. It held the faint aroma of her mother's perfume and she buried her face in it for a moment, breathing deeply. Palma Violets. The smell always reminded her of those nights when her parents readied themselves for a party, the theatre, or one of the orchestral concerts at the Town Hall. She and Lydia would sit there, on that same bed, watching Mummy as she dressed for the evening. Pretty gown. Lipstick. Dab of scent on the wrists. Dark mass of hair caught up with pins and clasps.

There had been a time when Mummy had bobbed her hair, like Mim, and worn her dresses short, showing her shapely knees. But lately she had let her hair grow long and curly again, and her dresses were different. Daddy had chosen some of the new ones. They had all gone to the dress shop, watching as Mummy tried on outfit after outfit, her father vetting each one.

'There, you won't look like a tart now,' Claire had heard him whisper later, as they were getting back into the car with the boxes of clothes and hats.

Mummy had halted, just for a moment, and stared at him, her face white. Then she had pulled on her gloves with savage little tugs and gotten into the car, and they had all been so preoccupied with finding their own seats that Claire had forgotten all about it till later.

'What's a tart?' she had asked Joe the following morning.'

'I don't know. Ask Mum,' he had shrugged and ran off.

But she couldn't. The word had been said with such depth of force, such hidden innuendo, that she couldn't bear to bring the subject up.

So many conflicting scenes and ideas floated through her head. So much concealed displeasure. Sometimes she felt as though she were on the outside of the family, seeing them all through a stranger's eyes: Joe preoccupied with boyish pursuits. Lydia self-absorbed and precocious. Her father almost a stranger to them. And her mother . . .

There were nights when Mummy sparkled, like a diamond in one of the rings she wore. Then there were other times when she seemed to drag herself around, barely able to dress herself, looking defeated before the night had even begun. And her father, tight-lipped and silent.

Claire closed her eyes, caught in other perplexities, other mysteries. Adults were such a confusing lot. Mim. George. Her own parents. Others who came to the dinner parties Mother organised for Father's clients. They all seemed to dance around each other, doing complicated little steps, parrying and thrusting. Playing stupid adult games that made no sense.

'Claire? Are you up there?'

Mrs Buchanan's voice.

She glanced at the clock on the bedside table. Over an hour had passed since she had come upstairs. Hurriedly she replaced the photos and stowed the box back on the top shelf of the cupboard. Then she let herself out the door.

CHAPTER 14

There was, Nina sensed, a restless unease brewing on the streets of Sydney. Wharf labourers and timber workers were on strike, and Frank's lorries carting wood to the work sites were often forced to have police escorts. Miners were locked out for refusing wage cuts and the price of coal soared. Queues at the employment office were longer than she had ever seen.

'Getting above themselves,' Frank told Nina, referring to the strikers. 'They don't know what it's like to be a boss.'

'*You* haven't always been a boss,' Nina reminded him quietly.

'No. But I've always believed in an honest day's work for an honest day's pay.'

'You're a fair man, Frank.'

'Hard but fair. I expect loyalty from my men.'

Policemen. Soldiers. There was a military air about the city, a sense of disquiet. As though all was not as it should be.

Despite Olive Buchanan, Nina found herself constantly pottering in her new kitchen, unable to stay away.

'I don't know why you bother,' said Mim.

'What am I to do with my time otherwise?'

'Get out more. If I had Mrs Buchanan, I'd never want to set eyes on a saucepan.'

Mim and George had moved to a house in the neighbouring suburb. It was larger and grander than the Carmody home, and Mim had gone to great lengths to show Nina the features.

'Of course it cost a small fortune, more than yours,' she confided. 'There are fireplaces in every bedroom.'

'It's lovely, Mim,' Nina replied, mentally reminding herself to go to Anthony Hordern's in the city and buy a suitable housewarming present.

Squalid tenements and beautiful mansions: to Nina, the city seemed a place of vast inconsistencies. Food prices and rents were high but, ensconced in her lovely home, she was scarcely affected. On the few occasions she accompanied Frank in the car, she stared from the window, seeing the houses with rotting weatherboards and rusted roofs as though for the first time.

Finding herself at a loose end during the day, with the children in school, Nina began involving herself in charity work. St Vincent de Paul. The Sydney City Mission. She was surprised to learn how many homeless people wandered the streets.

It was through the Mission work that she met Father Mulcahy. He was in his forties, a tall dark-haired man. 'You're a compassionate woman, Nina,' he said, the second time he met her. 'How long since you've been to church?'

It had been a lifetime since she had gone, before her marriage. 'It's been years, Father,' she replied apologetically.

'You might like to come along on Sunday,' he said with a smile as he walked away.

Against Frank's wishes she went, creeping from the house like an escaping prisoner, closing the front door softly after her as she left. It was early, and he was still sleeping off the effects of the previous night's grog. She found solace there, amongst the hymns and candles and the stained mullioned windows that diffracted the light. She closed her eyes and listened to Father Mulcahy's voice, strong and clear as it rang through the church. She heard voices soar as the congregation sang, the notes carrying on the air to some faraway exalted place. Where do the words go, she wondered, when we can no longer hear them?

Frank was angry when she returned. 'Your job is here, home with the children,' he said in a brutal undertone. 'Not bible-bashing with that lot of wowsers.'

When had their relationship turned so unpleasant? she wondered. The snide innuendos, the nasty remarks. What had he said to her that day getting into the car, after the shopping expedition for new clothes?

You don't look like a tart now.

She shuddered at the memory, remembering the puzzled look on her daughter's face. Claire had heard, even though Frank had kept his voice low.

The arguments and confrontations were becoming more frequent, more hostile. And where Frank was once careful what he said in front of the children, it seemed he no longer bothered. Coming home drunk, he would rant and rave as he tried to insert his key into the front lock; Nina had come to recognise the lead-up signs and sought ways to avoid any confrontation.

She'd push Claire forward. 'Go and get Daddy's dinner, darling. I'll just put Joe and Lydia to bed.'

And she'd take the younger children upstairs, lying on Lydia's bed until the child fell asleep and she was sure Frank would be snoring on the drawing-room settee. Only then would she tiptoe along the hallway to her own room.

He had taken to coming to her bed again, irregularly but insistently, forcing his way under the sheets and into her body. She lay, fixing her mind elsewhere until his thrusting movements died, mindful of the grip with which he held her. She knew there'd be bruises in the morning.

'He's drunk,' she told herself, knowing she was making excuses. She told no-one — who to tell anyway? — keeping the hurt, the utter humiliation to herself.

She'd tried to shield the children from all this, but the task was now beyond her. Only the previous week, after one such episode, Claire had come downstairs in the morning to find her sobbing in the kitchen.

'Why are you crying?'

Nina had dabbed at her eyes. No matter what problems she and Frank had, the children shouldn't bear the burden. 'It's nothing, really.'

'Father will be down soon. You know he hates it when you cry. He'd give you anything to make you stop.'

Nina raised her head and stared at her daughter. How perceptive! Frank *would* be down soon. He'd rummage in his wallet, as he had done the time before, and the time before that, and hand her a fistful of notes. 'There,' he'd say. 'Buy yourself something nice.'

Predictable Frank. No contrition. Never saying sorry. Just money. She felt like a prostitute. And in many ways she wished there *was* someone else, some other woman, as Mim had suggested. The young pretty secretary in the office, perhaps. Then, maybe, he'd leave her alone.

That same morning he'd come into the kitchen after the children had left for school. 'About last night ...' His voice had trailed off and Nina had noticed he couldn't look her in the eye. He had stood staring instead at the floor, at the big grey-and-white tiles.

Firmly. 'Let's not talk about it.'

He'd put his hand on her arm and she'd flinched away, walking towards the stove with little jerky movements. The thought, sudden and unexpected, had startled her: at what point had she been unable to bear his touch?

'Nina?'

'*Don't*, Frank!'

How far had they come from that sunny day in Tea-tree Passage when he'd let himself in the kitchen door? Aeons. A lifetime. They were a world away from what they had been then.

'Nina.' His voice had been insistent.

'Yes, Frank.'

'You never come near me.' Then quietly. 'Do you hate me that much?'

Her own voice, when it came, sounded weary, filled with defeat. 'I don't *hate* you, Frank, but sometimes I don't like what you've become.'

'I'm working hard for you and the children. You never go hungry.'

That same old cliché, mixed with undeniable truth. Nina, who had seen children begging in the streets, knew he was right. Frank *did* provide well for them. Lovely home. Car. Money. Her own discontent was the price she had to pay.

The church became her refuge. Often she went during the day, while Frank was at work and the children at school. She sat on a pew, watching the people hurrying in, crossing themselves in front of the altar, snatching a few quiet moments away from the bustle of the street outside.

During the second week in June, she went to the doctor. In the sanctuary of his office she put on the examination gown and lay on the hard table, trying to project her mind elsewhere as he thrust his fingers inside her, then fighting back tears as she heard the inevitable words.

Somehow she found her way to the church, to the claustrophobic confessional box.

'Is there anything you need to tell me?' came the voice on the other side of the curtain.

'I'm having another baby, Father.'

'Bless you. That's wonderful news.'

'Is it?'

'You don't want this child?'

'No.'

She remembered the promise she had made to herself years ago.

My children will be born of love and need and desire, not from any misdirected sense of duty or obligation.

Her pregnancy had been the result of lovemaking she had endured, but not enjoyed. In that regard she had already failed the fragile life inside her.

My children will be equally loved.

How could she love this child, created from a relationship clouded with such despair?

'Why don't you want it? It is your husband's?'

'*Of course.*'

'Jesus said, "Suffer the little children".'

'*I'm* suffering. You must guide me.'

'How?'

Testing. Saying the word. 'An abortion. I can't have this child.'

'That's against God's will.'

'I know.'

Later, walking home, she scarcely noticed the wind that sent the last of the autumn leaves dancing in its wake. Yellow and red leaves layering themselves in the gutters, spraying out from under the automobiles as they passed. The Carmodys, she thought wryly. Respectable upright citizens. But it was all an illusion. A lie.

* * *

'Nina's pregnant,' Frank said, taking a deep breath.

He'd waited all night, taking courage from several whiskys before breaking the news. Mim was quiet for a moment. 'Well, there you go,' she replied at last, pulling the sheets up, covering her breasts. 'Fancy that.'

'Mim, I am married —'

'You don't have to explain!'

'I never pretended —'

'That you don't *fuck* your wife!'

She turned away and he waited several agonising seconds. 'I'm sorry. I didn't want it to be like this.'

She gave a laugh and spun to face him. 'Like what, Frank? Making excuses? Playing Nina and I off against each other.'

'I don't do that!'

'What do you whisper in your wife's ear when you make love? The same things you tell me?'

She slid from the bed and walked across the room, pouring a tumbler of whisky from the bottle that stood on the dresser. Neat little arse, slim figure: the sight of her like that always caused those same old hardenings of desire.

'*Of course not!*'

She handed him the drink. 'We don't have any hold over each other, Frank. We're free spirits, remember?'

'I love you.'

She stared, sizing him up, then used words to wound him, as only Mim could. 'I allow myself the same freedom, you know. You're not the only one, Frank.'

He waited, watching her. Waited for the grin that told him she was teasing, playing games. But none came. Her face remained impassive. A wave of suspicion swamped him. Perhaps she was telling the truth? He couldn't bear the thought of that — Mim doing those same erotic acts with someone else.

She laughed, a brittle sound that ground against his senses. 'Surely you're not jealous?'

He drained the glass, feeling the grog spread warmly in his belly, and struggled with her words again as they danced through his consciousness. Running one hand through his hair, he sagged back onto the bed. Somehow he had to reassure her.

'About Nina. It means nothing.'

She came and sat next to him on the bed, trailing her fingers through the hair on his chest. 'Your wife's having your baby and it means nothing?'

'That's not what I meant.'

Her hand moved lower, towards his hardness. Oh, God! Don't stop!

'Then what *did* you mean?'

Those words again. Niggling. 'Tell me it isn't true.'

'About what?'

'Other lovers.'

She smiled, a secretive smile. 'Does your male ego feel threatened, darling?'

'I thought we had something special.'

A laugh bubbled in her throat. Teasing. Tormenting. Fingers worked at him, roughly. Annoyed, he snatched them away, bringing his own hands up until they enclosed her throat.

She was still smiling, mouth pulled upwards at the corners. Daring him. 'You're so naive, Frank.'

His hands tightened. For one impossibly long moment, he wanted to inflict pain, wanted to hurt her, as she had hurt him.

'Don't, Frank!' She began to struggle, pushing against his chest with her hands.

'Say you love me.'

'I love you.'

He released her and she scrabbled away from him, across the sheets. Her arms, folded across her breasts, made a barrier between them. 'Don't you ever, *ever* do that again.'

He dressed in silence and walked away, taking the bottle of whisky as he went. Out on the street, a light rain had begun to fall. He raised his face towards it and felt an inexplicable urge to cry.

What had he become? Angry? Disillusioned? He'd sought comfort from Mim, comfort Nina had failed to give yet, at every possible moment, she threw those tiny wounding barbs at him. I love you, she'd said. But he'd made her and the words meant nothing.

A headache threatened. He sat in the driver's seat of the car and raised the bottle to his mouth. Whisky. Neat. Numbing the pain. Taking it to some distant place.

Later, when he tried to think about it, he couldn't remember starting the car, steering it away from Mim's. And he didn't remember the corner coming up too fast, wrestling clumsily with the wheel, or the tree looming by the roadside. Remembered only the sound of breaking glass and his body still accelerating, colliding with the dashboard, the windscreen. And he remembered the anger that had pushed his foot more firmly on the accelerator.

'Next time you mightn't be so lucky,' said a doctor in a white coat, as he leaned over the hospital bed, examining Frank's bruises.

Lucky! In many ways he wished he were dead.

It was, Nina thought, a time of excesses. Dancing. Dinners. Frank's drinking. At least every weekend there was a party at somebody's place. Their social life seemed full to bursting, and she and Frank seemed to be out every second night. They were spending time together, of sorts, yet the gulf between them only seemed to widen.

Nina hated those social occasions. They were Frank's friends, not hers. Not even friends, really, merely business colleagues. Handy-to-know people whose acquaintance Frank cultivated, and they acted like everyone's best mate. Shallow. Predictable. Women kissing the air near her cheek. The 'darlings' and 'Nina, how are you, my dear?' wearied her.

Sometimes she felt as though she were part of an ongoing play. Acting. Professing interest in their children, their social mornings. 'You must come and have lunch with us soon,' they said, but no invitation was ever forthcoming.

Frank's capacity for alcohol both amazed and horrified her. A few drinks before leaving the house for the latest function. Numerous glasses later, while circulating amongst the guests. Only a few months earlier he had smashed the car into a tree while drunk, lucky to escape with bruises. The car had been damaged beyond repair and, the following day, he had purchased a new one.

Frank still suffered from nightmares but she had long ago stopped offering support. He had brushed her concerns away too often, discounted his own problems, reducing them to a trivial inconvenience. And perhaps they were. Maybe she was the only one troubled by their regular appearance.

So many events had come between them: the war, Frank's parents, Bill. All were still hovering on the periphery of their lives, though years had passed and those events should have been placed firmly in some sort of different perspective. But they hadn't been.

Mim threw a belated housewarming party. Nina hadn't wanted to go — she had been feeling off-colour all week — but Frank insisted and she went along to keep the peace. While he immersed himself in a group discussing business issues, she wandered to the back of the room, where she found herself talking to a serious young man.

Her back ached and the baby kicked mercilessly. She rested a hand on her stomach, feeling the movements, letting her thoughts drift from the man's conversation. After a while a waiter passed with a tray of canapés. 'Would you like some?' the young man asked politely.

Nina shook her head. The thought of food made her feel queasy. 'No, thanks.'

'Well, if you're sure ...'

He was looking at her expectantly over a pair of horn-rimmed spectacles.

'No, don't mind me,' said Nina, glad of his departure. Even the boring young men don't want to know me, she thought ruefully.

Through the fronds of a potted palm, she could see Frank. He was now in the centre of a group of women. One of them — Mim? — had her hand on his shoulder in a familiar way. She supposed she should feel some jealousy. That was the normal emotion, wasn't it? But there was none.

As though sensing her scrutiny, Frank glanced across and caught her eye, then made his way across the room towards her. How had he managed to tear himself away from those women? she thought with a sigh as she tipped the remainder of her drink into the pot plant.

'Are you enjoying yourself?'

Might as well be honest; she was tired of pretending. 'No.'

One of the men in the group standing next to them turned and stared at her, frowning. Nina recognised him as one of the bankers.

Frank pulled her back into the corner of the room. 'You would if you let yourself,' he hissed. 'If you stopped being so unsociable, so detached. These people only want to be your friends.'

'Let myself get involved with this pack of —'

Words failed her and she stood watching him. His forehead had creased into a mass of lines and the glass teetered precariously in his hand.

'These people are important to us!' he said through clenched teeth.

'They're dull, boring and predictable.'

'For God's sake! They're our bread and butter, our livelihood.'

'They're using you, and you're using them.'

'Nina!'

She left early, calling a taxi. Left Frank talking to a blonde woman with a huge bosom, who laughed and giggled and flirted, and hung off his arm in an overly familiar manner.

Walking in the front door, her anger dissipated. 'The children are all asleep,' the babysitter said. 'No problems tonight.'

Nina paid the woman and saw her to the door. In the kitchen she heated water for a pot of tea. It was quiet in there, except for the faint hum of the refrigerator. Leaning back against the bench, she hugged the shape of her child. As though sensing her attention, it moved sluggishly beneath her arms. Slow roll. Long shuddering manoeuvre.

Strange to be having a baby again after all these years; Lydia would be over six by the time it was born. Initially she hadn't wanted another child and, God forbid, she had even contemplated an abortion. But she had accepted the eventuality during these past few months, resigned herself. She would love it, she reasoned, no matter what. Perhaps it'd be another boy. Company for Joe, despite the age difference.

She poured a cup of tea and carried it through the house, looking in on the children. Claire, lying on top of the sheets, coltish and angular. Light from the hallway spilled across the bed, highlighting her dark hair and pale skin. Joe tossed restlessly on his bed, muttering in his sleep. Something about a fishing rod. Lydia: curled foetal-like, thumb in her mouth. Gently Nina prised it away and the child stirred, but did not wake.

She walked to the bedroom she shared with Frank. Stepping out of her clothes, she went through the nightly ritual. Face. Teeth. Glancing up at the mirror above the washbasin, she caught sight of her own naked reflection. Forty years old, yet still pretty in a faded weary way. Heavy pendulous breasts. Belly straining with the shape of the child.

Nina ran a hand through her hair, frowning at her physical image. 'There is more to me,' she thought. Publicly dutiful wife. Caring mother. Yet something of herself, her own essence, was lacking. She was living her life through Frank, pandering to his moods.

'What have we become?' she asked herself. And what *had* they become, she and Frank? Strangers almost. Two separate moving shadows, scarcely knowing each other, though God knows they'd tried.

CHAPTER 15

The violence in the streets continued. Despite the police presence, one of Frank's employees was killed in a fracas involving a delivery truck.

Nina insisted on visiting the dead man's wife. 'I don't think that's a good idea,' countered Frank. 'She lives in a pretty bad area. I don't want you going there alone.'

In the end she asked Father Mulcahy to accompany her. They walked along narrow laneways, past broken-down tenements whose windows were patched with brown paper and where the only plumbing was a backyard tap.

'What do you want?' asked the woman who answered Nina's knock on the front door.

'I'm Nina Carmody. I've come to say how sorry I am —'

The woman glanced at the priest. 'There's no need and I'll not be wanting charity.'

'I haven't come to offer you charity,' Nina said quietly.

'Well, then. You'd better come in. Can't hang around the front door or the blessed neighbours'll be gossiping.'

While Father Mulcahy waited in the front room, Nina followed the woman to the kitchen. It was dark in there, the window grimy. 'I don't know what to say,' she said to the woman's back. '"I'm sorry" seems so inadequate.'

'Too late to be sorry. What's done is done. Harry's dead and I've got four kids to provide for.'

Nina fished in her purse, holding forward several notes. 'Perhaps this might help.'

'I told you, I don't want charity!'

'Very well.' Nina replaced the money, not knowing what to say next.

The woman filled the kettle and placed it on the stove, then turned to stare at Nina. 'You're having a baby soon.'

'Another three months.'

There was silence, except for the slow drip of the tap over the sink.

'He doesn't deserve you.'

Puzzled. Whatever was the woman talking about? 'Who?'

'Your husband.'

What did Frank have to do with this? 'I don't understand.'

'I wasn't going to say anything, but now that I've met you, I think you deserve better. He's not faithful to you.'

The words echoed dully and she jerked her head up, staring at the woman. 'How do you know?'

'Everyone at work knows he's having an affair. It's common knowledge.'

Somehow she got through the visit, the dark swirling tea in the cracked cup and the piece of stale cake.

'Are you unwell?' asked Father Mulcahy as they retraced their steps later. 'You're very pale.'

Home again, she sat with Lydia on her lap, and buried her face in the child's golden hair.

'What's wrong, Mummy?'

'Nothing.'

He's not faithful to you.

'You look sad.'

'I'm not really. Just tired.'

He's having an affair.

She thought later that curiosity should have prompted her to ask who the woman was. Mentally she went through the list of possibilities, not picking any one in particular. It could have been any of them. She closed her eyes and shook her head.

'Better not to know,' she told herself. 'Say nothing.'

She had no right, no hold over Frank. She did not love him. Had perhaps *never* loved him. And God knows they both deserved something more than this dismal emotionless marriage.

Joe sat in the front seat of the car, next to his father, and watched the houses flashing by. 'Where are we going?'

'Like I told your mother, for a drive.'

They had set off from the house in the direction of the office. Father had taken him there several times,

174

showing him proudly through the rooms. 'One day this will all be yours,' he was fond of saying.

Joe wasn't sure he wanted to work in a stuffy office. He preferred being outdoors, sitting on the jetty at the bottom of their garden, fishing line dangling in the water. But he said nothing. It was years before he would leave school and perhaps Father would change his mind meantime.

But it wasn't the office, he realised, towards which they were headed today. Several blocks along, Father swung the car into a side street and headed in the opposite direction.

'This isn't the way to your work.'

'No.'

An explanation didn't seem forthcoming so Joe waited, watching until his father pulled the car into Aunty Mim's driveway.

Uncle George's car wasn't there, just Mim's, a red low-slung convertible. The front door was open and his father beckoned him through, not even bothering to knock.

They stood in the foyer, Joe hanging back against the wall while his father shrugged off his coat, laying it over the bannister. 'Mim!' he called. There was a flurry from the top of the stairs and she came running down, all pink and breathless, wearing a long shimmering gown.

'Frank,' she said, in an eager husky kind of way, meeting his father at the bottom of the stairs and kissing him on the mouth.

Yuk! thought Joe. Why adults did that was a mystery to him. The kiss went on and on, and he thought of his mother. She and Father never kissed like that.

'Hello, Aunty Mim.'

He stepped forward and she swung towards him, a surprised look on her face. Obviously she hadn't been expecting him. She glanced back towards his father, frowning. 'You brought the boy?'

Joe, he wanted to say. *My name's Joe*. But he knew he'd get a clip over the ear if he spoke out of turn.

Mim took Father by the arm and steered him into the living room. Joe waited, uninvited, not knowing whether to follow. He could hear them talking in a loud whisper.

'Why did you bring him here?'

'I had to. Nina's been acting funny lately, like she suspects something. It looks better this way. By bringing Joe —'

'What if he says something?'

'He won't. He's only seven, for Christ's sake!'

'Well, then.'

Father came back into the foyer and guided him into one of the small adjacent sitting rooms. He sat on the settee as instructed, his legs not reaching the floor. After a few minutes, Mim came in with a plate of biscuits and a glass of milk, a colouring book and a packet of pencils.

'Here.' She set them on the small table in front of him, then motioned towards a page of the book. 'I have to show Daddy something upstairs. We'll be just a little while. When we come down, I want to see this picture all coloured in.'

'I want to come upstairs, too.'

'Ah, no, son,' said Father, his face turning a strange shade of pink.

'You can't,' added Mim firmly. 'Just be a good boy and do as you're told. Then Daddy will buy you an ice-cream on the way home.'

His gaze slid between them. Mim frowning. Father glancing away. It was ages since he'd had an ice-cream. If his staying in this room while Mim and Father went upstairs meant he could have one, then it seemed a small price to pay.

Puzzled, he stood at the doorway and watched as they hurried up the stairs. Mim was a step or two ahead and she looked back, laughing, tugging his father by the hand. 'Come on. We haven't long.' Then they disappeared from view and he was left staring at the empty stairs.

He wandered back into the room and flicked through the pages of the colouring book. Fairies and dragons! he thought, disgusted. Girl stuff! All right for Claire or Lydia. He picked up a blue pencil and let it slide disinterestedly back and forth across the paper, careful to stay inside the lines.

The house was quiet, the only sound coming from the clock on the mantelpiece. He took a sip of the milk and nibbled at the edge of a biscuit. Bored, he wandered around the room, touching his fingers to the ornaments and photograph frames that cluttered every surface. Sepia faces stared back. Disapproving. Unsmiling. A pile of books sat nearby. On the top lay an embroidered bookmark. Miriam, it said, in neat little black cross-stitches at the top.

He slipped it into his pocket, his fingers encountering a boiled lolly as he did so. He pulled the lolly out, studying it. There were bits of fluff sticking to the surface but maybe if he found a bathroom and wet it under a tap, it'd all come off.

Although he had been to the house several times, he had never been upstairs before. The treads were covered with thick blue carpet and his shoes sank into the softness. Up and up he went, fingers tracing the curve of the bannister. At the top a hallway stretched ahead, doorways leading off to the left and right. Which one was the bathroom?

He found it easily, washed the fluff from the lolly, and popped it into his mouth. Continuing along the hallway, he peered into the rooms. They were bedrooms, mostly, with the occasional additional bathroom, and a study containing a leather-topped desk and chair, and bookshelves that surrounded the walls. He went to the window and looked down, onto the driveway. His father's car sat there, baking in the sun.

Father! Where was he?

The door to the last room along the hallway was closed. He stood outside it for what seemed like a long time, then silently turned the handle and peered in.

Another bedroom. It was dim inside, the curtains drawn, and it took several seconds for his eyes to adjust. In the half-light he could see shapes on the bed, and the white of his father's bare buttocks as they rose and fell. He was lying on top of Mim and the bed was creaking, alarmingly so, and he wondered if it might break under their combined weight.

He took a deep breath, confused. His father's bottom was moving faster now. Up and down, up and down. Mim gave a moan and threw her head back. Was he hurting her?

'Frank! Frank!' she whispered hoarsely.

He shouldn't be there, that much he knew. And if his father caught him, there'd be a thrashing instead of ice-cream. Soundlessly Joe pulled the door closed and ran down the stairs, waiting in the sitting room with the ridiculous colouring book and pencils. The lolly had almost dissolved in his mouth and he could feel the hard sharp edge of it against his tongue.

After a few minutes his father came in, adjusting his tie. 'Were you a good boy, Joe?'

'Yes, Father.'

'Let's be off, then.'

He took his coat and steered Joe towards the front door. Of Mim, there was no sign.

'What did Aunty Mim want to show you?' he said as the car turned the corner, remembering the bare bottom bobbing up and down and Mim's groans. Perhaps, if he asked, his father would explain.

But Father stared straight ahead, watching the road with unusual concentration. 'Nothing, son,' he replied briefly. 'It was nothing at all.'

Near the park Joe spotted the ice-cream van. 'Aunty Mim said you'd buy me one,' he reminded his father, who stopped the car and brought back a double cone.

Joe reached out his hand but the cone was held away, just out of grasp.

'Joe, about this afternoon. Best not to mention it to your mother, all right?'

It was a bribe, he knew that. Say nothing and you can have a reward. He stared hard at the ice-cream. The bottom layer was starting to melt.

'Yes, Father.'

Mother was lying on the bed when they got home. She looked tired, dark circles under her eyes. His own eyes followed the line of her body, the bump on her stomach. There was going to be another baby. Maybe it would be a boy.

'Where have you been?' she asked, looking worried.

'For a drive. Then Dad bought me an ice-cream at the park.'

Despite the question, it seemed she wasn't listening. 'Have you heard the news on the radio?' she said instead to his father. 'Something about America. Wall Street. The stock market's collapsed and everything's gone.'

CHAPTER 16

It seemed to Frank as though everything came to a grinding halt overnight. The banks froze business loans, refusing any further advances. Several dozen houses in the last estate were waiting to be sold, but the steady stream of buyers had miraculously dried up. And, to make matters worse, most of their profits had been invested in the latest subdivision, which was only half-completed.

'What'll we do?' asked George, who had been handling the firm's finances. 'We've a serious cash flow problem. We can't sell the land until all the roadworks are finished, and there's no money to finish the roads. Bit of a bind, really.'

'Have you explained that to the bank?'

'Several times. They don't care.'

'Shit!'

'There's something else. I was wondering if you could advance me a bit of cash. Mim and I have been living a bit high on the hog lately. There's a couple of blokes after me for money.'

'How much?'

'Ten thousand.'

'No way.' Frank shook his head. 'I can't lay my hands on that sort of dough. Most of my money's tied up in the business. You know that.'

'Come on, Frank. Just a small loan, then, to tide us over until everything starts rolling again.'

'That's not going to happen,' Frank replied quietly.

He felt bad refusing George, but it wasn't his problem, not really. He had himself to consider. The house was heavily mortgaged against the business, and there'd been a spate of doctor's bills lately. Nina hadn't been well and the baby was due shortly. No, he reasoned, George would have to sort out his own financial dilemmas.

The other problem was that Nina knew about Mim. It had been his own stupid fault, taking Joe to Mim's a few weeks earlier. It appeared that Joe had picked up a bookmark with Mim's name on it, and Nina had found it when checking the lad's pockets before doing the washing.

'Here,' she'd said, handing it to him later, her face expressionless. 'Joe had this. You might like to return it.'

He'd thought quickly, trying to fabricate some explanation, some excuse. But she had cut him off, saying, 'How you conduct yourself is your own business, Frank. But don't involve the children.'

He'd expected tears or threats — wasn't that how women reacted? — but there were none. No ultimatums. No recriminations whatsoever. Just God-damned bloody silence. He was drowning in it. Slowly.

'What did Nina say?' asked Mim when he returned the bookmark.

'Nothing.'

'*Nothing?*'

'That's what I bloody said! Why? What does it matter?'

'I just wanted to know. You needn't be so defensive.'

The guilt was making him explosive lately. It rose up inside him, lodging somewhere in his gut, a solid unmoveable mass. He didn't know how to handle the situation, was confused by it. Should he, he wondered briefly, end the affair, or at least tell Nina it was over? But he had admitted nothing to her, and to do so would acknowledge his own complicity.

Say nothing, he decided eventually. Pretend ignorance. Nina had other pressing things to occupy her lately. The children, the impending birth of the baby.

He took every available opportunity to be with Mim, no longer making excuses for his absences. There, in that quiet dark house, he made the inevitable comparisons. Neat and ordered home. No children yelling. Smooth svelte body not stretched and swollen by the processes of childbirth. No-one to interrupt them. Even George was seldom home these days.

George appeared at the office. One eye was bruised and puffy, and there were cuts to one cheek. 'Are you sure you couldn't help with a bit of cash?' he pleaded.

'What happened to your face?'

George touched a finger to a gash above his mouth. 'The blokes I owe the money to — they're getting touchy.'

'I told you I don't have that kind of dough.'

'But you've been happy to fornicate with my wife for years. Surely that's worth something?'

Flustered, Frank stared at the man's desperate face, not knowing what to say. But George went on, not waiting for a reply. 'Don't looked so damn shocked. I've known about it from the start. Mim told me. We don't have any secrets.'

'Obviously.'

'Well?'

He heard his own reply, words sliding into the space between them, shocking him. 'I fuck your wife, my friend, because she tells me you are unable to do so. Mim and I have no secrets either.'

George's face seemed to collapse, falling in on itself. Suddenly he looked old and vulnerable. 'I admit it, Frank. I'm a failure. I owe money all over the place. The business is in a mess. And you're right! I can't even screw my own wife. You know what those blokes said?'

Frank shook his head.

'They called me a bloody useless poofter. How do you think that felt? Then they said if I don't pay up, they'll spread it around town. Who'll want to do business with us then?'

He laid his forehead on the desk. Frank watched the back of his head, the shaking shoulders. George: crying like a baby. What could he say? What assurances could he give?

Disconcerted, he walked towards the door. 'I'm sorry, George. I can't help. There's no money.'

He trudged along the water near Circular Quay. The wind blew, carrying a salt tang, and he took in great lungfuls. Everything was falling apart around him, unravelling at an alarming pace. He wished he could simply walk away from it all. Nina. The children. What remained of the business.

And Mim? He could never leave her, he knew that. She intrigued him, fascinated him with her odd little ways. Yet she had that disarming habit of bringing him crashing to the ground with her barbed words. Unlike his association with Nina, he never knew, from one moment to the next, exactly where he stood with Mim. Was that the attraction — the uncertainty, the changeable nature of their relationship? Then he hated himself for trying to analyse and make sense of it all. They were two adults, he and Mim. They enjoyed each others' company. Sex was great. They hadn't deliberately set out to hurt anyone along the way.

The telephone call came at midnight. Who could be ringing at that hour? he wondered, opening one bleary eye to the clock on the bedside table.

Nina answered the telephone. 'It's Mim,' she said stonily, climbing back into bed. 'She wants to talk to you.'

Groggily. 'What about?'

'She wouldn't tell me,' she snapped. Then, after a momentary pause, she added, 'She sounds upset.'

He slid from the bed and took the call in his study downstairs. 'What is it? You shouldn't be ringing here!'

'I need you!'

Her voice had a desperate hysterical edge to it, and he sensed by the muffled tone that she'd been crying. 'Now?'

'Yes.'

'What will I tell Nina?'

'I don't bloody well care! Just come!'

She met him at the front door. Her eyes were red-rimmed and she made no move to kiss him — which, in itself was strange.

'For God's sake, Mim! What's wrong?'

She shook her head, blinking back tears and unable to speak. Took his hand, instead, and led him upstairs to one of the spare bedrooms. With each successive step, a sense of dread began to mushroom inside him.

He halted at the doorway, unable for a moment to go on. The light seemed unnaturally bright, highlighting everything in the room. George's body was slumped on the bed. A pool of dark blood congealed around his head. In his hand lay a small handgun. Tentatively Frank moved forward, taking hesitant steps towards the bed. He reached towards George — his first instinct was to feel for a pulse — but Mim pulled him away.

'It's no use. He's dead.'

'But why?'

The question was pointless; he already knew the answer. Agitated, he ran his hands through his hair, projecting his mind past the sight of the blood and George's lifeless body to the protocols of death. What to do now? Ring the doctor? Police? Mim was in no fit state. She sat on a chair next to the bed, running her fingers along George's arm. 'I was asleep. The sound of the gun woke me. Like an explosion. Oh, God!'

And she collapsed into a flood of tears.

It was hours before the police finished their report, and pale light tinged the eastern horizon as the undertaker and his assistant left, carrying the sheet-wrapped body to the waiting hearse. Frank stood at the front doorway and watched them pull away, looking for a long time down the now-empty street. Another day had begun and life continued as normal, yet he knew the direction of his own life had altered in a monumental way. Something inside him had changed, some spark diminished and made inconsequential by the night's events.

He felt exhausted, his mind numb, yet he knew he would have trouble sleeping. The events of the night were seared into his mind and would not be easily erased. Mim seemed disoriented, walking as though in a dream. He led her into the main bedroom, pulling back the bedspread and forcing several sleeping tablets, found in the bathroom cabinet, into her limp hand.

'No,' she hissed, trying to press them back. 'I don't need these.'

'You must sleep.'

'I don't want to sleep.'

'You need to forget what's happened.'

She rounded on him, eyes dark and huge in her face. 'My husband's dead. My world's collapsing around me and you want me to *forget*?'

'Just for a few hours,' he said gently. 'You've the next few days to get through and you'll need your strength.'

Reluctantly she took the tablets, washing them down with the contents of a tumbler of neat whisky. Her hand shook and the tears started anew. Frank helped her from her clothes and onto the bed. He pulled the curtains against the approaching dawn then lay beside her, one arm holding her protectively. Beneath his hand he could sense the panicky thumping of her heart, could feel the erratic rise and fall of her chest.

It occurred to him then that he should have rung Nina, to explain what had happened. But how to say the words? *George's dead.* Even now he could scarcely believe it himself. It was like a dream, a horrendous nightmare from which he might soon wake and find himself in his own bed in his own home.

Mim turned to him. 'There were so many good times, Frank. The sex didn't matter. In his own way George loved me.'

Was she trying to convince herself, Frank wondered, or him? 'Of course he did.'

'If I'd known what he was about to do, perhaps I could have stopped him.'

'Self-recrimination is such a futile emotion.'

Mim reared back as though stung. 'How could you say that? Of course I blame myself. If I'd spent more time, watched him more closely —'

He put his mouth over hers, silencing her words. Felt her tongue probe his, almost savagely. Her teeth bruised his lips.

'Fuck me, Frank!'

Reaching his own hand forward, he encountered breast and belly. Mim straddled his own body, urging him on. It seemed almost obscene to be making love to her, after all that had happened, but Mim clung to him, her body working hard and furious against his own. She threw her head back, her cries filling the room. Were they for him, or George? he wondered later.

Afterwards, they curled spoon-like on the bed. As the minutes passed, her breathing slowed and she whispered drowsily in a little-girl voice, the words echoing in his brain like the shriek of a train down a long tunnel: 'I don't want to forget. I want to remember.'

Soothing. 'Of course you will.'

'You won't ever leave me, Frank?'

'I'll always look after you.'

'Promise?'

'I love you. Somehow we'll get through all this.'

He'd lie there, he knew, until she slept. Then he'd let himself out the front door and return to his own home, to the chaos of children and interruptions and his own crumbling ambitions. Home to the inevitable questions and explanation he knew he must give — not wanting to and dreading it already.

Soon. I'll go soon.

The thought slid through his tired mind, dipping and swaying. He was aware of Mim's breathing and the curtains billowing with the dawn breeze. Lulling, lulling, lulling ...

*   *   *

He is running across the grey countryside, across those flat Flanders plains. The landscape is littered with shell-holes brimming with greasy water. Here and there are the swollen fly-blown bodies of horses that lie where they have fallen. Their faces are twisted with the agony of their death. Their teeth are bared, lips pulled back into a parody of a smile.

He zigzags as he runs, trying not to step in the water or the maggoty remains of the animals. The ground shudders beneath his feet. Brilliant flashes of light turn night almost into day.

'Frank!'

Someone is calling. The voice penetrates the fear and the pounding of his own heart, yet he is too afraid to stop. He must distance himself from all this: the chaos, his exposure to the guns, the gut-wrenching terror. Must distance himself even from the voice, which contains its own tone of fear.

'Frank! Frank!'

He is gasping for air, his lungs almost bursting. A pain has begun, deep within his ribcage, and each step brings unspeakable agony. Still he goes on, searching for some place to hide. In the intermittent lulls between the bombs, he can hear an ugly rasping sound. Then he realises, shocked, that the source of the sound is his own mouth.

Reaching the splintered remains of a small wood, he stops at last, bends over to catch his breath, holding his hands to his chest. Seconds pass. The pain subsides, fading into discomfort. As he stands upright again, a figure comes pounding up beside him. He raises his head, not believing.

It is Bill! Bill with half his head blown away, brains and blood spilling in a sticky mess down the side of his face. Bill with his skin an awful shade of bloodless grey, eyes like sunken hollows in his face.

It can't be real. He extends his hand, encountering his brother's arm. It is cold, like ice and, unlike his face, an odd colour. Not blue, not purple. Just a bewildering in-between shade that reminds him of childhood mulberry stains and the dark underbellies of the fish his father unloaded from the Sea-spray all those years ago.

Bill's mouth forms whispered words, barely heard. 'Help me!'

'I can't,' Frank replies, shocked, backing away. 'You're already dead.'

A putrid stench wafts towards him. The foul stink of it fills his nostrils and the contents of his stomach threaten to disgorge themselves.

'It's your fault, Frank.'

'No! I didn't know!'

'How will you explain?'

Sobbing. 'I don't know.'

As he watches, Bill's face changes. The features blur, melting together into a mish-mash of red and grey. Re-form. Become older. More pudgy. More tanned. It is not Bill at all, he realises, but George.

'It's all your fault, Frank.'

Same words. Different voice.

'NO!'

'Did it make you feel worthwhile, fornicating with another man's wife?'

'I love Mim.'

'She's using you. That's what Mim does. Uses people, then spits them out. You'll be next.'

'She loves me.'

Laughter ripples towards him, an insane snigger that reverberates on and on. The sound of it fills his head. 'Mim only loves herself. She's like a leech, sucking away at the very essence of you. What will you do when she bleeds you dry?'

'Go away! You're dead, too. You can't touch me.'

'I am your conscience, Frank. I can never leave.'

The scene sways about him, a moving kaleidoscope of hues. He sinks to the ground, head pressed against his knees, rocking backwards and forwards. The howl builds in his head and he opens his mouth, releasing it to the wind.

The sound of his own scream woke him. He sat upright in the bed, trying to gather his thoughts, feeling across the sheets in the darkened room for Nina. She had always been there, comforting him, after similar nightmares.

Then he remembered. It was not Nina's bed in which he lay, but Mim's. And the awful shuddering memory came jolting back.

CHAPTER 17

Frank was truly caught between the protocol of organising the funeral and needing to be there for Mim, and bearing Nina's eternal bloody silence. It was the silence he couldn't stand, that wretched self-imposed suppression. If only she'd flare up and bring the whole sorry mess into the open. He could deal with that. But she went about the house tight-lipped and non-committal, and he didn't know the words to start the conversation.

He scraped together enough to pay for George's funeral. It wasn't as lavish as Mim had hoped for. The casket was pine, not mahogany, and they used one of the work vehicles instead of a hearse. 'I am sorry about George,' he overheard Nina say to Mim at the grave-side. Then she walked away, head bowed, back to the waiting car.

He took Mim home, leaving her in the empty house at her own insistence. 'Please,' she whispered, looking drained. 'I just want to be by myself for a while. Go home to your wife.'

Back at the house, Nina ignored him. He hated that, the coldness, the lack of communication. But, he reasoned, he could only blame himself.

'We have to sell the house,' he said, finding her standing on the terrace, staring down towards the bay. She stood apart from him, arms folded across her chest, not looking in his direction.

He wished she'd say something, but she simply stood statue-still.

'There's no money,' he went on, despising himself, loathing the situation that had been forced on them. The bloody house was the only thing she'd ever wanted, and the only decent thing he'd ever been able to provide. 'And we have to repay the debts somehow.'

'The business?'

There was a slight inflection to her voice. Of hope? he wondered. He shook his head. 'All gone. Turns out George was helping himself. Gambling debts. That's why —'

He stopped, unable to say the words, then cleared his throat. 'We'll have to wind it all up. I'll give the workers the news tomorrow.'

Nina turned towards him, her face pale. 'If we have to sell the house, then that's what we'll do.'

'I'm so sorry, Nina.'

'Yes, well . . .'

And she left the words unspoken as she walked away.

A procession of would-be buyers tramped noisily through her home. They commented in loud voices on her lovingly restored handiwork, careless of being heard. She felt herself withdrawing from them, recoiling from their loud voices and unmannerly children who tore through the rooms.

'Please stop,' she begged two young boys, swinging from the drapes in the living room.

The mother looked at her coldly. 'Leave them alone,' she said in a sharp undertone.

The property was sold for a fraction of its value, scarcely enough to clear the mortgage. Mechanically Nina wrapped and packed the china, the precious knick-knacks she had collected over the years. The children, as though sensing her distress, tiptoed around the house, helping wherever they could.

It was a week before Christmas when she felt the first pains of labour. 'It can't be,' she cried. Claire watched with round eyes as she sank into a nearby chair. 'It's too soon. I've the rest of the packing to organise. If it could just wait a week, until we've moved.'

'It's all right, Mummy. Joe and I will finish.'

Frank took her to the hospital. She lay in the high bed, letting the pain overtake her, heedless of the hands that poked and prodded. In a way it was a release, taking her from the events of the previous weeks. George's death. The sale of the house. She gave herself to the unspeakable agony that shuddered through her like a knife. Gave herself wholly to delivering her child, letting the hours slide mercilessly into each other until, at last, it was all over and the child slithered between her legs onto the bloodied sheet.

She was exhausted. Too old, she thought, to be going through the rigours of childbirth. A nurse began to wash her, wiping a damp cloth between her legs.

'Is something wrong?' she asked, suddenly aware she had heard no loud wail, no frantic cry for air. And there had been no announcement of the sex of the child.

She levered herself onto her elbows. The doctor was standing at the end of the bed, shaking his head. 'I'm sorry, Mrs Carmody. He has ... certain problems.'

He? 'It's a boy?'

'Like I said, I don't think —'

'I want my child.'

'It's better if you don't —'

'I *want* my child!'

Wordlessly they handed him to her, a tiny fragile body wrapped in white sheeting. Pale bloodless face. Translucent skin. Eyes closed.

'Is he dead?'

'No.'

'Is he going to die?'

They were all staring at her. Nurses. Doctor. Standing still, waiting, staring with sympathetic eyes.

'Mrs Carmody —'

Panic welled inside her. 'Somebody answer me! I said, *Is he going to die?*'

'It's best if we take him now. This is too upsetting.'

She held the baby against her chest as though daring anyone to take a step closer. 'I carried him inside me,' she said, struggling to keep her voice even. 'I suffered the pain and pushed him from my body. And now, because he's not normal and perfect and whole, you want to take him away?'

'Mrs Carmody, I understand that you're upset.'

Upset? *Upset?* What sort of ineffectual useless word was that? 'He's my *child*.'

'Would you like me to call your husband?'

'*NO!*'

The doctor withdrew towards the door. 'Very well. If that's what you wish.'

'I will hold him,' she said determinedly to his retreating back, 'until the end. And if it takes a day or a week, I don't care!'

It seemed only seconds passed until a nurse took him from her arms. Mere moments to memorise his tiny face, those fine, yet imperfect, features. A fleeting scarce-remembered stretch of time to feel the weight, the scant substance of him. Nina was aware of them lifting him, aware, too, of the cold against her arms where his body had lain, and she wanted to cry out at the injustice of it all. Wanted to scream and scream and scream, never stopping, and felt an emptiness that turned in on itself, consuming her.

'I am to blame,' she told herself, the thought random, yet insistent. 'I did not want this child! Now I am being punished!'

The staff kept her in the maternity ward, where she was forced to watch the mothers with their newborn babies. Her breasts ached. They bound them with rough towels, stemming the flow of milk. A sense of grief engulfed her. She couldn't stop crying. Frank came to visit. 'You have to pull yourself together,' he said. 'Get over it.'

She stared at him in amazement. 'Don't you care? He was your son!'

Father Mulcahy called in to see her. 'I'm so sorry, Nina,' he soothed in a comforting tone. 'But you must remember, it was God's will.'

'God is punishing me,' she replied bitterly.

'Why do you say that?'

'I did not want this child.'

'You are a good mother.'

'He is my burden to carry.'

The sale of two precious Royal Doulton figurines paid for the funeral, the second Nina had attended in less than two months. She watched, numb, as the tiny casket was carried to the grave. Watched as the clods of earth fell and another part of her life lay buried.

'Best forgotten about, eh?' said Frank, taking her arm and leading her back to the car. 'We have to move on.'

Wearily she replied, 'Yes, Frank.'

By the time she left hospital, the sale of the house had been finalised, and Frank had moved the family to a rented flat. It was located in the inner city, two bedrooms with no carpet, only linoleum on the floors. It would, Nina knew, be bitterly cold in winter. Much of the furniture — her beautiful cherished pieces — was gone.

'I sold it,' said Frank matter-of-factly. 'Wouldn't fit in here. Besides, it just didn't suit.'

What had he done with the money? she wondered.

'Packing up, helping your father move — you've been so helpful,' praised Nina, gathering her remaining children about her. It was as though her life were moving in reverse.

'Aunty Mim helped,' said Joe importantly.

'Well,' added Claire with nine-year-old cynicism. 'She stood there and gave orders and *we* did all the work.'

Mim: hovering on the periphery of her life. Would she ever be free of her?

The flat was filthy, so she set to, polishing the knobs and taps, throwing buckets of hot soapy water at the walls, trying to wash away the dirt and misery of other people's lives. Occupying herself. Taking herself from her thoughts. It was, she thought, exhausted, one way of making herself forget.

Claire's ninth birthday had come while Mummy was in hospital. Aunty Mim dropped by with a present and a cake, and a hug from which she had squirmed away. Daddy had tried to put on a happy face but she had sensed the changes, and knew instinctively that nothing was as it should be.

It seemed her entire life had altered direction during those past few months. First Uncle George had died, though she wasn't sure why. There had been much whispering and secrecy, and her own questions on the subject had gone unanswered. And Aunty Mim, who had once been a regular visitor to the house, hardly came any more, certainly not when Mummy was there.

It was Depression time, that was what everyone said. She and Joe and Lydia had been taken from their exclusive private schools and enrolled at the public school, two blocks away. The house had been sold, and Father no longer had a business.

'No-one,' he told her sadly, 'has money to buy houses.'

'But someone bought ours.'

'We practically gave it away.'

'Why?'

'When you're older, you'll understand.'

That was Father's usual answer to her questions. *When you're older.*

Then there was the mystery about the baby. There had been one, Claire knew. It had grown inside Mummy's tummy. She had placed her hand there, several times, and felt it wriggling. 'Does it hurt?' she had asked and Mummy had laughed. Not a mean kind of laugh, like Aunty Mim, but a kind of chuckle that meant she thought Claire amusing.

But when Mummy came home from the hospital, home to the flat with only two bedrooms where she and Joe and Lydia had to share again, there was nothing.

'Don't ask about the baby,' Aunty Mim had instructed.

'Why?'

'Because he died.'

He? So it had been a boy. 'Like Uncle George?'

Aunty Mim had nodded, tears springing into her eyes.

The flat was cramped, with no privacy. 'We'll make the best of it,' Mummy had said the first time she'd seen it, trying to look cheerful. But Claire had noticed the sadness in her eyes and the lines of pain in her face.

Mummy kept her hair ribbons, combs and clips — things she no longer wore — in an old chocolate box. Lydia and Claire loved to pull them out and look at them, spread them on the bed, comb and braid each other's hair. Claire thought a lot about their life in the big house. Remembered the parties, her parents dressing for the occasions. Ballgowns. Tuxedos. Remembered the times spent on the jetty with Joe, casting that fine line into the water, and his excited shouts when he caught a fish.

She hated living back in the inner city. It was noisy and dirty, and she wished they could move to a different place altogether. Somewhere by the sea. To Tea-tree Passage, perhaps. Mummy had once said it was beside the sea. She spent hours dreaming about the place, trying to imagine an alternate life, one where everyone was happy and no-one died.

Frank wasn't sure when he made the conscious decision to leave, but knew it was the result of a festering discontent that grew and grew inside his head until it reached explosion point. Everything good about his marriage had gone. He and Nina scarcely spoke. The children were withdrawn and uncommunicative. He felt as though he had failed them all in some monstrous way. They'd be better off without him.

He walked to Mim's — the car had been repossessed the previous month — and stood outside the front gates of her house for what seemed like a long time, staring at the SOLD sign attached to her front fence. They were all moving on, making new lives. And *his* life involved Mim, above all else.

He opened the front door and walked inside.

'Mim?'

Her voice came floating down from the rooms above. 'Up here, darling.'

Up the carpeted stairs he went, past the room where they had found George, and whose door remained permanently shut. He could hear the sound of metal scraping and the slamming of a lid.

She was packing, randomly throwing clothes into several suitcases that sat open on the bed. Coat hangers lay strewn on the floor. Bottles of creams and lotions were scattered on the dresser.

'Bit early to be packing all this,' he commented, pouring himself a whisky from the half-full bottle on the bedside table. 'The house is still officially yours for another month.'

She shrugged and brought another armful of clothes from the wardrobe. 'No use waiting until the last moment.'

'Mim, I've been thinking.'

'Mmnn.' She was holding out a peach-coloured gown, one he had seen her wear several times, and not really listening.

'I'm leaving Nina.'

Her head shot up and she came to a halt, the gown discarded on the floor. 'Why on earth would you do that?'

'Because I want to be with you.'

She gave an odd little grimace. 'Well, that's

202

something I've been meaning to speak to you about. I'm going away.'

'Going away?' he asked stupidly. 'Where to?'

'England, darling.'

Her words chugged furiously in his mind, begging to be understood. *England*? Why would she go there?

'Bloody hell! *I* can't go to England!'

She walked towards him, wrapping her arms around his neck, bringing her mouth near his own. 'I'm not asking you to.'

'So when you say you're leaving, you mean to say you're also leaving *me*?'

She gave him a quick kiss on the mouth, a momentary meeting of skin, a fleeting touch. Then she moved back to her task, head down, not meeting his gaze.

'I don't want to stay here, darling, not after everything that's happened. Too many memories. Too horrid for words.'

Suddenly he was suspicious. 'You're going alone?'

'Don't be silly. Henry's coming with me.'

'*Henry*?'

'My friend, Henry. You know, the writer?'

'I know who Henry is, Mim. I just didn't think you were such good mates that you'd pack up and travel to the other side of the world with him.'

'There's a lot about me you don't know.'

He supposed there was, given the conversation. Defeated, he sat on the edge of the bed and ran one hand through his hair. 'So it's definite, then?'

'The steamer ticket's booked. We're leaving in two days.'

His world, his plans, were unravelling, and a sense of desperation filled him. Two days. Forty-eight hours. It wasn't too late. Perhaps he could persuade her to change her mind. 'Tonight,' he pleaded. 'We'll go out for dinner, just like old times.'

'Henry's already asked me.'

'Well, later then. I'll come around and we can —'

'We can *what*, Frank?'

He stood, staring at her. Her eyes glinted, cold and hard, and her mouth had compressed into a firm unyielding line. What had happened to that frivolous fun-loving Mim?

'So we can talk, for Christ's sake!'

'You think a fuck will change my mind, is that it?'

'No!'

She smiled, a deprecating grimace. 'Sorry, darling. Too much to do and not enough hours. Besides, it's the wrong time of the month.'

'So the going gets tough and you turn your back and walk away! What about all the years we've had together? Don't they mean something?'

'It's over. Time to move on.'

She took his arm and led him down the stairs to the front door. 'Goodbye, Frank.'

'So this is it, then?'

''Fraid so.' And she closed the door in his face.

He stood, stunned, almost not believing what had happened. All these years and now it had come to this. A brief goodbye. Not even a decent damn kiss.

'*Bitch!*' he yelled and thumped his hand against the door. 'You lousy bloody *BITCH!*'

An old woman, walking towards him along the footpath, stopped and waited, and he slammed his hand against his palm and moved off.

Every thought jangled. Her rejection stung. Her easy dismissal wounded, rubbed against his manliness. She had only been using him, Frank knew that now. And the words jostled back at him from the shadowy recesses of some almost-forgotten dream: *She's like a leech. What will you do when she bleeds you dry?*

'What *will* I do?' he muttered aloud. Thank God he hadn't told Nina his plan, burnt his bridges at home. He'd go back, pretend nothing had happened. Pretend that today had been like every other day and his pride wasn't deflated.

It was ironic, he thought, that Mim, who had needed the constant reassurance of Frank's own allegiance, had been the one to leave. And it occurred to him later, much to his shame, that Mim's treatment of him was equal to his own treatment of Nina. Callous and cold. Calculated. He'd been prepared to abandon her and the children. And for what? Mim hadn't even given him a backward glance.

CHAPTER 18

One by one, Nina sold her precious belongings: the figurines she had so lovingly collected, a few paintings, the last of the good furniture. She joined the hated food queues and accepted ration cards from imperious-looking officials at the dole office. Finally she made all sorts of excuses to the man who came to collect the rent.

'I've heard it all before, luv,' he told her wearily. 'Just pay the money or get out.'

Frank had trouble finding work. He scanned the newspapers every day and went down to the docks. Hoping. Hoping. Nina saw the despondency in his face, saw the humiliation. He was a proud man, not given to begging.

Then, miracle of miracles, he was offered a job as a delivery driver for a soft drink factory. He left at five in the morning, catching two buses and a tram to take him to the depot. Came home at seven, exhaustion making his face grey. He wasn't getting any younger and, despite their differences over the years, Nina's heart went out to him.

The job lasted two weeks. Frank arrived home, drunk and full of melancholy, at midday. 'I've got the sack,' he told her bitterly.

'What happened?'

'The boss found someone to do it cheaper.'

'They weren't paying you much.'

'And they're paying the new bloke even less. Do you know what the boss asked me? He wanted to know if I would match the other bloke's price.'

Resignedly. 'And you told him no.' The money had been miserable, but at least it had been something.

'I said, "You'd better take him on then."'

'What'll we do now?'

Frank shook his head and took off his jacket, hanging it on the peg on the back of the door, swaying a little as he stood. 'I won't beg, Nina,' he said fiercely. 'I won't bloody well beg.'

She managed to find a job, just a few hours a day, in one of the nearby laundries. It was hot laborious work, bending over the huge washtubs and lugging the wet fabric to clothes lines that seemed, some days, to stretch forever. The pay was miserable, scarcely enough to cover the rent. She came home exhausted, hands red and swollen, often to find Frank passed out in a drunken stupor on the settee. Without looking, she knew there would be money missing from her purse.

They stayed in the flat six months. Six months of avoiding the rent man, of not answering knocks on the door. Six months of wondering if they would come home to find their belongings on the footpath.

Finally they moved late one night under cover of darkness, using a horse and cart, hessian bags tied firmly around the horse's hooves to muffle the sounds. They owed two months rent, and Frank was insistent that the neighbours weren't to know where they were headed.

Their new home was a single-storey tenement, more cockroach-infested and dirty than the last. The front room — the living room — had a window covered by grimy curtains facing the street. The middle room had a skylight, and the back room faced the lavatory at the end of the yard.

Though she missed her beautiful home and leafy suburb unbearably, there were some aspects of their former life she was glad to be rid of. Frank's fawning acquaintances. The boring parties. And Mim. She had gone to England, or so Frank had said, very casually, months ago.

In the end, even that relationship had faltered. She supposed she should have felt something — relief or elation? — yet there was nothing. Inside she felt cold. Numb.

Sometimes Frank wondered if he were going insane. As he walked along the city pavements, the buildings seemed to lean towards him. They reared, huge and monstrous, threatening to topple, crushing him beneath their mass. The sounds of traffic assaulted his ears. Horns blowing. Squeal of tyres against wet tar. Too loud. Too shrill. On the harbour, the giant girders of the new bridge grew slowly towards each other, two perfect arcs, not yet meeting, outlined dark against the sky. And they seemed like bars on a cage, hemming him.

He passed the dole queues. Anxious eyes turned towards him, hopeful yet desperate. Beggars lined the tunnels leading to the underground railway stations. 'Spare a few bob, mister?' they asked as he passed, and he'd shake his head, knowing that only a year earlier he could have given the money and not missed a penny of it.

Occasionally a woman he saw in the streets reminded him painfully of Mim. Shapely legs. High heels. *Click*, *click*, *click* against the footpath. He searched the faces of passers-by, thinking that one day he'd see her again, hoping against hope she had come back. But as the months passed, he knew it was simply wishful thinking.

By the end of the year he'd had a variety of jobs, none lasting more than a few weeks. Door-to-door selling mostly, hawking needles, mothballs, packets of seeds; anything that was cheap and easy to carry. It was demeaning humiliating work. Knocking on strangers' doors. 'Excuse me, ma'am. I was wondering —'

And his words were invariably cut off by the slamming of the door.

The abuse was soul-destroying. Granted, some women were kind, spending a few pennies when he was sure they had little to spare, asking him in for a cup of tea and pushing a plate of home-made biscuits towards him. He was eating irregularly and he supposed he'd lost weight. Certainly his belt now tied a few notches tighter.

He had fallen to the bottom of the pit, and there was no way he could climb out.

He began staying away from home. Just one night at a time. Then two. Then weeks went past where he slept in bus stops and sheds, venturing further out of the city. A few sales guaranteed a meal in a pub, a hot shower and a couple of drinks. Nina and the kids would get by, he reasoned. She had her job, the weekly dole rations. And she had long since stopped asking his whereabouts, simply accepted his comings and goings in silence.

He wandered from town to town, no set destination in mind. Got to know the cafes that donated the leftover food, and the location of the bagmen's camps, near the river or local showground.

The camps were filled with men of all ages. Young. Old. Men like himself, who had been businessmen in their own right before this whole sorry mess. They clung together, got pissed together, hid together from their own misery.

Somewhere up near Grafton, he teamed up with a chap named Bob. 'Robert A. O'Halloran,' he'd introduced himself with a wink. 'But you can call me Bob. Pharmacist in my previous life.'

'And now?'

Bob had thought for a moment, head cocked to one side. 'Student of human nature, I suppose.'

He'd had a chain of city chemist stores to his name, he said, before the world had gone mad. 'Well, if you've gotta go down, then you might as well do it in a big way,' he confided to Frank with a laugh. 'Least I can say I had a go.'

Frank knew exactly what he meant. He swung his hand forward, indicating the camp. 'So what brings you to this godforsaken place?'

'They say misery loves company.'

He thought about that and supposed Bob was right. 'Yes, well, maybe you have a point.'

'You seem like a decent bloke. Come on. Let's get out of here.'

'Where to?'

'There's a train due about three. It's going through to Brisbane. Let's check it out.'

He stared down at his shoes. They were falling apart, soles coming adrift from the uppers. If he could get a needle and thread and some cardboard, he'd be able to manage another month out of them. 'Why not?' he said. 'Beats walking.'

They waited on the top rung of the pig pens just north of the station. Several others waited, too, figures outlined against a pale blue sky as the empty freight train shuffled past. 'Now!' yelled Bob, and they both jumped, landing with a thud in the empty carriage.

It stunk of cow shit.

'Christ!' Bob grinned. 'We've copped a right stinker here. The wheat trains, they're the best. You can burrow into the grain at night. It keeps you warm. Knew a bloke once who got down too far though. Suffocated.'

Frank couldn't decide which was worse, drowning in wheat or squatting in cow turds. He found a fairly clean spot and sat down.

The train rocked along, lurching over the points in a steady rhythm. The sides of the carriages were slatted, allowing a fragmented view. Glimpse of tree, of hill. Occasional farmhouse. Bob fished in his pocket and brought out a wrapped sandwich. Opened it and offered Frank half.

'So, got a family?'

'Yes.'

He waited expectantly for Frank to go on.

'The usual,' Frank added. 'Wife and three kids back in Sydney. But I'm not much use to them. Can't even earn a decent quid.'

Bob nodded. 'Makes a bloke feel real inadequate when he can't make a bob. Someone said there were jobs going up in Queensland. Fruit picking. Thought I'd give that a go.'

'So you're going just on the off-chance?'

'No harm looking. There's nothing going on down here.'

'S'pose not.'

He pulled a flask from his pocket, took a swig and handed it to Frank. It was gin. Smooth sweet gin. He took a mouthful and felt it slide somewhere inside him, warm and mellow, took another and handed it back.

The grog made him talkative. The two men chatted on, probing tentatively into each other's lives, exploring inconsequential details mostly, the flask passing between them at odd intervals. Bob, it turned out, had served in infantry during the war, in Gallipoli and later in France.

'No kidding!' said Frank. 'Pozières. Tincourt. We might have walked right past each other.'

They got to talking about the war. Tactics.

Campaigns and manoeuvres. Mates they had lost. Skirting around the bigger issues. Maudlin, bloody maudlin, Frank thought, depressed. Nothing had changed much over the years. His own life still resembled a battlefield.

'Had a brother. Bill. He was killed over there.'

He hadn't meant to mention the name, had avoided saying it until now. The sound of it sliding off his tongue shocked him and he heard it mingling with the clickety-clack of the wheels and the rolling thud of the carriages.

'How did he cop it?'

Frank was silent for a while, his mind forming words, explanations and reasons. 'Bullet to the head.'

'Fucking Fritz!'

'It wasn't a German who fired the gun.'

He pushed the memory back, unsuccessfully: Bill staggering towards him, blood and brains splattered across his cheek. Huge gaping hole. Hands outstretched, as though to save himself from falling. A combination of shock, pain and fear on what remained of his brother's face.

Why wasn't he dead?

Words, so long repressed, rose like gorge in his throat. 'Go on! Say it!' ordered an inner voice. 'Tell the bloody truth!'

'I killed my brother.'

Words never before uttered. Not to his parents. Not to Nina. Never, *ever*, to himself.

He was aware of Bob staring at him, head rocking with the rhythm of the train, snapping to and fro.

Aware of his unblinking eyes. Aware too of the mechanical sounds: creak of carriage, click of metal against metal, and the late afternoon sun pouring its suffocating heat into that stinking cattle pen.

There was a need to explain, to enlarge upon those wretched words. Though he scarcely knew the man, he couldn't bear to think Bob thought ill of him. 'We'd been in the trenches for days. No sleep. Disorientated. Ears ringing with the constant noise. You know how it was.'

Bob nodded soberly. 'Yair, mate. I know.'

'A few blokes had gone over the sandbags into No Man's Land. I was covering them, but must've dozed off. The next thing I knew, I jerked awake. There were men coming towards me, clambering over the side of the trench, sliding towards me through the mud. Someone yelled "fire!".'

He stopped for a moment, unable to go on. Swallowed. Closed his eyes against the sun and searched his mind for words, memories.

'So you did,' prompted Bob.

'Didn't know it was our own blokes. Just fired and fired and fired. And when it was all over ...'

His voice trailed away and he buried his face in his hands. He hoped for tears, something, anything to cleanse the memory from his consciousness.

'What happened then?'

Frank raised his head and stared at the sky, wishing the infinite blue would swallow him, take him from his grief.

'Nothing.'

'Nothing?'

'No-one else knew, except me and one of the other blokes. So we just shut up about it and went back along the trench to the rest of the men. And the next day the other bloke copped it, too. Bullet in the heart.' He paused and glanced down at his hands, which were shaking. 'Don't know why I'm telling you all this. Never told a single person before. Been bottling it up for a bloody long time now.'

'Well, your secret's safe with me, mate. Anyway, it's your own conscience you've got to live with.'

He must have slept, waking later to shouts and the sound of gunfire. The train had stopped and it was almost dark. 'Coppers!' yelled a voice from further along, and there was a mad scramble. Bodies scaled the sides of the cattle trucks, dropping to the ground below. There was a sound of thudding footsteps.

'Come on,' urged Bob. 'Let's make a run for it. If those bastards catch us in here, they'll rough us up.'

Through the slatted sides, Frank could see dark shapes running past, and torch beams snaking through the semi-darkness.

'Right-o, you blokes. You're trespassing on government property. Everyone out where we can see you!'

He came home to Nina with two black eyes and a broken nose. She answered his knock on the front door and stood for a long time, looking at him, saying nothing. Then she turned and walked away, leaving him standing in the doorway. Hating himself. Hating what they had become.

* * *

The months dragged by, slid insidiously into years. Years of scrimping and making do, of lying in bed at night aching for a decent meal, listening to the scurry of rats in the walls. Years of wondering when it all might end. But, Nina thought with constant despair, there was no end, no conclusion, in sight.

1931 had been a bad year. Several of their neighbours had been evicted yet, somehow, she managed to scrape the rent money together, going without herself so the children were fed. A run on the New South Wales Savings Bank saw its eventual collapse, and the housing industry had all but folded. Surely, she thought, it could get no worse. However, the following year, charities were overwhelmed with requests, and there was an outbreak of diphtheria. Frank was absent for months at a time and she worried about Joe.

She knew he skipped school, spending his days roaming the streets. Letters had come from the headmaster. He was only ten years old, but what was she to do? He needed a father's firm hand.

'Don't worry about me, Mum,' he'd say when tackled. 'I'll get by.'

The population was fed-up and there was a militant, mutinous air about the city. In March she had taken the children to watch the opening of the new bridge across the harbour. They stood in the sunshine, part of the throng, and temporarily forgot their troubles. In amazement they watched as the ceremony was disrupted by a member of the New Guard, Captain de Groot. After that, Joe began hanging around with the New Guard crowd and went to their meetings, despite his mother's pleas.

She wished she could take the children from the city. Away from the desolate crowds and grinding poverty. Away from that communal kind of life she hated, where children played in the streets on hot nights after supper and the men ambled down to the local pub looking for work. Women sat on the front steps, fanning themselves against the heat. The sight of them, gossiping over peeling rails, disconcerted her. Everyone knew the others' business, or thought they did. And she hated that, the prying eyes and the questions.

'Frank gone away again?'

'That boy of yours, Nina, he's gonna get himself into trouble one day.'

She could never get used to that way of life, coming from the suburbs where everyone kept to their own yards. So she refused to join them, preferring her own company. She knew they talked about her, considered her a snob. 'If I become part of them,' she told herself, 'I will never escape this life.'

She busied herself, instead, with her sewing machine, earning a few extra bob from the occasional repair job, and became a dab hand at making school blouses for Claire and Lydia from bleached flour bags, or Joe's pants from cut-down curtains.

'I'm inventive,' she told herself calmly. 'I can manage.'

Fence palings, a broken chair or rolled-up newspapers became firewood. The coal man, taking pity on her, gave her the scrapings left in the barrow. She went to church on Sundays, taking the children, thanking God for food on the table and the thin old blankets on the beds.

After a month's absence, Frank came home with a despondency that both stunned and angered her. She'd been managing — just — in his absence, but one extra mouth to feed stretched her resources beyond control. She took to missing meals herself, learning to live with the hunger that churned her belly. Precious pounds went missing from her purse. Frank left the house each morning on the pretext of finding work, and came home drunk and abusive from the pub.

'This can't go on,' she told him. 'There's no money for food, and the rent's behind.'

He stared at her, face impassive. 'What in God's name do you expect me to do?'

'You could ease up on the grog, for a start.'

'I don't drink much.'

He was lying. Nina knew it. Frank knew it. Yet there was a belligerent tone to his voice and she hesitated. 'You could ask your parents for help,' she added, voice low.

'I won't crawl to them.'

'Frank! Please!'

'I'll not beg,' he told her curtly. 'We'll manage.'

'You'd rather watch your children starve,' she asked in disbelief, 'than ask your family for help?'

'A man's got pride.' Then. 'You haven't kept up with those bloody letters?'

She shook her head. There had been no point;

Frank's parents had never replied and it had been years since she'd written.

It was a terrible argument, words and accusations grinding on and on. Nina was glad the children were at school and not witness to what they had come to, she and Frank.

As usual he had the last word. 'You're a cold woman, Nina,' he shouted and flung himself out the door, slamming it viciously in his wake.

She didn't see him for two days, until he came sheepishly into the kitchen with a large bag of fruit. 'Here,' he said gruffly, hardly able to look her in the eye. 'These are for the kiddies.'

Joe was late for school. Several showers of rain had sent him scuttling for cover under the shop awnings. As a result his morning paper round, which brought in a few pennies each week, had gone overtime.

He ambled along the footpath in the direction of school, wishing for a more pleasant destination, kicking a bottle top with his boots. They were tight, too tight, the shoes, the heel rubbing against his own until he was certain a blister had formed. The sole had come adrift from the upper and, as he took each successive step, he caught a glimpse of a sockless big toe.

'Bugger!' he mumbled under his breath. 'Bugger! Bugger! Bugger!'

Old Smithers, his form teacher, would have it in for him, being late. It was the third morning this week, and the prospect of the cane loomed threateningly. To make matters worse, hunger gnawed in his belly.

There'd been little on offer for breakfast. Dry toast and weak milky tea, which he'd chosen to forgo. Now, with the prospect of no lunch, he wished he'd been less fussy.

God, his foot hurt!

'Bugger! Bloody bugger!'

He stopped in the shade of a tree, hunkered down on the footpath and removed his boot. Carefully he twisted his ankle until he could see his heel and the red ugly bubble of skin. It stung and he pressed his thumb against it, wishing away the pain.

As he looked up, he saw his father walking along the footpath on the opposite side of the road. He was whistling, his hands shoved deep in his pockets. At the corner he turned and walked through an open gate, into a house.

Joe stared long and hard after the retreating form, wondering. It was just a small cottage, corrugated-iron roof and blue weatherboards, and a few straggly shrubs lining the fence. Similar to the rest of the houses in the street, not standing out particularly. But Billy Mathews, a sixth grader, had told him last week that the place was a brothel.

'What's a brothel?' he'd asked, puzzled.

'You know, a place where men go to be with women.'

He'd nodded, none the wiser, yet not wanting to appear too childish. 'How do you know?'

Billy had smiled, a secretive little smirk. 'I looked in the window. Want to?'

'No.' He'd shaken his head, memories tugging. Aunty Mim's place. Walking along the carpeted hallway. Opening the door at the end of the corridor. Aunty Mim and his father doing *that*.

Curious now, he stood in the shadows and waited. After a while a car pulled into the curb and two men got out, went into the house. Joe crossed the road, walked up to the front door and knocked.

A woman answered. Her mouth was a slash of red lipstick and her cheeks heavily rouged. She lounged against the doorway, regarding him with an amused indulgent stare.

'Hello, little boy. What do you want?'

She leaned forward, her low-cut dress revealing a swell of breasts that Joe found it difficult to drag his eyes from.

'I — I was looking for my father,' he stammered, feeling his face redden under the woman's stare.

'Well, now. And why would you think he's here?'

'I saw him.'

'No,' she replied, straightening up, folding her arms across her chest. 'You must be mistaken.'

Frowning. 'No. I'm sure it was my father. Frank Carmody. We live down —'

'Hop it, sonny.'

The door slammed in his face.

He retreated back to the shade on the opposite footpath and waited. After what seemed like about half an hour, his father walked down the front steps of the house, pulling on his coat.

Too late now for school, Joe decided, squinting his eyes up towards the sun.

Outside the fruit shop he ran into Claire. By rights she should have been at high school but his mother could no longer afford the fees. So she stayed home, helping about the house and queueing for the weekly dole rations.

Claire grabbed him by the collar. 'Mum's going to give you what for, wagging school again.'

'I don't care!' he declared, pulling away. 'She can't make me go.'

'They'll put you in a home.'

'Yeah, sure.'

'Okay, smarty. Just wait.'

'They've got to catch me first.'

She smiled at him, threw a playful punch. It was like that between them, this good-natured banter. Verbal wrangling. Thrust and parry. Get in first. 'Anyway, you're starting to sound just like Mum,' he added. That was sure to stop her.

But Claire was eyeing a tray of red plums, and hadn't heard. 'I'd give anything for some of those,' she wished aloud.

'Anything?'

'All I've got is a lousy shilling, and Mum wants some potatoes and beans for tea.'

He watched while she waited her turn at the counter. When he thought the proprietor wasn't looking, he snatched the tray and sprinted along the footpath, heading towards home.

'Hey! You rotten little thief!'

He heard footsteps pounding the footpath behind him, closer than he had anticipated. Clutching the tray of plums to his chest, he sensed some of them falling. What a waste! The blister hurt like hell, slowing him. Hands grasped his collar, his shirt, pulling him to an abrupt halt. Shaking, he stared into the man's angry face.

'I think we'd better go and see your parents, son.'

The man frogmarched him all the way home. Ashamed, he hung his head as his mother opened the door.

'Is this your boy?'

'What's wrong?'

'Bloody little thief. He stole a whole tray of plums.'

From the corner of his eye, he could see Claire, who had followed them home, looking smug. *Told you so*, she mouthed at him. He raised his head and watched his mother's features falling into a mask of despair and embarrassment as she battled to keep her composure. 'Is that true, Joe?'

'Yes.'

'Why?'

'I was hungry.'

'Where's the boy's father?'

He's been in the brothel, Joe wanted to say, checking himself just in time. He suspected that Mother would not welcome that bit of news.

Mother shrugged. 'Out looking for work.'

'He'd be better off staying home, teaching this boy a few manners. Needs a good belting, in my book.'

'Where are the plums, Joe?'

He shook his head. They were gone, the entire trayful. Smashed to a pulp on the footpath.

'They're worth seven bob,' said the man, letting go of Joe's collar.

His mother raised her hands in a gesture of hopelessness. 'I don't have seven shillings.'

'Well, someone's got to pay.'

'Oh, Joe.' His mother's mouth had become all lopsided, somehow uncontrollable. A single tear slid down her cheek and she made no effort to wipe it away.

'I'll tell you what,' said the man, the tone of his voice softening. 'The boy can do a bit of work in my shop after school. Repay the money that way.'

The pay was minimal but he stayed on in the shop, long after the cost of the plums had been repaid. The owner let him take the spoiled fruit home. It wasn't much, but it was something. Mother accepted it gratefully, made jams and chutneys, bottled over-ripe tomatoes.

Father went away again, taking off one cold morning, carrying a small battered suitcase. Had he even bothered to say goodbye? Joe couldn't remember.

'You're the man of the house while he's gone,' Mother said.

And the burden was a heavy weight on his small shoulders.

CHAPTER 19

Frank knew he was running. Physically and mentally. Purposefully. Running as though his life depended on it. At times he wondered what was the catalyst that drove him the most. Memories? His own failures? Shame? And no matter how hard he ran, how fast and furious, the memories and failures and shame followed, allowing no respite.

The same words ran unbidden through his mind. Teasing. Taunting.

Look how far you'd gone.

Now see how hard you've fallen.

The freight trains became a way of life, a means of escape. From Nina. From the memory of Mim. Residues of his former life. Leaping into moving carriages, avoiding the cops as they staged regular inspections; the danger excited him temporarily, freed him from constraints. He was reckless and bold, confronting his own mortality. It seemed nothing could kill him, though he wished long and hard that it could.

When he could afford grog, he drank himself into oblivion and the days rolled together into an untidy blur. Was it Monday or Friday? Weekday or weekend? It scarcely mattered. Each was the same.

The dreams continued, worsened. He became too afraid to sleep at night, sitting awake in empty freight vans, watching glassy-eyed as the dark smudge of scenery rolled by. Sometimes a silver moon lit the landscape. At other times the clouds churned in and emptied their watery mass, and the sky was lit by ragged lines of lightning.

When he did doze, lightning became the flare of gunfire, and thunder was the roar of bombs. The imagined smell of thyme and dust and salty air filled his nostrils. Where was he? he wondered, confused. Gallipoli or France? Then he saw soldiers sliding towards him through the mud. Pozières, he knew with certainty, a land of chalk roads and zigzagging lines of sandbags, as he recognised the momentary look of surprise on their faces. His own gun fired, vomiting bullets. Hands came up, too late. Bloody, *bloody* mess.

In the dreams there was always blood on his hands. His brother's. Other men's. Dark sticky clots clinging to his fingers, under his nails. Vainly he tried to wipe it away, but it was like a stain. Immovable.

Then he'd wake. Screaming.

He grew thin. Stared at himself in railway washroom mirrors, almost not recognising the man he had become. Grey stubble on his chin. The skin on his ribs hanging in folds over bone. Permanent frown etched on his brow.

Sometimes a railway guard took pity on him, invited him into the office and gave him something to eat. He'd wolf down bread and cups of tea, making up for all those hungry hours, filling his belly full to bursting.

He felt fractured, split in two, as though he were on a roller-coaster ride from hell. Sometimes, during those long lonely nights, he wished he could go home, back to Nina and the children, and erase all those awful, awful years that hung between them. But home was a dingy rented place, and he hated seeing the sadness and disappointment in her face. Hated the reproachful expression in her eyes, couldn't bear to see her thin undernourished body, or the gangly limbs of his children.

Nina. Forever the martyr. Going without herself so the children suffered less.

'Don't fuss,' she'd snap when, on the rare occasions he was home, he encouraged her to eat more.

He came home as winter approached, dreading the cold. Came home to his children's resentful faces, Nina's accusing silence.

'Where have you *been*, Dad? We were worried.'

Were they? He hadn't made any effort at contact for six long months. They were managing okay without him, as well as any other family on the street. Joe's job at the fruit shop. Nina's few hours at the laundry. Dole rations. Scrimping. Making do.

He felt superfluous. Not part of them. A phantom useless father. One Saturday night someone offered him a job playing a violin at a dance. The pay was ten shillings, which had to be shared with the pianist. At midnight the dancers took the hat around and collected another two shillings. When he finally begged away at 2am, he stumbled along the streets until he came to an all-night bar.

Dawn was almost breaking as he let himself in the front door. He tiptoed into the children's room and sat for a while by their beds, seeing their smoothed-out sleeping expressions in that early pre-dawn light, the small hollows and indentations of their faces.

In the room he shared with Nina, he looked down on the curled form of his wife, watched the shadowy rise and fall of her chest. A pain rose inside him, a mixture of despair and grief.

I can't stay.

The words flittered about him, demanding acknowledgement. Mechanically he took his few remaining clothes from the makeshift wardrobe: two rows of stacked-up fruit boxes with a string line between them. When he was done, only two threadbare dresses of Nina's remained. For one long moment he stared at them, two limp pieces of fabric, poor excuses for clothes. A fragment of memory came to him: those long-ago rows of dresses and coats, ballgowns and blouses. What had happened to reduce them to this?

Her voice came from nowhere, disturbing his reverie. 'What are you doing, Frank?'

He pictured her lying there in the almost-dark, watching him with those grey sorrowful eyes.

'Packing.'

'Where are you going?'

'Away.'

'You're not coming back.'

It was a statement, not a question, and required no answer. What to say, anyway? She was silent for a moment. Then. 'Is there someone else? Another woman?'

'No.'

'Don't lie to me, Frank. I'm tired of it.'

He gave a bitter laugh. 'There's no-one, Nina. Who'd want me, anyhow?'

A faint sigh escaped her mouth. 'How will we get by?'

'You'll manage. God only knows, you have until now.'

He snapped the lid of the suitcase shut and placed what was left of his night's earnings on the window-sill. 'It's not much, but there's a few bob to tide you over.'

She was lying propped on her elbows in the bed, a mass of dishevelled dark curls about her head. In that faint pre-dawn light, her face was a blur of white. Her mouth, when it opened, seemed a dark hole into which he might fall.

'Frank! Please!'

He wanted badly to kiss her one last time. Wanted to place his mouth against hers, to taste her skin and warmth. Wanted to say, 'I'm sorry', and try to explain the reasons he thought it had all gone wrong. But the years, and all those harsh and unretractable words, had become a barrier between them.

So he picked up the suitcase, testing its weight in his hand. 'Goodbye, Nina.'

Two words ending a marriage, aborting a lifetime of memories. Without any further sound, he turned and let himself out the door.

She lay there for a long time after Frank clicked the lock on the front door, her mind numb. The children would soon wake, demanding to know where their father was and she'd say, like so many times before, 'he's gone'.

What she wouldn't tell them was that he wasn't coming back. She'd play the game of pretence, protecting them. From what? she wondered momentarily. After all that had happened, there was so little left to shock.

It was mid-December. There was scant money for food and rent, let alone to buy gifts.

'About Christmas,' she said to Claire, Joe and Lydia.

'We know, Mum,' replied Claire. 'There's no money for presents.'

'We don't want any, anyway,' added Joe.

'Just something small would be nice,' countered Lydia.

Nina sighed. Lydia, now eleven and the youngest of her small brood, caused her small amounts of worry. Only last week she had found her dancing in front of the bathroom mirror, lipstick a bright slash across her mouth.

The lipstick had been Nina's, worn in her previous life and now kept in the box with her few remaining trinkets. Frank had hated the colour, saying it made her look like Mim. 'All tarted up,' he'd said, and the irony was not lost on her now.

At her mother's entrance Lydia had turned and smiled. 'I'm going to be a famous actress when I grow up.'

'That's nice, dear. Now take off the lipstick, there's a good girl.'

'No.'

'Lydia!'

'You can't make me.'

Lydia had continued preening, turning this way and that in front of the mirror, her mouth forming a practiced pout, ignoring Nina who, for one brief moment, wanted to slap her.

'We could get a tree, make some decorations,' Claire said now, breaking her reverie.

'I know where I can get a good one,' added Joe.

'Just as long as it's legal,' cautioned Nina.

In the end, they were invited to Christmas dinner by Father Mulcahy. There were presents, small bags of lollies for the children, and a feast of chicken and turkey and baked vegetables, followed by little fruit mince pies and a plum pudding laced with brandy. Later, Nina remembered little of the night, except for the joyous faces of her children.

Only after they had left, walking back along the street towards their dingy house, did she break down. She heard herself saying, in a woolly distant kind of voice: 'He is so kind, so kind.'

Claire's bony arms went around her, comforting. 'It's all right, Mum. Everything's all right.'

She felt the tears slide down her face and her mouth, somehow uncontrollable. Her faltering steps took her back to the nightmare she had become part of. Her own life, her children's: would the suffering ever end?

It took a few months for the rumour to circulate that Frank wasn't coming back. The local storekeeper began to refuse Nina credit. 'Money up front,' he said. 'Can't afford to be subsidising everyone around here.'

Joe, on one of his rare days at school, came home with his clothes shredded. Standing there, staring at his bruised face and ruined shirt, a sudden anger consumed her. 'For God's sake, Joe! Can't you keep out of trouble for a change?'

He waited, sullen, mouth tight.

'Answer me!'

Lips barely moving. Expression resentful. 'Yes.'

'Yes, what?'

'Yes, I can keep out of trouble.'

'Where will I get the money to replace these clothes?'

'I'll find new ones.'

'Stolen from someone's clothesline, no doubt!'

'You don't trust me!'

She stopped, stunned. 'I'm sorry, Joe. Of course I trust you. I just don't know why you can't —'

'Can't what? Be less like my father?'

'You're nothing like your father.'

Joe backed away, a resolute look on his face, as though he hadn't heard her words. 'They said Dad isn't coming back.'

'Who said?'

'The kids at school.'

So that was what the fight had been about. Joe standing up for Frank, protecting himself from all those hateful truths. Nina glanced away, unable to bear the sight of her son's angry face.

'Well,' he went on, 'it's not true, is it?'

She forced herself to look at him. 'Yes.'

He flew at her then, beating his twelve-year-old fists ineffectually against her chest, tears streaming down his face. She let him cry himself out, waiting until the tears stopped and were replaced by the occasional hiccup. Despite his pretences, she thought, he was really still a child, a baby in some ways.

'Things will get better, I promise,' she said at last. 'At least we've got each other.'

He considered that for a moment, then nodded his head. 'But Dad's got no-one.'

'That's the choice your father's made.'

'Doesn't he love us any more?'

He gave her a soul-destroying look, and his words made her eyes swim. She had to reassure him, make it right. 'In his own funny way, your father loves us, Joe. Whether he realises it or not, it's himself that he's running away from.'

All through that winter of '34, Nina thought she would never get warm. Thin blankets and old coats on the beds. Huddling together at night. Miserable poverty grinding away until she feared she might go mad with the constant reminders of it. The strain of forcing herself to keep cheerful, for the children's sake, drained her.

She felt trapped, caught like a fly in a spider's web. In her darkest moments, she hated Frank with a furious ferocity, resentful that he had gone, simply walked out, leaving her with the full burden of responsibility. She was kept there, in that hated dismal house by the children, by the lack of money. Once Frank had promised her the world. Now she had nothing.

'I hate this!' she said. 'I just want to be normal.'

'What, Mum?' asked Joe, looking up from the table.

'Nothing,' she answered resignedly and gave him a hug.

One of Frank's acquaintances called in, the first time she had seen the man since her world had fallen in, almost five years earlier. 'Harry James,' he said, extending a hand as she met him at the front door. 'Remember me?'

'I remember,' she replied warily.

'I'm looking for Frank.'

'He's not here.'

'That's a shame.'

'What do you want him for?'

'Just catching up. Old times.'

'Just like that?'

It was hard to keep the sarcasm from her voice. Hard, too, to imagine what this man could want from them.

'Come in. Have a cup of tea,' she offered, more out of politeness than friendship.

Harry glanced about the kitchen, not trying to hide his curiosity. 'Bit of a come down from the big place,' he said as Nina poured hot water over tea leaves.

'Bigger people than us have fallen,' she replied, stone-faced. 'Better to have had and lost than never to have had at all.'

'That's a very noble sentiment. I find, myself, that it takes a lot of getting used to, being poor.'

'I have my children.'

'And Frank.'

No use pretending. 'Actually Frank doesn't live here any more. It's just us these days, me and the kids.'

Harry was quiet for a moment. 'So you're all alone. That's a pity.'

Stiffly. 'We manage.'

'I could move in if you like, help out a bit.'

Nina eyed him warily. 'In what way?'

'Think about it. You're an intelligent woman,' he said, giving her a conspiratorial wink.

'You mean sex?'

'I wouldn't have put it so bluntly.'

'No!' she retorted sharply. 'You'd rather put out silly little insinuations that only serve to demean both of us. Credit me with a little more common sense.'

He rose from his seat at the table and came towards her. She stood, teapot in hand, bringing it up as a barricade between them. His hands were on her arms and he brought his mouth towards hers, clumsily, trying to kiss her.

She stepped back, lifting the teapot higher. 'Don't touch me!'

'Come on. Just one little kiss.'

'Get out!'

'I fancied you, Nina, back in the old days. Frank always said you were cold, but I knew that underneath that cool exterior was a passion just waiting to be unleashed. It just needed the right man.'

'Is that so?' She thrust the teapot forward, pressing it against the man's fleshy hand.

'Ouch! No need for that. I was paying you a compliment, that's all.'

'Then, since you've said it, you can leave.'

Later, sipping a cup of lukewarm tea, she was surprised to find her hands shaking. *Cold*! Was that how Frank had described her to his mates? The word was so ... calculating, so ... emotionless. And she was none of those.

She felt curiously betrayed. Let down. Harry had been right. Underneath that straight-laced public exterior, she did feel passion and desire; indeed she felt an intensity about things that was sometimes hard to put into words. Perhaps, if Frank had been a different man, more sensitive to her needs, he would never have described her so.

The following day she answered a knock on the front door. A woman from the welfare office stood there, folder and pencil in hand. 'Mrs Carmody, we've come to inspect your home.'

'Why?'

But the woman was pushing past her, walking purposefully along the hallway and peering into the rooms. She stopped at the doorway to Nina's room. 'Is this your bedroom?'

Nina crossed her arms across her chest, a defiant gesture. 'Excuse me, but why are you here?'

'We've had a report that a man is living here. He was seen leaving your house yesterday.'

She stared at the woman incredulously. 'There's no man living here! That's a lie!'

The woman pointed to several men's overcoats that covered the bed. 'Then where did they come from?'

'They came from St Vincent de Paul's, months ago. They're all I've got to keep me warm. The children have the few remaining blankets. You can take them if you like and bring me back some decent ones.'

'Now, about this man. You're claiming welfare when you're being supported, and you know that's against the rules. Was it your husband?'

Angry now. 'No, it was *not* my husband, and there's no man living here. I had a visitor, that's all.'

The woman raised her eyebrows. 'A visitor. That's not what we were told.'

Nina ran to the window and threw back the torn curtains. '*Who* told you? Which of my so-called friendly neighbours?'

'I'm afraid I can't answer that. It's confidential.'

'*Confidential*! Any of the prying busybodies in this street can go to your office and spread stories about me, and you believe them?'

'We have to follow up all leads.'

The woman knocked on several neighbouring doors and talked to the occupants before leaving.

The following day a large parcel arrived. It contained, Nina discovered with surprise, four new blankets.

It had been, Frank thought, an unreal kind of day, the kind of day that made you stop and take note, as though through some faint and far-off possibility, it might be your last. An overcast day, spitting rain. The train stop-started at various sidings along the way. Water dripped from the timber slats that lined the sides, creating mucky puddles on the floor. At one stop an owl flew into the freight van, stunned, flopping beside him in the dung.

'Look at that!' Frank cried, touched in some inexplicable way that it should happen to land next to him.

The bird sat there for a while, staring at him with age-old eyes. Tentatively Frank reached out his hand. The bird didn't flinch. He stroked its damp feathers, running the underside of one finger along one wing. The owl shifted, but didn't move away. Gently he picked it up, nestling it on his trousers.

He sat there for a long time, feeling the sway of the van, hearing the clickety-clack of the wheels as they lumbered along the track, and closed his eyes against the grey rushing scenery.

Perhaps he slept. Certainly his mind seemed to be elsewhere, caught in a horribly familiar warp.

The bird is flying against his face, catching him with its wings. They are sharp, the wings, like razors, cutting him with every beat. The bird's beak snaps close to his ear. He pulls back, bringing his hands up to protect himself.

'I'll help you,' says his brother Bill, lurching from the shadows, clutching his mangled face. He brings forward a gun. It is, Frank knows, a Lee Enfield .303. Regulation issue.

Bill points the gun at the bird.

'No!' Frank cries. He hears the sound of his own voice echoing on and on, as though finding its way down a long tunnel. 'If you shoot the bird, then you will kill me, too.'

'Then we will be even.'

Bill cocks the gun and points it at Frank. He can see, back along the barrel, Bill's eye squinting with concentration.

'I didn't mean to kill you.'

'But you did.'

Noise explodes around him. Hands bang at the side of the freight vans. 'Come on, you blokes. Everyone out!'

He is caught, trapped between sleep and wakefulness, mind fuzzy. 'Go on,' says Bill, nudging him away with the gun. 'You've got to get out of here.'

'Where will I go?'

Bill shakes his head. 'You can't escape. Not really. You've been trying to for years.'

He feels an urgent need to flee. Away from the noise. Far away from Bill, who will — he knows from experience — always follow him. Suddenly he is climbing up the wooden side slats. One foot after the other. Pushing his feet into jagged toeholds.

He reaches the top slat and peers over the side. Several policemen run alongside the carriages, carrying guns. Yelling. 'Come on, you bastards! No use hiding. We'll have every one of you.'

He crouches. Poised. Ready.

'Go on!' orders Bill. 'Jump!'

Without warning, the train lurches forward. Frank's hands grab for support. Miss. Fingers scrape against splintery wood. He is sliding through air, clutching ineffectually as he falls.

His body hits the ground with a thud. Air rushes from his lungs. Wheels grind. Metal against metal. Closer. Closer.

'Frank!'

Bob O'Halloran's voice.

Or is it Bill's?

He hunkers down against the ground, rolling himself away from the hated noise. There is something hard against his back and a roaring sound in his ears. A pressure on his legs, followed by an all-encompassing pain. Pain meshes away at the very core of him — rearing up, dark and ugly and full of fear. Men scream, pull at his arms, his chest. Try to drag him from the unspeakable agony.

'Christ! He's under the wheels.'

'Someone get help!'

Frank hears the sound of someone retching, close by.

'His legs are gone. Oh, Lord!'

The sky has turned a shade of khaki and the sun peers through the hazy half-light. Voices, noises fade *into some distant place. Muted. Heard but not registered.*

In the distance he can hear a bird.

'It's an owl!' exclaims Bob.

Nina and the children walk towards him through the haze. Claire holds the bird in her hands. Her palms are cupped, cradling it. But it is dead, feathers dull and lifeless, ruffling in the breeze. 'Look,' she says. 'I brought you a present.'

'Father,' Joe beckons. 'We've come to take you home.'

Home: roaring fires, family, tea and crumpets on cold rainy afternoons. Frank feels their arms around him. He sees their smiles, their bright young faces. Nina's mouth is on his. A warm, warm whisper.

I love you ...

The rent was two months behind, and there was scarcely enough food in the cupboard to last the week. Sometimes, in desperation, Nina simply laid her head on the kitchen table and cried, allowing the hot tears to roll unchecked down her face. At times like these, the children gathered around her, saying nothing. What could be said, anyway, that hadn't already been mentioned before? *Something will come up*, or *at least we've got each other.* Meaningless words and phrases offering little hope. It would take a miracle to restore life to the way it should be, had been.

She was returning from the welfare office with the children when she saw a van parked outside her home. Two men were lugging furniture onto the footpath.

'Mum!' yelled Joe urgently. 'Look what those blokes are up to!'

'Hey! That's my stuff! What do you think you're doing?' she cried, tugging one of the men by the arm.

The man rummaged in his pocket and showed her a piece of signed paper. 'That's the repossession order, luv. You haven't paid rent in God-only-knows-how-long.'

She surveyed her belongings — a miserable lot, really. The children's beds. Mattresses. Kitchen table and four chairs. A little cane chair that belonged to Lydia, bought for her by Frank years ago.

She pointed to the mattresses. 'What'll we sleep on?'

The man shrugged. 'Sorry, luv, but I've a job to do.'

Lydia lunged towards her chair. 'You can't take that! It's mine!' She clung to the cane arm, sobbing.

'What could you possibly want with that?' Nina pleaded.

'Orders are orders. The owner says he'll be around in the morning to change the locks. If I were you, I'd be gone by then.'

They trudged into the house. Nina flicked the switch, but no light came on. There was no gas for the stove or bath heater. Cut off, she thought desperately. What'll we do?

'I'll get some wood, Mum,' said Joe, as though reading her mind. 'We can light a fire and heat some water out the back.'

He took an old baby's pram down to the timber yard and filled it with off-cuts. Nina watched him return. It was early evening, the colour of the sky caught somewhere between black and indigo, the first of the stars flickering against its dark mass. Wordlessly he threw the timber into a pile.

'Oh, Joe,' she whispered, coming up behind him as he finished, laying her hand on his shoulder. 'What will we do?'

'Dunno.'

A figure appeared in the back doorway, holding a candle. It was Claire. 'Mum! There's a policeman at the front door!'

Resignedly she followed her daughter back inside, along the darkened hallway. The man waited on the front verandah and she took the candle from Claire, shooing her back inside.

'Mrs Carmody?'

'Whatever you've come here for, it wasn't my boy,' she said, pushing past the man and walking out onto the step. 'He's been with me all day.'

'Mrs *Frank* Carmody?'

She stopped, turned, aware of a certain urgency to the man's voice.

'Yes.'

'I'm afraid I have some bad news.'

'Is it about my husband?'

'Would you like to go inside? It might be more comfortable in there.'

'I doubt it. But you'd better come in anyway.'

Mechanically she walked back through the front door, her hands clasped tightly around the candle. The flickering light lit the dreary hallway and threadbare carpet, the peeling wallpaper causing

243

small random shadows along the walls. *Don't think*, she commanded herself. *It might be minor*. Then reason intervened. The police wouldn't have sent someone for something trivial.

She beckoned the man into the sitting room, now empty. If he noticed the lack of furniture, he did not say, and Nina was thankful for that. 'Well?'

'I'm sorry. Your husband's dead. There was an accident on a goods train ...'

His explanation rattled past, scarcely heard. She stood still, letting that one word sift through her consciousness. *Dead*. Odd little word. Small. Concise. Not halfway. Dead was *dead*.

What did that mean? she wondered. No more Frank. No father for her children. She tried to think of the pleasurable times, but couldn't remember a single one. There must have been, she thought dully.

'Mrs Carmody?'

Jolting back to the present, she was suddenly aware of the policeman again. He probably wanted to get back to his own family, neat warm house and aroma of supper cooking. 'Yes.'

'Are you all right?'

She nodded. 'I'll be fine.'

'About the body. I take it there's no money for a funeral?'

Are you kidding? I can't afford to feed my kids!

'No. None.'

'Then we'll arrange something.'

Distractedly. 'Fine. Fine.'

'I'll just get along then.'

Wooden words. Disjointed. 'Thank you for letting me know.'

The front door closed behind the policeman and the children gathered around. They were silent, their eyes wide and dark. 'We heard,' said Joe at last. 'What'll we do now?'

Claire's shoulders were shaking. 'Hush,' Nina whispered, holding her close. 'Don't cry. We'll think of something.'

'I'm hungry,' said Lydia.

'But what are we going to do?' Joe's voice was insistent.

'We're leaving,' said Nina resolutely.

Lydia's head shot up. 'When?'

'Tomorrow. As soon as I've made arrangements.'

'Where are we going?' asked Claire in a small voice.

'Home.' Nina's voice was louder now, bolder.

'Home?'

'Home to Tea-tree Passage.'

PART FOUR

Tea-tree Passage

1938

CHAPTER 20

Joe sat in the dinghy, fishing line held loosely in his hand as he glanced upwards. The sky stretched away from him. Was there an end to it? he wondered. There were other stars and planets out there, millions of miles away, or so one of his teachers had once said. Yet he could see nothing but a sea eagle hovering, a dark smudge circling on an unseen current of air, and the brilliant blue beyond that made his eyes ache.

Slowly his gaze lowered and fixed on the low tussocky hummocks of Turtle Island. A flock of gulls hovered above its mass. Past one end of the island, he caught a glimpse of the horizon where a few clouds shredded away, leaving a fractured trail of white. On the other side of the bar the waves were breaking, discharging a surge of foam. Further out, past his line of vision where the water was dark, lay the deep channels where the men took the fishing boats, returning with boxes full of whiting and snapper.

A *plop* broke the silence and a wash of circles radiated from beside the dinghy. Joe stared hard at the water below. Late afternoon sun reflected off the mirrored surface and everything suddenly seemed gold. Water. The dinghy. Even his hand that held the line. What had caused the ripples? he wondered idly. A brightly coloured parrot fish, perhaps?

For three years he had been fishing Tea-tree Passage. He knew every little inlet, every stand of trees along its banks. Knew the deep holes where dugong grazed on the sea grass below, and the way the fish came in with the tide, pulled against their will over the sandbar that divided the rough water from the smooth. He knew the patterns of the moon and the tides, the idiosyncrasies of the weather. Yet every day on the water seemed a fresh experience and there was always something new to discover. Like a few months previously.

He'd known that any day the whales would pass, heading south for the summer. And that morning he'd seen his first of the season, a mother with a calf. During the next few weeks there'd been dozens, seen clearly from the shore as they moved through the passage, rolling and breaching in the water.

Idly he let his thoughts drift back to his arrival in Tea-tree Passage — well, to the events of one particular day leading up to his arrival, actually. And despite the passing years, the details were still vivid in his mind, as clear as though they had occurred the previous day.

* * *

The bailiff arrived, taking most of their remaining furniture. Then a policeman knocked on the front door to tell his mother that Father had been killed. Joe remembered her face, white and set, remembered thinking, 'Why doesn't she cry?'

The next morning Mother took them all and left the house.

'Where are we going?' Lydia asked as they made their way down the footpath.

'Just somewhere.'

'Why?'

'Little girls should be seen and not heard.'

'Are we still going to Tea-tree Passage?'

Mother clamped a hand across Lydia's mouth and peered along the street at the other houses, as though waiting for a telltale swish of curtain. 'Lydia! Please be quiet.'

'Why?'

'I don't want anyone to know.'

In the pawnshop Joe watched, silent, as she handed her wedding and engagement rings to the man behind the counter. The man studied them under a magnifying glass for a very long time. 'I'll give you five pounds,' he offered at last.

Indignantly. 'They're worth more than that.'

The man shrugged. 'Not to me they're not. No-one's got the money for this sort of thing these days. They'll probably sit here for months.'

Mother bit her bottom lip, and her forehead creased into a small frown. She seemed to be weighing up her alternatives.

'Make your mind up. I don't have all day!' the man snapped, pushing the rings towards her.

But she waved them away. 'All right, I'll take the money.'

They continued on to Central Railway Station, where she bought tickets from a man in a glass booth, then treated them to meat pies and a comic each.

'Are we really going to Tea-tree Passage?' Joe asked as the train pulled from the station.

'Yes.'

He remembered the trip, hours and hours of monotonous bush broken by the occasional siding or station. There were towns where dogs ran alongside the carriages and children hung off the level crossing gates, waving at the passengers. He felt important there, high up, seeing the world from that elevated rocking perspective.

After what seemed like a lifetime, but was merely days, the train pulled into a station, and Mother gathered their belongings and ushered them off.

'Is this Tea-tree Passage?'

'No. This is *town*.'

'How far is it to Tea-tree Passage?'

'Not far.'

'How will we get there?'

'We'll have to walk.'

'Walk!'

Carrying their few bags and suitcases, they set off, Lydia complaining, 'Are we nearly there yet?' with what seemed like every step.

'Stop whingeing,' Joe said, feeling sorry for his mother.

'Mum! I wasn't!' Then. 'My shoes are rubbing.'

'Be quiet, the pair of you!'

Joe bit back a retort. The hole in his own sole was huge and he could feel the sharp stones through his sock.

Presently a lorry came along. Stopped. 'Want a lift?' called a voice from the cabin. 'I'm going out to the Passage.'

'Yes, please,' Lydia piped up. 'That's where we're going, too.'

'Hop in, then.'

Joe, Claire and Lydia clambered up into the back, while Mother sat in the cabin with the man. There were old nets lying on the floor of the tray, as well as crab pots, and everything stank of raw fish. Lydia wrinkled her nose as the lorry rocked along the road, seeming to aim for every pothole in the rough surface.

There was no glass in the rear of the cabin and Joe heard the conversation between his mother and the man clearly.

'You from around these parts?'

'A long time ago. And you?'

'Nope. From further around the bay. Just heading out here to fix up someone's boat.'

'Fishing's still good then?'

'It's regular.'

The conversation continued in the same general vein. Joe felt his eyes close, made sleepy by the warm sun that beat down on them and the rhythmic jolting. He tried to imagine the place they were headed to, tried to form a picture of his grandparents, their house. Would his mother be made welcome, he wondered, by these relations he had never met?

At last the truck drew to a halt outside a rambling house. The man helped them down and stacked their bags by the front gate. 'So long, then,' he said, and was off, leaving a cloud of dust in his wake.

Mother stared, past the bags and the front gate, a puzzled expression on her face. The house, on closer inspection, appeared closed up, with the windows boarded over and the gate hanging lopsided on its hinges. Weeds grew over the front gravel path.

'Who owns this house?'

'Your grandparents.'

There. He felt that swift surge of suspense again, a tingle of anticipation. What were they like, these mysterious parents of his father? But from the appearance of the house, it seemed unlikely he was about to meet either of them.

'It doesn't look as though anyone lives here now,' he said carefully, not wanting to upset Mother.

But it was as though she hadn't heard. They trudged up the path, through the long weeds, and she knocked on the door. No reply. Knocked louder.

Joe tugged on her arm. 'I don't think anyone's home, Mum.'

Desperately. 'There has to be.'

'In fact, I think it's been an awfully long time since *anyone's* lived here.'

He watched as his mother glanced wildly around, bringing her hand to her temple as the boarded-up windows and cobwebs registered. The day was ending, long purple shadows straddling the ground. Already the air was becoming chill.

Suddenly a voice came floating towards them from down the road. 'Ahoy there! Looking for someone?'

A large woman waddled towards them, wearing a floral print dress. Joe thought he would always remember that dress, pulled tight over belly and thighs, and it was all he could do to suppress a laugh.

'Maudie?' Mother gasped, flinging herself in the woman's direction. 'Oh, thank God! It's Maudie.'

The woman peered at them, one by one, her face breaking into a smile. 'Well, blow me down, if it isn't young Nina.'

'Not so young anymore,' Mother replied ruefully.

'And these must be your kiddies.'

Mother introduced them and Maudie insisted on bestowing sloppy kisses on every cheek. 'Well, don't you all look a sorry sight,' she said, standing back and giving them the once-over. Then she asked, 'Where's Frank?'

Mother's eyes filled with tears and her face took on that odd lopsided look again, as though it were collapsing under the strain. 'He's dead.'

'Dead? Frank's dead? No!'

'We're desperate, Maudie. We need a roof over our heads.'

Maudie glanced towards the house. 'The old folk,' she said slowly, 'passed away a couple of years ago. John tried to contact you, but we didn't have an address, any idea where you were. The place has been locked up since then. It'll be a right old mess, but you're welcome to it.'

Maudie trudged up to her own place and brought back a key, inserting it into the lock with a scrape of metal. For one impossibly long moment, Joe sensed he was standing on some kind of threshold. Not merely the doorway to his dead grandparents' home, but poised on the next journey of his short life and holding a desperate kind of hope. Sydney, and now Tea-tree Passage. His father's death. In the past few days, so many things had altered, moved on, and nothing would ever be the same again. Please God, he thought, for Mother's sake, let this new life be better than the old.

Then, as quickly as it came, the feeling disappeared and he joined his sisters as they raced through the house, flinging open doors and unboarding windows, letting light flood the shadowy rooms.

The next few weeks had been a blur of work. The house had smelt stale inside, a mixture, he remembered, of death and decay. Dust lay inches thick on the sheets that covered the furniture, and vast shrouds of cobwebs linked every available surface. Mother had poured bucket after bucket of hot water from the copper in the outside laundry, then she'd dusted and cleaned and polished until the place positively gleamed. In the aftermath, he himself had taken the job of clearing the build-up of leaves from the gutters and weeding the gardens, and Claire had begun marking out the beginnings of a vegetable plot in the weed-infested soil behind the house. Now, three years later, he couldn't for the life of him remember what Lydia's contribution had been.

Tea-tree Passage. Until that time, it had only been a name, not real at all. A hushed whispered collection of words, a mysterious place. Foreign. Yet, as Joe reflected now, their arrival had felt like a homecoming of sorts, as though they belonged in that place they had never before seen. Belonged amongst the tea-trees and mangroves, the fishermen's cottages, the sandy track that ran down to the sea wall and the jetties where the boats were tied. He had an impression that they were meant to be there, and that their life until that moment had merely been a series of detours, leading them eventually to this final destination.

It was, he considered sometimes, as though they were somehow intrinsically bound up in the place, from some faraway time, before his own birth. He could sense it and, he supposed, in a way they were. This collection of fishermen's cottages had been part of his own parents' childhoods. Mum and Dad had grown up here, and fallen in love.

During that first year, Joe had been sent away to a boarding school in Brisbane. It had been Maudie's idea and she had provided the money. 'Too many women in this house,' he had overheard her say. 'The boy needs discipline.'

'Joe's a good lad,' his mother had replied defensively.

Maudie had let out a snort. 'Joe's been hanging around with some of the New Guard mob in town.

Do him good to get a decent education and mix with boys his own age.'

Right from the start he'd hated it. All the other chaps had come from well-off families, except for a serious little twerp called Paul, who had scraped in on a scholarship. They had given him a hard time, expected him to keep up with them, and he'd been forced to bludge off them to do so, which he'd hated. Maudie's generosity with school fees hadn't extended to pocket money.

It had started innocuously enough with an invitation. 'Come on out for afternoon tea,' one of the chaps said one Saturday.

'I can't. I don't have any money.'

'Poor Joe's broke.'

'I could lend you some,' offered another.

'No thanks.' How could he ever pay it back?

'We're going to those tearooms in town. Cream cakes.'

It had been weeks since he'd tasted anything but bland school fare.

'I'll shout,' offered another.

In the end he'd gone, thankful to escape the rigid timetables for even a few hours. They'd had milkshakes and lamingtons with cream centres, and tiny little sandwiches that seemed to melt in his mouth.

Later, the boy who'd offered the money had sidled up to him in his room. 'I've figured out how you can repay me,' he'd said with a smirk.

'You told me it was your treat.'

'I changed my mind.'

'I don't have any money.'

'I know that.'

'What do I have to do?'

'I'll let you know.'

Three nights later, after lights out, the boy had let himself into Joe's room. 'I've come to collect,' he'd said, climbing into Joe's bed.

An image had come to him from somewhere in his past and he'd felt a hot shame. Watching his father and Mim through that open bedroom door, his father's bare arse bobbing up and down. Abruptly Joe had backed away, pushing himself across the sheets.

'Get lost!'

'You're scared!'

'Am not!'

'The other blokes said you wouldn't.'

'Then they'd be right.'

The boy had slid from the bed and walked to the doorway. 'I'll get you, you little prick.'

The following afternoon someone had reported a sum of money missing. Joe had known even before they opened his locker that it would be there, the coins nestled in a shirt he'd thrown on the locker floor after cricket.

The headmaster had called him to his office, threatening to tell his mother. That night he'd let himself out the window and made his way to Roma Street Station, smuggling himself on the next train north.

He'd played cat and mouse with the conductor, locking himself in the lavatory for inordinately long periods of time. Back at Tea-tree Passage, he'd hidden in the old boat shed, relying on Claire to bring him supplies.

His escape had lasted exactly four days. The school had contacted his mother who, Claire had informed him, was worried sick. Then Claire relented and told Mother who had marched down to the boatshed and dragged him from his hiding place.

'I don't want to go back! I won't go back!'

'Ungrateful little wretch,' Maudie had grumbled.

'It's what your father would have wanted.' This from Mother.

'My father's dead!'

He'd said the words with such force that he'd seen his mother recoil and move one step back. He'd hated himself for hurting her, but how could he tell her the truth? Better to lie or bluff it out. Concentrate on smaller issues.

'I'm doing the best I can to support you all,' Mother had said in a low voice, her face a mask of defeat. 'Cleaning other peoples' homes. Washing their dirty clothes. Cooking. Ironing. Sometimes we have to do things we don't particularly enjoy, Joe, just to better ourselves.'

He'd known she hated her job in town. At night she arrived home, feet swollen from standing all day, her hands red and raw. 'I can stay here, help you instead,' he'd offered.

'Why don't you want to go back? Tell me, Joe.'

Joe had glared mutinously at his mother. 'I hate it there.'

'Why? It's a good school.'

'Well, you'd hate it, too. The other kids all have money, Mum. They come from rich families. I feel like the poor relation.'

'You can't force him,' Maudie had said abruptly, in a surprising about-turn. 'He'll only take off again.'

In the end, Mother had relented and hadn't made him go back. But, he thought now with a sigh, over two years had passed since then. His sixteenth birthday had come and gone and life had improved somewhat. He had part-time work at the pub, helping the cellarman. Claire was almost eighteen and had a job at Mainwaring's general store. Several nights a week, at Nina's insistence, she was studying typing and shorthand at evening college in town. Lydia was still at school, struggling with Arithmetic and English.

The boat rocked with the tide, lifting on the swell, swinging around until he faced the shore. Absent-mindedly he stared towards the paint-peeling jetties nestled amongst the tea-trees. The *Sea-spray* was there, tied to a pylon. It had probably once been a smart little boat but the years of neglect were showing. One day, when he'd saved enough money to do the necessary repairs, he'd take the boat out again, be a fisherman like his father had once been, and his father before him.

Past the jetties he could see the faded roofs of the shacks, and smoke curling into the sky from the occasional chimney. Maudie's place was the first, closest to the water. It was a bit of a dump now, having gone downhill since Great-Uncle John had kicked the bucket two years ago. Maudie was getting past looking after it now.

The next house along belonged to the Melvilles. It had been empty since the old lady had passed away the previous winter, but her son, Hal, had moved in a few months back. Hal was the eldest of three Melville boys. One had been killed in the war and another, Jimmy, had lost the use of his legs. Occasionally Jimmy came back to the Passage and Joe had seen him down at the jetties, pushing himself along the path in his wheelchair.

Hal was a doctor and had recently replaced the old medico in town who had retired. A widower, he had two sons. David was twenty, three years older than Joe, and was a fisherman like most of the blokes around. His older brother, Alex, whom Joe was yet to meet, was in the city studying to be a doctor. Since the younger Melvilles had moved in, there had been a constant parade of workmen's trucks to the cottage, accompanied by a commotion of hammers and saws. Now, the work completed and the house boasting several new rooms and a fresh coat of paint, the Melville place made all the other cottages look shabby by comparison.

Claire and David Melville had been keeping company for a while. David was a good sort of a bloke, the type he wouldn't mind having for a brother-in-law one day, if they ever decided to get married. His mother, he knew, approved of David, too.

The line in his hand was still slack. No fish today, he thought with a sigh. The tides weren't right, or the wind, perhaps. Even the bait. He wound in the line and picked up the oars. They dipped almost silently into the water, spraying fine droplets as he brought them around in a rhythmic cycle. Dip. Pull. Dip. Pull.

As he came closer to the shore, he could see a girl in a red dress sitting under the nearest clump of tea-trees. It would be Claire, he knew, pencil in hand. She was always sketching these days, every spare minute. They were landscapes mainly, where water merged with sky and trees were a muted green. Mother thought they were wonderful and pinned them up on the kitchen walls, proudly showing them off to any visitor who happened to call in. And the sketches weren't bad either, he had to admit.

As he watched, a figure, tall and lanky, squatted down beside his sister. A stranger: Joe had never seen the man around these parts before. They were talking. A murmur of voices floated across the water, although Joe was too distant to make out the thread of the conversation. Just some passer-by, he thought, lost and wanting to find his way back to town.

CHAPTER 21

Claire sat near the water's edge under the sparse shade of a clump of trees, watching Joe as he manouevred the dinghy around the headland with a deft swing of the oars. His brown arms brought the paddles forward, pulling with steady strokes. His dark head was bent against the wind.

Idly she picked up the pencil again, letting it hover over the thick paper. She was trying to capture the essence of the scene — boats tied at the jetties amongst the tea-trees, the headland and the pandanus palms that grew there, and the tide washing in below. She had roughed most of it in — hulls sleek with age and the coils of rope that lay abandoned on the decks — but something wasn't right. The light, perhaps? She hadn't quite managed to depict the brilliance that came with summers at Tea-tree Passage, that white eye-squinting sunlight.

A shadow fell across the page and she stared upwards into a pair of blue eyes. 'That's a very passable sketch,' said a mouth located somewhere below the eyes.

Embarrassed, she pulled the paper towards her, as though shielding it from his gaze. 'It's average.'

'I happen to think it's very good.'

'The colour's not right.'

'Why do you do that?'

Puzzled. 'Do what?'

'Demean yourself.'

'I don't do that!' she replied hotly, wishing he'd either sit down or go away. Her neck was starting to ache from looking up at him.

He laughed, revealing a set of white teeth. 'I give up,' he replied, raising his hands, palms out, towards her. 'Anyway, I suppose you must be one of the Carmody girls. Let me guess.'

He made a pretense of it, tilting his head and studying her, a thoughtful expression on his face. 'Claire,' he said eventually. 'You must be Claire.'

'How did you know?'

'Those dark mysterious eyes.'

Exasperated. 'Don't tease.'

'It was David, if you must know.'

'David?' She stared at him, confused. 'David Melville?'

'I'm his brother,' he offered by way of an explanation. 'Alex.'

Realisation dawned. So this was David's brother — though two men couldn't look less alike, she thought with surprise. David was dark-haired, with skin tanned to a deep brown from the hours spent out on his fishing trawler. Alex, in comparison, was fair.

'The doctor,' said Claire, affording him a grin.

'Ah, I see my name and reputation precede me. Well, I'm still doing my internship. Another few months and I'll be able to go out by myself, if I choose.'

'I'm impressed, *Doctor* Melville.'

'David tells me you two are an item.'

'We're friends,' she said carefully.

'He also tells me it's your birthday next week.'

'I'll be eighteen.'

'Ah,' he replied with a grin. 'An old maid already.'

David Melville had been calling at the house for several months now, occasionally taking her to the picture theatre in town. He was a pleasant man, good company. And although Claire thought of him more as a mate than an admirer, they enjoyed an easygoing friendship, born of common interests. She said as much.

'That's not what I heard.'

'Then you heard wrong. Anyway, if you're going to stay here talking, you might as well sit down. It's making my neck ache, looking up at you.'

He flopped down beside her, arranging his leggy frame against the sand, took a twig and traced the ridges and small hollows, the tiny crab holes. He was wearing a shirt with the sleeves rolled up, and a pair of baggy shorts. Sandy hair fell in an untidy shock across his forehead, and she fought back a sudden and unexpected impulse to brush it away.

She shook her head, dispelling the thought. 'Funny, you don't look like a doctor,' she said instead, diverting her attention to a more general subject.

'And what are doctors supposed to look like?'

She shrugged, not knowing. 'You and David don't even look like brothers.'

The pale skin on his forearm was already turning pink and he rubbed at it, absent-mindedly. 'No. I take after my mother, or so everyone says. And all my work's indoors, so I don't get much of a chance to get out in the sun.' He shielded his eyes with one hand and stared out over the water. 'God, I love it here. So peaceful.'

'It is, isn't it? You know, the first day I ever set foot in this place, it was like coming home.'

'We used to come here as kids, David and I, stay with our grandmother. We always thought of this as our summer home. Dad bought us a little dinghy and David was always out in it, mucking about. He always said he'd come back and live here one day, be a fisherman. But I suppose he's told you that already.'

Claire nodded and moved to pack her artwork away. Alex put a hand on her arm, stilling her. 'Please don't stop. Let me watch.'

Her attention travelled from his hand, along his length of arm, to his face, somehow drawn to his eyes. They were crinkly at the corners, as though containing a smile, some joke of their own. He caught her gaze, her eyes unable to break from his scrutiny for what seemed an inordinately long time, until she blinked and turned her head back to her task. She felt winded and out of breath, as though she had been running for miles. Confused, she picked up a pencil, the lead a grey-green in colour.

She had been sketching the tea-trees, masses of leaves against the papery trunks. Somehow she thought she had managed to capture the essence of the bark, those layers of paper-thin wood peeling from the trunk in chunks, sepia shadows falling beneath their mass. Tentatively she moved the pencil across the paper. It felt odd to have someone watching her as she drew; it made her feel like a child again, trying to colour in while staying inside the lines.

Steadfastly she refused to think about him, and the pencil flew over the paper. A stroke here, a line there. Slowly the sketch began to form definition.

'Have you ever had lessons?'

'No. I'm self-taught.'

'You could be a professional artist.'

She glanced up, eyes narrowed against the glare. 'Who'd pay good money for something like this?'

'There you go again.'

'What?'

'Demeaning yourself.'

'It's the truth.'

'I'd buy it.'

'You would?' Then. 'You're just saying that.'

'How much would you charge?'

'Don't be silly.'

'Fancy a swim?' he asked, standing and stretching his arms as he changed the subject. 'It's warm enough.'

Claire tucked her pencils and sketchbook under a rock, where the pages wouldn't be scattered by the wind. Together they walked down to the water's edge, across the wet corrugated sand. Alex pulled his shirt over his head, revealing a sprinkling of hairs on his chest and smooth pale skin.

For the first time ever, she felt self-conscious removing her dress. She imagined him watching her, felt almost naked under his gaze. Why, Claire didn't know. He was David's brother, after all, and she'd never felt embarrassed stripping off to her bathers before. But when she turned, he was facing away, as though affording her a measure of privacy. Relieved, she threw her dress on the sand and ran down to the water, wading out recklessly, calling to him as she went.

Later, picking up her drawing gear from under the rock, Claire handed him the sketch. 'Here. It's yours.'

He stood looking at the piece of paper for a moment, then thanked her and walked away. She stood, watching as he went along the sandy track towards the houses. And after he had gone, when nothing remained but the breeze sighing through the she-oaks and the tide still creeping relentlessly up the sand, she wondered if she had, in fact, dreamt it all.

Nina, walking along the sea wall, saw them in the water. She shielded her eyes with her hand, watching as Claire swam with strong practised strokes out to the buoy that marked the channel. Dark hair streamed behind her as she moved, like ribbons of seaweed. Yards from shore, she clung to the float and tossed her head, shaking the strands of hair from her face. Even from that distance, Nina could hear her call, 'Beat you.'

A man surfaced beside her and they clung to the buoy, mere inches apart, laughing. Nina wondered fleetingly who he was, then remembered. It must be the older Melville lad, David's brother. Maudie had said he was home for the summer holidays.

She turned and stared along the length of the Passage, watching as Joe brought in the dinghy. He looks like Frank, she thought, not for the first time. That same long-legged gangliness, large hands and feet. That same sense of purpose.

Of all her children, it was Joe who concerned her at the moment. He was growing up in a rambling old house full of women, his mind fixed firmly on the *Sea-spray* rotting down at the wharf. He was saving hard, she knew, planning to restore the old tub, though God only knew why.

Nina had tried to focus his energies in other directions. Thanks to Maudie's generosity, she had gotten him as far as a boarding school in Brisbane, but he had run away, and she had been reluctant to send him back.

'I'll take off again,' he'd argued, 'and next time I won't come home.'

'I only want what's best for you,' she'd remonstrated.

'This is the best place for me. Tea-tree Passage.'

That had been two years ago.

Momentarily she closed her eyes against the glare, and against the possibility that Joe was travelling down the same path as Frank. She wanted more for him than the life of a fisherman. Perhaps she had been wrong to bring the children back to this place that held so many terrible memories. But, she assured herself, she had had no choice.

For a long time after Frank's death, she had experienced pangs of inexplicable and unexpected grief. They always came quietly and insidiously, thrusting themselves on her when she least expected it. A song, the smell of roses, the tilt of Joe's head — all serving to remind her of what she'd had, and lost.

There were times when a guilt rose up inside her like bile, and she wondered if she could have done more for Frank. If they'd spoken more, communicated. If she'd been more loving, more understanding, if she'd closed her eyes to things she hadn't wanted to see. If he hadn't met Mim. If, if, if . . .

Occasionally she wondered about the other woman. Had Mim, travelling to faraway countries, ever found the happiness she had sought? Nina doubted it. And now, years later, she knew she held no grudge against her. Mim had been a catalyst for the events that had unfolded, not the deep-seated cause. Everything that had happened between her and Frank, all the wrongs and injustices and abuse, had somehow begun much earlier, on that day of Frank's return after the war.

In her mind's eye she could still hear the screen door wheezing open, could still see him standing in that kitchen, lost for words, almost a stranger. And that was how they'd spent their lives, she thought now: as strangers. Two people coming together at odd moments, over the children mostly.

Though she wanted more for her family, for herself she had no ambition. She was content to be there in that quiet unhurried place. Life at Tea-tree Passage had a steady rhythm, no days outstanding from the others. It was an existence of habits, of predictability, and any small diversions in routine were treated as exciting events. At least they were all fed and clothed, had a roof over their heads. The worst years were behind them now, their Sydney life merely a memory.

It had been a hard slog, getting the family back on its feet again but, somehow, she'd managed it. Taking in sewing. Cleaning houses in town. Scrimping and making do. The Returned Soldiers' League had been a wonderful help, too. Under Joe's supervision, the garden yielded up an endless supply of vegetables, and there was always a fish to be caught in the waters of the Passage. Life, by comparison, was generous, and she was happy to share her good fortune.

Even the passing swaggies testified to Nina's kindness and, over the past three years, she had seen hundreds of them. They were hungry men, with mournful eyes and shamed faces at the circumstances that had led them to these country roads. Many had been well-to-do businessmen before the nightmare they called the Great Depression had begun. Upholsterers. Carpenters. One had even been a high court judge before he had fallen on hard times and the booze.

At first the children had been wary of these men. 'Don't be afraid,' she had told them, gathering them around her. 'They're mostly family men who've left their kinfolk in the city to find work on the land.'

'Like Father?' asked Joe.

'Bloody hawkers!' said Maudie.

'Hawkers, swagmen — call them what you will. They'll not harm the children. Most likely they've little ones of their own. Perhaps it's like a little piece of home, having a child to talk to. Let them have their small pleasures. They get little else.'

No-one was turned away from Nina's door. Often they stayed for a day or two, receiving food and a bed with clean sheets on the verandah, in exchange for odd jobs such as chopping wood or weeding the vegetable garden, gladly accepting a spare loaf of bread to take on the road with them when they moved on.

'Why do you do that,' asked Maudie, 'when you've scant enough for yourself?'

'I don't know. Feel sorry for them, I suppose.'

'So, give them food and send them packing.'

She'd glared at Maudie, long and hard. 'These men crave to be needed,' she said firmly. 'They don't want handouts and they hate the idea of charity. They want to feel like they've earned whatever I give them.'

'Well, you can't feed the whole blessed countryside.'

'It's little enough help.'

But it wasn't the whole truth. How could she tell the older woman that she saw Frank in every one of their lean faces? And she knew that, like Frank, somewhere along the way they'd lost their ability to settle, these men, probably tugged onwards by the memories of a woman, or a child.

'Kindness breeds kindness,' she had said to Maudie later. 'And there have been times when people have been so very kind to me.'

She liked to think that somewhere, before his death, some woman had offered Frank the makings of a meal, provided a shed to sleep in, kept him from the rain. Liked to believe that someone had given him a load of wood to chop in repayment, making him feel like a whole man again. And if so, she was only repaying that same kindness in a small way.

But there were fewer swaggies on the roads these days. The economy was improving, or so the newspapers said, and her worries had shifted from the logistics of feeding her children to worrying about their futures.

Lydia was the only one left at school. Nina despaired over her sometimes. She was reckless and impulsive and inclined to be, what Maudie called, flighty. 'Flirting with the men down by the jetties,' she'd told Nina the previous week. 'You'll have to keep an eye on that one.'

Defensively. 'How would you know?'

'She reminds me of myself at the same age,' answered Maudie forthrightly. 'Looking back, I suppose I was a right little tart.'

'My daughter's not like that.'

'Lydia's too mature for her own years.'

Although she admitted it only to herself, Nina knew Maudie spoke the truth. Only yesterday Nina had found her younger daughter in front of the bathroom mirror, painting her lips a bright red.

'Where did you get the lipstick?'

'I bought it. Sixpence at the chemist shop in town.'

'You're only fifteen. Far too young!'

'Don't be an old stick-in-the-mud. All the girls at school are wearing it.' She'd pursed her lips and smiled, turning from her reflection towards her mother. 'Fiery Glow, it's called. I think it looks sexy.'

'*Lydia!*'

She'd laughed then, defiantly. 'You can't make me take it off,' she had said in a low voice, challenging her mother. Then she'd flounced out the door without a backwards glance.

'Have you seen Lydia?' Joe had asked, coming in a few minutes later. 'She looks like a painted doll. Tell her to take that muck off her face.'

Joe — the only male in a houseful of women — seemed unsettled. All in all, he was a good lad. He had a part-time job at the pub in town and gave her most of what he earned each week. But Nina wasn't happy to have him mixing with the crowd that congregated there. They were much older and he was at an impressionable age and, she suspected, easily led. He scarcely talked about his father, the way he had deserted them but, Nina knew, it had had an effect on him. At times he seemed withdrawn, closed into his own small shell, and she worried constantly about him and those invisible unmentioned scars.

Then there was Claire. She was a delight, really, and Nina always thought of her as the responsible one of the family. She was working at the store in town, doing secretarial studies at night. With a bit of luck, old Parsons the solicitor might put her on when she finished. And she'd been keeping company with David Melville, a good sensible lad, from all accounts. Perhaps he'd ask her to marry him, in a year or two, when she was older. They'd settle down in the Passage, have babies, grandchildren that Nina could spoil.

'Hey, Mum!'

Joe's voice broke her reverie. He had tied the boat to the jetty and was clambering up the wooden ladder. She walked down the last of the path towards him. He turned to her, a smile slapped across his face. 'Nothing today, Mum. What say we go into town for supper, instead? Fish and chips. My shout.'

Claire stood naked in front of the bathroom mirror, frowning at the reflection of herself in the light from the single globe above the handbasin. Too thin, she thought with annoyance, and her mouth looked odd against the rest of her face. Too wide, perhaps, too upturned in the corners, as though she wore a perpetual smile.

Why couldn't she look like Lydia? Already at fifteen, her younger sister had the sort of curvaceous figure Claire would die for, with a pale milky skin that made her own seem dark by comparison, and a bosom that strained at the buttons on her school uniform. And Lydia could talk easily to anyone, from the old fishermen who gathered down at the wharves to the children who arrived from town on the weekends to have a picnic lunch and play ball games on the sand until, fractious with fatigue and sunburn, they left for home.

Claire frowned again and bit her lip. No use wishing for what could never be, commonsense told her. Think of the positives: that was what her mother would say, always trying to look for some good in everything. Her hair, she supposed, was thick and shining. Her teeth were white and straight. There was not an ounce of fat on her frame — unlike Lydia who was inclined to plumpness.

She gave an involuntary sigh. Good sensible Claire. Almost running the general store, although she had only been there a year, and scoring top marks in her secretarial course at night school. A job at Parsons' solicitors was almost guaranteed when she finished. David — wonderful, predictable David — was waiting in the wings. One day, a few years from now, he'd ask her to marry him. Would she say yes because there'd be nothing else? No alternatives. No other options. Already she sensed the inevitability of her life.

At random moments she thought about the house they would live in, probably a few doors up from her present home. She thought about the babies they'd have, snug wriggling bundles. Imagined a life of fishing and being subservient to the weather and tides and the leaky hull of an old boat. Washing and ironing. Cooking robust meals for her growing brood. David making demands on her spare time. No opportunity for her drawing.

You could be a professional artist.

Alex's words jolted her and immediately she dismissed them. How would her mother react, or Maudie, if she repeated them?

'Stuff and nonsense!' she could almost hear Maudie say. 'That's no way to make a quid! Better off marrying a rich man.'

And her mother: 'No use filling your head with wild dreams.'

Her mother's desires, Claire knew, had died long ago.

Slowly she brought her hands up, running fingers lightly across her belly. How would it feel, she wondered, to have a child? She tried, but failed, to imagine her skin hard and taut with it, like the women who came lumbering into the store to be served, their carefully clad bodies evidence of their productivity. She cupped her breasts, pushing them up until they formed firm mounds. Like Lydia's, she thought grudgingly.

Why did she keep comparing herself to her sister?

She closed her eyes, aware only of her own hands against skin, that soft touch. Involuntarily she let her thoughts drift, imagining what it would be like to have a man hold her in the same way. Not the furtive grappling in the picture theatre with David, darkness hiding her burning face as she brushed his hand away with a hushed, 'Don't!' There had to be more to life than that. But hands that caressed and promised sensuality, fingers that would rouse in her those desires that had, until now, lain dormant.

Who would he be? David? Someone she had yet to meet? However, she thought with surprise, it was not David's face that flitted through her subconscious, or some stranger's, but Alex's.

CHAPTER 22

Town was a twenty minute walk, or five minutes if you had the good fortune to own a car. Maudie usually hitched a ride with the lorry that carted the fish.

'Can't complain about the stink,' she confided breathlessly to Claire, 'when it saves me legs.'

Nina preferred to walk, saying she liked the scenery and the chance to be by herself.

'Bloody independent, that's what you are,' declared Maudie with a reproachful sniff. 'Don't know why you bother. You're just wearing yourself out. Always someone willing to give you a lift, if you ask.'

Claire found a rusted bicycle under Maudie's house. Joe straightened the wheel spokes, painted it bright red and put on two new tyres. Every weekday morning she could be found wobbling her way to work. Down the dusty main street in town she went, past the School of the Arts hall which incorporated a library and a room for band practice, past the picture theatre, newsagent, butcher and hotel.

Town was an orderly place, with streets all running at right angles to each other and houses that didn't look slapped together, like most of those at Tea-tree Passage. The train passed through twice a day, a dirty locomotive pulling decrepit carriages, leaving a plume of steam in its wake. Often Claire stood at the railway crossing as it passed, leaning against her bike. Children waved from the windows, noses pressed flat against the glass. Adults glanced up from behind newspapers, affording the town scant attention. Then, as suddenly as it came, the train would be gone, rattling away down the track, lurching from side to side. She'd stare after it until it rounded the bend and disappeared, only the clackety-clack sound and the memory of a child's face lingering in her mind.

People passing through her life. There one moment, gone the next. Like her father, she considered. Homeless. Going from place to place. Not feeling he belonged anywhere, especially at home with his family.

Why was that? Hadn't he loved them enough to stay? Had they disappointed him in some way? She didn't know. She was aware only of a sadness washing over her like a tide when she thought of him. He'd been a strong man, and weak: a mixture of good and bad, right and wrong. She was not blind to his faults.

'He was still my father,' she whispered fiercely to herself. 'No matter what, I loved him.'

The general store where Claire worked stood at the far end of town. It was a grey lopsided building, the original having been added onto numerous times. Charlie Mainwaring was the present owner, a cantankerous old fellow whose dark moods, Claire thought, matched the gloomy interior and heavy cedar shopfittings.

The store carried all manner of items, from groceries to hardware, to haberdashery and confectionery. Stock feed was housed in a little side shed, presided over by Paddy, an equally dour chap who sewed the sacks of wheat with a large curved needle held in knobbly fingers. He was fond of singing, Paddy was, his mouth working around a roughly rolled cigarette held between tobacco-stained teeth. To Claire's dismay, his repertoire consisted of three songs, of which he knew few words.

Claire stood at the scales, weighing and packing biscuits from the bin under the counter. Already she'd finished a dozen packets, more than enough for the next few days, but her attention wasn't on her task. It was her birthday and David was collecting her later, after he sorted the fish. He'd promised to take her to the pictures and, although it wasn't likely, it would be nice to get home early for a change so she could indulge in a bath first.

'Hello, again.'

Surprised, her head shot up, just in time to see Alex Melville take a Scotch Finger biscuit from the pile in front of her. 'Mmmm, nice,' he said, biting into it.

Claire stifled a laugh and glanced towards the back of the shop. 'Don't let old Charlie catch you eating the profits or I'll lose my job.'

'If he catches you calling him *old Charlie*, you'll lose it anyway.'

'I'd find another one.'

Alex wiped the crumbs from his fingers. 'Ah! Such confidence can only come with youth.'

Challenging. 'I'm not a child.'

A thought slid into her consciousness: who was she trying to convince, herself or him?

'Of course not. You're a beautiful and desirable woman.'

The words shocked her into momentary panic. What to say? How to react? Her thoughts were in disarray. Her tongue seemed glued to the roof of her mouth. Was he laughing at her naivety, making fun of her? Not knowing, she bent over her task again, furiously ladling biscuits into a bag. Hiding her confusion. Hoping her employer couldn't hear the conversation. 'You say the silliest things.'

'Anyway,' he said, changing the subject, 'where would Charlie Mainwaring find someone as efficient to replace you?'

She brought her head up, facing him, ready to challenge his statement. He really was testing her, seeing how far he could push her! But a smile lingered at the corners of his mouth. Maddening. Infuriating. 'Where, indeed?' she replied.

Charlie came ambling from the back of the shop, carrying several tins. He stared at Alex with suspicious eyes. 'You gonna work today, Claire, or just stand around chatting? These sardines gotta go with that new order.'

She took the tins and turned back to Alex, her

manner suddenly brisk. 'Is there anything I can help you with?'

'I've a list, although I've probably left heaps off. If you don't mind, I'll just look around while I'm here.'

Alex walked around the shelves, picking up packets of tea and sugar, iced vo-vo biscuits, tins of camp pie and salmon. He seemed to be marking time, Claire thought, spinning out the selection of goods.

'Suppose that'll be Doc Melville's son,' said Charlie, watching Alex's progress along the shelves. 'Got a girlfriend, has he?'

Had he? Claire didn't know. 'I wouldn't have a clue. Why don't you ask him?'

Charlie mumbled a half-heard reply, something about the youth of today and insolence. Alex brought his purchases back to the counter and Charlie tallied up the cost in a small notebook, using the pencil he kept behind his ear. 'That'll be six shillings and fourpence.'

Alex handed Claire the money, winking at her. She stifled a laugh and went to the cash register. The coins felt warm in her hand and, for some inexplicable reason, her face burned.

Alex turned to go but, at the last minute, swung back. 'I almost forgot. I need a bag of chook feed.'

Charlie glanced across at Claire. 'Paddy's finished up for the day. You'd better go out back,' he said.

It was warm in the feed shed and the smell of pellets and hay hung heavy in the air. Dust motes hovered, caught in a stray sunbeam that bounced off the rough wall. A few stray chooks scratched and pecked at a stream of spilt wheat on floorboards worn smooth by the heavy sacks dragged daily across their surface.

'Shoo,' said Claire, sending the hens scattering with a thrust of her hands.

A striped marmalade cat came running from behind a drum of molasses. Tiger, the hay shed cat, was kept at the store to catch mice. She bred with wild abandon every spring, and now her latest batch of half-grown kittens followed her.

Alex scooped one up, holding it at eye level. It was pale grey in colour, with darker stripes along its back. 'I should take you home,' he said. 'There's a plague of mice in our garage.'

'That'd be one less Charlie would have to find a home for. He's been wondering how he'll get rid of them.'

Claire went to pull a sack of feed from the corner but Alex put out a hand to stop her. 'Don't. It's too heavy. I'll get it. Here. Take the kitten.'

As he handed her the cat, their hands brushed and they both came upright at the same time, facing each other. 'Oh,' she said, trying to sidestep him.

'Claire.'

He was blocking her path. The light made his skin seem golden, matching his hair which still fell in that maddening shock across his forehead, giving him a little-boy look. He looked serious for once, no smile playing across his mouth.

'You look so pretty in this light,' he said, brushing a stray wisp of hair from her face. 'Pretty little Claire.'

His mouth was mere inches from hers. She saw his lips working at the words and felt a sudden rush of heat to her face. Embarrassed, she dipped her head. 'Oh, nonsense,' she said, trying to step around him, her voice unnaturally cross as she tried to hide her confusion.

The kitten dug its claws into her shoulder, trying to lever itself to freedom. 'Ouch!' she winced, lifting the animal away. 'Rotten little thing.'

Alex took a step back, apologising. 'I'm sorry, Claire, I didn't mean —'

'Think nothing of it,' she snapped. 'Now, can we get this bag of chook feed out?'

He loaded the bag into the car, then took the kitten from her. 'Sure it's all right if I take him?'

'He's a *her*, and no, Charlie'll be glad to be rid of it.'

'What time do you finish work?'

'Six o'clock. Half an hour.'

'Good. I'll wait around, give you a lift home.'

She remembered her bicycle, propped against the shed, and the half-hour walk she'd have to get to work the next morning. Then she thought about the evening ahead and the promise of a long hot bath first.

'Thanks. That'd be lovely.'

Back in the shop she hurried through the last of the orders for the day, which Charlie would deliver on his way home. That done, she untied her apron and ran a comb through her hair at the mirror at the back of the shop. For some inexplicable reason, her heart was racing.

She glanced up to see Charlie staring at her. 'You making yourself pretty for him?'

'Don't be ridiculous!'

'What's David going to say?'

'He's David's brother, for goodness sake.' She was fighting to keep her voice level. Why was Charlie making her feel so damned guilty? It wasn't as though anything was about to happen. 'He's only giving me a lift home. I don't know why you're making such a big deal about this!'

'I only asked a simple question,' Charlie shrugged. 'You're the one getting all churned up.'

Hands shaking, she collected her bag and walked to the shop door. Alex was sitting in the car, staring pensively down the stretch of roadway, absent-mindedly stroking the kitten which was clinging to his shoulder.

'Hey!' She slid in beside him, taking the cat. 'Have you thought of a name?'

Alex started the car and eased it from the curb. The kitten miaowed with fright, clinging to Claire's dress. 'I thought you might like to choose.'

She thought for a moment, stroking the animal's soft fur. 'She's a pretty grey colour. What about Smoky?'

'Smoky it is,' he replied with a grin.

The car bowled along, easily covering the distance between town and Tea-tree Passage. Dusk was approaching and lights were coming on in houses. Dark shapes moved behind curtains. Claire nursed the tiny mewling bundle on her lap until it curled into a tight ball and went to sleep.

They chatted about general topics: the weather; Claire's job; how Alex would finish his internship in a few months. The kitten stirred and stretched, slept again. After what seemed like mere moments, Alex pulled the car to a halt at the front of Claire's house.

He made no effort to get out, open the door for her, so she sat, wondering what to do. When she glanced across at him, she saw he was smiling.

'Happy birthday.'

'How did you know it was today?'

'David told me.' He tilted his head to one side, watching her, and the kitten gave a small miaow. 'I bought you a present.'

'You didn't have to do that.'

'I wanted to.'

'You hardly know me.'

'You know, Claire, there are some people you know all your life,' he said, looking serious, 'yet you feel as though you don't really know them at all. Then sometimes there are others whom you have barely met, yet you feel comfortable with them. Do you know what I mean?'

She nodded.

'And I feel very comfortable with you.'

He leant over into the back seat and brought forward a small wrapped present. Handed it to her.

'What is it?'

'Go on,' he prompted, his eyes twinkling. 'Open it and see.'

She peeled back the wrapping. It was a box of watercolour paints, dozens of small tubes of varying colours.

'Oh!' She gave a cry of surprise and sat looking at the gift. Words failed her and she felt ridiculously like crying.

'I hope you like it?'

'It's — it's wonderful. Thank you.'

The words sounded so inadequate, not really conveying her gratitude at all. She'd been looking at the box of paints for ages in the newsagent's window but the price had been hopelessly beyond her budget.

'Well,' he went on, 'pencils are fine for amateurs, but if you want a decent amount of colour, you'll need these.'

'I *am* an amateur.'

'There you go again —'

'I know, I know,' she laughed, raising her hands in defeat.

'You're a damn fine artist, Claire. One day maybe you'll realise that.'

'Oh, my!' said her mother when Claire showed her Alex's gift. 'That must have cost a pretty penny.'

'One pound five shillings and sixpence,' replied Claire. 'I saw them in the newsagent's window.'

Nina regarded her quizzically. 'Why is he buying you presents? You hardly know him.'

Later Lydia took the tiny tubes from the box and arranged them on the dining table, graduating the colours. Black to brown, orange then red, through to purple, blues, then yellow-green. 'It looks like a rainbow,' she said.

'I can't wait to paint with them.'

'Why did Alex buy you these?'

'It's my birthday.'

'No. I mean *why*. It's not like you're friends or anything.'

'Why would you say that?'

'You only met him a couple of days ago.'

'Lydia, some people you know all your life but you feel you don't really know them at all. Yet others, whom you have barely met, you feel comfortable with. Do you know what I mean?'

'No.' She was silent for a moment, then: 'Do you like Alex?'

'He's very nice.'

'Nice enough to marry?'

'Lydia!' She felt herself blushing.

'Just testing.'

David walked into Alex's room after he came home from the pictures with Claire. Alex was lying on the bed, reading, although his attention wasn't really on the book he held in his hand. The image of Claire's face kept blotting out the words, that look of surprised delight as she opened the present he'd given her earlier. Then he'd thought of the two of them, Claire and his brother, alone in the darkened theatre — was David holding her hand, kissing her? — and felt a surge of irritation.

'Alex?'

He snapped the pages of the book shut, tried to keep his voice even. 'Good movie?'

'Passable.' David paused for a moment, as though selecting words and, when he spoke, his voice was monotone, lacking warmth. 'Claire told me you bought her a birthday present.'

'That's right. A set of paints.'

'Why?'

'I thought that was obvious. Because it's her birthday.'

'You scarcely know her.'

'True, but I happen to think she's a talented artist.'

'*Artist*! Where's the sense in that? Art doesn't help to pay the bills.'

'Some people make a good living from it.'

'And some make a living through hard work.'

'I happen to think her talent needs encouragement. Do you have a problem with that?'

'So you're being *Mr Benevolent*.'

There was an inflection to the words that troubled Alex, made him wary. His brother was building up to something. 'Don't play word games, David. If something's the matter, then come straight out and say it.'

'Claire doesn't want your presents.'

'Did she say that?'

'No! I'm saying it for her.'

'Isn't that a bit presumptuous?'

'I'm a bloody fisherman, not a fancy doctor, and maybe I'm not as good with words as you, so I'll keep it simple. Back off! Claire's mine!'

David's eyes were dark with anger, and Alex was sure he'd never seen him so furious. 'A woman isn't a possession,' he replied in what he hoped was a reasonable tone. 'Doesn't Claire have a say in all this?'

'Of course she does. She's young, that's all, and she doesn't need you filling her head with fancy ideas. In a few weeks you'll be gone, back to the city. So don't mess with our lives meanwhile.'

'And after I'm gone?'

'We've something going, Claire and I, and I don't want you jeopardising that.'

'Just exactly what have you got going?'

'I plan to marry her.'

'Does Claire know?'

'I haven't asked her yet, if that's what you mean.'

Alex shrugged. 'Fine. Have it your own way. But you're barking up the wrong tree, brother dear. As far as Claire's concerned, she doesn't even know I exist.'

CHAPTER 23

To Claire, the summer of '38 was hot and indolent, and emotions were brittle and flyaway as autumn leaves. Sensibility was at odds with shiftlessness. She felt restless, out of kilter. An unfulfilled energy propelled her through each day, her thoughts constantly shifting and realigning themselves.

Even the weather was fretful. Storm clouds gathered on the horizon each afternoon and, as night fell, lightning flickered away in the east. Dry thunder filled the heavy air, yet there was not a drop of rain. The grass at the front of their house was bleached colourless and the tea-trees stood still under a listless sun. Even the fish had disappeared.

The fraying time. That was what Maudie called it.

It was an apt name, Claire thought. She felt ragged at the edges, worn out. No longer was she whole. There seemed to be two parts to her, neither meeting. The various layers of herself were peeling away, leaving a soft core. Exposed. Defenceless.

During the lull between customers in Mainwaring's store, as she ladled flour or sugar into bags, she let her mind drift. Perhaps she was like the buoy in the middle of the channel. For one extraordinarily real moment, she felt the water lapping at her as she was dragged along by the currents and tides, felt the seaweed and tiny fish brushing past her skin.

'Hey, Claire! That last order packed yet?'

Charlie Mainwaring — breaking her thoughts into fragments where they lay shattered on the worn linoleum that covered the counter.

Christmas had come and gone with a rush of heat and good humour. It was tradition for the residents of Tea-tree Passage to spend the day together, and that year the venue had been Maudie's house. Besides Nina's own brood, Hal Melville had been there with his two sons, plus the O'Reillys and Sharps from further up the road.

Maudie's home was testimony to the deprivations of the Depression. Sugarbags — boiled in the copper with sunlight soap and a handful of washing soda until they turned a pretty shade of cream — had made an array of frilled curtains and matching cushion covers. Every surface of the furniture was covered in an assortment of gaudy dust-covered keepsakes, mementos of Maudie's younger life. Rubbish, most of it. Fit for the bin, as Nina often said, itching to get her duster and mop.

The one thing Claire loved about Maudie's house, though, was the fantastic collection of marine bric-a-brac. There were abalone shells, tritons and spindles, cowries and murex. Conchs of all shapes and colours, and smooth coiled nautilus. The dried remains of a sea-horse, fragile as brittle glass. Sea sponges and starfish, hard and dry, and a set of shark jaws with jagged teeth that set her own teeth on edge. They fascinated her, those shells and, occasionally, she brought her sketchbook to Maudie's living room to capture the delicate faded colours, the flared lips with pink pearly coatings.

As she had walked towards the dining table on that Christmas Day, past the shells and dried marine life, David had held a small branch of tea-tree above the doorway. 'I couldn't find any mistletoe,' he'd grinned. 'Will this do, instead?'

And he had kissed her, right there and then, in front of everybody. Aware that the others were watching, Claire had blushed bright red. When she looked up, she had seen Alex observing in silence. His lips were caught in a smile but his eyes had been hard.

After lunch — unbearable with Alex sitting opposite and Claire trying purposefully to avoid eye contact with him — David had asked her to walk down to the jetty.

'Just want to check on the boat,' he'd said, and it had seemed churlish to refuse.

He had kissed her again under the shade of the casuarinas, long hard kisses that hurt her mouth. 'I hope you don't mind what I did before, kissing you like that in front of everyone,' he had said. 'I just wanted to let them know you were mine.'

What did he mean? '*Mine*? That makes me feel like a possession. Something to tout around, show off.'

'I didn't mean it to sound like that. You know me, never good with words. I love you, Claire. I just want it to be us. You and me.'

The words had swayed fitfully around her, filling her with restless energy. She had jerked away, making an excuse to go back to the house. 'I have to help with the washing-up.'

It had sounded pathetic, even to her own ears.

Later, while the women were gathered around the kitchen sink, Nina had said: 'Alex will be going back to the city soon. I expect he'll forget all about this place.'

'There won't be much to remember,' Claire had answered.

'That's not how I see it,' interjected Maudie, diving her hands into the sudsy water.

Claire had given her great-aunt a long look. 'What's that supposed to mean?'

'I might be old, but I still have eyes.'

She'd felt herself colour for the second time that day. 'We're friends, Alex and I, that's all.'

'I don't think David sees it that way.' Maudie had set the last saucepan on the draining board and pulled the plug, letting the tea-coloured water gurgle down the drain. 'Anyway,' she'd added, 'you could do a lot worse than marry a doctor.'

'Maudie!' Nina had stood, gobsmacked, staring at the older woman.

'Well, there ain't. Better'n a fisherman,' she had said pointedly. 'Look where fishing got us.'

'The Carmodys have survived for years from the fish,' Nina had remonstrated. 'It's honest work.' Then she had glared at Claire. 'And you'd be better off forgetting about doctors and the like. Concentrate on young David. Now there's a nice boy.'

'Hey!' Claire had declared, throwing her hands up in mock defeat. 'I'm not about to marry anyone. Fisherman *or* doctor. Okay?'

David and Alex: two brothers who pulled her in different directions.

Now, two weeks later, she tried to examine her thoughts analytically. On one side, there was solid reliable David. He was her mate, literally. He'd lay down his life for her, she was certain, yet he had never bought her paints or encouraged her to be creative. He was a man of more practical matters. Boats. Fish. Tides and full moons. From the start there had been an easy camaraderie between them, and they had slid into a relationship of sorts.

Then there was Alex. He was smart and amusing, sensitive to her needs. There was an attraction between them — Claire had seen the interest in Alex's eyes, recognised it — a mutual immediate response that hadn't surfaced between herself and David. Why was that?

Her thoughts kept drifting back to that afternoon of her birthday. Alex in the car, smiling at her, the kitten asleep on her lap. *I feel very comfortable with you.* The sense that, spiritually, she'd known him for years, even though they'd just met.

She remembered the way he'd handed her the gift of paints. Silly, she thought now. It was probably just a random act of kindness. Yet, whenever she saw him, thought of him, something woke inside her, some previously unknown response that made her breathless and left her feeling as though, somewhere along the way, she'd lost control.

She gave a grimace, thinking how Lydia would revel in the same situation — the attention of two men — though her sister, with her flippant attitudes and devil-may-care approach to life, would get more satisfaction in playing them off against each other, not wanting to get deeply involved at all.

The situation: that was how she had come to know it. It made her uncomfortable, angry with herself, as though it were within her own power to settle it. I won't even talk to Alex again, she vowed, yet she knew she couldn't keep that promise. Somehow she was drawn to him. *Some people you meet you feel you've known all your life*. How well she understood — she who had only known Alex for a few weeks yet was so consumed, so absorbed by him.

There were days when she wondered if both men were avoiding her. David stalked moodily around the deck of his boat and Alex was nowhere to be seen. Part of her wanted to be up-front and direct, yet words failed her and she found she could say nothing to either of them. It was too personal, too unresolved even in her own mind. There had been a confrontation of sorts between the two men, she knew that, but neither would discuss it.

'It's nothing,' said David when cornered. 'I just told him to back off. And don't even suggest I'm jealous.'

Somehow, unwittingly, she was responsible for it all. She, Claire, who had never hurt or upset anyone in her entire life, had caused the brothers to be at odds with each other.

The following day was a Saturday and she finished work at two o'clock. Gathering her bag, she walked outside into bright sunshine to find Alex lounging against the verandah post.

'Hello.' He gave her a lazy smile.

Though she tried to act nonchalant, her heart had begun an erratic thumping in her chest. 'Hello, yourself.'

'Wondered what you might be doing after work.'

David was out on the boat and the afternoon stretched in front of her. 'Nothing really.'

'Come over to the pub, then. There's a few of us meeting there.'

She badly wanted to go, yet something held her back. *A few of us.* Who did he mean?

'You might be over twenty-one but I'm not.'

'So?'

'So I suppose you'll order me lemonade and everyone will laugh at Claire the kid who's not old enough to drink.'

The smile faded and he studied her, his eyes probing hers. 'I won't let them.'

'Promise?' She was teasing, bantering: she knew that. Trying to lessen the intensity of his gaze with words.

'Cross my heart.'

The only hotel was The Pacific. It stood on the hill, overlooking the town, a rickety two-storeyed affair that appeared to lean precariously sideways, the sort of place that parents frowned on. The owners had added a dance hall to the side of the building some years earlier and, on Saturday nights, music echoed from its interior down the empty streets. The young adults of the town gathered there to tell a few jokes, to dance, to fish small flasks from their pockets. Supper was tea and sandwiches and cakes filled with cream. Claire knew, because Joe had brought some home the previous weekend, after he'd finished work in the cellar.

As they walked towards the pub, heat fell on them in waves. Claire was aware of Alex next to her, his height, the square set of his shoulders, aware of his shadow spearing out beside hers.

Joe was outside on the footpath, helping the cellarman unload barrels from the lorry; they tilted them on their edges, shuffling them along, rolling them down the wooden plank that led to the cool cavernous underbelly of the building. He nodded towards the front door. 'You two going in there?'

'Yes.' Head tilted defiantly. 'What of it?'

'I'll tell Mum.'

'You wouldn't! She'd have a fit if she knew!'

He grinned at the expression of alarm on her face. 'Silly. Of course I won't. Just joking.'

Claire had never been inside the pub before, and she glanced curiously around. There was a slow trade at present — just a man polishing glasses at the bar that ran the length of the back wall, and one rowdy laughing table of customers.

Alex introduced her to the others: two of his friends and their female companions who had motored up from Brisbane for the day. They were older, sophisticated city people, and the girls were both smoking cigarettes. One girl, introduced as Harry — 'Short for Harriet, darling, but that's too boring for words,' she told Claire with a grimace — offered her one and Claire took it. She positioned it between her forefinger and middle fingers, acting as though smoking were something she did regularly. Alex shot her a warning look and she stared defiantly back at him. *Just try and stop me.*

Teddy, one of Alex's mates, leant forward with a match and she inhaled. The smoke caught in her throat, a tickle that made her cough. She sensed her face reddening. *How embarrassing!* The others laughed, as she had known they would, and then Teddy said, 'I remember my first fag,' and they were away, recounting their own stories, Claire temporarily forgotten.

Alex took the cigarette from her hand and stubbed it out in the ashtray. She shot him a grateful glance. 'I suppose you'll say, "I told you so".'

'Never,' he replied with a smile. 'Now, about that lemonade.'

Someone bought a packet of potato crisps and a bag of peanuts in their shells. Drinks all round. Talking and laughing. Getting to know Alex's friends. They were a down-to-earth bunch, she realised as the afternoon wore on. Friendly and gregarious, with the ability to laugh at themselves.

'Alex, when are you coming back to the city?' Teddy asked later.

'Another week. Then it's nose to the grindstone again.'

Claire found it hard to draw breath. A week! Mere days and he'd be gone, miles away. Already she missed him unbearably; the days, weeks and months stretched emptily ahead. Suddenly she couldn't bear staying in the room, listening to the chatter. It seemed so paltry, so inconsequential, when all she could think about was Alex's leaving.

She pushed her chair back, excused herself and went to the washroom. Stood in front of the basin and splashed water on her face, trying to quell the sense of rising panic. *Stop it*, she told herself. *We have no ties to each other. There's nothing there. Nothing! Nothing! Nothing!*

The door opened behind her and Harry came in, leant over the basin and expertly applied lipstick to her mouth. She pressed her lips together to distribute the colour evenly then stood back, running a comb through her hair. Glancing idly at Claire, she said, 'Teddy and I are planning to get married when he finishes his internship. Don't you think he's gorgeous?'

'He's a darling,' replied Claire. 'Have you known him long?'

'Years. Not like you and Alex. We let *him* out of the city for five minutes and already he's smitten.'

'Smitten?' She gave a shaky laugh. 'I think you've got the wrong idea there.'

Harry gave her a sideways look. 'Well, you can deny it all you want, but the pair of you have it written all over your faces.' She fluffed her hair around her cheeks and gave Claire a wink. 'Come on. Confess.'

Claire shook her head. 'There's nothing going on. Truly.'

'Well, all I can say is that if I weren't so keen on Teddy, I'd be jealous,' Harry laughed. She walked towards a cubicle and shut the door, leaving Claire alone at the mirror, still staring at her own reflection.

CHAPTER 24

'Mum?'

'Yes, dear.'

Lydia suppressed a smile and calculatingly tossed the question at her mother. 'Who do you think Claire will marry? Alex or David?'

The words had the desired effect. Nina's hands came to a halt, poised above the bowl of shredded coconut next to the tray of iced lamingtons. 'Why on earth would you ask that?' she replied tersely.

'Well ...' Lydia tilted her head to one side as though appearing to think, spinning the words out for maximum effect. It was a gesture, designed to confuse, that she'd practised several times in front of the bathroom mirror. 'I think she likes Alex better than David.'

'Nonsense.' Briskly Nina slapped another square of sponge cake in the chocolate icing. 'And you've other things to be putting your mind to, young lady.'

'Such as?'

'Your last year at school. What you'll do when you leave.'

Lydia gave a yawn. 'I'm not planning to *do* anything. I'm going to marry a rich man. A lawyer or a doctor would be nice.'

'Like Alex Melville?' grinned Joe, coming in the kitchen door and letting it slam in his wake. 'Too late, kiddo. I think Claire's beaten you there.'

Exasperated, Nina pushed the hair from her forehead with the back of her hand. 'Will you two stop that!'

'It's true. They were at the pub together the other day. Oh, don't fret,' he added, seeing his mother's startled face. 'There was a whole group of them, and Claire was only drinking lemonade.'

Nina set her mouth in a resigned way and shook her head. Joe put his arm around her shoulder. 'I know you don't like me working down there, but it helps to pay the bills.'

'I'm not complaining,' Nina retorted sharply. 'I take the money, don't I?'

'But you don't like it.'

'I don't have to like it.'

Lydia dipped her finger in the icing. Licked it. 'You haven't answered my question. Who do you think Claire will marry?'

'I don't think Claire's about to marry anyone. She's far too young to think of such things. She's simply having a good time, that's all.'

'Good! That's what I wanted to hear.'

'What, dear?' asked Nina absentmindedly, scraping the last of the icing from the bowl.

'That she's not going to marry Alex. Perhaps Joe's right. I think I will, instead.'

Her mother laughed, a short sharp sound, and Lydia tossed her head. She quite liked the thought of Alex as part of the family. He was an attractive man, with his crinkly blue eyes and sandy hair. As a doctor's wife, she'd have a certain prestige, wherever they lived. And money! That'd make a change. God, how she hated being poor!

Claire had told her that Alex was twenty-three, years older than either of them. Twenty-three, she thought now. Very grown-up. And she was certain he liked her. He always ruffled her hair and didn't call her 'kiddo', like Joe and David. 'Princess,' he said instead, and made the name seem almost magical as he rolled it off his tongue.

'As if Alex'd even look twice at a little squirt like you.' Joe laughed.

'I'm nearly sixteen.'

'Sweet sixteen and never been kissed.'

Defiantly she placed her hands on her hips. 'And how would you know, Joe Carmody?'

Joe gave a knowing grin. 'All the boys at school —'

The conversation wasn't at all going how she had planned it. 'Mum! Tell him to stop!'

Affably. 'Leave your sister alone, Joe.'

Behind his mother's back, Joe screwed up his face at her. 'Poor little Lydia.'

In a huff, she flounced out of the kitchen, up the hallway, and slammed the bathroom door behind her. 'And don't be long in there, either,' she heard Joe call after her. 'There's others who want to have a bath.'

Pooh! She'd make him wait for being mean.

She stood before the mirror and stared at her reflection. Pale skin. Chubby face with large blue eyes that creased in the corners when she smiled. Blonde hair that had mostly come away from its clips and hung in wisps. She pouted, pursing her lips in what she hoped was a seductive manner, and her reflection pouted back. Attractive in an unusual kind of way, she supposed. Not like Claire who was dark-skinned and pretty, and whom all the boys seemed to like.

Claire: the bane of her existence. If it weren't for Claire, she'd have both Alex and David dancing attention on her. She sighed. It wasn't fair being the youngest! Claire was eighteen and almost a world away, doing her typing course, soon to be a secretary in one of the new offices downtown. Sometimes, when she slipped out of the school gates at lunchtime, bored with the day's work, Lydia watched the secretaries stepping along High Street, red-lipped laughing girls with high heels clacking along the pavement, wearing tight-fitted suits and jaunty hats. Claire longed to be a secretary and wear one of those trim hats, Lydia knew. And Joe knew what he wanted, more than anything. He was saving up to do a few repairs on the *Sea-spray*, and wanted to be a fisherman, like his grandfather.

And Lydia. What did Lydia want? Money. Prestige. Eventually a husband. She was in no hurry. She could wait. 'Mrs Melville,' she said, watching the movement of her mouth in the mirror. 'Mrs *Alex* Melville.'

She liked the sound of that.

'Hey, Lydia!'

There was a loud banging on the door and the sound of Joe's voice. She jumped, startled at the intrusion. 'What?'

'Hurry up. A bloke's got to get ready for the party. Or are you going to stay in there all night?'

Hal Melville had organised a farewell get-together for Alex. Nina and Maudie had made sponge cakes and trays of sandwiches, not to mention the lamingtons that Lydia had watched her mother ice earlier.

Quickly Lydia bathed and changed, pulling the brush through her long hair and pinning it up again. She thought it made her look older, more sophisticated. A bottle of Evening in Paris perfume sat next to the basin. It was Claire's; David had bought it for her birthday. Carelessly she splashed it along her wrists and behind her ears. Then, at the last moment, she dabbed a coating of Fiery Glow on her lips.

Claire wasn't home from work when Lydia and her mother went over to the Melville place. 'You can help me get the food ready,' Nina had said, and Lydia had gone along willingly, hoping to spend some time alone with Alex before the other guests arrived. But, to her annoyance, he was nowhere in sight. There was just Maudie and her mother, and the woman from town who came to clean the Melville's house. Too bloody boring, she thought, taking the grey kitten and wandering out into the yard.

The men arrived at the party with bottles of drinks under their arms. Lydia persuaded young Bert O'Reilly, from one of the cottages further down, to top up her lemonade with beer, careful to hide the glass from her mother's prying eyes. Alex arrived and they all sat on the back verandah, facing the ocean. A few of his friends were there, city folk. She flirted with one of them — Teddy, he said his name was — until his girlfriend intervened and dragged him away.

There was a note on the table in her mother's handwriting. *We've gone to the Melville's. Come down when you get home.*

'Alex's going-away party,' Claire said with a sigh, dropping the piece of paper on the kitchen bench. She hated the thought of saying goodbye, couldn't imagine what life would be like when he left.

'Stay away,' an inner voice prompted. 'You're only setting yourself up for disappointment.'

But how could she avoid going? It would appear odd if the entire Carmody family turned up minus Claire. And David would want to know why. Perhaps she could plead a violent headache or a stomach upset?

She walked across to the window and stared along the track that led down to the sea wall. The Melville house, newly painted, was just visible, a few cars sprawling in the shade of the tea-trees in the front yard. Music carried towards her on the breeze. The party was obviously underway. Alex was there, somewhere. Perhaps, if she wished long and hard enough, he would walk out into the front yard. But the scene in front of her remained empty.

The minutes dragged by. She should change, go and join the others, but was somehow reluctant. Not of seeing Alex — she found the minutes spent apart from him interminable — but the agony of having to share him with his family and friends, of having to smile and pretend, of having David monopolise her attention.

'I'll just go down for a swim first,' she told herself, knowing she was delaying the inevitable.

It was approaching dusk as she donned her swimsuit and ran down to the foreshore. She waded into the water and it swirled across her legs, up her thighs, momentarily cold as it hit her belly. Taking a deep breath she dived in and swam underwater, towards the buoy, until lack of air forced her to the surface. Then, head down and arms rotating, she swam with strong practised strokes, holding her breath until, with bursting lungs, she came up next to the marker.

Was it only a few weeks earlier she and Alex had raced each other there? She rolled onto her back and swished her feet. The sky stretched above, medium blue darkening to indigo in the gathering dusk, a slash of red on the western horizon. She closed her eyes and felt the warm soothing flow of water around her body, imagined the depths of it below. Wished for the umpteenth time that day that she didn't have to go to Alex's party at all, but knew she had to. 'Duty calls,' she muttered to herself eventually and swam towards the shore.

She trudged up to the house, bathed and washed her hair. Padded through the empty house naked then, back in her room, she slipped on a dressing gown. Collecting the clothes she would wear, she laid them on the bed, surveyed them, wishing instantly she had been financial enough to buy a new dress for the occasion. Something bright to counteract her mood.

'Claire?'

There was a voice at the window and she spun towards it, unsure. Alex was waiting there, hand on the timber frame. 'I'm sorry if I startled you.'

'That's all right.' Suddenly aware of her own lack of clothes, she pulled the gown tighter and folded her arms across her chest.

'I did knock at the front door but no-one answered. Then I saw your light on.'

'There's nobody home, except me. The others are up at your place.'

Alex climbed over the ledge, levering his lean frame into the room which seemed to shrink with his presence. He was wearing long trousers and an open-necked shirt, and Claire could see a sprinkling of fair hairs on his chest. 'Aren't you coming to the party?'

'I know I'm awfully late, but I was hot when I got home from work, so I went down for a swim and then I had to have a shower to get the —'

'Claire!' he broke in.

She stopped, knowing she was babbling, making words to fill the space between them. Mother always said she talked too much. Not knowing what to say, she turned back towards the mirror and picked up her hair brush, pulling it through her damp hair. Droplets of water sprayed over her hand, trickled down her neck. He reached one hand towards hers, removed the brush. 'Can I do that?'

She could see herself in the mirror, Alex behind her as he tentatively pulled the brush through her hair. Hand moving slowly, wrist brushing her cheek. She felt the warmth of him, the solid comfort and laid her head back against his chest.

He was watching her in the mirror, his eyes locked on hers. 'Do you mind?'

'No.'

'Truthfully? You'd tell me if you did?'

'Why are you here, Alex?'

His hand slowed, then stopped. He spun her around until she faced him. 'I wanted to talk to you. Alone. We won't get much of a chance tonight.'

'No.'

'So I'll not waste words. I'm here because ...' He paused for a moment, as though gathering his thoughts, then ploughed on. 'I need to know how to feel about you and me.'

His words came at her thickly, in slow motion. Agonising words. Promising hope, yet snatching it away. Claire watched his mouth form them, watched his lips move and wondered, not for the first time, what it would be like to kiss him.

Violently she forced the thought from her mind. What was she thinking of? 'Don't make me do this.'

'Claire, I need to know!'

'Know what?' she cried, and her own voice sounded as though it hadn't been used for years. 'There is no you and me! There can't be!'

The brush dropped onto the floor with a thud, and the sound echoed dully. He made no move to retrieve it. Instead, his hands came up, gripping her shoulders, and he stared at her long and hard, eyes searching her face as though for some sign.

'Because of David?'

What a mess! What a damnable bloody mess! She nodded, sensing her eyes fill with tears. The colours in the room washed together to form a watery blur. 'Alex, please,' she whispered, glancing away. 'Don't do this.'

'Do you love him?' Alex went on brutally, allowing her no escape. One hand came under her chin, forcing her to face him again. His eyes were dark and held the look of a man tortured beyond endurance. 'For God's sake, Claire! *Do you love my brother*? If you tell me yes, then I'll walk away, never speak of this again!'

'I'm very fond of him.'

'But you don't love him.'

Not like I love you. She shook her head, the words unsaid.

'So how do you fit into the whole picture?' he went on relentlessly. 'Can you marry a man you don't love? Is that what you want?'

'I don't know. It's what everyone expects.'

'Everyone?'

'David. Mum . . .' Her voice trailed away, unsure.

'Bugger them!' he exploded, his voice savage. 'This is *your* life we're talking about! What do *you* want?'

How could she say the words? How could she put into meaning the thoughts that had been scrambling around inside her for weeks now? Claire: the good girl. Claire: the responsible one. Claire, who badly wanted to be with Alex, no matter what the consequences. But how could she abandon David for his brother, without an overwhelming feeling of guilt? It would destroy any relationship between the two men and make life uncomfortable for both the Melville and Carmody families.

Impatiently. 'Claire! Answer me! Before I go away, I need to know if there's any chance of a future for us!'

She started, shocked at his directness, her mouth refusing to form words. He wanted decisions, commitments. And he wanted them now, not giving her time to think. She couldn't think, anyway. Heart thudding. Breath coming in shallow gasps. Stunned into silence by the unexpectedness of the conversation and the immediacy of him.

'There's something magical, mystical, between us,' he went on. 'You know what I'm talking about. It was there from the first time we met.'

She nodded. 'From that first day, I loved you, Alex.'

On a deep sigh, he drew her towards him and she closed her eyes, waiting for the touch of his mouth. Yet when the touch came, it was not on her own lips but along the outer ridge of her neck.

In that seemingly eternal moment, she was aware for the first time of desire. Warm lips brushing warm skin, the merest sensation, barely felt. That same warmth rushing through her, taking her beyond care. 'I love you, Alex,' she whispered again, guiding his head down with one hand, shuddering as his mouth found the soft hollow at the base of her throat.

Her whole being was enclosed in that room, yet she was conscious of external sensations. The shrill chorus of the cicadas from the trees at the back of the house. Curtains billowing at the open window, and the breeze that came at them in little gusts. From the direction of the surf, she could hear the dull *thud, thud, thud* of the waves against the sand, mixed with a few chords of music.

The party!

As though reading her thoughts, he pulled away, gazing into her face. 'We belong together, Claire. We both know that. And we shouldn't have to worry about hurting other people.'

She couldn't bear his scrutiny, the overwhelming intimacy, knowing he was about to walk away from her. Confused, she glanced away.

'Claire?' He cupped his palm under her chin, brought her face around to his. 'I can't bear to think of David being with you, kissing you. He might be my brother, but I need you more.'

'Oh, Alex,' she whispered. 'Don't make me choose.'

He touched his mouth to her forehead, releasing her. 'I'm sorry. Perhaps I shouldn't have said what I did. And I had no right, barging in here expecting answers.'

'Alex, I —'

But he cut her off, saying, 'I'd better go before everyone wonders where I am.'

Claire sat on the bed, staring at the window through which he had gone. The room still looked the same: bed and dresser, chair in the corner, the desk that held her paints and sketchbook. The curtain still billowed inwards with the breeze. Night crickets chirped. Yet something inside her had altered in a monumental way. *Alex wanted her*. Hadn't he told her so?

We belong together . . .

I need you . . .

She walked to the window and stared out. Music floated towards her from the direction of the party. Alex would be there now, mingling with the crowd, saying his goodbyes.

Suddenly she surprised herself by bursting into tears.

Somehow, after Alex had gone, she managed to dress and walk down the path towards the party that was Alex's farewell. With each successive step, she longed to turn and run, back to the confines of her room. Wanted to be alone to remember his mouth moving down her skin, those shuddering erotic sensations. Wanted to savour the emotions, letting them fuse in her mind.

At the Melville's she busied herself, carrying around trays of sandwiches. It was supposed to be her sister's job, but Lydia was in the corner talking earnestly to Teddy, Alex's friend and, by the expression on Harry's face, she was about to break up the conversation. Claire caught herself looking in the hall mirror as she passed. Outwardly nothing seemed different yet, inside, her emotions were churning. How could she ever appear normal to anyone at the party? Surely they could see some difference, some alteration in her?

Lydia was suddenly beside her. 'Jealous cow,' she muttered, inclining her head towards Harry. 'What's wrong?'

'Nothing!' Then, nose twitching, Claire cried, 'You little sneak! You've been into my perfume, the one David gave me.'

'Have not.'

'Don't try the big-blue-eyes-I'm-innocent routine with me, Lydia. I'm not Mum. Besides, I can smell it twenty yards away. You must have used half the bottle.'

Lydia shrugged, obviously bored by the conversation. 'Evening in Paris,' she muttered. 'There are much nicer, more expensive perfumes in the chemist's in town. I'd rather a man bought me Elizabeth Arden.'

But Claire was walking away, towards the kitchen, scarcely registering Lydia's words. She felt shredded, torn in two. Traitorous on all counts. While she offered around the tray of lamingtons, her eyes sought and found Alex in the crowd, and he gave her a tentative smile. I understand, he seemed to say.

He beckoned her over and she went, on the pretext of taking him cake. He bent his head low, whispering in her ear. 'I'm leaving on the midday train tomorrow. Will you come to the station and say goodbye?'

Without hesitation. 'Yes.'

'I'll see you there, then.'

Music from the gramophone crackled out from the living room across the lawn into the warm night, and the clink of the beer glasses sounded lethargic. It was an effort for Claire to drag her gaze from him, but David was suddenly by her side, demanding her attention. 'If you don't mind, old cock,' he said tersely to his brother, taking the plate of cake from

Claire's hands and placing it firmly in Alex's, 'I think this dance's mine.'

David took her elbow, planning to steer her away. She raised her eyes to Alex's, wanting badly to stay.

'David —'

'I'm sure Alex won't mind me dragging you away. Now, let's dance.'

'Not at all,' said Alex affably, staring down at the plate in his hands. 'I'll just do the honours with this lot.'

She danced with David on the verandah to the scratchy tunes, and he kissed her, right there under the light, where she was sure everyone, including Alex, could see.

Later she sat on the back steps, listening to the music and staring out through the darkness, across the grassy dunes towards the surf. Her head spun. She felt giddy, out of control. Mentally she counted the hours until tomorrow. Somehow she'd get time off work, say goodbye to Alex. Unbearable thought. *Goodbye*. So final. So permanent.

With a hammering heart, Claire took an early lunch break and made her way to the railway station fifteen minutes before the midday train was due. It was hot, with a gusty wind blowing, and she felt the perspiration on her forehead as she stepped onto the platform.

At first glance it appeared the station was deserted, and a wild hope sprang into her mind. Perhaps Alex had changed his mind, was not leaving after all. But there he was, she saw at last, stepping around his suitcases as he rose from the seat to greet her.

She was glad she'd been able to get away. David, she knew, was out fishing, and Hal Melville was busy with the lunchtime rush at the surgery. It would be miserable to be leaving somewhere with no-one to say goodbye.

'Thank God, you've come. I was thinking you couldn't leave the shop.'

'Charlie was okay. I've got to make up the extra time in the morning.'

Morning. How bleak and far away it seemed without Alex! Meanwhile, he lounged against the wall and they chatted, meaningless dialogue that only served to fill the minutes. Later, when she tried to remember the thread of the conversation, she recalled nothing of the words, but saw, instead, only those blue eyes and the crinkles at the corners of his mouth when he smiled. She longed to put her fingers there, on that mouth, and trace the outline of his lips. But she knew that to do so would unleash all those emotions from the previous night. So she folded her arms across her chest, erecting a barricade between them, not allowing herself to think.

After what seemed like mere minutes, the train came swaying along the track towards them. 'This is it, then,' said Alex, gathering up his suitcase.

Claire felt a sense of dread settle in her stomach. She swallowed and bit her lip. 'God, I hate goodbyes!'

'I'll write.' He smiled, then his expression became serious. 'Look, Claire. It's only a few more months until I finish my internship, and there's a few loose ends I have to tie up in the city. I'll get back as soon as I can. Promise me you won't do anything silly in the meantime.'

'Such as?'

'Marrying my brother, for one thing.'

Despite herself, she laughed. 'That's not likely.'

The train pulled into the station with a hiss of steam. 'Don't forget to write,' she said on a deep breath, as passengers clambered down the steps and porters carried luggage. Activity, people milling about her. Busy bustling lives. Yet her own life had ground to a halt, made eventless by Alex's imminent leaving.

Unexpectedly he bent his head, kissed her in the middle of the thronging crowd, and she brought her hands up, touching them for one brief moment to his face.

'I can't bear your leaving.'

'I have to go.'

'I'll miss you.'

The guard came along, closing doors. 'Come on, then,' he winked at Alex. 'All aboard.'

Alex released her, swung himself easily up the steps and leaned out the door. She swayed for a moment, finding her balance. 'Promise me you'll wait?' he said, and she felt absurdly close to tears.

'Cross my heart.'

'And . . .'

'Don't forget to write.'

'I'll write!'

'And, Claire —'

He broke off, as though he had been going to say something but changed his mind. The train gave a jerk forward, wheels slowly turning. A gush of steam clouded the platform.

'What?'

He smiled and shook his head. 'Nothing. Take care, that's all.'

The whistle blew and the train jerked forward again, wheels grinding, straining at the tracks. For one absurdly long moment, she thought she'd launch herself towards the carriage that contained him, wrench open the door, tell Alex she was coming, too.

The carriage moved slowly at first and she found herself walking along beside it, anxious to maintain contact. 'Goodbye, Claire.'

'Don't say goodbye. I can't bear that word. It seems so final.'

'*Au revoir*, then. It's French,' he added. 'It means "till we meet again".'

'Have a good trip.'

'I love you, Claire.'

The train was moving faster now. She stopped, unable to keep pace, and stared after Alex's retreating face. He raised his hand and waved. Tears blurred her eyes and she blinked, rubbed her hand across her face, anxious not to miss a moment. But by the time she could see clearly again, the last carriage was rounding the bend and Alex was lost to view.

She stood, staring down the length of empty track until the station master came along, rattling his keys. 'Come along, Miss. That's the last train until tomorrow, and I've got to lock up now.'

CHAPTER 25

Back in the store, the afternoon passed poisonously. Claire had never known such heat before. It rose in suffocating waves, making every chore arduous. Packing orders, sweeping the floor, making small talk with the customers and trying to keep her voice light, when inside she was crumbling to dust; with every passing hour, the pain of Alex's leaving became more acute, more intense.

Images of those last few minutes spent together kept scrambling back. The crowded platform. Shrill whistle. Carriages jerking forward, taking Alex away from her. The way the train had gathered momentum, leaving her behind and slamming her to a halt, breathless, as though the air had been sucked from her lungs.

I love you, Claire.

She remembered his mouth, the way his lips had formed the words. Four treasured words that were momentous in their simplicity, their unexpectedness.

Then she remembered David's words, weeks earlier. *I just told him to back off.*

Two men, and now she had to choose.

Should she follow her heart? Commonsense told her that she would, but how could she deal with the inevitable antagonism between the two brothers? How could she divide the family and live with herself? She shook her head, not knowing, wanting to cry out with the impossibility of it all.

After work she cycled lethargically back to the Passage. Lydia was sitting on the back verandah, skirt hiked above her knees, fanning herself with the hem.

'Where's Mum?'

'Up at Maudie's, helping her cut out a dress pattern, or something.'

Distracted, she wandered up to her room and collected the box of watercolours. Back in the kitchen, she filled a jar with water, found a brush and paper. Arranged the tubes of paint on the table, then sat in the chair. She stared at them hopelessly, unable even to open them. Today, she had no heart for it.

Alex: she couldn't erase the name from her mind. It clung there, tenaciously, teasing her with sly sentiment, flinging itself at her in unexpected moments. Her reaction to his leaving surprised her. Claire: the strong one. Claire: the sensible one. That was what everyone said. Yet his departure had reduced her to a different level of consciousness. Several short weeks, that was all she'd known him, yet somehow he'd shaped her life, given her other awarenesses.

'Bloody hell!' In frustration she threw the paintbrush on the table and scraped the chair back.

Skirting around the house to escape Lydia's attention, she wandered down past the Melville's. The windows were closed, curtains limp behind polished glass. Hal Melville's car wasn't in the driveway, and Claire could see from the front fence that David's boat wasn't tied to the usual jetty. He was out, somewhere beyond Turtle Island, fishing.

Compared to the previous night, the place looked forlorn, abandoned almost. A dozen or so empty beer bottles were arranged in a neat pile next to the front step. The blue-purple hydrangeas that lined each side of the front path drooped in the heat. As she watched, a woman came down the front steps, a pair of garden shears in her hand, followed by the kitten, Smoky. She was, Claire knew, Doctor Melville's housekeeper from town.

'Hello,' she said, seeing Claire. 'Haven't I seen you around here before?'

Claire scooped up the kitten and held it for a moment against her cheek. 'I was here at the party last night.'

The woman nodded, her face creased into a smile.

'I just live down the road,' added Claire, pointing to her own home.

'Anything I can help you with, then?' the woman asked amiably.

'I was just admiring the flowers,' she mumbled in reply. Then, dumping the kitten on the grass, she fled along the sandy track in the direction of the sea wall.

The days passed slowly, drawn out and made unbearable by the heat. Nights were spent tossing to the eternal buzzing of mosquitoes. Seconds, minutes and hours multiplied, separating her from Alex. Patiently she waited for his letter to arrive, scanning the post box every day, but none came. One week passed. Two. Disappointment tracked through her, making her irritable. Surely he'd had time to pen a few words, however brief.

Erica was waiting outside the flat when Alex arrived, pacing along the length of the footpath. 'Thank God, you're here,' she snapped, taking the key from his hand.

'Hello, Erica. Nice to see you again,' he replied affably.

She flung the door open and marched inside. 'It would have been nicer if you'd returned my phone calls. I left three of them with your father.'

He kicked the door shut behind him. 'Whatever it was, I thought it could wait until I got back.'

She brought her hands up onto her hips. 'Oh, bloody lovely! Don't spoil Alex's holiday, is that it? Well, I'll get right to the point as I don't want to waste your precious time. I'm pregnant!'

He dropped his suitcase and the thump echoed through the flat. 'Are you sure? I — I mean — how long?'

'Two months, according to the doctor I saw last week.'

'Bloody hell!'

'*Bloody hell*! Is that all you can say? For a doctor, Alex, your bedside manner's damn atrocious. A little sympathy wouldn't go astray. It might interest you to know that while you've been off having your little holiday fling, I've been stuck here with my head in a bucket.'

'Holiday fling? Who told you that?'

'Harry said you'd taken a girl to the pub. Claire, wasn't that her name?'

She was furious, he could see that, but was her anger directed more at him or herself? He raised his hands, begging her to stop. 'Okay, okay. Let's discuss this rationally, shall we?'

'I'm pregnant, and you want to be *rational*? I trusted you, Alex. You said you were using precautions.'

'I was. They're not foolproof, though.'

'Obviously not!'

'Have you said anything —'

'To my parents?' She shook her head. 'You've got to be joking! But I can only keep up the I've-got-a-stomach-bug charade for so long before they get suspicious.'

He closed his eyes, allowing his memory to take him back to the first time he'd met Erica. It had started out as a bit of a joke, really, with Teddy saying Alex was working too hard and needed a bit of fun. 'Look, there's a few of us going to the theatre on Saturday night. You'll be the odd one out, so I'll ask Harry to bring a friend.'

'A blind date, don't you mean?'

Teddy had shrugged. 'Whatever. You'll enjoy yourself, old cock, if you just forget about work for a few hours.'

The night at the theatre, Alex had to admit, had been better than expected. Harry's friend Erica was blonde and willowy, and looked stunning in a simple black dress and high-heeled shoes that emphasised her long shapely legs. They had soon discovered that, besides Harry and Teddy, they had several friends in common, and shared a love of classical music. Afterwards, over a cup of coffee in a nearby cafe, they'd talked for hours about mutual interests.

In the car, as Alex had drawn up outside her home, she had reached over and kissed him — a lingering unsolicited kiss that had told him she was definitely interested and that he was, judging by the way his body reacted, impressed.

'There are a few of us going on a picnic tomorrow,' she had said. 'Up Mount Coot-tha. Would you like to come?'

The following day had been cool, with clouds scudding over an autumn sky. Alex had watched Erica as she ran down the steps towards the car, picnic basket slung over one arm. She had looked striking in a pair of white linen trousers and a pink shirt, her hair pulled back into an elegant chignon, and her eyes hidden behind a fashionable pair of dark glasses.

The day had passed agreeably. At odd times Alex had watched her, Harry's friend, thinking that maybe Erica would be an asset to a young up-and-coming doctor. She was attractive and laughed at the right moments, could tell a half-decent joke. Her father, Erica had told him, had started a manufacturing business during the war and had made an obscene amount of money from locomotives and rolling stock. He was also, it turned out, a director on the board of the hospital where Alex was serving his internship: a blustery, florid-faced man, known through the workplace corridors for his ill humour. Luckily, so far he and Alex had maintained a cordial relationship.

She had kissed him again when he took her home. 'Would you like to come up for a drink?'

'Your parents, they won't mind?'

'They've gone away for a few days.'

The implication had been obvious.

Expertly she had mixed two martinis, which were long and cool and tasted exquisite. 'Would you like to dance?' she'd asked, slipping a record on the gramophone.

He'd walked towards her, held her, and moved slowly across the carpet, rocking to the strains of the music. She'd felt warm in his arms, compliant, and he had sensed the beat of her heart through the delicate substance of her blouse.

When the record came to an end, she had stopped, laced her fingers at the back of his neck and pulled his mouth close to her own. 'Kiss me, Alex.'

He had obliged, aware of that same hardening in his groin as her breasts flattened against his chest. 'May I?' he'd asked, taking the first of the pins from her hair, watching as the mass of silver blonde tumbled about her face.

'You're a very attractive man, Alex Melville.'

'And you're a very desirable woman.'

One hand had moved down, along his belly and the ridge of his hip, finally cupping the hardness in his groin through the fabric of his trousers. She had put her mouth on his again, flicking her tongue past his teeth with little darting movements that made him ache with the nearness of her.

'Prove it to me,' she had whispered, taking his hand and leading him from the room.

Nursing a monumental hangover, Alex had woken the next morning in Erica's white four-poster bed. He'd felt embarrassed to be there; she had seemed amused. And he hadn't been able to ask her, either then or during the times they'd since shared, if he was the first she'd taken there. Somehow, given her level of proficiency, he doubted it.

That had been almost twelve months ago. They'd maintained a somewhat erratic relationship since, meeting at his place or a convenient hotel, when time and desires and finances allowed. 'No strings attached,' she'd maintained. 'It's a sexual thing. Just because I'm a woman it doesn't mean I can't admit to such indulgences.'

Erica was the 'loose end' he'd told Claire about on that last day at the station. Once back in the city, he'd known that the first step towards any future with Claire was to end the relationship. But with Erica standing before him now, shocking him with the news of the baby, it seemed all his plans were crumbling.

He took his car from the garage next to the flats and drove her home. She sat in the passenger seat, staring out the window, not talking. 'Look, this is all a bit of a shock, and I'm just as concerned as you,' Alex said as they pulled up outside her home. 'Let's sleep on it, come up with some decisions in the morning. One more day won't make any difference.'

Two hours later, Teddy stood in front of Alex's desk, hands on hips. 'What do you mean you "don't want to come to the pub?"'

'I've got some case histories to write up before I go back to work tomorrow,' he answered stubbornly.

'So, we've all got the same workload. You need a break.'

'I've just had a break. Four weeks.'

'Christ, mate! What's gotten into you? You're no fun any more.'

Alex glared back at Teddy, wishing his friend would disappear, and shrugged.

'It's Claire, isn't it?' Teddy went on relentlessly. 'Missing her already?'

'No, it bloody-well isn't Claire. It's Erica, if you must know. She's pregnant, although that's not for general public knowledge.'

'Christ!' Teddy sat down in the chair with a thump. 'Wouldn't like to be around her old man when he finds out. What are you going to do?'

There were no sparks, Alex admitted to himself, but Erica was pleasant company and perhaps that was all he could ever expect. 'What choice do I have but marry her?'

'Is that what Erica wants?'

'I don't know what Erica wants. All I know is what she doesn't want, and that's a baby.'

'She could always have an abortion. I know someone —'

Alex shook his head. 'Too risky. I'd never forgive myself if something went wrong. And she can't simply have the child. Imagine her father's reaction. My name'd be mud around here.'

'So you're going to do the *honourable thing*?'

'From where I'm standing, it doesn't feel very honourable. Forced or obligated might be a better description.'

'What about Claire? Where does she stand in all this?'

Wearily Alex ran his hand through his hair. 'I was going to break it off with Erica, if you must know. But now . . .'

'Out of sight, out of mind,' Teddy ribbed. 'Maybe Claire's forgotten about you already?'

'She isn't like that.'

'Alex, have you thought that maybe it was just a holiday fling? You know, all that sand, water and sunshine stirring up the old hormones. Besides, you've only known each other for a few weeks, not like Harry and I.'

'That's different.'

'Bullshit!'

'You and Harry —'

'Our families have been friends for years.'

'Okay.' Alex threw his hands up in defeat. 'I understand all that. What I want to know is when did you *know*?'

'Stop being obscure. Know what?'

'That Harry was the one, that you loved her. I knew the minute I met Claire.'

'Love?' Teddy gave an amused laugh. 'What's love

got to do with all this? We're doctors, right? For appearances' sake, we need wives who are smart and beautiful.'

'Claire's smart and beautiful.'

'Of course she is, old cock. But she's a country girl. Unsophisticated. Unused to the ways of the world. Erica, though, will make a wonderful hostess for your dinner parties when you're head of cardiology.'

'Don't be crass.'

'And,' Teddy went on, undaunted, 'as you've told me several times in the past, she's a bloody good fuck!'

'Evidenced by this *bloody* predicament I find myself in.' Alex gave a wry grin. 'Touché! You know how to wound a bloke.'

'So, now you've made the decision, how long are you going to sit around moping about it?'

'I'm not moping. I told you I've got case histories —'

In the end he went, and succeeded in getting himself very drunk. He remembered little of walking home and letting himself into the flat, remembered only taking the sketch Claire had given him, that first day they had met. He sat on the side of the bed, staring at the blur of colour. Boats tied at the jetties amongst a profusion of tea-tree, the headland, pandanus palms that thrust spikes into the pale sky. Tide washing along the rocks, white foam spewing upwards. It was rough, the sketch, unfinished, yet it showed promise.

Furious, he resisted the urge to crush the paper in his hands, to toss it on the floor. Through necessity, whatever he'd had with Claire was over, finished, burnt out before it had had a chance to develop. Erica and the baby were his first considerations now.

Carefully he took the sketch, laid it between the pages of one of his books, then let himself fall back on the bed. He closed his eyes, trying hard not to think of the future: marriage to a woman he didn't love, fatherhood, a child he hadn't planned.

When he woke, it was morning.

'Write,' she'd said. And he did — several letters that at varying stages of their creation ended in the bin. He'd made promises, which he was unable to keep, and she deserved an explanation. But what to say? *How* to say it? Even the opening words confused him.

'Darling Claire,' he wrote, and immediately scrunched the paper into a tight ball. No, that sounded too assuming. Besides, he couldn't say that now.

'Hi, Claire.' Too casual. She meant more than that, dammit! That piece of paper met the same fate as the first.

Meanwhile, a letter arrived from David, full of local news.

Joe's started working for me on the boat. He's a deckhand, cum general rouseabout, and loves every minute of it. Must be in the blood. Claire's finished her typing course and has been offered a job at Parsons' solicitors. Dad's thinking about taking another doctor into the practice. Says there's too much work for one. Pity you're so settled in the city or you could come back. I can just see the sign —

Melville and Son. Dad would be so proud. What a difference a few weeks make!

'I don't know why she can't wait and get married in a church like a proper bride,' Erica's mother said to Alex, as though blaming him for the speed with which the wedding was organised. As an only child, her daughter had obviously failed to live up to parental expectations. 'You young people! Always rush, rush, rush.'

Erica's father slapped him on the back, several times. 'Welcome to the family, son.'

The wedding was a low-key affair at a local registry office, with just Teddy and Harry, and Erica's parents. Alex hadn't even told his own family. Erica looked pale, but lovely, in a white linen suit, carrying a bunch of pink lilies and baby's breath. She smiled tremulously at him as they made their vows. Afterwards they went to a nearby hotel, where Alex's new father-in-law treated them to a slap-up lunch.

Two days later Erica lost the child.

He hadn't realised, until it was all over, how attached he'd become to the idea of being a father. Instead, he mourned alone for the tiny scrap of life that had fought so hard for existence, and lost.

Erica, once she had recovered, was quite blasé about the whole episode. 'Bloody good timing! Saves all the busybodies counting up the months between wedding and baby,' she announced. 'Too damn dreary for words. Thank God we didn't tell my parents.'

She could, he thought bitterly, think only of herself.

*   *   *

Lydia dawdled all the way to school, wishing her mother had let her stay home. It was picnic day, to be held at the next beach around from Tea-tree Passage, a treat for the little kids really. It would be dreadfully tedious and she didn't want to go.

Lydia was one of the oldest at the school and she hated being there. Hated the lessons, the uniform that hung halfway down her calves. Hated having her hair tied back. Too many rules and regulations, she thought as she trudged along the road, kicking a stone with the tip of her shoe.

She wanted to leave, had been pestering her mother for ages, but Nina insisted she stay. 'You can't get a decent job without qualifications,' she argued.

'But, Mum. Claire's going to work for Parsons, so there'll be a job going at the shop.'

'No! You'll stay at school, young lady. Finish the year out.'

It was so unfair. One whole year! Twelve months! Three hundred and sixty-five days! *Boring*! *Boring*! *Boring*!

She reached school just as the bus, laden with excited children, was about to depart for the beach. Casually she swung herself through the still-open door, throwing her towel onto the rack above the seat. Then she sulked all the way, staring morosely out the window.

Lunch was sandwiches and cupcakes, laid out on trays under the shade of the trees. Lydia hung back as the younger children gathered around. She'd been on a diet for weeks now, trying to slim down. If only she were as thin as Claire, then she wouldn't have to worry, she thought with irritation, eyeing the dollops of cream on the cakes. Later the ice truck arrived, dispensing tubs of Peters ice-cream. Lydia wasn't interested in the ice-cream. Instead she stared with interest at the driver. Pete was his name, a new employee at the Ice Works in town.

The foot races were starting. She hadn't planned to enter but, knowing Pete would be watching, she wandered over to the starting line, took off her shoes and felt the sand hot between her toes.

'On your marks,' yelled the starter and she hitched the hem of her uniform under the elastic of her undies, baring her legs.

'Go!'

Easily she sprinted to the tape that marked the end of the race, long hair flying behind her as she ran. Then she untucked the hem of her skirt, letting it fall against her thighs, and wandered over to the ice truck to claim her ice-cream.

'Hello,' she said to Pete, smiling provocatively.

'That was a good run.'

'It was okay. Did you see it?'

'Sure.'

'So, do I get an ice-cream as a reward?'

'If you're nice to me, I'll give you two.'

'Nice?'

'How about coming with me to the matinee in town on Saturday afternoon? My treat.'

She eyed him lazily. He really was quite good-looking. 'It's a deal.'

One month passed. Two. Claire waited on tenterhooks for Alex's letter, but none came. What now? She'd admitted to Alex how she felt, laid herself bare, and it had not been easy. *I love you* — words she'd never said to any man, not even David.

The outpouring of emotion had left her feeling vulnerable, exposed. Niggling doubts came creeping in, overriding sensibility. What if Alex had changed his mind about her? Now, back in the city with his friends, had he discovered their relationship had been a summer romance, nothing more? What if she never heard from him again?

Stop it! she told herself, angry for doubting him. Trust. That was what relationships were built on. And more than anyone, she trusted Alex.

Meanwhile, the days dragged on. She started her new job in the solicitor's office: filing, typing letters, making morning tea. The position kept her busy and paid well so, to cheer herself up, she splurged her first few pay packets on new clothes.

'Have to look the part now, Mum,' she said, arriving home with two linen suits and a pair of black pumps.

'And don't you look smart to boot?' Maudie added, watching as Claire tried them on, pirouetting in front of the mirror in her mother's bedroom. 'Quite the young lady.'

Despite the new job and pretty clothes, the anticipation of any future with Alex crumbled daily. Desolation replaced hope. Expectation spiralled in a long downward loop. David called routinely. He was full of good humour. The trawler was doing well and he'd put a proposition to Joe: now that the boy was working for him, he'd help get the *Sea-spray* up and running, and then they'd form a partnership.

'He's a damn good worker,' David told Nina. 'Just needs a bit of capital to get started and he'll make a fine fisherman.'

David was waiting outside the office for Claire late one afternoon at the end of April. 'How about the pictures tonight?'

'What's on?'

'Abbott and Costello.'

'Okay.'

'You needn't sound so enthusiastic.'

'It's not that. I'm tired, that's all.'

'We could make it another night.'

'No. I'll be fine. Just give me half an hour to freshen up.'

The movie made her smile for the first time in weeks. They were the last to leave their seats and, by the time she and David stumbled onto the footpath, the street was deserted. Winter was coming and already Claire could feel a chill to the air. The summer memories were fading, had been for weeks. There were days when she thought she must have imagined it all: Alex's homecoming, lazy conversations, that day at the railway station.

Past the newsagent and barber shops they walked, towards David's car. After a few steps, he slung one arm across her shoulder, pulling her close. It felt snug there, walking, hips brushing, shadows from the streetlights looming before them, pulled into odd angular shapes.

They paused in front of the jeweller's display window and David pointed to an array of engagement rings. 'You'd only have to say the word, Claire, and I'd buy you one.'

She gave a forced smile. 'Is that a marriage proposal?'

He moved in front of her, placed his hands on her shoulders. 'Yes. Marry me and you'll make me the happiest man alive.'

'You're supposed to talk to my mother first, then go down on your knees,' she bantered, not knowing how to reply, searching for time to frame a decent refusal.

'Is that a "no"?' he asked astutely.

Sadly she shook her head, knowing her words would cause pain. 'I'm sorry, David. Marriage is a huge step and I'm not ready for that.'

'Don't think I'll give up easily,' he replied, kissing her lightly on the mouth. 'I'm a persistent man, in case you hadn't noticed.'

'Have you heard from Alex?' she asked later as he opened the car door for her, trying to keep her voice casual.

'Dad had a letter last week. He's doing okay.'

Grief bit deeply, rendered her momentarily breathless. Alex had found time to write to his family yet, somewhere between Tea-tree Passage and the city, he'd forgotten her. *I love you, Claire —* those had been his parting words, promising hope, a future shared. But they had been empty, she knew now, and the declaration had meant nothing.

*   *   *

It was early June. A blustery southerly had been blowing for days and the sky was a perpetual shade of grey. Occasional downpours of rain laid a veil of white over the landscape, reducing Turtle Island to a dark blur. Local creeks poured coffee-coloured water onto the beach, which was littered with tree limbs. A ridge of yellow foam sat along the high tide mark.

During a break in the rain, Claire wandered down to the jetties. The mullet had been on the run and she hadn't seen David or Joe for days. Now, Joe was just docking the *Sea-spray*, securing the hull to the wharf with thick coils of rope.

'Hey, sis,' he waved at her, beckoning her over. 'Message from David.'

'Where is he?'

Joe indicated the rough water out past the island. 'Still trawling. He'll be in later.'

'What's the message?'

'Alex is coming home.'

She stopped, suddenly unable to draw breath. 'Alex?' she asked tentatively, wondering if she had misheard.

Joe wound the last of the rope and jumped down onto the planks of the wharf. 'Saturday's the day. There's a party up at the Melville's place to celebrate, and David wants you to come.'

Saturday. Four days away. How could she contain herself? She swallowed hard and grinned at Joe. 'I'd love to.'

CHAPTER 26

Claire counted the days until Alex's arrival, and never, ever, had the hours passed so slowly. And while one part of her couldn't contain her excitement at seeing him again, the other was apprehensive. Months earlier, at the railway station saying goodbye, she had felt they were two people who shared a common destiny, that her future was somehow fused with his.

There's something magical, mystical, between us.

We belong together, Claire.

I love you . . .

She imagined conversations, reasons why he hadn't written. Maybe there was a perfectly logical explanation. *I've been sick.* No, that was unlikely. David would have said something. *I've had heaps of work.* Rubbish! she thought morosely. If he'd wanted to write, he would have kept his promise, made the time. Somehow.

Now that she was employed at Parsons', Claire had the weekends to herself. On Saturday morning she washed her hair, manicured her nails, and surveyed every dress in her meagre wardrobe, undecided what to wear. They were work clothes mostly, or casual shifts worn to the beach. Perhaps she should have bought a new party frock for the occasion?

Finally she settled on a pale green linen sheath and a pair of extremely high-heeled pumps, ones that Nina was certain she would overbalance in and break a leg. At various times she went to the window that overlooked the Melville's house. David hadn't mentioned what time Alex was arriving, but Claire thought she might catch a glimpse of him. But there was nothing, until late afternoon when she noticed a strange car had pulled onto the grassy patch next to the front gate. Of Alex there was no sign.

Tentatively she dressed, butterflies threatening. She brushed her hair, pinned it up from her face and applied a smear of lipstick. Dabbed the last of the Evening in Paris behind her ears.

David met her at the Melville's front door. 'You look gorgeous,' he whispered. 'Clearly the most beautiful woman here tonight.'

'Stop that,' she smiled, secretly pleased at the compliment. She hoped Alex would think so, too.

A happy buzz of voices met her as she walked into the crowded living room. Someone thrust a drink into her hand. 'Champagne,' she whispered to Nina, taking a sip. 'What's the occasion?'

Nina shrugged. 'Haven't a clue.'

Claire's eyes searched the room for Alex. She saw him at last in the corner, talking to Maudie, and she steeled herself to walk over and say hello. Hi, she'd say casually, as though nothing had ever passed between them. But Hal was approaching, smiling. 'Glad you could make it.'

'The champagne,' she said again. 'What's the occasion?'

But Hal Melville was moving away, clapping his hands for silence. 'Well, I think that's about everyone here now. Let's get the preliminaries out of the way and then we'll eat.'

He signalled Alex forward, and Claire watched that well-loved rangy frame move across the room. He hadn't seen her yet.

Hal put his arm companionably over his eldest son's shoulder. 'We're here to welcome Alex home, but this time he didn't come alone.'

He beckoned to someone standing close. A woman moved forward, blonde and reed-thin. She was smiling. Not at Hal, but at Alex. Claire sensed a knot of apprehension building in her stomach. A throbbing had begun at the base of her throat. This was not how she had imagined the evening. She forced her attention back to Hal.

'Well, folks, I'd like you to meet Erica, Alex's new wife.'

Everyone clapped, exclaimed a response, and the noise vibrated around her. Speechless, Claire stared at Hal, wondering briefly if she had heard correctly. At that precise moment, Alex's gaze met Claire's. She gave a start, then closed her eyes for a moment against the sight of him, trying to calm herself. When she opened them again, he had turned away, talking to his father. The woman named Erica — *his wife* — had draped her arm possessively through his.

Hal raised his hand, calling for quiet again. 'That's not the only news, folks,' he went on. 'Alex has agreed to come into the medical practice with me. It's going to be a real family affair.'

'Hear! hear!' called a voice from the back of the room.

Hal smiled, focusing his attention on his older son. 'Now for the real surprise. I've decided that my wedding present to the newlyweds is this house.'

Alex stared at his father, his face pale with shock. 'No,' he began, moving forward. 'This wasn't what we planned —'

But Hal was shaking his head, waving him away. 'No arguments, now! I insist! I've bought a place in town for David and myself.' He raised his face to the remainder of the crowd. 'I know that Tea-tree Passage will be a great place for my son and his wife to raise a family, so I hope you'll make them both welcome.'

Somehow she made it through the remainder of the evening, although she felt as though she were walking through a fog. Talking to Alex again, shaking Erica's hand, congratulating them both. 'Welcome to Tea-tree Passage,' she murmured to Alex's wife, swallowing hard. Making appropriate sounds and gestures. Not letting anyone see she was crumbling inside. Pretending the evening was like any other.

Anger and grief collided sickeningly. *How dare he!* she raged inwardly. Coming back here, acting as though nothing had happened between them.

Another thought: how long had Alex known Erica? Maybe she had been waiting for him in the city while Alex stood on the railway station professing undying love to Claire? *How could he?*

The party broke up early and David suggested a drive into town, to the pub. Claire accepted, glad to be gone. She waited on the front steps while he collected the car from the lean-to garage at the rear of the house. She heard David start the car, let it idle in the dark. It was cold outside and she shivered, wishing he'd hurry. In the darkness, the front door opened behind her and someone moved down the steps. She knew it was Alex, even before he spoke.

'Claire?'

She smiled bravely, hoping he couldn't hear the heartache in her voice. 'Alex, I'm so pleased for you. Erica's lovely.'

He ignored her words. 'I need to talk to you.'

'I know you'll be very happy together,' she went on, knowing she was babbling. 'Erica will find it different here after living in the city.'

'*Claire!*' he said urgently, anguish in his voice.

Her mouth trembled and she covered her face with her hands. 'Alex, please go.'

Gently he prized her hands away, held them in his own. 'I need to explain —'

'Whatever it is, I don't want to know! Not now. Not ever!'

'I didn't know about Dad giving us this house. You have to believe that!'

As they stood confronting each other, faces outlined in the light that pooled through the windows, Claire fought back the impulse to cling to him, beg him to tell her it was all a terrible mistake. But David's car was approaching down the side of the house, sweeping headlights lighting the road. Her head jerked towards the sound. *'For God's sake, Alex! Let me go!'*

He pulled his hands away, turned, walked back up the stairs. Back to Erica and his new life, she thought miserably. Back inside the home he would share with her. She moved towards David, who waited patiently in the car, slipped in beside him and tried to slow her breathing.

'What were you talking to Alex about?' he asked, frowning in the light from the dashboard.

May God forgive her for lying. 'Nothing much. I was telling him how much I liked Erica.'

'She's a great woman, isn't she?' David enthused as the car pulled away. 'So let's go and toast their happiness, just you and I.'

The next morning Claire found her mother in the kitchen. Nina was pulling on gloves in readiness for her usual sojourn into town, to church. 'I'll be back later,' she said brightly. 'Hal's giving me a lift today.'

'I don't know why you bother,' grumbled Claire. She'd hardly slept a wink all night and a headache threatened.

'It's a comfort to me.'

'Religion never got *us* anywhere.'

'Now you sound like your father.'

She stopped, stared at her mother. 'Perhaps he was right.'

'Oh, for goodness sake, Claire. What's eating at you today?'

'It's Alex,' Lydia said with a smirk, sidling past to the breakfast table. 'Now he's married, Claire's dying of a broken heart.'

'Lydia!' Mortified, she chased her sister around the table. 'You little bitch! Take that back! Mum, tell her to stop!'

During the following week, a removalist's truck arrived to take Hal Melville's belongings to a new house in town. The next morning, a different one had taken its place.

'You should see the furniture going into Alex's,' called Lydia, almost falling out the window in excitement. 'It's all brand new. Wardrobes, dining table and chairs. Not to mention the biggest bed I've ever seen.'

Claire glared at her sister. What was Lydia trying to do? Make her jealous? She walked to the window, watching the removalists as they lugged the last of the suitcases and trunks up the front path while Erica hovered, fussing. Alex was nowhere in sight. Probably gone to town to settle into the surgery with his father, Claire surmised, leaving his wife to oversee the unpacking.

Uninvited, Lydia went over to the house with an offer of help. When she returned, hours later, she was full of information. 'Erica's dresses!' she exclaimed. 'You should see them. There's dozens and dozens. And blouses. And handbags. And ...' For a moment words failed her. 'And ... about thirty pairs of shoes.'

'Don't suppose she'll get to wear them all here,' commented Nina dryly.

Slowly, teasingly, Lydia let slip tiny bits of information, eking them out, one by one, as though she knew Claire was greedy for any morsel. Erica was twenty-two, two years younger than Alex, who had celebrated his twenty-fourth birthday on their wedding day. They had known each other for over a year. 'And they're deeply in love,' she whispered in conspiratorial tones.

A year! Although it answered none of her questions, that knowledge angered Claire. Alex had already known Erica last summer; they'd met long before he'd come to Tea-tree Passage.

Knowing Alex was so close, yet so unapproachable, Claire found that first week interminable. Days dragged. Nights were sleepless pools of darkness where her thoughts ranged through possibilities and probabilities. The following Sunday she was sitting on the sea wall, sketching, when Erica ambled down.

'Good morning. It's Claire, isn't it?'

Claire snapped the sketchbook shut and muttered a reply. Being generous to Erica wasn't part of her agenda at present.

Erica was wearing slacks and a fitted shirt, with expensive-looking loafers on her feet. A diamond stud earring glittered in each ear lobe. 'Do you like them?' she asked, seeing Claire looking at them. 'They were a wedding present from Alex.'

Claire glanced away, embarrassed at being caught staring. 'They're lovely. Bit out of my price range, though.'

'They cost an absolute fortune. Still, it's not every day a woman marries.'

'No,' admitted Claire. 'I suppose not.'

'May I see?' asked Erica, pointing to Claire's sketchbook.

Reluctantly Claire opened it at the page she had been working on. She'd roughed out a silhouette of the island, with the gulls wheeling overhead and the water, all choppy, washing at the nearest rocks.

Erica awarded the page a quick glance. 'Mmnn. Pretty,' she said without conviction. 'Alex told me you like to paint. That's a nice safe hobby.'

Nice? Safe? What did she mean by that? And why would Alex have mentioned anything about me, Claire wondered? She bit back a reply, asking instead, 'How do you like living at the Passage?'

Erica gave a conspiratorial grimace that somehow implicated Claire. 'It's okay. Nothing much to do though, is there?'

It was a criticism of sorts, and Claire bristled. 'Well, there's town, and I suppose you'll be busy with the house and shopping, things like that,' she replied defensively.

Erica stifled a yawn. 'Alex's promised to get a woman in to help with the house, so I'll have plenty of time to fill. Anyway,' she added, changing the subject, 'Alex tells me you're going steady with his brother, David.'

'We're friends.'

Erica raised one finely plucked eyebrow. 'Just friends? No marriage plans of your own? We're not about to become sisters-in-law?'

'Plenty of time for all that.'

'Someone told me you and *Alex* were friends, too.'

She'd put a slight emphasis on the word, and it held an implied warning of sorts. Back off! He's married now! Was that why Erica had followed her down to the sea wall, plying her with small talk before letting Claire know that she was aware of their past relationship and would tolerate no interference?

'Who told you that?' she asked, more sharply than she had intended.

'Lydia mentioned something about it the other day.'

Blast Lydia! Causing trouble again. She had no right to say anything. And what exactly had she told Erica? Claire shook her head. Short of asking Erica directly, she'd never know. And there was no way she'd do that.

Claire gave a wan smile. 'Alex and I are simply friends. And speaking of Alex, isn't that him coming down the track?'

Erica watched, shading her eyes against the glare as Alex ambled down. 'I was wondering where you'd gone,' he said to his wife.

'Just getting some fresh air, darling,' she smiled, slipping her hand through his arm. Claire glanced away, feeling uncomfortable. 'So I was just talking to Claire. You know she could be your sister-in-law one day?'

'Is that so?'

He gave Claire a short sharp look, or was she just imagining it? She shook her head, confused, knowing she couldn't be analytical where Alex was concerned.

Knew, instead, it was unbearable to be near him, to watch him standing next to his wife.

Quickly she gathered up her book and pencils. 'I've got to go,' she said. 'Jobs to do.' And she hurried up the path towards the house, wanting to run, to distance herself from them. Erica with her smug self-satisfaction and diamond earrings. Alex with his quizzical looks. He didn't own her and she owed him nothing. Tears smarted and she wiped them angrily away. Why, of all places, did they have to move to Tea-tree Passage?

David took her to town, to the newly opened restaurant there. He bought her a corsage which he pinned to the lapel of her dress. Sitting in the car afterwards, he turned to her, held out a small velvet-covered box.

Reluctantly she took it, opened the lid. Inside, nestled on a bed of blue satin, was the most stunning bracelet she'd ever seen.

'Why?' she asked, turning it over in her hand. 'It's not my birthday, or Christmas or —'

'Because I love you. Just say the word and I'll make it a ring, instead. I've spoken to your mother.'

'What did she say?'

'She said it's your decision.'

Your decision. What did that mean?

'For God's sake, Claire. I'd crawl across broken glass for you.'

He would, too, she knew that. She knew also that an acceptance of his proposal would somehow demean him. He was a good man who was worthy of more, who deserved the love of a woman, not the kind of half-hearted attention that was all she was capable of.

'Don't you love me, Claire? If not, just say the word and I'll disappear. A bloke can only take so much rejection.'

How well she knew! And why couldn't she come out and tell him the truth? I don't love you. I love your brother, though that's a hopeless self-destructive obsession, something I'll never learn to live with. And staying here, being part of this place will only tear me to shreds too.

'I'm too young,' she said instead, hating herself.

'Almost nineteen. My mother had already had Alex by the same age.'

She placed the bracelet back in the box. 'I'm not your mother, and I can't accept this.'

'Claire, please. We're so right for each other. You, me. Belonging here. Bringing up our children.'

'There's going to be another war, that's what the newspapers say. I don't think this is the right time for marriage, bringing babies into the world. There's too much unrest.'

David started the car and they drove home in silence, the bracelet in its box on the seat between them. 'I love you, Claire, but I can't wait forever,' he said as he pulled the car to a halt at the front of her house. 'And I won't ask you again. You tell me when you're ready, all right.'

She nodded. 'Goodnight, David.'

* * *

Alex let himself into the darkened house. He was late, he knew, but not late enough for Erica to have taken herself to bed. Mrs Jamieson's first baby hadn't been due for several weeks and it had been touch and go for a few hours, trying to delay the labour and then, when it became obvious the child was determined to arrive early, attending to the mother.

It had been a difficult delivery and, although he felt physically drained, now he experienced a kind of sustained elation. Hearing that first squall, seeing the tiny limbs move — the miracle of childbirth never ceased to fascinate him. And although they hadn't really discussed it, hopefully it wouldn't be long before he and Erica had a child of their own.

He dumped his bag on the hall table, glancing into the living room. She was sitting in an armchair there, visible from the light of a single table lamp. Sitting staring at him, tapping her fingernails on the wooden chair arm.

'Hello, darling.'

She gave no return smile, simply sat there, her face an unreadable mask. 'Where have you been?'

'I'm sorry I'm late. Had a bit of an emergency —'

Her voice rose an octave. 'You could have let me know!'

'I'm sorry, there wasn't a telephone —'

'Dinner's ruined.'

'We'll eat it, anyway,' he soothed, walking towards her, taking her hand and pulling her to her feet. 'Come on, let's not argue. The meal's not important. I love you.'

'It's important to me.'

Afterwards, as she stood before the mirror in the bedroom, brushing her hair, he came up behind her, cupping his palms around her small breasts.

'Don't!' she snapped, jerking away. 'I'm too tired.'

He stood, not knowing what to do or say. He hated arguments and dissension, knowing she was punishing him in the worst possible way. 'Come on, Erica, be reasonable. I'm doing the best I can.'

She threw her hands up in mock defeat. 'I know, I know. A doctor always puts his patients first.'

'It's my job. I tried to tell you what it would be like before we married.'

'Well, I didn't imagine it would be like *this*.'

Suddenly she sagged, the fight going out of her. She wound her arms around his neck, planting kisses seductively along his jawline. 'Don't be angry with me.'

'I'm not angry. I just happen to think you're being unreasonable.'

'Of course I am. Unreasonable. Hideously jealous. Possessive. I don't want to share you with anyone, especially patients who keep you out till all hours. I want to spend every minute with you. Alone. Making love.'

The abrupt turnaround baffled him. 'You just said you were too tired.'

'I changed my mind.'

She led him to the bed, compliant and indulgent. She had obviously dismissed her earlier irritation and was eager to please, attending to his needs as well as her own. Though the argument had dissipated, he was left with a niggling feeling that she was playing along with him, but for what?

He cast the thought aside and gave himself wholly to the pleasure. Brush of mouth along her throat. The sweet, sweet taste of her. Moving as one, flesh seared together. Rise and fall. Beautiful explosive dance. Never ever had he felt so whole, so joined to another. He came then, unable to control his aching body, shuddering into her with a feeling akin to grief.

Later he said: 'I didn't tell you where I was tonight.'

'No,' she said, nuzzling his ear, one hand moving across the matt of hair on his belly. 'Tell me, darling.'

'Mrs Jamieson's. Her baby came early. Erica, it's the most wonderful experience, watching the birth of a child, holding a tiny life in your hands.' His own hand moved down, kneading the taut skin on her belly. 'There's something magical about a pregnant woman. And I can just see you, big-bellied, carrying our child.'

She reared back as though stung, knocking his hand away. 'Come on, Alex. I'm certainly not ready to have a baby. Horrid, smelly little creatures. Anyway, you're taking care of all that.'

Ignoring her, he grazed his mouth over her breast, feeling the rise and fall of her chest. 'That's what marriage is all about. Loving each other, having children.'

'But I want to *live* first. When do you get holidays? Let's plan a little trip away.'

He lay there in the dark, awake long after his wife slept, wondering, not for the first time, if he had done the right thing bringing her here to Tea-tree Passage. Compared to the city, it was tranquil but secluded, shuffling along at its own pace. Though he himself was content to be here, he was concerned for Erica. Apart from Claire, who was a few years younger, there were no other women here his wife's age.

Claire: his thoughts turned to her, as they invariably did. He remembered her on the night of his return, looking beautiful in that pale green dress, her hair pulled up, making her look older than her years. He had felt a stab of ... What? he wondered now, trying to put a name to the emotion. Regret at not pursuing their relationship. Guilt, for being so easily led towards Erica. He had wanted to explain his actions to her but she had been so ... so ... He searched his mind again. Confused. Upset? Angry? That was the word. She'd been *angry*. Understandably so.

Erica stirred beside him and he brushed a strand of hair from her face. No use thinking of the past. The future: that was the important consideration now. He and Erica, the children they would one day have. It had been a sudden and dramatic change, moving here, and he'd have to ease her into small-town life more slowly. Perhaps she was right. Having a holiday to look forward to would allay some of her misgivings. On Monday he would send away for some brochures. Somewhere further north. One of the islands. Surprise her.

'Dull little backwater,' Erica confided to Maudie, weeks later. 'There's no excitement in Tea-tree Passage.'

'We make our own fun. Always have.'

Erica yawned, looking bored. 'I think I'm going to hate living here.'

'Too late now. You should have thought of that before you agreed to come,' replied Maudie bluntly.

'I thought being with Alex was all that mattered. But you know what doctors are like: all work and no play.'

Maudie eyed Erica's slim waist. 'Perhaps you need a baby to occupy you. No time to get bored then.'

'A baby! Ouch!'

'Nothing wrong with having kids. Would've had a whole bunch myself if I could. Me innards,' she added, patting her ample stomach. 'Something not right there.'

'I don't want a baby. I want a bit of excitement in my life. Time enough for children later.'

'She won't stay long,' Maudie told Nina later. 'She's a city girl, born and bred.'

'Don't you think you're being a little unfair?' offered Nina, arranging the cups and saucers for afternoon tea. There were a few women expected. 'Give the girl a chance to get to know us. If she loves Alex, she'll settle.'

'Pshaw!' Maudie gave a derisive snort. 'She's not interested in us, that one! The only thing Erica loves is money. Thinks she can live quite well on a doctor's salary.'

'For goodness sake, Maudie! Just try and be sociable to the girl.'

'I'll be the perfect guest.'

Maudie stood back and admired Nina's handiwork: she really had a way of making things look nice. One of Frank's mother's lace throw-overs covered the traymobile. The teapot and milk jug — complete with glass-beaded cover — sat on the timber tray. There were plates of tiny wafer-thin sandwiches and scones, with pots of jam and cream. Maudie's own contribution had been a sponge cake — light as a feather, even if she said so herself.

The afternoon passed quickly, sandwiches, cake and cups of tea being consumed with gusto. Hal Melville called past. 'Can't seem to stay away. I miss this old place,' he said to Maudie, and they invited him in for a cuppa. Nina turned the radio on. There was, as usual, talk of war.

They were washing-up when the announcement came on the wireless. 'Sshh,' hushed Claire. 'Listen.'

From amongst the static and crackle came the words, sending a chill into Maudie's heart as they gathered around the wireless. It was the Prime Minister, Menzies. 'Fellow Australians, it is my melancholy duty to inform you officially that, in consequence of the persistence of Germany in her invasion of Poland, Great Britain has declared war upon her and that, as a result, Australia is also at war.'

Nina sank into the nearest chair. 'Dear God, no,' she said, holding a hand over her heart.

Later, at dusk, Nina walked with Hal Melville down to the sea wall, a nauseous feeling rumbling in her stomach. They sat there, on the rocky ledge, dangling their feet over the side. The tide was on the rise. She could see the water inching along the sand with each successive wave.

It was the last war happening all over again. 'Remember last time?' she said.

Hal nodded. 'Last time,' he mused. 'I was lucky. The Army medical corps was relatively safe compared to the soldiers on the front lines.'

'Bill dead at Pozières. Your brother Paddy at Mons. Jimmy missing a leg. What a waste!'

'Pozières. Mons. I've never been there, but I feel I know those places.'

Nina nodded, agreeing. 'It's a sort of association. Names bringing it all back. By the way, how is Jimmy? I hear he got married?'

'To a widow with two kiddies. She's a good woman but he can't settle, poor sod. Bloody hard getting about with one leg. No-one wants to employ him.'

The intervening years telescoped away. 'I remember the war as though it were yesterday: the parties, the dances. Afterwards everyone was gone. Scattered or dead. We didn't feel much like celebrating. Will it be like that again?'

Hal shrugged. 'God forbid. You were lucky, though. Frank came back.'

She stared at him through the gloom, closed her eyes for a moment against the memory — screen door wheezing shut, Frank standing there. *Nina*? The name weaving towards her through the hot still air.

Hal's arm was on hers. 'Nina? Are you all right?'

She nodded, found her voice. 'It wasn't Frank who came home,' she said sadly, 'but someone else. War changes people, makes strong men weak. And it'll be our sons who are affected this time. Alex and David. Joe.'

Hal was silent, looking out over the water, his face silhouetted in the light from a pale moon that had risen over the waves. Nina touched him lightly on the shoulder. 'Say a prayer tonight, Hal.'

'What shall I pray for?'

'Please God, we get this war over with quickly.'

PART FIVE

Shifting Sands

Brisbane

1940

CHAPTER 27

Prime Minister Menzies called for two thousand infantry volunteers to be trained under the command of Major-General Thomas Blamey. Munitions factories were placed on wartime alert, and defence personnel took up strategic stations around the countryside. Newspaper headlines screamed, *War*! *War*! *War*!

In Tea-tree Passage, Christmas and New Year came and went without the customary festive fuss. Suddenly it was January, 1940. The boat carrying soldiers of the Second Imperial Force — an advance guard of the Sixth Division — steamed out of Sydney Harbour as crowds on the nearby headlands waved farewell. Claire heard it all on the wireless, solemn voices proclaiming what she already knew; the war was changing all that was safe and familiar.

The war also provided the perfect opportunity to escape. Life at Tea-tree Passage had become unbearable. Seeing Alex and his wife together, trying to hide her feelings from David — it had all become too much of a strain. As soon as calls came for women to help the war effort, she told her mother she was leaving.

'Where will you go?'

'Brisbane.' Claire glanced away, unable to bear the anguished look on her mother's face. 'It's not too far away,' she added, already consumed with guilt.

'It's far enough.'

'You could come down sometimes, stay with me.'

Nina sighed, her mouth set. Claire knew she hated the war and everything that went with it. 'We won't be a proper family any more.'

'I feel useless here. In the city I can do something worthwhile.' Excuses. Saying anything to escape.

Maudie bought her a new suitcase. 'A sort of going-away present, if you like,' she said. 'I'll miss you, Claire. You were always my favourite.'

'As a great-aunt, you're supposed to be unbiased,' Claire replied with a grin. 'But thanks for the case. Mum's old ones are only fit for the dump.'

She packed carefully, layering her clothes, a few treasured photographs, sketchbook and paints. Said goodbye to David.

'I'll miss you, Claire. Are you sure you won't change your mind and stay?'

She shook her head. 'The world awaits. Come and join me.' Platitudes. Saying the right thing. Hoping he wouldn't follow. She wasn't ready for that.

'I might just do that.'

He took her to the station and she was reminded of that other time, when Alex had gone. She knew what it had been like to be left behind, forgotten. But this time she was the one leaving.

'Keep in touch, Claire. Write as often as you can. And if things don't work out then I'll be here, waiting for you.'

She remembered the scene later as a series of snapshots — faces and gestures printed indelibly on her mind. David carrying her bag into the carriage. Grey overcast sky threatening rain. Her mother holding a handkerchief to her mouth which was pulled into an odd uncontrollable shape, trying to stem the tears. Then, as the train pulled from the platform, drops of rain rolled down the glass, obscuring everything outside behind a veil of white.

Crowded with service personnel, the train barely crawled along. The carriages were old and decrepit, and had obviously been brought from retirement. The journey was stop-start, with tedious hours spent waiting at sidings for crowded northbound troop trains to pass. The soldier sitting beside Claire tried to strike up a conversation. He was young and fresh-faced, probably not long out of school, and made her think of Joe. 'What's a nice girl doing in a place like this?'

'I'm going to Brisbane.'

'Been away from home before?'

She shook her head. 'No. This is the first time. Is it so obvious?'

He laughed and offered her a cigarette, which she refused. 'So what made you leave home?'

'I'm going to help with the war effort.'

Later she picked up her book, tried to read, but couldn't settle. Her mind was distracted, randomly flitting from one idea to another. She stared pensively out the window and wondered, not for the first time, precisely what had driven her away.

She was running, she knew that. Running from Alex and David, from the predictability of her life. Running from the safety of Tea-tree Passage. The decision to leave, made hastily, was now weighing heavily. She had left her family and friends and was heading to a place where she knew no-one. Had she done the right thing?

'You won't regret it,' said the soldier, as though reading her mind. 'I remember what it was like, the first time I went away. I was scared but, at the same time, excited. And I can remember thinking: this is *my* life.'

My life. She liked the sound of that. It offered a sense of freedom, of pleasing herself, a feeling of not being bound by any one person or place. For the first time she understood how her father had felt, leaving home during those last months before his death, putting worries and responsibilities behind him.

The trip took almost three days. There were cold cups of coffee and bland meals from station refreshment rooms. Nights were spent curled on the seat under a blanket. People came and went from the carriage, providing fleeting encounters with travellers she knew she'd never meet again. Yet nothing could dampen that feeling of excitement. *My life*: the words had continued in her head long after the soldier had alighted at some godforsaken siding.

On that last morning she woke, wiped her hand across the smeared window and stared at the city outskirts. She could see farms and green valleys, and roads that wound down hillsides like lethargic snakes around the occasional cluster of houses. The train seemed to be gathering speed, as though eager to reach its destination.

She picked her way down the corridor, across the jumble of sleeping bodies on the floor, to the lavatory at the opposite end of the carriage. Peed, then stared at herself in the fly-speckled mirror. Her face was unnaturally pale and dark circles ringed her eyes — a legacy of scant sleep. Her hair was an unmanageable tangle. Carefully she ran a comb through it, teasing out the knots, smoothed the creases in her skirt and wished long and hard for a bath.

Roads ran alongside the railway line now. Buildings became less flung out. Row upon row of houses blended together, roofs blurring into one solid colour. At Roma Street Station, the train shuffled to a halt. Claire heard the sounds of footsteps running alongside and doors being flung open. Passengers spilled onto the platform in one solid mass, glad to escape the confines of the carriages. Eagerly she swung her suitcase from the overhead luggage rack and stumbled after them.

As the crowd surged past, she stood on the footpath at the entrance to the station. What to do first? Somewhere to stay was a priority, but a job was equally important. Someone gave her directions to the Manpower office and she lugged her suitcase onto a passing tram.

The interview was brief.

'What experience do you have?'

'Office skills. Typing.'

'Shorthand?'

'Yes.'

'Excellent. The war office is looking for someone. I'll send you over.'

She was given an address on a piece of paper and a taxi took her to another building in the centre of the city. The second interview was longer, more in-depth.

'This job, it's war work. Classified. No discussing it with anyone. Remember, idle tongues —'

'Cost lives,' Claire interjected with a smile. 'I know all the protocol. I'm trustworthy and I'll be an asset to your organisation.'

'Very well, then,' the woman said, snapping her book shut. 'When can you start? We're awfully short-staffed and could do with someone right away.'

'Now?'

'That's the general idea.'

Not waiting for an answer, the woman beckoned one of the typists from behind the glass doors of her office. A young woman, not much older than Claire, looked up, pushed her chair back and came towards them. She was tall and fair-skinned, with red hair and a face liberally sprinkled with freckles.

'This is Kathryn,' the older woman said. 'You'll be working together. Would you like to show Claire around?'

Kathryn smiled and steered Claire in the direction of the far door. 'It's almost morning-tea time and you look famished. We'll eat first, then I'll take you on the grand tour. And, by the way, if you call me Kathryn, I'll scream. It's Kath. Okay?'

'Sounds fine by me.'

In the canteen Kath ordered a large plate of sandwiches and a pot of tea. 'So where do you live?' she asked between mouthfuls.

Claire was reminded of her suitcase waiting with the lobby attendant downstairs. 'Nowhere yet. I've only just arrived. Thought I'd find something today, get settled in.'

'There's a spare room at the boarding house where I'm staying. One of the other girls — the one whose job you're taking — got pregnant and left. As far as I know, the room's still vacant.'

'Why are you staying at a boarding house?' asked Claire, eyeing the wedding ring on Kath's finger.

'My old man's away, up north,' she said. 'So it seemed silly to rent a house just for one. No use wasting money. We're saving for a place of our own, when this whole rotten war's over.'

'So what's the boarding house like?'

'It's nothing fancy, but the rent's cheap. Girls only: no blokes allowed past the downstairs lounge. The locals call it "The Nunnery". There's a dining room although the food's awful.' She pushed the almost-empty plate towards Claire and nodded towards the offices on the floor above. 'Here, have another sandwich. You'll need it, before we go back up there.'

The boarding house turned out to be in a nearby working-class suburb, a two-pence tram ride from the office. There was a general store on one nearby corner and a pub on the other. The building was a rambling affair that straddled two house blocks. It was low and clung to the ground, and the front yard was bare of trees except for a huge plumbago that dropped a carpet of purple on the path.

Claire lugged her suitcase into the room shown. It was austere, unfurnished except for a bed, a wardrobe and a small dressing-table. The view from the window was the brick wall of the house next door.

'I know it's not much, but you can add your own touches, pretty it up,' encouraged Kath, giving Claire a quick hug. 'Oh, I'm so looking forward to your being here. It'll liven the place no end.'

'Hey, over here!'

Joe waved at Jane as she made her way down the track towards the jetty, admiring her neat figure and swinging hips as she walked, and the mop of chestnut hair. She was wearing a pair of shorts, very tight, and a sleeveless cotton blouse, the hem of which she'd tied in a knot at her midriff, revealing brown skin.

He'd met her the previous Friday afternoon when he'd shown up at Parsons' solicitors. It had been Claire's last day at work before heading off to the city.

'I'm in town, delivering the fish for David if you'd like a lift home,' he'd said to Claire, poking his head around the office door. 'It's only the smelly old truck, but it'll save pedalling. You can throw your bike in the back.'

'Lovely. Oh, Jane, this is Joe, my brother.'

A young woman stepped forward, holding out her hand. 'Hello,' she'd said brightly, and her handshake was firm and confident.

'Jane's taking over my job. Now, if you'll just excuse me for a minute, I'm off to the loo.'

'Haven't seen you around before,' he'd said when Claire had gone.

'I'm new in town. My parents own a place further back up in the hills. An orchard. Half an hour's drive away.'

'Where are you staying?'

'I've a little flat. Bedsitter, really. Too small to swing the proverbial cat, but it's fine for one.'

'Boyfriend?'

She laughed, and the sound was musical. 'What's with the inquisition?'

'Well, I don't want some bloke chasing after me if I ask you out.'

'Would you?'

'Would I what?'

'Ask me out.' She stared unblinkingly into his eyes, as though daring him.

'I might.'

She smiled, challengingly, revealing a perfect set of white teeth. 'Well, go on, then.'

They'd made a date: the following afternoon at the pub. Sitting in the beer garden on that warm Saturday, they'd talked and talked, not realising the time. It had been late when they left, dark, and they'd wandered down to the cafe and bought fish and chips. Jane had spread them out on the grass in the park and they had eaten quickly, blowing on the slivers of hot potato. Laughing.

Later he couldn't remember what had led them to the grassy hollow behind the bandstand. Had she suggested it? And, if so, how? He couldn't remember the words. Hadn't needed words, anyway. He had only known that it felt right, Jane's taut willing body beneath his. He had felt as though he belonged there, her curves fitting snugly into the contours of his own, her body arching under his, determining their rhythm. And later, when it was all over, she hadn't made him feel awkward or embarrassed, although he knew his own skills had been lacking.

'You're supposed to start apologising now,' she'd said, licking her tongue along his neck. 'Telling me it was all a big mistake, but you still respect me.'

Vehemently. 'Of course I still respect you! Why wouldn't I?'

'It's a joke, silly,' she had chided gently. 'That's what blokes do. Talk a girl into having sex, then run a mile when it's all over.'

'I'm not like that.'

'No, I don't suppose you are.'

He was reminded later of his father and Mim in that huge echoing house, all those years ago. He remembered walking down the hallway, opening the door, seeing them there. He hadn't understood at the time, but now he knew what had driven them together, that feeling of need and desire.

He blinked in the bright sunshine, dragging his mind from the past. Now, watching as she walked towards him, that same feeling of wonderment returned. Jane! Liking him, plain old Joe Carmody the fisherman.

She climbed down the ladder at the side of the jetty and ran along the length of deck towards him, laughing. Wrapping her arms around his neck, she kissed him, and he felt that same old hardening in his groin. 'I missed you.'

'We saw each other last night. And the night before that.'

'I know. And the night before that. And all the hours in between, I missed you.'

Joe untangled himself from her embrace and slung the ropes away. The boat drifted from the jetty, small waves thumping against the hull. He went to move up into the engine house to start the motor and Jane gave him a knowing smile. 'I'll be down below, waiting. Come down when we get out past the island.'

Claire settled easily into the work. The hours were long and hard, typing letters and memos. As she had been initially warned, the contents were classified, so she blocked her mind to the words, not wanting to know.

Weekends with Kath were fun. They went out to the pubs, the pictures, walks in the park. Kath's life was fractured, compartmentalised by the letters that arrived irregularly from her husband who was somewhere 'up north'.

'Don't you want to know where he is?' Claire asked.

'It's best not to. I'd only worry more.'

Doubtfully. 'I suppose so.'

'What about you, Claire? Is there a boyfriend?'

'Sort of.'

'What sort of answer is that? Either he is or he isn't.'

'We've been friends for years but I'm not sure I want to marry him, if that's what you mean.'

'Is there someone else, then?'

A sudden image of Alex rose up, overwhelming her. Lanky frame, sandy hair flopping over his forehead. Blue eyes with tiny creases on the outer edge. 'No!' she said quickly, closing her mind against the recollection. 'There's no-one.'

She lay in bed at night, listening to the muted sound of the traffic, the air-raid sirens. Remembered the quiet lapping of water at Tea-tree Passage, the cry of a lone gull, Nina moving about the kitchen late at night, the sound of the oven door opening and the aroma of baking bread — images and smells and sounds jostling randomly against one another, taking her back, not forward.

She tried harder to fit into city life. 'I can't go back!' she told herself. 'I simply can't!'

The months passed. She wrote home regularly, neat condensed letters to her mother and David that gave little indication of the homesickness she felt. Nina's replies came quickly. Lydia was counting the months until she finished school. Joe was doing well on the boats. Did Claire know a girl named Jane who worked at Parsons? She and Joe had been keeping company.

Keeping company. Claire smiled at the quaint phrase.

David's letters were full of family news, fishing. I miss you, he wrote. When are you coming home?

She was required to work back two nights a week. It was strange coming onto the roads after dark. The ongoing blackouts meant no streetlights, and bicycle and car lights had to be hooded. One of the men in the office always escorted the girls to the tram stop.

She came downstairs one night to find David waiting in the lobby. He was wearing a khaki uniform, the implication of which she realised immediately.

'You've joined up?' she said, kissing him.

'Catalina Squadron. Monoplane flying boats,' he went on, in response to her raised eyebrows. 'Wing span about one hundred and forty feet. Two engines. Crew of eight.'

'Okay, okay,' she laughed, raising her hands in a gesture of surrender. 'I believe you. I just hate to think of you getting involved in this wretched war.'

'Don't worry, we won't be in the thick of it. The Cats aren't fighter planes. They're so slow they're the only planes to get hit from behind by birds. We'll be doing coast-watching mostly, up north, and some air-sea rescue work.'

'You didn't have to join up. Fishing's a protected industry. What about the boats?'

David shrugged. 'Too much of a struggle, what with the fuel rationing. Anyway, Joe was keen to take over, and I know they'll be in good hands.'

They were on the footpath now. 'Have you eaten?' Claire asked, pulling on her coat. 'I'm starving, and I've missed dinner back at the boarding house.'

They found a cafe where they had meat and vegetables, bread and a pot of tea for two shillings and sixpence each. Between mouthfuls, they traded news.

'Joe has a girlfriend.'

'Mum wrote and told me. What's Jane like? I didn't get to know her before I left.'

'Nice. Pretty. They seem fairly keen on each other.'

'And Lydia's itching to leave school.'

David gave a chuckle. 'Lydia can't wait to get on with her life. Your Mum's going to have her hands full there. She organised a party for her seventeenth birthday.'

'I know. She told me.'

'Did she tell you all the guests were boys?'

Claire laughed. 'No.'

'Maudie isn't well. Dad says it's her heart. Your Mum's been looking after her.'

'She's getting on, the poor thing.' Then, needing desperately to know: 'How are Alex and Erica?'

He was silent for a moment, as though organising thoughts into words. 'I sometimes get the impression that she's unhappy.'

'Why do you say that?'

He shrugged. 'Don't know, really. It's just an impression, that's all.'

He was, Claire thought, the most amiable man, and looked quite handsome sitting there in his freshly pressed shirt and trousers. Even some of the other women diners, she saw, had noticed him.

The meal finished, he walked her back to the boarding house. 'I'd ask you in but it's fairly awful. No men allowed past the lounge.'

'I've got to get back myself. By the way, it's only a few months until Christmas. Are you going home?'

Was she? Hadn't thought about it really, but the news of Maudie's ill health concerned her. How was Nina coping? And that remark of David's. *Erica unhappy?* Claire needed to see for herself. If there were a chance that the marriage might be over ...

'I'll see if I can wrangle some leave,' she said, taking a deep breath.

She and David managed to board the same train. It was night-time and they sat in the crowded carriage opposite each other, knees touching. The air was dense, oppressive, with rain threatening. After a while, Claire put down her book and walked out into the corridor.

She threw open a window and let the warm air brush past her face, blowing her hair around. Stood there, rocking slightly with the movement of the carriage, watching the scenery drag by: dark humps of hills and trees, the lights of an occasional house. Cinders spewed along the side of the track like fireflies.

There was a movement behind her and she turned. It was David.

'Claire?'

He gathered her into his arms, crushing her against his chest. 'I've missed this. Missed you.'

Lightly. 'Me too.'

He released her, stood looking at her for one long moment. Then he bent his head and kissed her — long hard kisses that bruised her mouth — urgently, like a man too long denied.

'I know I said I wouldn't ask again, but I love you, Claire. For God's sake, marry me!'

She stared at him through the gloom. 'I'm not ready.'

'When will you be? I can't wait forever!'

There was an anguished tone to his voice, a hint of desperation. Suddenly she hated herself. Why not give in? He was a wonderful man. Courteous. Loving. She could do a lot worse than marry David.

Because I don't love him.

The words flew at her, battering themselves mercilessly against the logic of her thoughts, rendering her momentarily speechless. Wounding words. Soul-destroying and sharp, like tiny knives cutting into the very core of her. She'd lie, rather than say them. *Couldn't* say them. *Couldn't! Couldn't! Couldn't!*

'I don't know.'

'Why are you stalling?'

Because I'm hoping Alex will tell me his marriage is over, that he's made a mistake.

'I'm not waiting around forever, Claire. A man's got pride.'

The Christmas Day celebrations were held at Alex and Erica's. It was the first time Claire had been in the house since Hal had moved out. Despondently she tried not to stare at the expensive furniture, the lovely drapes.

'Put your bag in on the bed,' said Alex, and she blocked out the thought of the two of them there, Alex holding his wife in his arms, bodies intertwined, loving each other the way she wanted to be loved.

Erica was pale and untalkative, barely saying hello to Claire. 'What's wrong with her?' she asked Nina.

'Erica's pregnant. She and Alex are going to be a proper family now. Only a few of us know. They're going to announce it after lunch.'

'That'll be lovely,' said Claire automatically, telling her mother the sentiments she knew she wanted to hear. She smiled, feigning happiness, heedless of the lie. Couldn't, *wouldn't*, let anyone see how upset she felt.

'A new Melville baby at Tea-tree Passage. What a pity Alex's mother isn't alive to share in this,' Nina went on, oblivious to Claire's distress.

So Alex and Erica were to be parents. Nina's words echoed inside her head and she felt a surge of anger. Anger at herself, her own naivety. She had to face the truth. There was never any likelihood of a relationship with Alex, hadn't been for a long time. Yet it had taken the news of the child to make her realise that. No use waiting around for some miracle that might release him; she had to get on with her own life.

She walked towards the window. From her vantage point, she could see David down near the jetty. He was standing still, hands in his pockets, staring out over the water. Consciously, painfully, she dragged her mind past the conversation with her mother. After Christmas, back in the city, what then? She had already lost Alex. What if she lost David, too? Perhaps he'd tire of waiting for her, meet someone else?

Mentally she ticked off the positives. He loved her. He was honest and decent. And a marriage didn't have to be all fireworks and breathlessness, did it? Familiarity and being comfortable with one another had to count for something, and maybe the breathlessness faded to that, anyway, over time. Perhaps she and David had simply skipped that initial stage, settled into relaxed closeness, instead.

Mind made up, she set off along the track towards him. Running. Hair flying out behind her. 'David!'

He turned towards her and caught her within his grasp. 'What's wrong?'

She took one of his hands in hers, brought it to her mouth. The hand of a working man, rough, calloused by the nets and ropes.

'About what you asked me,' she said.

He looked puzzled.

'About getting married,' she reminded him. 'The answer's yes.'

He laughed and swung her around. 'Tell me again.'

'Yes! Yes! Yes! A thousand times yes!'

'I love you, Claire. And I can't wait to tell everyone.'

'Let's wait until after dinner,' she cautioned. 'It'll be our secret. We'll surprise our families then.'

Erica had excelled herself, Claire thought, looking at the table decorations. Matching tablecloth and napkins. The best crockery and cutlery. Wine. Christmas carols playing on the gramophone.

After the meal was eaten, David rose from the table, banging for quiet with a spoon. 'Claire and I have an announcement to make.'

'Sshh,' hushed Maudie. 'Let David speak.'

'Claire's agreed to marry me.'

There was a general uproar and murmurs of approval. Hal slapped David on the back. 'About time, son.'

Claire glanced up to see Alex frowning at her. For one brief second, their eyes met; then he glanced away and rose to his feet. 'I'd like to propose a toast,' he said, raising his glass in salute. 'To my brother and Claire.'

Afterwards he cornered her in the kitchen. 'Welcome to the family, Claire. It's about time.'

'Thanks.'

'When's the big day?'

'We haven't decided. Soon, I suppose.'

Someone had a camera and they all took it in turns to have their photographs taken. David and Claire first, of course. Then the host and hostess: Alex with his arm around his wife's shoulders; Erica smiling uncertainly into the camera lens.

After tea, as soon as they could, David and Claire escaped. He slung his arm around her waist as they made their way across the grassy dunes. Behind them, the music tumbled into the night air, spilling and rushing behind them.

'Some news, eh?' David laughed as he lifted a wisp of dark hair from her cheek. 'That stopped them all in their tracks.'

His lips brushed her shoulders and she thought of Alex and Erica earlier, the way he had held his wife, and thought she might die from wanting him so much. *Stop it*, she told herself angrily. *It can't ever be.*

She let David kiss her and run his hand inside her blouse. Fingers exploring, teasing. But all the while it was Alex's face she saw, Alex's hands she felt. Would the nightmare ever go away?

It wasn't until later, after she was in bed, that she realised neither Alex nor Erica had mentioned the baby.

'Why don't you wait until after the war, till you both come home?' Nina said the following morning.

'Why?'

'It's silly, that's all. Rushing into it.'

'We're not rushing.'

'You are.'

Brutally she retorted, 'Like you and Dad?'

Nina closed her eyes for a minute and, when she opened them again, they were filled with unshed tears. 'Yes,' she said simply.

'It's not like that.' Claire walked across the room and sat on the settee, her mouth firm and unyielding. '*We're* not like that.' Then. 'Did you love him?'

Nina did not reply, just stared at her daughter.

'Well,' demanded Clare, 'did you?'

Nina shrugged. 'It was different then. The war, the uncertainty: we did things that normally we wouldn't have entertained the thought of. Thinking back, I scarcely knew your father. It was so hurried, so rushed. Get married before —'

'I said, "did you love him"?'

Nina was silent for a moment and, when her voice finally came, it was soft, almost inaudible. 'I thought I did, at the time.'

'And later?'

'Claire!'

'I need to know!'

'Your father came back from the war a ... a different man. War changed him. Afterwards he could never really relate to normal life again. But we made the best of it. He tried to be a good father —'

'Drunk!' she interrupted. 'He was always drunk.'

'No! Not always!'

'It seemed like that,' replied Claire defensively. 'All I remember were the nights when he came lurching home along that stinking alleyway, and you saying, "Go to him, Claire, there's a good girl. Fetch Daddy his tea." And you and Joe and Lydia hiding in the bedroom. And I'd go, do what you told me to, and I'd be shaking so much I'd almost drop the plate.'

Her mother seemed to sag under the accusation. 'I didn't know.' Then she added. 'It was the only way I knew. He didn't *hit* you.'

Slowly. 'No, he never hit me. Not physically. But him standing there, swaying, babbling on and on like a lunatic — it was like a slap in the face.'

'He loved you, Claire. In his own funny way, he loved you.'

They were opening old wounds, hurts that had been festering away for years, yet not resolving anything. You could go on like this forever, Claire thought, round and round. 'I'm not you,' she insisted, wanting the conversation to be over. 'And David is not my father. We're different people and these are different times. We'll make it work.'

'Do you love him?'

It was Claire's turn to be silent. She stood, staring out the window towards the beach. Water lapped at the sand. A lone gull pecked along the waterline. She thought of Alex and Erica, heard her mother's words. *Erica's pregnant. She and Alex are going to be a proper family now.* Alex had his own life, a wife and soon a child. She had to let go, move on. No use hanging on to the past. And maybe, with David, she could do that.

Nina walked towards her daughter, placing a hand on each of Claire's shoulders. 'I know why you're doing this. It's because of Alex, isn't it?'

Was she that transparent? Claire swung guiltily around, sending her mother slightly off balance. 'Don't be bloody stupid! What's Alex got to do with this?'

Nina stepped back. 'You're my daughter and I can see things. Okay, go ahead and marry David. And if that's what you really want, then you have my blessing. Just be certain you're doing it for the right reasons. I don't want you making a mistake, and David doesn't deserve to be second best.'

'Mother!'

Nina's face was impassive. 'I've said my piece, for whatever good it's done, and I'll never speak of it again.'

CHAPTER 28

February in the city was hot and humid, and scarcely a breeze blew. Claire found herself thinking longingly of the Passage and the blue-green ocean, wishing she were back under the tea-trees where she belonged.

David wrangled two days' leave and they scoured the windows of the local jewellery stores, finally settling on a simple solitaire diamond ring. Afterwards they went to the movies: Bette Davis and Charles Boyer in *All This And Heaven Too*. There was a stale smell in the theatre, an odour of chocolate and popcorn and despair. In the noisy half-dark interval before the movie started, he put the ring on her finger.

'There. It's official. Now all we have to do is set a date.'

'I don't know when I can get time off. What about you? When's your next leave due?'

'Who knows? It could be months.'

Nothing was resolved. The curtain went up and they sat through the newsreels, Claire aware of the solid comfort of his arm around her shoulders.

They came out of the theatre to a dark sky threatening rain. 'What time do you have to be back in barracks?' she asked.

David glanced at his watch. 'Half an hour. I'll have to run.'

'Till next time, then?'

'I wish it didn't have to be like this. I want it to be us. You and me. No timetables. No war. Nothing keeping us apart.'

He kissed her at the front door, hungry kisses that demanded something she was unable to give. It all seemed unreal. She was engaged to be married; the ring on her finger bore witness to that. Yet there was no permanence, no stability about their relationship. Hurried meetings. Rushed goodbyes. Not knowing when they'd see each other again. How could they make plans?

She undressed and climbed into bed, lay rigid, listening to the city noises: traffic, blare of car horns, someone laughing in the corridor outside. Sleep seemed miles away. She went over in minute detail everything that had happened in the last two days. Dissected phrases and sentences. Tried to remember David as she had seen him last, racing along the road towards the tram stop. And now, long after he had gone, she could still feel the pressure of his mouth on hers, and the weight of responsibility of her commitments.

Claire marked the passing days on a calendar hung on the back of her door. Slowly the months dissolved into each other, no days standing out as separate and distinct from the next. Summer became autumn and leaves began to fall in the gutters, swept along by cool winds that raced along the river. Work kept her busy. Kath's husband Tom had been sent to Singapore and Kath wasn't taking it well. So, in their meagre amount of spare time, the two of them had lunch at little out-of-the-way restaurants and saw every movie available, trying to forget, if just for a few hours, that there was a war on and everyone's lives were in turmoil.

'Anything,' as Kath said 'to help fill in the hours and take my mind off what might be happening up north.'

They had friendly arguments over who was the better actor. Kath preferred Clark Gable and Robert Taylor. Claire thought no-one could compare to Gary Cooper.

Claire tried desperately to put Tea-tree Passage, and all that had happened there, behind her. It was in the past, and she had moved on. Alex had made other choices and she had to live with that. Her relationship with David: that was the most important thing now. Somehow, she'd make a decent fist of it.

The occasional letter arrived from David, heavily censored. He was involved in coastal patrol work, she knew that much. 'Don't you worry about him being up there?' Kath asked.

'It's pretty safe. Everyone says so.'

During the first week in June, Kath came into her room. 'Phone call for you downstairs.'

'Who is it?'

Kath shrugged. 'Haven't a clue.'

Tentatively she walked down the hallway and picked up the telephone. 'Hello.'

It was Alex: she would have recognised his voice anywhere. 'Hi, Claire. Seeing you're almost part of the family now, I wanted to let you know that Erica's had the baby.'

She closed her eyes, fighting back sudden tears. 'That's lovely, Alex. Boy or girl?'

'A boy! We're going to call him Joshua, but I expect he'll get Josh. Seven-and-a-half pounds. I can't believe it. I have a son. I'm a *father!*'

She could imagine him holding the receiver with one hand, running his other hand excitedly through his hair. And he *was* excited: she could hear it in his voice.

'I'm happy for you, Alex.'

And she was, wasn't she?

Claire replaced the receiver and stood, staring at it. Moments earlier it had carried Alex's voice across the miles. Now it lay silent. Her thoughts turned to the child. Joshua. That was a nice name. She tried to picture them as a family: Alex, Erica and Josh. Alex would make a good father, involved and attentive. And Erica . . .

She paused, undecided. Somehow she had the feeling that baby Josh was going to cramp Erica's style.

A few days later, she sent a note of congratulations. It seemed churlish not to do so. As she sealed the envelope, it was like an ending of sorts. Alex had his own family. There would never *ever* be room in his life for her.

* * *

In September David telephoned Claire at work. She hadn't seen him since that February day when he'd slipped the engagement ring on her finger. 'I've got three days' leave.'

'When?'

'Next week. From Wednesday.' He paused for a moment, then went on. 'I was hoping you'd be able to get a few days off, too. We could get married.'

What had she thought, that she could put off the actual moment forever? On a deep breath, she replied: 'I've got some leave owing. I'm sure it'll all work in beautifully.'

'Are you sure you can arrange everything in time?'

'I'll keep it simple.'

The family had to be notified, the church and minister booked. Kath gave her a hug and offered to organise flowers. 'I want you to be my matron of honour,' insisted Claire.

'What about a wedding dress?'

'What about it?' Claire shrugged.

'You're not going to wear your uniform!'

'Why not? Seems the most sensible thing to do. It's all unnecessary expense and with all the war-time restrictions — I don't fancy mosquito netting for a bridal veil!'

Kath shot her a defiant look, then laughed. 'Forever bloody practical, even on your wedding day!'

They were married in a church in the city; it was three months before Claire's twenty-first birthday. She remembered little of the mid-morning ceremony, recalled mostly running down the front steps of the church into sunshine, wearing a starched uniform and highly polished shoes and holding David's hand while throwing her bouquet.

They were all there to congratulate the couple. Nina and Maudie showering them with rose petals picked that morning from some unsuspecting garden. Joe looking uncomfortable in a suit. Lydia. David's father Hal. Alex and Erica and baby Josh, who slept right through the ceremony. Kath, who was a most efficient maid of honour.

Afterwards they went to a nearby pub for lunch. Everyone was laughing, chatting. It really was a happy day, Claire thought. She caught Alex's eye. Look at me, she wanted to say. I don't need you. I can be happy with David.

Erica sat next to her, holding Josh when he woke from his nap. 'Would you like a nurse?' she asked Claire.

She held out her arms for the child, felt the weight of him. He was three months old already, pink-cheeked and bright-eyed. She reached out her hand, watched as he hooked one of his fingers around her own, inhaled deeply, stared down at his perfect small features and took in the aroma of soap and talcum powder.

Nina had sat in the front pew, watching her daughter as she vowed to 'love, honour and obey', struggling to hear Claire's softly spoken words. It was like deja vu, she had thought. A re-run of her own rushed wartime marriage to Frank.

Part of her had fought back the impulse to step forward, put an end to the ceremony. Claire wasn't in love with David, she knew. They were friends, nothing more. So why try and pretend?

She had glanced across at Alex, standing next to his wife, already knowing the answer to her question. But Alex was married now and had a family of his own and, whatever had happened during that long-ago summer when he and Claire had first met, whatever emotions he had stirred in her daughter, were now best forgotten. 'It's Claire's life,' she had told herself silently. 'She can make her own choices.'

David surprised Claire by renting a small weatherboard cottage perched on a sand dune overlooking the sea at Coolangatta. They caught the mid-afternoon train down, leaning out the window and laughing like schoolchildren. David carried the two small cases up the rise to the cottage, after collecting the key from the real estate office next to the railway station.

By the time they arrived, sun streamed from a clear blue sky and gulls screamed noisily overhead. The air was filled with the tang of salt. A warm breeze fanned the trees, threatening to carry off Claire's straw hat. She held onto it with one hand as she ran up the path leading to the front door, while the wind whipped her gathered skirt, pleating the fabric to her legs.

David loaded the cases into the small bedroom, which was mainly taken up by a white canopied bed.

'Oh, my,' whispered Claire, suddenly self-conscious as she sat tentatively on one side of the mattress, dangling her feet.

David pushed her backwards across the cover, bringing his lean frame parallel with hers. 'Which side do you want?'

'Does it matter?'

'Witch! You're supposed to give me an answer, not ask another question.' He ran a finger from her hairline down the length of her nose. 'I can't believe that after all this time we're actually married.'

'It does seem strange,' she agreed with a smile. 'Strange, but nice.'

'You *do* mean that?'

'Of course.'

'Mrs Melville,' he whispered, teasing, touching his mouth briefly to hers.

'Now, *that* seems strange. *Mrs Melville*.'

'Why don't you unpack the bags while I pop down to the shops before they shut? We'll need something for dinner.'

'Tomatoes. Bread. Cold meat and cheese,' said Claire, mentally ticking off the ingredients for supper. 'And some milk and tea for breakfast.'

'Or we could go out, if you'd rather,' David offered. 'Down to the pub instead.'

'No. We'll throw together something here. Then we'll have the whole night.'

'You and me. No interruptions.' He smiled at her meaningfully, leant forward and lightly kissed her on the nose. 'And the sooner I go, the sooner I'll be back.' And he bounced from the bed and walked from the house, the screen door banging behind him.

The furniture was spartan and worn, but the overall feeling in the cottage was one of cheerfulness. Late-afternoon sun streamed in the windows. From outside Claire could hear the warbling of a bird. The rooms had a musty, lack-of-use smell, so she threw open the windows to admit the salty breeze which whipped the curtains and made them dance. Leaning out, she took deep lungfuls of air. Watched the waves inching up the shoreline. Later they'd go down there, she and David. Walk for miles with the sand beneath her bare feet, letting the salt settle on her skin.

She glanced back into the cottage: their own place, if only for three days. In the bedroom she unpacked their clothes, placing them in the dresser drawers. It seemed strange, handling David's belongings. Shirts and shorts, underwear, shaving gear: thoughtfully she rubbed the bristles of the brush across her cheek. They all seemed so personal, such a part of him. Three days. So many things to get used to, if only they had the time.

The glint of gold caught her eye and she raised her left hand, studying her wedding ring. Rose gold to match the other ring he'd given her, months earlier. Plain band.

Mrs Melville.

She smiled, remembering the words, then thought how little her life would really change now she was married. In three days' time she'd go back to the boarding house, back to Kath and work, and the same old humdrum existence as before. God only knew when she'd see David next. The next few days would have to sustain them both for an uncertain number of months ahead.

She lowered the blinds, making the room gloomy, yellow-tinged, subdued. Slowly she unfastened her blouse and skirt, letting them fall to the floor. Then she lay on the bed in her slip, stretching her legs until her toes touched the cool timber of the mahogany bed-end.

She stretched her arms above her head, then drew a cigarette from a pack on the bedside table and lit it. Chesterfields: the smoking was a habit she had acquired since she'd moved to the city. She folded her left arm under her head and drew steadily on the cigarette, watching the wisps of smoke curl lazily from her mouth.

She and David would have a child, Claire promised herself, thinking of Josh. A baby would bind them together, turn them from a couple into a family. Perhaps they'd start one tonight, God willing. A little girl, maybe.

She stubbed out the cigarette and closed her eyes, heard the soft hissing of the waves beyond, and waited for David to return.

Alex lay on the bed in the hotel room, watching his wife. Erica sat in the chair on the opposite side of the room, Josh nuzzling hungrily at her breast. Her eyes were closed and there was a bored, impatient expression on her face, as though she couldn't wait to be finished. The room was quiet, infernally so, except for the ticking of the clock on the bedside table and Josh sucking.

'It was a good wedding,' he said, breaking the silence.

Erica's eyes remained shut. 'It was all right.'

They'd motored down, using some of Alex's precious allowance of fuel that his medical occupation afforded. Tomorrow they would spend the day with Erica's parents, and head home the following day, taking a leisurely drive. Josh, as usual, would probably sleep all the way.

Lazily he slid from the bed and moved closer, watching as Josh's mouth moved furiously at Erica's nipple. He reached out and slid one finger across his son's downy head. A sense of tenderness welled up inside him, a feeling close to grief.

At his father's touch, Josh pulled away from Erica's breast and let out a wail. Erica opened her eyes and gave him an angry glare. 'Now look what you've done!'

'Come on, darling. It wasn't intentional.'

She rose to her feet and dumped the screaming baby unceremoniously in his cot. 'You try and settle him, then. I've had enough!'

'You haven't finished feeding him,' Alex responded patiently. Erica seemed prone to sudden outbursts since Josh's birth, and it usually required all his tact to calm her.

'I'm tired of all that. It takes up so much *time*.'

'No more than if you gave him a bottle,' he said amicably. 'It's all part of having a baby.'

'Well, he's not just *my* baby, he's yours, too. So I'll buy a bottle and we can take turns.'

'Fine. Whatever you want.'

'This whole motherhood thing's grossly overrated, if you ask me. Look at my stomach!'

'There's nothing wrong with your stomach.'

'And my breasts are sore,' she went on, as though she hadn't heard.

'That'll pass. Give it time. Three months isn't long enough to undo nine months of pregnancy.'

'I don't want to wait. I want my life back. Now!'

She flounced off to the bathroom, nightgown slung over one arm. Alex sighed, went to the cot and picked up his son. Sturdy arms flailing, face puckered and red. He laid him against his shoulder, feeling the boy's legs jerking upwards. 'He's got colic,' he told Erica when she came back into the room.

Erica pulled the covers back and slid into the bed, not even looking towards them. 'Actually, that's a good idea.'

'What is?'

'Buying a bottle. I'll do that tomorrow morning. I've had enough of breastfeeding. Time to get my body back in shape.'

'If that's what you want.'

'There's another thing you might as well know. You have a son, someone to carry on the Melville name so, as far as I'm concerned, my procreating days are over. No more children!'

'Aren't you being a little unreasonable?'

'Not in the least.'

'And how are you going to prevent that?'

'You're a doctor, Alex. You figure it out.' And she rolled on her side, presenting him with a view of her back.

Josh was calming, his wails reduced to a hiccup. Alex walked across the carpet, back and forth, soothing him with whispered words until he slept. He felt the solid weight of him against his chest, and was amazed, yet again, by his depth of feeling for the child.

CHAPTER 29

Lydia was supposed to be sweeping up but she was more intent on singing along to the gramophone. It was the third time she'd played 'Wish Me Luck as You Wave Me Goodbye'.

'Excuse me, ma'am.'

Lydia paused in her singing and swung towards the voice. A soldier stood outside the screen door, hat in hand.

'There are three of us here,' he added. 'I think your Mom is expecting us.'

During the last few months, Nina had begun taking American servicemen into the house, and Lydia had watched the passing parade with a mixture of dismay and delight. Dismay because she was expected to help with the extra work, and delight because somehow, for a few brief days, these men gave her a link to the outside world.

It was called rest leave, or 'R&R' — 'rest and recreation'. Lydia wasn't particularly interested in the 'rest' part, but she was certainly interested in the 'recreation' side of events. Especially as the soldiers were mostly young and good-looking. And this one, waiting at the door now, was decidedly handsome.

'Come in,' she said with a smile, opening the door to admit them. They introduced themselves. Hank was the one she had spoken to. Then there was Tex and Ellis, who was older than the other two and their superior, though Lydia promptly forgot his rank.

They were, as Nina confided to Lydia later, 'Lovely polite men. A credit to their country.'

And polite they were. They stayed for several days, always saying, 'Thank you, ma'am, for a lovely meal,' every time Nina put plates of food in front of them. Then they'd shoo her out of the kitchen while they washed up, helped by Lydia, laughing and talking as they worked, mesmerising her with their voices, their accents.

Afterwards, when Jane and Joe came in, they all sat in the living room with Nina, listening to the wireless, or lugged the gramophone out onto the verandah and danced to the scratchy music.

'Don't you think Hank's cute?' Lydia asked Jane while they were in the kitchen later, making hot cocoa.

Jane poured boiling water into the cups and her face was momentarily obscured by steam. 'Cute, but dangerous.'

Lydia gave a languid amused chuckle. *Dangerous?* 'Why would you say that?'

'Because he's a Yank. You know what they say about them? Overpaid, oversexed and over here.'

'Hank isn't like that.'

'Of course he is. He's a normal man.'

'Like Joe,' Lydia thrust back. 'Just what do the two of you get up to out on that boat? You were gone for hours today.'

Jane coloured slightly and picked up two of the steaming mugs. 'At least I know Joe's going to be here tomorrow, next week, next month. He's not some fly-by-nighter.'

The following night the three men went into town, to the pub. Hank asked Lydia along and, after a cautioning from Nina, she was allowed to go.

They walked along the road, the men taking it in turns to sing. They were war songs mostly, the words of which everyone knew. Hank reached for her hand in the dark, squeezing her fingers. 'You don't mind, do you?' he asked.

'No.'

'Have you got a boyfriend?'

'Not at the moment.'

'But you have, in the past?'

'Of course.'

Boyfriends. She supposed she could call them that. They *were* boys and they had been *very* friendly, just for a short time, until Lydia had given in. The sex had been hurried and frantic: fumbled couplings in the back seat of some car or behind the lunch shed at school; she had been left feeling empty inside, as though she were capable of more.

The sex didn't bother her, one way or the other. It was simply a means to an end, a temporary escape from her mundane existence and the predictability of her life. She'd had a taste of the city at Claire and David's wedding, and had liked what she saw. The streets had been full of Yanks since the American Navy had come to Brisbane earlier in the year. Lydia had seen the newsreels at the picture theatre in town: crowds welcoming these men in Queen Street. Now, back in Tea-tree Passage, she was bored senseless. They were using her, these *boyfriends*, Lydia knew, just as she was using them.

At the pub, Hank sat beside her, slung his arm proprietorially around her shoulder, and she succeeded in getting very drunk on the tequila that came from a small flask in his coat pocket. Eventually the room began to swim and her voice sounded disjointed.

She and Hank were the last to leave, and the barman gave her an odd look as she walked past. 'You all right, miss?' he asked.

'I'm fine. Just going home now,' she slurred.

They walked around the back of the pub. There were no streetlights there, simply black pools of darkness. She leaned against the wall, head spinning. Hank kissed her, rough kisses that bruised her mouth. Dimly she felt his teeth digging into her lip while his hands undid the buttons of her blouse. He lowered his head, nuzzling flesh. She moaned, pulling him closer, demanding more.

'Did anyone tell you how beautiful you are?' he asked.

'I bet you say that to all the girls.'

'No, only you.'

They were meaningless lying words, she knew. She smiled in the darkness as he pushed her skirt up around her waist and then fumbled impatiently with her knickers. She heard the sound of his belt being undone, sensed him tugging at his trousers. He cupped his hands around her buttocks, drawing her close, lifting her, and she felt his first rigid thrust.

The movements, hard and furious, made her feel nauseous. Accommodatingly, she stifled the urge to vomit, focusing her mind on the present. She didn't have to wait long. 'Jesus Christ, Mother Mary!' he grunted, making one final lunge.

While he pulled up his trousers, she retrieved her knickers from the ground where they lay, tucked them into her handbag and hurriedly pulled down her skirt. Smoothed the creases from the fabric, not wanting to alert her mother, who she knew would be waiting. Ran her hands through her hair, untangling the curls.

They walked home, not touching, footsteps thudding down that empty length of road. Hank was silent, for which Lydia was thankful. Her head was pounding and the road swam in and out of focus. Nina was in bed when they arrived home, the house dark and unwelcoming. Hank went off to his bunk on the verandah and Lydia slid between her own sheets. Putting her hand between her legs, she felt the moistness, smelt the scent of male. What was it all for? she wondered. Five minutes of grunting and shoving that left her feeling disappointed and unfulfilled. But what more could there be? It was an animal act, and she felt nothing.

Erica, Josh perched on her hip, swung along the track that led down to the beach. Past Maudie's house she went, where the fat old cow was hanging her rags of washing on the clothes line. Grey pillowcases and sheets, almost threadbare. Christ! Didn't she ever think to buy new ones? Maudie gave a wave but Erica kept her head down, watching her unobtrusively from the corner of her eye, hoping the old woman wouldn't follow, wanting to talk.

Out in the channel she could see Lydia swimming out to the marker buoy with long lazy strokes. Someone was following her, one of those Yankee soldiers that Nina was always taking in, probably. Little slut, Erica thought now, watching through narrowed eyes as the younger woman reached the buoy and clung there, shaking blonde hair from her face. The sound of her laughter carried across the water, followed by the deeper baritone of the man's reply. You didn't need much intelligence to work out Lydia's type. At least she could be a little discreet, Erica thought, if nothing else.

She had a book under one arm, a towel and a bottle of juice for Josh. Reaching the beach, she sat her son on the sand and spread the towel under the shade of a clump of pandanus palms. Then she pulled the loose shift over her head.

She was wearing a swimsuit underneath, purchased the week before from Claudia's Apparel in town. It was low-cut and daring, the neckline revealing the swell of her breasts and that dark cleft between. Needless to say, she hadn't bothered to show Alex. He would only have nodded and said, 'That's nice, dear,' without really looking. There was little she told him these days.

She sat on the towel and Josh crawled towards her, grinning, spreading sand as he went. 'Stop it!' she admonished, wagging her finger at him. 'Don't do that, Josh baby. Mummy'll get cross.'

She scooped him up and pointed him in the direction of the water, yards away. Watched him with a mixture of pride and annoyance as he swung away, moving with a curious sideways motion, like a little crab. A sturdy child with a thick crop of sandy-coloured hair like his father, he was six months old now, crawling everywhere and always into mischief.

With a sigh she opened her book and glanced at the first page. She had found it so much easier when Josh was younger and slept most of the time. These days he confined her more. Trips into town or to the beach often had to be cut short because he needed his morning or afternoon nap. He became grizzly when tired — bloody unbearable, in fact.

And Alex wasn't much better in the entertainment stakes. He was always busy with work and, by the time he got home late most evenings, he was too exhausted to go out.

'Let's drive into town to the pub after dinner,' she'd said only last week. 'Have a couple of drinks. Socialise.'

'We can have a drink here. The bar cupboard's full of grog. And as for socialising, I've already seen half the town's folk in the surgery this week.'

'It's not the same.'

'What about Josh?'

'We could take him, or get a babysitter. I'm sure Nina could do with a few extra bob.'

'Could we make it another night? I'm bushed.'

She'd walked away, pretending to be busy with some task, trying to hide her frustration.

'Erica? You don't mind, do you?'

'Of course I bloody mind!' she'd exploded, rounding on him, hands on hips, knowing her voice was shrill and sounding like a fishwife's. 'We never do anything, go anywhere! You're always too tired. Alex, I swear, if you'd told me what it was going to be like living here, I'd never have come.'

'You don't give the place a chance. You're always criticising, running everything down.'

'Rubbish!'

He'd stood, staring at her, an angry expression on his face, and the thought had occurred to her that their relationship was faltering. What would she do if it ended? Ask for a divorce? Go home to her parents? Take Josh or leave him with his father? So many decisions.

On the other hand, society had a tendency to look down on divorced women, and life with Alex was comfortable financially. Mostly he left her to her own devices, and she was free to come and go as she pleased. He gave her a generous allowance and never asked about her whereabouts during the day.

'Admit it,' she said to herself now. 'You're bored and restless. Bogged down in this bloody hick place.'

She was eager to take her life off hold and, she thought now, she could easily add a little spice to it, if necessary. Like Lydia. Except she'd be a damn sight more prudent. But there was still the problem of Josh. She counted the months. He would start school when he was five, but that was more than four years away. Blast!

A shadow fell across her and she glanced up. A man stood there, holding her wriggling son. It looked like the same chap who had been swimming with Lydia earlier, although she couldn't be sure.

'Here, ma'am,' he said, handing her the boy. 'He was getting mighty close to the water, and I guessed the little tyke couldn't swim.'

'Thanks,' she replied graciously, appraising the tanned body and muscular physique. 'American, are you?'

'That's right, ma'am.'

'My name's Erica.'

'Erica. That's a pretty name. Mine's Hank.'

'Staying up at the Carmody place, are you?' She patted the towel beside her, indicating that he should sit there. 'America. I always wanted to go there. Tell me, what's it like?'

She watched her son, shoving fistfuls of sand in his mouth as Hank talked. His voice was melodious, soothing, and he spoke of faraway places she'd never seen. There was a magic about that, an air of mystery.

The sun beat down, and the glare reflected by the sand hurt her eyes. There was no sign of any other living thing, except for the gulls that circled overhead. Josh crawled onto the towel next to her in the shade, closed his eyes and slept.

She saw Hank eye the ring on her left hand. 'Married, are you?' he asked, after a while.

She gave him a long look. 'Yes.'

'Husband off at war?'

'No, but he might as well be, the precious little I see of him.'

He gave her a disarming smile. 'Did anyone tell you how pretty you are?'

'Not lately.'

'Well, I'm telling you now.'

'I bet you say that to all the girls.'

'No, only you.'

She smiled and stretched, enjoying the banter, knowing exactly where the conversation was leading. Felt a warm rush of anticipation and desire. It had been weeks since Alex had touched her.

She wasn't expected home, and Alex planned to be at the surgery all day. There was no-one to report to or watch her movements, and Josh would sleep for an hour at least. Maybe two. She leaned forward, traced the outline of Hank's lips with the tip of one finger. 'Tell me again,' she murmured lazily.

Japan, declared the city newspapers, was on the move. American aeroplanes and depots at Pearl Harbor were bombed in early December. Raids had been made on Singapore and Malaya. In Tea-tree Passage, there had been reports of a submarine seen in the ocean, further out. 'The Japanese are coming.' Those were the words on everyone's lips.

Amidst all this, Joe disappeared.

He had tried to enlist in town, twice, and had been refused entry. Fishing, like mining and farming, was an exempt occupation, and everyone around the area knew him, knew what a great job he was doing keeping the boats going through this difficult time of labour and fuel shortages.

'No way, mate,' said the enlisting officer, the last time he'd tried. 'I'd lose my job if I signed you up. Go back to your boats and thank God you're safe.'

'I'm not bloody safe. If the Japs take over this place, we're all done for.'

'That won't happen.'

Furious, he'd marched away, vowing to try a different approach.

He hitched a ride to Brisbane on a passing lorry. No one knew him at the enlistment office there. He was simply Joe Carmody: dark hair and brown eyes, one hundred and forty-five pounds and nineteen years of age. His next of kin was given as his mother, Nina Carmody. His address: Tea-tree Passage.

He passed the medical easily. Was sent to be kitted out, then dispatched back home to wait for orders. The following day he arrived home, dressed in khaki. Wordlessly his mother shook her head, her face pale and her mouth flattened into a tight unyielding line, and instantly he hated himself for the reaction he had provoked.

'Oh, Joe,' she said with a deep sigh. 'Why didn't you tell me?'

'Because you would have tried to talk me out of it.'

'You think war hasn't ruined our lives enough already?'

'Someone's got to stop those bastards.'

'And you're going to stop them all by yourself? Joe! No! You're a fisherman. It's a protected industry. No-one would blame you for not going. We need you here.'

There was a harsh tone to her voice, unrelenting. 'I'd blame myself,' he tried to explain, 'for not doing my bit.'

'What about the boats? Who's going to run them?'

Joe named several of the men who were working for him, O'Reilly and Sharp boys mostly. 'They're good blokes and straight. They'll look after things till I get back.'

Till I get back. Was that his way of reassuring her that things would be all right? But there was no way of knowing. Greater men than him had died on foreign battlefields in the past.

She made a pot of tea and put a plate of biscuits on the table. Poured him a cup, sugared it just the way he liked. Watched as he sipped the steaming liquid, her eyes dark and filled with pain.

There was an uneasy silence between them, punctuated only by the ticking of the clock on the wall. Hands measuring out the passing seconds and minutes, bringing him closer to that final leave-taking. When would that be? Days, weeks or months from now? He'd been given no indication.

'What's Jane think about all this?' his mother said at last.

'She doesn't know. She's coming out here after she finishes work. I'll tell her then.'

Abruptly she rose, busied herself about the kitchen. Took the makings of a meal and arranged it on the bench. Refused to look at him, to acknowledge further what he had done.

'I'm not sorry, Mum.' The words sounded loud against the silence, and she could not fail to hear. 'I want to go and do my bit, like all the other blokes. A man's got pride.'

'You're only nineteen. Your father wasn't much older when he went away to war.'

Her voice was flat, devoid of any emotion. Her face, when she turned, seemed frozen, her mouth barely able to move. She eyed him steadily, for what seemed like ages, then turned and walked from the room.

Jane arrived after supper, pedalling furiously up the track. She dropped her bike near the front gate and rushed up the front steps. When she saw him waiting in the shadows for her, still wearing the uniform, she came to an abrupt halt.

'Oh, my God! What have you done?'

'Just tell me you like a man in uniform,' he grinned at her.

They walked along the track, down to the sea wall. A faint breeze had sprung up, trying to dispel the heat of the day. Overhead, a formation of ducks flew, their cries echoing along the Passage, hauntingly sweet.

Joe reached for her hand, feeling its warm solidity, and tried to find the words to explain. They came haltingly, waiting for acknowledgement, acceptance even. She smiled hesitatingly when he had finished. 'If that's what you want, Joe, then you have to do it,' she answered, putting his fears at rest. 'I'll support you, you know that. But I'm going to miss you like crazy.'

'Do you mean that?'

She wound her arms around his neck and kissed him soundly. 'Does that answer your question?'

'A little. I might still need some more convincing, though.'

She gave him a playful punch. 'Later. Okay?'

He led her to the end of the rock wall. 'Come on. Sit down. We need to talk,' he began tentatively.

'What about?' she asked as he slung his arm around her shoulder, pulling her close.

'Us.'

'Exactly *what* about us?'

Her voice came as a whisper, barely heard above the swish of the surf. He could see the outline of her face in the reflected light spilling from the marker buoy out in the middle of the channel.

'I was thinking we might get married before I leave.'

He felt her stiffen, then she drew imperceptibly away. 'I don't think that's wise.'

'Why not?'

'We're too young, for a start.'

'I'm nearly twenty.'

'And I'm only eighteen.'

This conversation wasn't going the way he had planned. Somehow he had to convince her that his idea was sound. 'Look! They're only numbers. It's what we *are*, inside, that counts. I love you, Jane, plain and simple, and I don't have to wait years to know that. We don't need a fancy ceremony. Just a few family and friends. We'll keep it simple —'

'No!'

'Why not? Don't you love me?'

'Because none of us know what's in store. You could end up . . .'

Her words wavered and caught, and she was unable to go on. She clung to him, buried her face against his neck. He could feel her chest rising and falling, and knew she was crying.

'Dead,' he said, and the word sounded flat and emotionless.

'Yes,' she hiccupped. 'I don't want to be a widow, and I don't really want you to go away. If circumstances were different, you wouldn't even be asking me like this. A spur-of-the-moment wedding isn't the best way to start married life. Look at Claire and David. They're a prime example.'

'That wasn't spur-of-the-moment. They've known each other for years.'

'And they've seen each other twice in the last year.'

'That's what love's about, though. Carrying you through the rough times. As long as they love each other, that's what counts.'

'Claire doesn't love David. It's Alex she loves.'

'Alex? He's married.'

'That's what I mean. It's Alex she wants, but she can't have him. So she's settled for David, instead. Second best.'

'How do you know that?'

'Haven't you seen the way she looks at Alex, how she jumps when she hears his name? Any fool can see that.'

'It's not like that with us, is it? I'm not second best?'

'Of course not, silly. I just want things to be right, that's all, not have a half-hearted attempt at a

412

wedding just because you're going away. We don't even know when we'll see each other again.'

He cupped her face with his hands, staring into her eyes. 'Will you wait for me?'

She nodded, and he could see the hint of a smile.

'Promise?'

Solemnly. 'I promise.'

He closed his eyes and felt a hum of anticipation. His world was changing, moving on. Jane couldn't be part of that, but it was enough to know she'd be here. He felt secure, comforted.

The flow of the conversation rose and fell in his mind as he remembered what Jane had said earlier. Claire loving Alex? It seemed unreal, unimaginable. Who else knew? With his heavy workload, he'd seen so little of his sister in the months before she went away. What a damnable, unenviable predicament that would be, he thought: loving someone, and not having that love returned. Thank God he and Jane weren't like that!

Jane. He felt for her in the darkness, seeking those warm familiar places. She came to him, compliant and willing, as always. And afterwards, as he lay beside her, all he could hear was the sound of the waves, thudding, on and on in the darkness, sounding like a drum roll in his head.

CHAPTER 30

It was customary in town that when each of the local lads went to war, a dance was held in their honour. And Joe was no different. Nina prepared for the night in silence. He hated that, the not talking. But what could he say to her, anyway? I love you, Mum. I wish I wasn't going but I have things to prove. To myself. To you and Jane. I'm no longer a boy, but a man.

She kept her thoughts to herself, walking about the house straight and tall. Stoic, he thought. Hiding it all away like she always had done, even when he was a child. If only she'd yell at him, let it out.

The night of the dance arrived, warm and sultry. Storm clouds hovered above the eastern horizon. Lightning flickered away far out to sea. A hot breeze blew as they ran up the steps of the local hall, where members of the band were tuning their instruments.

He danced with Nina and Maudie first, then kept the remainder for Jane. Waltz and barn dance. Pride of Erin. Highland Schottische. She looked pretty in a

414

lemon chiffon dress, cut down for the occasion from an old frock of Nina's. While she tried to keep up with him in the foxtrot, he noticed that her cheeks were pale and her eyes were bright with unshed tears. 'Slow down, Joe,' she whispered, but her words were lost in the music and tramp of feet, and he saw her mouth working wordlessly, uselessly.

He himself was moving faster, faster, as though in doing so, he could somehow speed up time. The sooner he left, the sooner he could come back to her. That made sense, didn't it? His feet slid across the polished crows'-ash floor, slipping, gliding, pulling her in his wake. Other dancers whirled past in a confusion of colour, while the music seemed to be going at a furious pace.

There was a lavish supper: savouries, cold chicken and salads, followed by pavlova, trifle and fruit salad. Nina came over with a plateful and, to please her, he tried to eat. Pushed it around on the plate, mostly, rearranging it with his fork. But his appetite had gone.

Everyone wanted to talk, to wish him well. He was caught in their mass, jostled from one group to another, answering questions. The music started again — 'Under the Spreading Chestnut Tree'. It was a silly fun dance, one of their favourites, and he glanced around for Jane. He couldn't see her, so he waited by the door, tapping his feet in time to the music. Perhaps she'd gone to the ladies' room.

The dance finished and there was still no sight of her. Alex walked past, on his way to the bar. 'If you're looking for Jane,' he said, 'I saw her go outside ages ago.'

Joe sprinted down the front steps of the hall, eyes searching the gloom. He walked through the haphazard array of automobiles, calling, 'Jane?'

The band was playing another song: 'Lambeth Walk'.

'Jane? Where are you?'

There was a movement by the clump of trees and she stepped forward into the half-light. Head held defiantly, dress limp. Hands hanging, clasped, in front of her.

He walked towards her and put a hand on each shoulder. 'There you are. I was wondering where you'd gotten to. Alex said you'd left.'

'I don't know how you can bear to stay in there,' she said. 'It's maudlin. It's — it's predatory. Everyone coming to say goodbye. You can see it in their faces, all wondering if they'll ever see you again. Yet they're all smiling and laughing. And next week or next month, they'll say "Joe who?", and it'll be as though you never existed.'

'Come back inside,' he soothed. 'You're upset, that's all.'

She pulled away from his touch. 'I've been thinking about it, Joe, how damn selfish you're being. Walking away from your business and your family. Walking away from me and everything we've got.'

He flinched, stung by the savagery in her voice, then retaliated. 'And exactly what is there between us? I asked you to marry me and you said no.'

She was stepping backwards now, towards the dark safety of the trees. 'I hate war.' Her voice was soft and deliberate, mingling with the music that swayed out across the dirt parking area.

'None of us like war, Jane.' Placating, soothing words. Bloody useless, really.

'It's so senseless and destructive, ripping apart lives and families. And when it's over, what then? All those same old platitudes will come out, about getting on with it, making the best of a bad situation, for those of us who are left.'

'If it makes any difference to you, I don't *want* to go away.'

'Why go, then?'

'Because I have to,' he replied simply, hoping she'd understand.

'And afterwards, what will become of us, you and I? The more I think about it, I know our relationship won't ever be the same.'

'Of course it will.'

'It can't. There'll be too much separating us. Too many differences.'

'My parents managed it,' he said stiffly.

She gave a scornful laugh. 'That's a load of shit, Joe! Ask your mother what it was like after the last war, how she coped with trying to make a shattered man whole again.'

'Will you come back inside?'

'I just wanted you to know how I felt, that's all. It isn't all hunky-dory, waving your man off at the railway station.'

'Don't spoil the evening. Come and dance.'

'I promised I'd wait for you.'

'And ...'

Her conversation had a purpose, a destination, he suspected then. Words and sentences were leading towards some weighty disclosure. 'I don't know if I can keep that promise, or if I want to.'

'Why ever not? You said you loved me.'

'I do, I do.' She was crying, great gulping sobs that tore into her words. 'It's just that we can never go back to what we have now. It can't ever work.'

He held her to him until her tears dried and her sobs were reduced to a hiccup. 'The war can't last much longer; that's what everyone says. I could be home again in the blink of an eye, and we'll look back on tonight and wonder what all the fuss was about.'

He led her back into the hall in time to see the customary purse being passed around, everyone adding their donation. Later, when he counted it out, there was over ten pounds. 'Here. This is for you,' he said, handing it to his mother. 'There won't be as much money coming in while I'm gone. This will keep you going for a while.'

The last dance was 'Goodnight Sweetheart'. He held Jane close, rocking her gently in the centre of the floor, trying not to think of her earlier outburst. She was upset, that was all. Her words were wild and off-base. Nothing could come between them, neither separation nor war.

The music ended on a nostalgic note. Then the band broke into a strident National Anthem and everyone stood to attention. Joe glanced about him, feeling proud. He was surrounded by friends and family. He was going to fight for his country, his flag. And when it was all over, when the whole sordid mess had died down, they would, as he had told Jane earlier, look back and wonder what all the fuss was about.

It seemed the whole town had turned out to farewell the group of lads leaving on the midday train. Kitbags lay strewn along the platform; people mingled, calling out goodbyes as the carriages lurched towards them along the track. Someone had borrowed the flag from the police station and draped it from the railway sign.

But behind the joviality hung a sense of sadness. As Nina stepped back, allowing Joe time to say goodbye to Jane, she was poignantly reminded of the last war. Standing in that same place, waving goodbye to Bill and Frank, not knowing when, or if, she'd see them again. And now, years later, she was still caught up in that endless cycle of loss. Here was Joe leaving in much the same circumstances, acting so like Frank these days that sometimes it was painful to watch. Had she failed him in some way? she often wondered. He was a man of scant education, of simple needs: a boat, fishing line, the company of a good woman. But he'd have none of these where he was going. And if he survived the war, how would he cope? Would he come back with the same frailty and failings as his father?

The guard came along the platform, blowing his whistle, ordering the travellers aboard. Joe stepped away from Jane, still holding her hand. He looked across at his mother. I won't cry, won't be emotional in public, Nina thought, fighting back tears. At home, later, she could allow herself the luxury of grief.

It was dark when she finally walked onto the front verandah and glanced along the track towards the other houses. Lights were blazing in the Melville place, faint strains of music coming to her on the breeze. The frangipani were in flower and she breathed deeply, inhaling the heady scent. *Come back safely, Joe. We'll miss you while you're gone.*

A stream of gold light slid effortlessly across the water of the Passage, highlighting the tidal ripples. 'Ah! There's the moon,' she sighed, thinking of other moons, other times. Lonely moons, living in that same house with Frank's parents, waiting for him to come home. And that pale luminescence bathing their bedroom on the first night of his return — her watching him as he slept, wondering how she would ever pick up the pieces of her life, make them whole. But she had, eventually, if just for a while. And now this other new war was tearing her family apart again. Claire was gone, and now Joe. Lydia was restless, Nina knew, longing to escape to the city. How long could she keep her here?

It seemed life was tucked into two separate compartments. On the home front there was the daily grind of restrictions. And she did her bit. Knitting blankets for the war effort, organising Comforts' Fund boxes. She and several other local women had been packing Christmas parcels since the beginning of the year.

'December's a long way off,' Maudie had said at the time.

'Well, there are a lot of soldiers,' she'd replied,

stowing away the biscuits and packs of cards, handkerchiefs, chocolates and cigarettes.

At home she took pride in serving up eggless cakes and meatless meals, making blackout curtains and taping her windows. At first Lydia had been horrified by the crisscrossing of grey adhesive on the glass. 'It's in case of attack,' Nina had told her.

'Who'd bother to come here, to Tea-tree Passage?'

'You never know, dear.'

Patriotic, Lydia said, was her middle name.

There were days when she had to remind herself that across the sea there was a war going on; it was so unimaginable, so far removed from the deprivations of her own life. Listening to the wireless, watching the newsreels at the picture theatre: the brutality of it all was thrust at them, shocking senses. As she watched the rows of celluloid soldiers marching across the screen, she reminded herself that they were someone's sons, husbands and fathers.

Looking back, it seemed these war years were comprised either of partings or reunions, comings and goings, uncertainties. Vera Lynn singing 'We'll Meet Again' on the wireless. The small brooch the authorities sent her after Joe had enlisted — a map of Australia with a crown on it — that was presented to all mothers and wives of servicemen serving overseas. She couldn't bear to wear it, so she packed it away in her small box of trinkets, with the old photos and letters and reminders of that other war.

She focused her gaze back on the water now. The moon had risen higher, paled, bathing everything in silver. The tide was almost ready to turn, the water high on the sand. A faint breeze shifted the leaves of the tea-trees. She felt it, soft on her face. A new year was almost here. 1942. What would it bring? Heartache? Tears? She couldn't begin to imagine.

The war in the south-west Pacific was moving closer. Malaya fell to the Japanese, followed by Timor. In mid-February, the seemingly impregnable naval base of Singapore was overrun. Thirteen thousand Australian soldiers, members of the 8th Division, were forced to surrender. Kath's husband, Tom, was amongst them.

She was beside herself with worry. Claire wished she could help in some way, but there was nothing she could offer except the usual platitudes, useless words that seemed to serve no real purpose: 'Cheer up. It mightn't be as bad as they say. You know the newspapers.'

Kath stared at her with a tear-stained face. 'Don't patronise me! You don't believe that!'

'I don't know what I believe any more.'

'I feel so damn useless. The waiting and not knowing — it's killing me. I don't know what I'll do if anything happens to him.'

'You'd cope,' said Claire pragmatically, 'because you wouldn't have a choice.'

'Do you know Milly from the office?' asked Kath suddenly, changing the subject. 'Her husband's up there, too. But does she care? No! She's having an affair with a bloody Yank!'

'You've got to keep faith, for Tom's sake. If you don't, you might as well give up now.'

Four days later, Japanese bombers delivered their deadly loads over Darwin. 'They were lucky,' Claire said to Kath later. 'It could have been much worse. The newspapers said only seven people were killed.'

'And you believed that?' asked Kath incredulously.

'Of course.'

'Don't kid yourself. The newspapers only tell you what they want you to read. We're living in an information brown-out. I can just see all the editors sitting in their offices. "Tell them nothing," they say. "Keep the masses quiet." There's more going on than you or I know. Look at us! Digging air-raid shelters in our schools, taping windows, blacking out our windows at night.'

Claire nodded in agreement. 'We've become prisoners in our own homes. And I worry about the unthinkable: invasion.'

Her thoughts were often of Nina in the old house at the Passage. If the worse happened, she'd bring her and Lydia down to Brisbane, find them a room somewhere. God! The prospect was so overwhelming it didn't bear thinking about.

In picture theatres, the newsreels showed lines of allied soldiers being led through tropical jungles. Kath scanned their faces for a sign of Tom, ever hopeful. Rationing was introduced for food, clothing and petrol. Housewives were asked to cook only one hot meal per day to conserve fuel. Through it all Claire worked, ate and slept, her life bound by timetables and fear.

Two months after the fall of Singapore, Kath received notification that Tom was missing. She was devastated, pacing up and down the small expanse of floor in Claire's bedroom, her mood alternating between fury and despair. Several weeks later, she was informed that, officially, he was a prisoner of war.

'He's alive,' she sobbed on Claire's shoulder. 'Thank God, he's alive.'

She was, the authorities told her, allowed to write a letter to him once a week. 'No more than twenty-five words, though!' she raged to Claire. 'What can I possibly say in twenty-five words?'

'You'll tell him that you love him and you miss him,' replied Claire, slinging an arm around her friend's shoulder. 'And that the day he comes home, you'll have the biggest baked dinner waiting. Peas and gravy and roast meat —'

'Stop it!' cried Kath, her mood brightening, shaking her head at Claire. 'My mouth's watering just thinking about it.'

Intermittent letters arrived from David, heavily censored, and she had no clue as to his whereabouts. Six months had passed since that sunny September day when they'd run down the church steps together. Sometimes she found it hard to recall his face, his easy smile. She had to remind herself that she was a married woman: it all seemed so unreal. Living apart. An abnormal life. She knew exactly how Kath felt.

'I love you, Claire,' he wrote. 'I think of you constantly and am counting the minutes till we can be together again.'

She and Kath went to see *Boomtown*, starring Clark Gable. Afterwards they decided to go to one of the clubs. 'Silver Hut, the Riverside or Dr Carver's?' asked Claire.

'The Riverside,' chose Kath. 'They have the best bands. Not that I feel like dancing.'

The room was crowded with servicemen. As the two women sat at the bar, sipping cocktails, one of the soldiers sidled up and tried to make small talk with Claire.

'She's married,' said Kath bluntly. 'So eyes off, buddy.'

'Kath!' exclaimed Claire, shocked.

'I've got to watch you, for David's sake,' she laughed. 'You're so damn pretty every man here would take you home if he could.'

Lydia loved the vibrancy of the city. She'd had a taste of it the previous year, when she'd come down for Claire's wedding, though Nina had kept a close watch on her. Now, alone and unchaperoned, she revelled in the thronging sidewalks, and the men in uniform who whistled as she sashayed past.

The American General, MacArthur, had arrived in Brisbane in July, setting up his headquarters there. Since then American troops had been flooding into the city, spreading out into hastily converted camps, pubs and servicemen's clubs. The tiny aerodrome at Eagle Farm had been transformed into a huge airfield for transport and war planes.

Despite the rationing, never had she seen so many shops and such a vast array of goods. T. C. Beirnes was her favourite store, and she loved standing in the centre of the shop watching the cashiers on their raised platform, and the series of wires and pulleys that sent the money, invoices and receipts whizzing overhead.

A job had been the main priority, and a soldier she had met on the train coming down had given her some good advice. 'Try and get a position yourself,' he had told her. 'If you go to Manpower, they expect you to take any job going. You could end up in a munitions factory, and that's hard dirty work. Dangerous, too.'

So she had gone directly to Somerville House, where she knew General MacArthur had set up headquarters. The man behind the desk there had offered her a position as a waitress in the Officers' Dining Room. The pay was three pounds a week, a pound more than she'd earned working in the general store back home.

She enjoyed her job, the easy banter with the servicemen, and she was never lost for a date on Saturday nights. In her spare time she joined a theatre group, helping out behind the stage, moving the props between scenes. She had always been plump, since she'd been small but, miraculously, the weight started falling away. Even Claire, to whom she made a duty visit every few weeks, commented on her changing appearance.

She had found a little one-bedroom flat close to work, but far enough away from Claire's digs to avoid scrutiny. The last thing she needed was constant lectures by her older sister about her social life and drinking habits. The flat was tiny and was a constant clutter: wet stockings hanging over the bathroom rail; unwashed dishes in the sink; last week's magazines scattered over the floor. But Lydia didn't care. It was hers, and no one could interfere.

One evening at work, as she was walking back to the kitchen with an order, someone grabbed her hand. 'Hey! Don't I know you?'

'That's an old pick-up line,' she said, trying to extricate her hand. 'You'll have to come up with something more original than that.'

'No, I'm serious. I've met you before.'

She frowned, looking blankly at the man's face. Dark blond hair. Crinkly blue eyes that seemed to smile as he talked, and the kind of rugged good looks that make older men attractive. Realisation dawned. Tea-tree Passage, the previous year. Hank and Tex and Ellis: three of Nina's refugees.

'Ellis!' she said now, surprised he had remembered her. He had been the older of the three men, more reserved, and they'd had little conversation.

'How's Nina?'

'She's fine. Still muddling along up there. The Comforts' Fund and Red Cross keep her busy. Joe's joined up, did you know?'

She spent several minutes talking to him until a warning frown from the head waitress sent her back to the kitchen.

'See you around, sweetheart,' he said, and she waltzed away, thinking that he was at least forty, much too old. When she came back to his table again, she noted that it was empty.

As she was leaving at the end of her shift, she was surprised to find him waiting at the front door. 'I have a car. Thought you might like a lift home.'

'I don't live very far,' she said doubtfully. None of the men she had met had ever offered her a ride before.

'It's no trouble.' He steered her towards the waiting vehicle. 'I'd enjoy the company.'

Within minutes the car pulled up outside Lydia's flat. 'I have tickets for a show. Perhaps you'd like to come with me?'

'When?'

'Saturday night. Unless you have other plans.'

'No,' she replied quickly. Someone at work was sure to swap. 'I could go. But are you sure you're not asking me just because ...' She let her voice trail away, gave him time to reply.

'Because of last year, when your mother was so kind to us?'

She nodded and crossed her legs so her skirt rode higher, revealing her knees. Ellis was staring, but she made no move to smooth it down. She knew she was flirting but couldn't help herself.

'I'll pick you up on Saturday, say six o'clock? We could have dinner first.'

'That'd be lovely.'

He walked around and opened the door for her. Helped her out of the car. As she did, she caught her leg against the upholstery.

'Damn.'

'What's wrong?'

'Another stocking gone, and I've already used all my clothing coupons.'

He gave her a wry smile and held her hand for a fraction longer than necessary as she steadied herself on the pavement. 'With legs like that, who needs stockings?'

She laughed, knowing he was teasing her — light-hearted banter to put her at ease. 'See you Saturday, then?'

'Saturday. It's a date.'

She ran up the stairs to her room, let herself in the door and felt a flutter of excitement. Compared to Ellis, the men she had been involved with up until now had been mere boys, fumbling and inexperienced. Ellis had class, and the sort of style and sophistication that comes with age. And Saturday, as far as Lydia was concerned, couldn't arrive quickly enough.

CHAPTER 31

Thankfully, training was brief; Goondiwindi in summer was hot and dry. There was no sea-breeze to cool the air and no Jane to make life bearable. After a few weeks, Joe found himself heading north towards New Guinea on a small Dutch East Indies freighter. Conditions on board were primitive. The wooden decks were held together with pitch, which became very hot and sticky during the day. Instead of bunks, the men slept on sheets of plywood which were stacked against the bulkheads when not in use. Meals were eaten twice daily, fairly awful fare after Nina's cooking, and he was glad when they eventually reached land.

The work was arduous in the hot humid conditions, and daily downpours of rain left them drenched. In his spare time he wrote letters, scribbled missives that, he was certain, kept the censor busy.

Dear Jane,
*   We're on the south-east tip of New Guinea,*
at a place called Milne Bay, and we're part of

*the anti-aircraft artillery battery at Gurney
Airstrip. The Japs come over several times a
day, but don't worry. We've got the RAAF
here, with their Hudsons and Kittyhawks for
air cover. And we've all learned how to use the
Bofors guns. The trip up is best forgotten,
although conditions here aren't much better.
Missing you and loving you always.
Joe*

He waited for a reply, but none came. Daily he
watched while the mail was dispensed. There were
letters from Nina and Claire, and a small postcard
from Lydia, who had, she informed him, gone to live in
Brisbane and was having a 'fabulous time'. He wrote
again. *Darling Jane. I miss you. Why won't you write?*

Waited.

Worried.

Lydia spent an inordinately long time preparing for
her night at the theatre with Ellis. She borrowed a
dress and hat from Ellen, the girl in the flat across
the hall.

'Don't know if it'll fit,' said Ellen doubtfully.
'You've lost so much weight lately, it'll probably
hang on you.'

Ellen worked part-time in the theatre, too,
understudy for one of the actresses. She had the most
amazing wardrobe of clothes, made-over things from
all sorts of fabric.

The dress was cream chiffon with cabbage roses
in varying shades of pink, and suited Lydia's pale

complexion perfectly. She pulled in the waist with a wide sash. 'It looks fabulous,' she said to Ellen, appraising herself in the mirror.

'What about gloves?'

'I've got some somewhere.'

'Stockings?'

Lydia pulled a wry face. 'Laddered my last pair getting out of Ellis' car. I've a bottle of that rub-on stuff somewhere, and I'll draw on some stocking seams. It'll be night-time, so no-one will notice.'

She washed her hair and spent ages in front of the mirror, carefully applying make-up. Not too much, though; she didn't want to look like the tarts that paraded up and down the streets of Fortitude Valley.

Ellis called promptly at six o'clock. He was carrying a small box, which he handed to her. Inside was an orchid, pink to match her dress.

'How did you know?' she cried, delighted.

'Lucky guess,' he smiled. 'May I pin it on?'

The base of his palm brushed against her breast as he secured the flower to her neckline. A fleeting touch — there, then gone — and she felt a shiver of excitement.

'And that's not all,' he said with a grin, handing her a wrapped parcel.

'What is it?' No-one ever gave her presents, and now she was receiving two in the same night. 'It's not my birthday.'

'No,' he laughed, seemingly amused by her surprise. 'Open it and see.'

There were stockings inside. Not one pair, but

three. 'Silk! How lovely!' she exclaimed, delighted, holding them for a moment against her cheek. She thanked him by standing on tiptoes and kissing him on the cheek.

He took her to Lennon's Hotel. A doorman met them at the car, snapping his fingers at the parking attendant. In through the front door she swept, feeling like a princess on Ellis's arm. Everywhere she looked there were vases of flowers and chandeliers glittering from the high ceilings.

A waiter ushered them to a cosy alcove and Ellis held the chair out for her. 'Would you like a drink before dinner?' he asked when they were seated.

'Thanks. That'd be lovely.'

He ordered martinis and took a cigar from his pocket. 'You don't mind, do you?'

'Of course not.'

Lydia had never been in such a fancy hotel. She glanced at the women parading past wearing stylish hats, escorted by men in smart suits or neatly-pressed uniforms. Strains of music floated towards them from a nearby room, a snappy jazzy number that set her feet tapping. She thought about dancing with Ellis, imagined his strong arms guiding her across the dance floor and his body pressed against hers. And afterwards ...

'Drink, madam.'

The waiter had returned with the martinis, interrupting her thoughts. Tentatively she sipped the cool liquid. It tasted sweet and exotic. Ellis reached over and took her hand. 'I'm glad you could make it tonight. Enjoying yourself?'

She took another sip, stared at him over the rim of her glass, challenging him. 'What do you think?'

'I think,' he began, staring into her face, 'that you're a beautiful woman who deserves the very best. Best food and wine. Best music.'

'And the best man?'

He laughed. 'Flattery will get you everywhere, my dear. Anyway, it's just occurred to me that there's one thing I haven't asked you.'

'And what's that?'

'Your age.'

'I'm nineteen.'

'Just a baby,' he teased, 'compared to an old man of thirty-eight.'

'You're not old. Besides,' she added, tracing one finger along the back of his hand, 'I prefer mature men.'

She found the combination of Ellis, the pungent aroma of the Havana cigar and the martini overwhelmingly erotic, yet perplexing. No man had ever gone to this much trouble on her behalf. Flowers. Stockings. Expensive drinks and dinner. He certainly believed in paying his way.

Ellis ordered the meal. Lobster and prawns, and tiny bowls of salad served separately. Ordered another round of drinks. 'This reminds me of home,' he said as dinner was served. 'Buying fresh shellfish from the lobster boats in Boothbay Harbor.'

'Tell me about yourself,' Lydia prompted, spearing a prawn.

He talked about his boyhood in the States, growing up in Portland, Maine. Lydia, meal finished, listened, her chin cupped in one palm, to the musical cadence of his voice, the soft rise and fall of words. It all sounded so wonderful, so far away, so fascinating.

'Now it's your turn,' he said at last, as a waiter removed the empty plates.

'Nothing to tell,' she replied. 'Anyway, what time does the show start? Shouldn't we be leaving?'

He looked apologetic. 'Actually, I have a confession to make. There is no show. Are you disappointed?'

'Not particularly.'

'I could organise tickets ...'

'It's okay. Really. I don't mind.'

'The truth is, I wanted you all to myself. I want to sit here and look at *you*, not some silly play.' He was silent for a moment, watching her, and she had the craziest urge to glance away, not stare at him boldly as she had been. There was a moment's discomfort, as though he had touched some raw nerve inside her. 'You're very pretty,' he went on, reaching forward to brush a stray strand of hair from her face. 'I suppose all the men tell you that?'

Lydia nodded, suddenly unable to speak. The touch of him was like fire, and she fought back a desire to place her hand there, where his own hand had been seconds before.

'Well,' he said, breaking the spell and pushing his chair back. 'Let's go dancing. What do you fancy?'

'The jitterbug. It's my favourite.'

They went downstairs to the dance hall. Ellis was more than adept on the dance floor and she knew other women were watching them as they passed.

The band played the music of Glenn Miller, Duke Ellington and Benny Goodman. 'Not bad,' called Ellis as he spun her across the floor. 'For a small-town band, they've got a big sound.'

Eventually they fell exhausted into the street at some ungodly hour of the morning. 'It's three o'clock,' said Ellis, glancing at his watch. 'Don't know about you, but I'm ready for bed.'

Sex: that was all the other men had ever wanted, and she waited for him to initiate the invitation. *My place or yours?* But the words weren't forthcoming. 'Come on,' he said instead. 'It's time I took you home.'

He stopped the car outside her front door. 'Thanks for tonight, Lydia. I enjoyed myself.'

'Me, too.'

'Can we do it again?'

'I'd love to. When?'

Ellis laughed and the rich baritone of it filled the car. 'Whoa there, precious. Let me catch up on some shut-eye. I'll call you, okay?'

Inside, Lydia tossed her clothes on the floor and slid between the sheets. But sleep was not forthcoming. Instead, her mind went over the evening, searching out small details. She smiled to herself in the dark, secretly puzzled. Ellis had been the perfect gentleman. He hadn't even tried to kiss her goodnight, had simply held her hand to his mouth for the briefest moment.

'I don't know what I've done wrong,' Lydia complained to Ellen as she lit up a Chesterfield. 'He said he'd ring and it's been three days. I've scarcely left the telephone.'

'There *is* a war on,' replied Ellen dryly. 'Perhaps he's been busy. And I'll have my dress back, if you don't mind. There's a do on, over at the club.'

'There's a stain,' said Lydia dismissively. 'I'll have it cleaned.' Then. 'What if he didn't enjoy the evening? He seemed to, but I couldn't be sure. He's a lot older than the men I usually go out with.'

'How old?'

'Thirty-eight.'

'Bloody ancient.' Ellen stubbed the butt of her cigarette in the pot plant on the table.

'You wouldn't say that if you met him. He's one of the nicest, sexiest men I've ever met,' she retorted defensively.

'And he didn't even kiss you goodnight! Come on, Lydia. He must be retarded or something. All normal blokes want sex!'

Lydia was called in to the theatre on her day off work. One of the girls in the show had left and she was asked to audition for the part. She felt confident. Acting, singing, dancing: they couldn't be too difficult. She was certain she had a reasonable voice, and Nina had always said she was a great actress. Ellis hadn't complained about her dancing, although he hadn't bothered to call.

She warbled her way through two songs, accompanied by a man on the piano. Was asked to lift her skirt above her knees and waltz across the floor.

'Voice isn't great.'

'It's passable.'

'Acting needs a bit of work.'

'Great legs, though. That's what the blokes want.'

'If you don't mind,' Lydia interrupted, 'I'm not a piece of meat in a butcher's window.'

'You got it in one, love.'

'So, what's the verdict?'

'The job's yours.'

Ellis phoned that night. 'I've been out of town for a few days and haven't had a chance to call. What about Saturday?'

'What about it?' She was still smarting from his absence and his easy dismissal of it.

He laughed. 'Sweetheart, I'm sorry. I should have let you know. Okay. Point taken. Forgiven?'

'Forgiven.'

They went to the horseraces at Albion Park, part of a group of American soldiers and their girlfriends. They made a gay party, all jokes and bubbling laughter. The day was sunny, with not a cloud to mar the interminable blue of the sky. She backed one winner, with Ellis' help, boosting her funds by almost three pounds.

Afterwards there was dinner at a nearby cafe, followed by a taxi ride home. 'Would you like to come up for a drink?' Lydia offered, certain he would. But he surprised her.

'Can I take a raincheck on that, sweetheart? Busy day tomorrow, I'm afraid. Maybe next time.'

'He's homosexual,' said Ellen the next day.

Lydia resigned from her waitressing position. Practised like mad at rehearsals, watched and learned from the others. Worried herself sick before her opening show, a week later.

Afterwards, Claire came to the dressing room. 'I thought I'd catch your first performance.'

'Did you see me?' Lydia had only a small part and, to her dismay, had been placed at the back of the stage.

'Of course. You were very good.'

'You're just saying that.'

Claire ignored the remark. 'Don't know about the skimpy costume, though. Mum'd have a fit if she saw you like that.'

'Well, she won't know unless you tell her,' replied Lydia darkly, pulling on a stocking.

Claire picked up the other stocking. 'Real silk! Where did you manage to get these?'

'A friend. He's an American.'

'Some friend.'

'He's gorgeous. Mature. The nicest I've met in a long while.'

'How mature?' asked Claire suspiciously.

'Thirty-eight. And don't tell me he's too old.'

'Would you listen if I did?'

Who was Claire to give her lectures on men? Her own life was in chaos. In love with Alex, Lydia was still certain, yet married to his brother. What a tangled mess! Quickly she changed the subject. 'Speaking of clothes, I've used all my coupons and there's a pair of shoes I've had my eye on.'

Claire opened her purse. 'You might as well have my spares. I don't need anything fancy these days, now I'm an old married woman.'

'Thanks.' Lydia grabbed the coupons and gave Claire a quick peck on the cheek. 'These should be just enough.'

It wasn't until Claire was leaving that she let slip the information. 'Did you know Alex has moved to Brisbane?'

'No! What about Erica? Is she here, too?'

Lydia shook her head. 'Back in Tea-tree Passage, and none too pleased about him going, apparently.'

'So where, why —?'

She shrugged, casually. 'An army hospital somewhere. Mum did say, but I forget.'

Alex turned up on Claire's doorstep a week later. She'd been queuing for much-needed art supplies at T. C. Beirnes department store in Fortitude Valley, and her feet were aching and tired. He was waiting in the lounge, talking to Kath who raised her eyebrows questioningly as Claire came into the room. Nice one, she seemed to say, before disappearing down the hallway to her room.

'What are you doing in the big city?' she asked, in what she hoped was a casual voice. Her heart was thumping so loudly that she was sure he could hear.

'I've joined the medical corps.'

He had, Alex told her, wanted to contribute to the war effort, to 'do his bit'. So now he was working at the Australian General Hospital at Greenslopes, the largest army hospital in Queensland. Hal was back home, managing the medical practice there as best he could. 'I've got the night off, which is pretty rare. So I thought you might like to go out for dinner.'

She paused, considering the protocol. Surely David wouldn't mind. Alex was his brother, after all.

'I know it's short notice. We can make it another night if you'd prefer.'

'No,' she said quickly. 'Dinner's fine. If I see one more meatless meal I think I'll scream. A nice juicy steak, that's what I fancy.'

'How about the Riverside Club?'

'Perfect.'

They walked through the city, side by side. The streets were filled to overflowing with men and women in uniform, cafes spilling tables and patrons onto footpaths. Laughter and conversation mingled in the night air. Cars crawled past, headlights hooded as demanded by the blackout restrictions.

They found a table and ordered a drink. In that yellow lamplight, Alex's face looked grey with fatigue. Concerned, she reached a hand across the table and took his. 'Are you all right?'

'Tired, that's all.'

'How's Erica?'

'Fine. Fine.' He looked away for a moment, unable to meet her gaze. A slight frown creased his forehead and he seemed distracted.

'It's not fine, is it?' she asked in a soft voice.

'No.' Shook his head. 'Damn difficult, really, what with me being down here. She wanted to come down, too, bring Josh. The thing is, I'm supposed to live in the digs provided. And I'm working such horrendous hours at the hospital I'd hardly ever see them.'

'Don't you worry about them being up there?'

'They're a hell of a lot safer in Tea-tree Passage.'

'Do you really believe that? I'm worried about Mum. Been wondering if I should bring her down here.'

'If the Japs do attack, it's going to be on a major city, not some little town. So, as for Tea-tree Passage not being safe — I think it's a load of *hogwash*, as the Yanks would say.'

He drawled the word, American-style. Claire laughed and changed the subject. 'Lydia has an American boyfriend. He brings her silk stockings.'

'Lucky Lydia! She never did handle deprivations well.'

'I think she's in love.'

He raised his eyebrows, staring at her with an amused expression on his face. 'Lydia wouldn't know the meaning of love.'

'I know. She's a selfish little pig. But she is my sister and blood's —'

'Thicker than water,' he finished for her with a smile, then changed the subject himself. 'So, how do you fill your time while David's away?'

She shrugged. 'Work, mostly. Plus I spend a few nights down at the town hall, packing boxes for the Comforts' Fund.'

'And your artwork?'

'When I get the chance. Supplies are so hard to get these days it hardly seems worth the bother. So how's my little nephew, Josh?'

At the mention of his son's name, Alex's face lit up. 'If only you could see him. He's a beaut little kid. Loads of fun. Had his first birthday not long back. But of course you know that: you sent a present.' He fished in his pocket, pulling out a crumpled photograph. 'It's a few months old now, but it's all I've got. Erica did promise to take some new ones.'

His voice trailed away, and Claire wondered if Erica were punishing him in some devious way. What were a few photographs, after all?

They had dinner and several coffees. Talked about David and her war office job, conditions at the hospital. 'It's crazy. Everyone's running at breakneck speed. Not enough sleep. We're like walking zombies. Speaking of which, I'd better take you home. Tomorrow's another day and I'm exhausted.'

He took her to the front door of the boarding house, stood holding both her hands in his. 'Thanks for tonight, Claire. I really enjoyed myself.'

'Me, too.'

'This is the first chance I've really had to talk to you alone since —'

He stopped, the sentence unfinished. Mentally she supplied the words. *Since that day at the railway station when you told me you loved me.*

She closed her eyes against the sight of him. 'Don't, Alex. I don't want explanations or excuses for what happened. It's all in the past.'

'Is it?'

The question hung between them, heavy in the night air. 'Yes,' she replied firmly, reaching up to kiss him on the cheek. 'We've both moved on, made a new future for ourselves. So, thanks for a lovely evening. We must do it again.'

Somehow she was walking away from him, not looking back. Walking away from that familiar much-loved man to her cold lonely room. He was married — so was she — and she'd made vows to David which she would never break. There could never be anything between her and Alex now.

She lay in bed, wiping away the tears, hating herself, her own morality. Determinedly she crushed that need to be held, to be loved, into the hard core within. Claire: the good girl. Claire: the strong one. Why couldn't she be more like Lydia? Snatch any opportunity that came along; live life for the present: those were her sister's mottos. And maybe there was nothing wrong with that method of thinking. The way the war was progressing, God only knew what was in store.

Ellis called for her in the staff car. 'We're going on a picnic up in the mountains, so bring something warm,' he warned.

He'd brought a hamper, packed with all sorts of delicacies. Ham and cold pork pie, cheese, bread rolls and sweet red tomatoes. Tiny custard tarts and, for after, a bottle of whisky.

He laid a chequered rug in the sunshine. They were on a hilltop and had a commanding view of the valley below. Small farms dotted the scene, neat fences dividing the land into picturesque squares. Lydia breathed in the fresh air and twirled around, holding her arms to the breeze. 'The countryside. I just love it here. Let's not go back. Ever.'

'My commanding officer would have something to say about that.'

'Well, let's stay a day. A week.'

He raised his eyebrows. 'We passed a little guesthouse further back. Perhaps they've a vacancy for the night.'

A passer-by stopped, asking directions. Ellis handed the man his camera, instructing him on the use. Then he put his arm around Lydia. 'Smile,' he said, and she obliged. The man took several shots and went on his way.

Later they stowed the picnic gear in the car and trundled back down the hill, stopping at the guesthouse nestled into the side of the hill. Yes, the woman at the desk informed them. There was a vacancy. One room only.

'We'll take it,' said Lydia.

The room was small — the bed seemed to take up most of the space — but cheerful. A log fire snapped in the grate. From the window, late afternoon clouds could be seen hanging in the valley. Lydia felt she could reach out and touch them, they appeared so close. 'Well, what do you think?' asked Ellis, sitting on the chair next to the fire. 'Does it suit, madam?'

'Oh, silly. It's lovely. Cosy. Private.'

'Ah, private. That's important.'

She came across the room towards him, watching his now-familiar face. He smiled and she knelt beside him, placed her mouth on his. Felt his lips move, mouth open to accept hers. Sensed his arms encompassing her.

'I've wanted to do that for a long time,' he said, drawing away at last.

'Why didn't you?'

'Because it has to be right.'

'And this,' she indicated the room with a sweep of her hand, 'is right?'

'Yes.'

A knock on the door: their hostess informing them that a meal was being served in the dining room. Ellis escorted her downstairs. Damask tablecloth, red candles dripping wax along their length, roast beef and vegetables accompanied by wine; another fire, this one larger than the first. Lydia was scarcely aware of it all. She was anxious to return to their room, her nerves taut like fine wire. Impatiently she sipped the wine and pushed the food around on her plate, scarcely eating. Her attention was centred on Ellis. Her eyes scarcely left his face. She was watching, waiting. Her body ached for the touch of him, desire building inside her like an all-consuming heat.

Just when it seemed she could bear it no longer, he pushed his chair back and rose, led her back along the hallway to their room. Her legs felt weak — was it from desire or the wine? — and her breath seemed shallow, almost non-existent.

'Ellis,' she whispered as he closed the door behind them. 'I can't bear it any longer. Don't keep me waiting.'

They fell together on the bed, fully clothed, kissing. She grappled with his belt, cupped her palm around his hardness. 'Slow down,' he whispered, stilling her with his hands. 'There's no rush. We've got all night.'

446

One by one, he removed her clothes. Dress. Petticoat. Bra and undies. Rolled the silk stockings down the length of her leg, pausing to plant tiny erotic kisses along the arch of her foot. Mouth teasing. Hands arousing. Time played out, slow-moving minutes. The fire crackled in the grate, dying low.

Helped by Lydia, he removed his own clothes, guiding her hands over buttons and zippers. Pausing. Waiting. Punctuating her movements with his mouth on her breasts, her belly and thighs. In the firelight his eyes were like dark hollows in his face and she felt like a flower opening to the sun. But he was the warmth, the heat, teasing and tormenting until she cried out with the desperate wanting.

Her body opened to receive him, and the sensation was like nothing she had ever experienced before. This was no hurried coupling, skirts pulled up and hands pushing aside the buttons of her blouse, bruising her breasts, like she'd been used to. But slow and rhythmic, Ellis taking time to please her as well as himself.

Pace quickening. Senses alert, poised. Long drawn-out sigh coming from his mouth. One final explosive movement and unexpected pleasure jolting through her.

'Oh my God! Oh my God!'

Words tumbled unbidden from her mouth at the wonderment of it all, the whisper of it reverberating around the room.

Afterwards Ellis held her, whispering the words she had longed to hear. 'I love you, Lydia. Oh, God! I love you.'

They talked for hours, lying in the bed, a warm tangle of arms and legs. Cocooned away from the world and the ever-present threat of war, firelight casting rosy shadows along the walls.

'Was it worth the wait?' he asked later, tracing one hand along the ridge of her hip.

She smiled, shaking her head at him. 'Of all the perverse, deliberate —'

'Lydia, sex is like a fine bottle of wine or exquisite food. To be enjoyed properly, it can't be taken anywhere, any time. You have to prepare for it, plan ahead. Anticipation is part of the excitement.'

'Anticipation!' she said, kissing him again, 'makes me impatient. Now, where were we before? Oh, here, I think.'

And she ran her hand along his belly, light teasing movements that brought him to hardness again.

CHAPTER 32

Built on a rise at Forty-six Hawthorne Road, Halcyon was a three-storeyed Mediterranean-style villa which had been commandeered during the course of the war for the use of American officers. Lydia loved the house, soon knew intimately the quickest route to Ellis's room. Sprinting up the wide staircase, she would peek her head around his door; the way became as familiar to her as her own heartbeat.

'A man who owned a heap of shoe shops built it,' Ellis told her as they lay on the wide bed, looking upwards at the ornate cornice work.

'Must be money in shoes,' Lydia replied with a laugh, stretching her legs and thinking of the pair of black pumps she had bought a few weeks earlier, compliments of Claire's commandeered ration coupons.

From the bedroom window there was an unobstructed view of New Farm Park. By leaning out over the sill, Lydia could see the wide sweep of lawn dotted by trees, and couples strolling beneath the shade. Inside, in the cool dark confines of the room, Ellis taught her about love and desire and indulgence, playing her out until she was desperate for his taut tanned body. He filled the needy components of her, made her feel wanted, adored. For her own part, she felt incomplete and fragmented without him.

'When this whole rotten war's over, we'll get married,' he said, sliding from the bed and walking towards the window, watching the scene below. 'Fancy living in the States?'

Lydia watched the firm lines of his buttocks as he moved, thinking lazily how she had cupped them in her palms, drawing him into her, less than an hour earlier. 'I might.'

'We'll have a nice house, a few kids. You'll love my folks.'

'Sounds heavenly.'

Idly she let her mind wander back. The past two months, since she had first made love with Ellis, had passed quickly, days sliding into each other in quick succession. He had spared no expense during their courtship and his generosity knew no bounds. He had the use of a staff car and a seemingly unlimited supply of petrol. There were trips to the pictures with expensive Dress Circle seats, and dinners followed by dancing.

Daily he brought her presents: stockings and whisky, cigarettes and boxes of chocolates. He waited at the stage door for her after work, escorting her through the darkened streets. Sometimes they stopped in an all-night cafe for coffee, dawdling over the menu. Laughing. Whispering. Lydia reaching out, touching his hand. 'I need you, Ellis. Make love to me.'

'Now?'

'Now. Let's skip coffee.'

Running hand in hand down the hill towards the park. Ellis teasing her body with his own on the soft grass. Afterwards, walking home, hand in hand, leaning against him. In that short time he had become her rock, her support.

'I don't expect to be gone long. Will you miss me?'

She propped herself on her elbow on the bed, drawing her mind back to the present and his words.

'What did you say?'

'We're pulling out.'

'When?'

'Tomorrow morning.'

'Where are you going?'

'I'm not allowed to say. Remember, idle talk —'

'I know, I know! How will I contact you then?'

'I'll write.'

'Promise?'

'Have I ever lied to you?'

'Of course not.'

'I love you, Lydia. This past two months has been fantastic. Wait for me. I'll only be gone a few weeks.'

She sat on the bed wearing one of his shirts, watching in dismay as Ellis packed, meticulously laying his clothes in the suitcase. He took his brush and comb from the dresser, and then the photographs — the ones he'd had taken that afternoon up in the mountains, the first day they'd made love — and handed them to her. 'Look after these until I get back. They might get crushed in the case.'

'You're taking everything?' she asked in surprise.

'There's not really that much to take.'

'I suppose not.'

'When we come back, we could have different billets. Meanwhile, they'll need this room for someone else, I expect.'

She tried to think of another man in the room, a stranger, invading that private place they had both shared. Sudden images came to her. Ellis making love to her on the rumpled bed. Leaning from the window at dawn, seeing the mist lying in the park. Watching in the mirror above the dresser as Ellis had come up behind her, stroking her nakedness.

What if something happened to him? What if he didn't — couldn't — come back to her? Was this how every woman felt, this utter desolation, when their menfolk went away to war? Lydia didn't know. It was new to her, this loving business, putting others before herself, thinking of someone else's needs.

Sleep eluded her. She lay, her body curved spoon-like against Ellis, wishing the night would never end. But too soon it was morning, the first tentative rays of dawn stealing into the room. Ellis stirred and slid from the bed. She could hear him moving about the room, dressing. Pull of fabric against skin. Snap of belt buckle. She went to get up, but he gently pushed her back on the bed. 'No, don't move. I want to remember you like that, lying there amongst the sheets, all rumpled and half asleep.'

He dropped a kiss lightly on her forehead. She closed her eyes again, feeling the warmth of his mouth. Heard the scrape of a suitcase being picked up, his footfalls. Heard the final click of the door. The sound of his footsteps as they receded down the hall echoed like a drum roll in her head.

She lay there for a long time, eyes squeezed shut to stem the flow of tears, and unable to move. Those last few moments replayed themselves in her head, like a movie. Sounds, movements. Memories. Besides a few photos, nothing remained.

Nina felt as though she were living in a twilight zone, on constant tenterhooks, waiting for something — the unthinkable — to happen. After sunset they lived in the gloom of brown-out. Windowpanes were taped against the possibility of bomb blast, and householders were supposed to keep buckets of sand handy for smothering incendiary bombs. Rationing made life difficult. She was tired of making eggless cakes and preparing chokoes so they looked like pears.

Maudie, of course, refused to comply. 'What would the Japs want with an old duck like me?' she said to Nina with a wry smile. 'I'm too bloody old for all this mucking about. And some days I think a bomb would be a blessing, put me out of my misery.'

Maudie was going downhill fast. She seldom went further than her own yard these days, a plump stooped figure with a bland face, once-blue eyes pale and clouded over with cataracts. She was inclined, increasingly so, to be forgetful, often referring to Joe and Claire as children. Lydia's name she never mentioned. When Nina gently reminded her that Claire was married now, a grown woman, a look of such puzzlement crossed her face. Nina helped her keep the house tidy as best she could — or as much as Maudie would allow — and regularly took over a casserole or cake. The only highlight to her days, she told Nina, was listening to Jack Davey and his quizzes on the wireless.

Nina was also concerned for Alex. There had been rumours circulating about Erica; she had been entertaining American soldiers in her home, going with them to the pub in town.

'It's not right,' said Maudie in one of her rare lucid moments. 'A young woman by herself with a child, entertaining men. What would Alex say?'

'He's not here, is he?' replied Nina, a resentment against Erica building inside her.

'He's a doctor!' Maudie snapped back, a look of exasperation on her face. 'There are certain proprieties —'

'Well, you can be the one to tell him.'

Eventually she tried to talk to Erica. She met her along the track one day. The boy, Josh, was walking beside her, a miniature replica of his father with his lean frame and sandy-coloured hair.

'I haven't seen you for a while, Erica. How's Alex?'

She seemed bored and restless, and Nina was almost certain she'd been drinking. Her eyes had a glazed, disinterested look. 'I wouldn't have a clue. Stuck in this place, I never know what's going on.'

'Why don't you go down to the city, spend a bit of time with Alex and your parents?'

'And why don't you mind your own business?'

The memory spun at her, taking her breath away. She, Nina, handing Frank the bookmark she had found in Joe's pocket. *Mim's* bookmark. Remembered the sick feeling in the pit of her stomach, the knowledge that she had been betrayed. Not only by her husband, whom she had trusted implicitly, but by a woman who had claimed to be her friend. Remembered the look in Frank's eyes when she had handed the bookmark to him. Warning her away. *Why don't you mind your own business?*

Calmly, purposefully, she said, 'There's talk around town, Erica. I'm not saying I take much notice of gossip, and how you conduct yourself is your own business. But don't involve the boy.'

Erica looked momentarily stunned, picked up Josh and sat him on her hip. Shrugged. 'Have you tried to get a travel permit lately? Someone has to have died before they'll give you one. There are signs up all over the station walls, saying "is this trip really necessary?" Anyway, Alex is working such long hours I'd hardly get to see him and, as for living in my parents' house — I'd feel like a child again.'

Nina took Maudie for her fortnightly visit to Hal. He seemed greyer around the temples than before, his face pale. Exhausted, she thought, the poor man's exhausted.

'Just battling on,' he said after he had examined Maudie. 'It's awkward with Alex being away, but it's difficult times all round. I'd gotten used to another pair of hands around here, that's all.'

* * *

Joe wiped the sweat from his forehead with his shirt sleeve and held out his hand for the letter. He stared at the writing. Jane. Four bloody months and only now had he received word from her.

He'd tried not to think about her, had attempted to immerse himself in his work, but it had been damn difficult on mail days, when the other chaps had letters from their girls. Hard, too, to hide his disappointment, and forget the words she'd said the night before he'd left. *I don't know if I can keep that promise, or if I want to ... we can never go back to what we have ...*

Now, letter in hand, he walked away from the other men, turning it over in his hands. Part of him wanted to rip the envelope open, devour the contents, yet another secret part of him was wary. There'd been no word from her for months, so why now?

Taking a deep breath, he slit the top of the envelope with his nail and drew out the paper. There was only one page. His eyes scanned the few miserable sentences in disbelief.

> *Dear Joe,*
> *I want you to know that whatever we had is over. I've met someone else. I'm sorry, but I can't help what's happened.*
> *Jane*

Shock rendered him motionless; his lungs felt suddenly devoid of air. He stared, devastated, at the words on the paper until they dissolved into a blur, and he squeezed his eyes shut, blocking them from his sight. How could she take all that was precious and sacred between them, and fling it in his face like this! How could she reduce the relationship they'd shared to these paltry inadequate words! *Whatever we had.* What was *that* supposed to mean? He'd loved her, damn it! Totally and unequivocally.

'Bitch!' he said, crushing the page into a tight ball and lobbing it into the nearest clump of bushes, out of sight. '*Traitorous bloody bitch*!'

It wasn't until later, when he could think more rationally, that the questions came, thrusting themselves mercilessly at him like tiny knives. Whom had she met? When? Where? He thought about that day with his father at Mim's, years earlier: walking along the hallway and opening the forbidden door; his father's bare buttocks moving up and down; Mim moaning. Thought about Jane doing that with someone other than himself, and a pain rose up inside him, deep in his chest. Bloody hell!

He tried to write back, picked up a pencil and paper at odd times, but the words wouldn't come. What to say anyway? Please change your mind? I love you? Don't debase our love into some sordid temporary affair?

No, he decided at length. He wouldn't beg. Jane had made her choice and he'd have to live with that. He couldn't alter the fact, anyway, stuck here in this wretched jungle. But he'd never let it happen again. No way! If he got out of this damn war alive, he'd never let himself love another woman, never be bound by anyone again. Live life for himself, that was what he'd do. To hell with the rest of them!

Lydia sat motionless on the edge of the bed, holding the calendar in her hand. Disbelief flooded through her. Two bloody months! Why hadn't she noticed?

Too caught up in it all, she thought, thinking of the visit to the doctor earlier in the day. Lying on the hard bed, her feet in stirrups and his hands probing her. Words confirming what she already knew, shocking her into uncustomary silence.

There was a knock on the door. 'Come in,' Lydia called.

Ellen swung into the bedroom. 'Why so miserable? Anyone would think you'd lost a shilling and found a threepence.'

'Guess,' she said glumly, then shook her head. 'No, you probably wouldn't. I'm preggers. Up the duff. Bun in the oven —'

'I get the picture.' Then. 'How do you know? Maybe it's a false alarm.'

'I'm two months overdue. I've spent every morning during the last two weeks with my head down the loo. And if that isn't enough evidence, I've just come from the doctor. "Well, Miss Carmody," he said, in a very condescending tone. "I'd say by about next June, you'll have a bouncing baby." Shit! The last thing I want is a kid.'

'Well, as my mother used to say, if you play with fire then you're likely to get burned.'

'Thanks.' She screwed the calendar into a tight roll and threw it at the wall. It bounced onto the floor and she sat looking at it, fighting back the urge to scream.

'What'll you do now?'

'Tell Ellis. It's his problem, too.'

'You've heard from him, then?'

Lydia shook her head. 'Not one bloody word since he left.'

'He might be some place where it's impossible to contact you.'

'I keep telling myself that.'

The following afternoon she went to Somerville House and spoke to one of the American officials. Asked after Ellis's whereabouts.

The man checked through a file on his desk. 'There's no-one of that name posted in Brisbane at the moment.'

Trying to stay calm, in control. 'I know that. I need to contact him urgently.'

'Why?'

'That's personal.'

'Well, I'm sorry. Without —'

Desperately. 'Can't you give me a contact address?'

'That's classified.'

'I told you. I need to contact this person urgently —'

'You could write a letter care of the Central Bureau of Intelligence. Maybe they could forward it on.'

'I might just do that!' she cried, frustrated.

She was walking back down the stairs when she heard a familiar voice. 'Hank!' she cried, grabbing his arm. 'I need to find Ellis. He said he'd come back for me, but he's been gone ages and there's been no word.'

She knew she was babbling, not making sense, but Hank was her only hope. He gave her a cheeky grin. 'He won't be back for you, darling. They've shipped him home to the States.'

'Home?'

'It wasn't a surprise. He knew where he was going when he left.'

Ellis had known, yet he hadn't told her? Why?

'He was a bit of a dark-horse, old Ellis,' Hank went on. From the smirk on his face, he was obviously enjoying himself. 'Like as not there were other secrets he didn't tell you.'

'What more could there possibly be?' she replied wearily.

'The guy's married. Has been for years. There's a couple of kids and a wife back in California.'

'California? He told me he came from Maine.'

'You didn't fall for that one, did you?'

Speechless, Lydia felt her way down the stairs, her mind churning. Her legs threatened to buckle under her. There was a tight feeling across her chest, and she wondered momentarily if she were about to faint. She paused at the bottom of the stairs to catch her breath. 'Are you all right?' asked a voice at her elbow.

It was one of the porters. Mutely she nodded and moved on. Bloody hell! What would she do now? Ellis was gone. He'd lied to her, on several counts, and she'd trusted him. Given him her heart and soul. How *could* she?

'You bastard!' she muttered under her breath. 'You rotten stinking bastard.'

'You could get rid of it,' Ellen said later. 'My cousin got in the family way last year, with her husband overseas and all. She had an abortion.'

'How much did it cost?'

'Fifty quid.'

Almost four months' wages. Lydia groaned. 'I don't have anywhere near that amount of money saved.'

'Couldn't you borrow it?'

She thought hard. Nina didn't have that kind of spare money, and Joe was overseas. So no luck there. Maudie would probably have the dough but there was no way Lydia would ask that old cow, letting her gloat over her predicament.

That left Claire.

She would ask her sister out for lunch, plead her case. Throw in a few well-chosen remarks about protecting the family name and not letting Nina find out. Surely to God, Claire would come through. It was her only hope.

Claire found Alex waiting downstairs when she finished work the following evening. It was months since she'd seen him, since they'd had dinner together. 'Surprise,' he said, kissing her lightly on the cheek. 'I've got passes for the Trocadero, so I've come to take you dancing.'

It was late December. Shop windows sported Christmas trees and coloured lights. Buses painted in camouflage colours trundled past. Crowds thronged the footpaths, intent on last-minute shopping. Everywhere Claire looked, it seemed there were women in uniform — VADs and WAAAFs mainly.

'Will you get home for Christmas?' she asked while they were waiting for the traffic to clear, so they could cross the road.

'I'm scheduled on over the holiday break. It means I'll miss Josh opening his presents. What about you?'

There was, Claire realised, no mention of Erica. She shook her head. 'At least Mum and Maudie have each other. Bit miserable to be spending it by yourself. A few of us from the boarding house were planning on going out for lunch. And I keep thinking that somehow David might get leave, although that's probably wishful thinking.'

'How is my brother? Have you heard from him lately?'

'The occasional letter. He's well, missing everyone. They keep him busy on the Catalinas.'

'What about Lydia?'

'I haven't seen her for weeks. She only lands on my doorstep if she wants something.'

They both agreed it was too hot to eat first, settling instead for a couple of drinks at the bar. Then, with the band starting up a popular tune, he led her onto the dance floor. She felt his arms around her, protective and strong, reinforcing how much she missed intimacy in her life. It had been over twelve months since her marriage to David, and she hadn't seen him since those four glorious days by the beach. It should be her husband here with her, she thought with a stab of certainty, not Alex. She needed someone who would love her wholeheartedly. She craved that tenderness and affection. Needed sex.

They danced a Palais Glide, Hokey Pokey, and a Boomps-a-Daisy. The music ended with a flourish and Alex pulled away, laughing. 'Don't know about you, but I'm thirsty. Drink?'

'That'd be lovely.'

She sat on an empty seat and watched as he threaded his way through the throng towards the bar. He was tall and square-shouldered, not unattractive, and she noticed that several women also watched his progress across the room, until he was lost in the crowd. A couple of WAAAFs she knew went past, stopped to chat, then moved on. She glanced around, seeing only the faces of strangers and, despite the crowd, she suddenly felt lonely. Lonely for home and the sound of the surf, the sighing of the tea-trees. Lonely for familiar faces — her mother's, David's.

'Oh, God,' she whispered to herself. 'When will this nightmare ever end?' But what precise nightmare did she mean, she wondered. The war? The separation from her husband? This hopeless, helpless attraction she still felt towards Alex?

She found herself searching the room for him, for the sight of his friendly face. Finally, there he was, coming back towards her, a drink in both hands. At that moment he looked up, caught her gaze, and came to an abrupt halt for what was merely a fraction of a second, but felt like hours — a long, drawn-out period of time when she was unable to look away. Then he smiled, breaking the spell.

It was late when they left. 'Hungry?' he asked, steering her towards the river front and a late-night pie stall. 'I often come down here when I finish late, have a bite to eat, sit and look at the water.'

They sat on a bench near the river, munching on pies. The water was an inky black, slapping against the banks. The occasional car trundled past. There was a sound of laughter, somewhere beyond her line of vision.

'How's Erica?' Claire asked, confronting the issue.

Alex was silent for a while and, when he finally spoke, his voice was soft and low, holding a note of anguish. 'Have you ever made mistakes in your life, Claire?'

'Yes.' *Falling in love with you, for a start.*

'A mistake so terrible that it ruins everything you believe in?'

'I don't understand —'

He turned to her, taking her hands in his, words tumbling from his mouth in an effort to be heard. 'There are so many things I've wanted to tell you. Erica was pregnant when we married. That's why —' He paused, tightening his grip on her hands. 'Anyway, she lost the child, but there it was. Too late to unravel all those words and promises. Now there's Josh, although Erica hasn't adapted well to motherhood. But, God, I love that boy. If anything was to happen —' His voice choked. 'What I'm trying to say is, that my life has gone down a road I would never have willingly chosen, but there's absolutely nothing I can do to alter it now.'

'Alex —'

Determinedly she withdrew her hands from his grasp. She had to break the moment, put an end to his words. She didn't want to hear how unhappy he was, or listen as he explained the desperate futility of his life. It seemed such a waste, such wanton destruction. One wrong decision, years earlier, and so many lives affected. Hers and David's. His and Erica's. Josh's. Consciously, she closed her mind to it all, to Alex's confession, his need to explain his actions.

Abruptly he changed the subject. 'But you probably don't want to hear all that. It's all in the past and I have to get on with my life, make the best of it.'

She nodded, unable to speak.

'So let me know when David gets leave. Perhaps Erica can come down and we'll all go out together. Just the four of us.'

'That would be lovely,' she said, trying unsuccessfully to muster enthusiasm for the idea. The thought was unbearable to her, spending time in close proximity to both brothers, Erica inserting herself between them.

They walked back to Claire's boarding house along darkened streets, not talking. She didn't know what words to say to break the silence between them. Thunder rumbled, surprisingly close. Lightning lit the sky, great jagged forks of it.

'It's going to rain. Would you like to come in for a drink?' she asked as they came to her front door and the first of the drops began to fall, warm on her skin.

Alex glanced down at his watch. 'I'd love to, but I'm on duty early tomorrow and I don't want to miss the last tram. If you'll excuse the pun, can I take a raincheck?'

She smiled. 'Of course.'

The evening was obviously at an end, and the disappointment was palpable. Claire rummaged in her bag for the key, inserted it and the door swung open. 'Thanks for a lovely time.'

'I enjoyed it, too.'

She turned to go but he moved, blocking her path. She stared up at him, puzzled. 'Claire?' he said, cupping her face with his hands. It seemed so right, his mouth on hers, and she stood on tiptoe to receive his kiss. A dizzying rush of emotion surged through her, reminding her of the need to be held, touched. She was conscious of her own hands at the back of his neck, pulling his mouth hard against hers. She was conscious also of the sudden tension, a sexual urgency, lying between them like a coiled spring; she was aware of Alex's needs and her own surprising, acknowledged desire to satisfy them.

It would have been so easy, so damn effortless to take advantage of his hurt and misery, and their shared loneliness. Spiriting him up to her bedroom, emotions and fantasies played out against rumpled sheets and warm flesh. Sharing the night, bodies and secrets. No-one else would have to know. Neither Erica nor David. So easy, because of the circumstances, to console each other, fulfil needs and passions normally kept tightly bound.

So what was stopping her? Her own marriage vows. A little boy named Josh. The knowledge that any sexual relationship she had with Alex could never be anything more than an affair, sordid and grubby, demeaning to both of them.

Abruptly he pulled away, stared at her for what seemed a very long time, and she felt her face burn under his scrutiny. 'I'm sorry, Claire. I had no right to do that.'

He turned and walked away. She stood in the doorway, watching, unable to close the door on his retreating form. A heavy downpour of rain had begun and he turned his collar up against it, bowed his head against its onslaught, finally disappearing into the dark.

Kath met her at the door to her room. Her friend's eyes were ablaze with excitement, and it was the first time Claire had seen her smile in months. 'I was wondering when you'd be home,' she said, beaming, waving an envelope at Claire. 'Guess what! I've had a letter from Tom. Listen.'

She read the brief contents and Claire kissed her friend, held her close. 'That's wonderful! See, I told you something good would happen. And the letter says he's being treated well by the Japanese.'

'Bullshit!' exploded Kath, her happy mood collapsing. 'They're brutal. Everyone says so. I feel so helpless. I want to do something, but I can't.'

'You *can* do something. You can keep writing.'

'This letter's six months old. Anything could have happened since then. Chances are he's not even alive. I feel as though I'm writing to nobody.'

Kath's eyes began to fill with tears and Claire grabbed her, shook her gently. 'Hey, no time for crying. Of course he's alive. You have to hang on to that thought. And your letters will be the one thing that'll get him through all this.'

And herself? she wondered later as she lay in her bed. What would get Claire through this whole miserable war? David? The promise of a life together after it was all over? The children they would some day have? A baby, she thought with sudden certainty. Part of them both, steering her thoughts away from the past, the might-have-beens. The future! That was the important consideration now. Herself and David. She owed him that much.

CHAPTER 33

The next morning Kath came to her room brandishing a telegram. 'The landlady said to give this to you.'

Claire stared at the envelope in Kath's hands, suddenly afraid. 'It's David,' she said, backing away. 'Something's happened. I just know it.'

'Of course it's not David. He's up north somewhere, not overseas.'

'Maybe it's Joe.'

'Your mother would have rung,' Kath reasoned. 'Anyway, you'll never know what it's about unless you open it.'

She thrust the envelope towards her friend. 'You do it.'

'Oh, for goodness sake!' said Kath in exasperation, tearing the paper open and reading the contents. 'Home on leave on the twenty-third for four days. Love David.'

Claire felt a surge of delight. 'The twenty-third! That's only two days away! He'll be here in time for Christmas!'

They cried and hugged each other, celebrating the previous night's letter from Tom as much as David's imminent return. Then Claire got busy in the bathroom, plucking eyebrows and shaving legs.

Later, when the excitement had settled to a bearable level, she thought about her own surprising reaction to the telegram. She had experienced fear there, real fear. How would she cope if something did happen to him? What would her reaction be? 'Silly,' she told herself with a laugh. Kath was right. David wasn't working in a designated war zone. Nothing could possibly happen. After this wretched conflict was over, they'd have the rest of their lives together.

Lydia telephoned that evening, wanting to meet for lunch. 'We haven't seen each other for ages and there's a lot to catch up on.'

Lydia's cheerfulness, Claire thought, sounded forced. 'Sounds good,' she agreed, 'but David's due home for a few days and we're planning to spend some time together. What are your plans for Christmas? Perhaps you'd like to spend the day with us?'

'What? Play stooge to the pair of you? I don't think so.'

'There'll be others there, I expect,' Claire assured her sister, thinking of Kath and Alex. 'Don't be silly. We'd love to see you.'

But Lydia, it appeared, had already made other plans.

At Kath's insistence, she had booked a hotel room. It was small and cramped, all she could manage at such short notice, but she didn't care. She and David were finally together again. He was as warm, romantic and tender as she had remembered, bringing her flowers on their first night together. She woke the following morning to the sight of them in a vase on the bedside table. Lilies and baby's breath, a scattering of red roses. She touched a hand to his hair, his face, reassuring herself he was really there and not some figment of her imagination. Tried to memorise his face, his features, committing them to memory. After the next few days, God only knew when they'd see each other again.

Later, devouring toast and tea in bed, she said: 'I want a baby, David. Our own child.'

He took her empty cup and sat it on the table next to his own, then laid a hand across her stomach. 'I can picture you,' he laughed, 'warm and round with it.'

'We'll have a boy first, then a girl.'

'Only two?' Then. 'What if we've started one already?'

She stretched, pulling his mouth in alignment with her own, oblivious to the crumbs that dotted the sheets. Ran her tongue along his top lip. 'What if we haven't?'

His hand closed over her breast, gently kneading. He bent and took her nipple in his mouth, flicking his tongue across its hardness, teasing. 'Then we'd better try again,' he said, pushing her back on the bed.

Alex invited Claire and David to spend Christmas Day with Teddy — his old university friend — Harry and their two children. Kath came along as well, to make an even number. Dinner was a festive affair, a real party with bonbons and shiny decorations. In the living room, the Christmas tree reached almost to the ceiling.

Everyone brought a present, set it under the tree. After lunch was dispensed with, Teddy's eldest child, a little girl, handed them out.

It was potluck whose gift they received. Alex, Claire knew, had brought hers. She had seen him carry it inside, place it with the others. She peeled back the wrapper to reveal a pewter photo frame. 'Oh, it's lovely!' she cried, holding it forward so David could see.

The four days passed in a blur of activity. Hotel lunches. Late-night movies. Dancing. A picnic in the Botanic Gardens with Alex and Kath. Making up for all those months they'd been apart. 'Claire and I are trying for a baby,' David told them, trying to hide his delight and failing miserably.

It was a sad, yet happy, time and, for David's sake, she made every minute count. Inexplicably, when she thought of his leaving, tears kept springing into her eyes and she'd look away, pretend to be preoccupied with something until the moment passed, not wanting him to see.

On that last day, he bought her a gift — a silver christening mug. 'It's for our child,' he said simply, reducing her to unexpected tears. 'Oh, hush now. I didn't mean to make you cry.'

'It's all right,' she hiccupped, trying to smile. 'I'm emotional these days.'

'Hey, chances are I'll be able to get back in a

couple of months and we can be a boring old married couple again.'

'You're not boring,' she replied fiercely, trying to keep the tears in check.

They made love with a ferocity she hadn't known she possessed. But somehow it was Alex's face she saw in the dark, Alex's exultant cries she heard. 'Love me, Claire,' David whispered, jolting her back to shocking reality. 'Love me till we're old and grey.'

In the morning she watched him dress, shrugging his shirt and trousers over his lean body. Coming up behind him as he brushed his hair, she laid her face against his back. 'It's been a perfect few days. I don't want it to end.'

He swung around, caught her in a powerful embrace. 'There'll be more.'

'After the war —' she began, catching herself too late. 'Oh, I don't ever see an end to all this!'

'But we have to believe there will be,' he said, 'or how could we ever go on?'

He escorted Claire back to her boarding house and Kath met them at the front door. 'Good luck, David. Come back safely.'

He kissed her warmly on the cheek. 'You're a good friend to Claire. Look after her for me.'

Claire felt the slow brush of his mouth against her own, felt her own arms encircling him. She held him tight, not wanting to release him. And when she did, her skin felt cold where his hands had rested, despite the heat of the day, and she shivered. He walked away, back straight, shoulders squared. And Claire watched him go with a sense of grief.

'He's a lovely man,' Kath said, giving her a hug. 'You really are very lucky.'

'I know.'

Past the pub he went, the general store, not looking back, until he rounded the corner and was gone. She felt empty inside. Numb. Tears streaked her face and angrily she wiped them away. 'I hate this!' she cried. 'Perhaps if I had a child and my own home, I'd feel different. But when he goes away, there's nothing to show for the time we've been together.'

Please God, she thought, staring along the empty street, let there be a child. A part of them both to cherish and hold. She had so much love to give. So much wasted, *wasted* love.

It was dark outside when the nurse summoned Alex to the telephone. Through the window next to the reception desk, he could see the lights of several ambulances illuminating the driveway outside. Distractedly he rubbed the back of his neck, easing away the day's tension. Almost knock-off time, and all he could think about was bed.

'Melville here,' he said into the receiver.

'Alex?' It was his father's voice. Tired, like his own. Worn out. 'There's some bad news, I'm afraid —'

He was instantly alert, the exhaustion forgotten. 'Josh! Erica! They're all right?'

'No, they're fine. It's David.'

'David?' he said stupidly, puzzled. 'I saw him yesterday. He only left this morning, heading back up north.'

'There was a mechanical problem and the Catalina

went into the sea, somewhere up near Palm Island. There —' His father's voice broke and there was a momentary silence. 'There were no survivors.'

'It's official, then?'

'The telegram came here. This was the address David had given for notification when he joined up, before he and Claire were married.'

David dead? The idea seemed inconceivable. Only yesterday they had all been together, laughing and joking, making plans for the future. *Claire and I are trying for a baby.*

Shock rendered him momentarily speechless, and he was unable to catch his breath. He held the receiver slightly away from his ear, staring at it, wondering if this were some monstrous prank, or some nightmare from which he would soon wake.

'Alex?'

His father's worried voice slid through the suffocatingly thick air towards him.

'I — I'm here.'

'Claire will have to be told. I *could* ring, but it'd be better coming from someone face to face. Alex, you're down there. Could you —'

Oh, God! How could he find the strength?

'I'll go,' he replied brusquely.

Claire came to the front door. 'Kath said you wanted to see me. Come into the kitchen and I'll make coffee.'

'No, if you don't mind, I'd rather talk out here.'

He turned, hat held in his hands, and walked down the steps onto the grass. Claire followed, hesitating. 'What's wrong?'

He shook his head, wondering how to frame the words.

'It's David, isn't it?' she asked, her voice sounding wooden and far away.

Alex nodded, staring past her, unable to meet her gaze. The mauve plumbago and the slash of colour from the flowerbeds, just visible in the light spilling from the doorway, rolled into grey mist. A wave of despair seemed to wash over her, and she appeared to sag. 'What happened?'

'The plane crashed into the sea.'

'Is he missing, or is he —'

'He's dead, Claire.'

She brought her hands up, covering her face. Stood perfectly still.

'Are you all right? Is there someone I can call? Kath, perhaps?'

Stiffly. Voice muffled. 'I'll be fine.'

'I don't think —'

She brought her hands down, held them out, palms facing him. *No more*, said the expression on her face. *I don't want to hear.*

He didn't know what to do. She looked so stricken, so vulnerable, that he longed to hold her, shield her from further pain. But she'd brought up a barrier between them with that clipped dialogue and the hardened veneer of her face.

'Claire!' he begged. 'I want to help. Just tell me what to do.'

'I said I'll be fine. Just leave me, please! There's lots to organise. *Just go!*'

She walked away from him towards the front

door. At the last moment she turned, facing him. 'If you don't mind — I've a frightful headache. I'm just going to take some aspirin and lie down for a while. I'll let you know about the funeral.'

'What about Lydia? She should be told.'

Claire's mouth trembled. Her face seemed to be collapsing in on itself. 'I don't know ... I can't think ...'

'Would you like me to tell her?'

She turned, ran inside. He made to follow but Kath was there, blocking his path. 'What's wrong?'

'It's David —' he began. 'There's been an accident. Someone should be with her.'

And Kath was gone, sprinting along the hallway. 'I'll ring you,' she called over her shoulder.

Numbly Alex walked away, leaving Claire in Kath's capable care. Down the dark empty road he went, until he came to the pub on the corner. It was dimly lit inside, smoky, and he sat at the bar. He ordered a drink, drained the glass, then had another.

He closed his eyes, listening to the murmur of voices and clink of glasses. Images of David danced in his tired mind. Childhood recollections, boyhood memories. David on the boats, in his air-force uniform. David and Claire's marriage. *Claire and I are trying for a baby.* Bloody hell!

He was, he had considered, used to the transience of life. He saw death every day, was made weary and — he often thought — callous by its constant presence. But the soldiers he treated at the hospital had become, through necessity, names on badges, faces he sought to remove from his mind when he left work each day, or he'd have gone mad with the thought of the uselessness, the insensibility of it all.

But he'd been wrong. He couldn't block it out, no matter how hard he tried. All those names on badges were mothers' sons, husbands or lovers, brothers. Their passing had left the same feelings of devastation and loss he was experiencing now. Someone, somewhere, had mourned their deaths.

He lowered his head onto the counter and felt the cool timber against his skin. 'Are you all right, mate?' asked the bartender, touching a hand to his sleeve.

Unable to bear the concern, he stumbled outside. The hot night air assaulted his senses as he gazed blankly around. What now? he thought with dismay. Find Lydia? Tell her the awful news? He shook his head, wishing he could simply go home and sleep until dawn. In his current frame of mind, his sister-in-law was the last person he wanted to see.

The lights were on in Lydia's flat. She answered the door dressed in a loose kimono. It was pink, he noticed numbly, with a smattering of darker pink hibiscus. Her hair was tousled. Her eyes held that sleepy sensual look he knew a lot of men found attractive. For himself, he couldn't help thinking it was something she had purposefully cultivated for her own benefit.

'Alex! This is a surprise!' she cried, pulling him inside.

'It's not a social call,' he said stiffly, closing the door behind him. 'I'm afraid I've got some awful news.'

Lydia tilted her head to one side. 'Bad news at this time of night? What on earth could it be?'

'David's dead.'

The words fell like poison from his mouth, echoing dully in his mind. Lydia paused for a moment, glanced down at her nails, then stared directly into his eyes. 'Would you like a drink? Scotch?'

Alex nodded. Lydia hadn't, he noticed, asked for any details.

He sank onto the settee, cupping his chin in his palms. Lydia put a record on the gramophone, turned the volume down low, then went to the drinks' cabinet, pouring generous measures into two glasses. As she walked, he watched the provocative swing of hips, the way the flimsy fabric of the gown clung to her buttocks and legs.

'How's Claire taking it?' she asked idly, carrying the glasses back across the room.

Alex took a sip of the drink — whisky and ice, with just a dash of water. He felt the liquid burn a path down his chest and thought, not for the first time that evening, that he had already consumed too much alcohol for one day. He set the drink on the low table in front of him, then ran his hand through his hair.

He was stalling, he knew that. How could he possibly put Claire's reaction — especially in the face of Lydia's indifference — into words? Suddenly he wished he hadn't come, that he'd left this whole sorry task to someone else. But it was too late. Lydia was sitting next to him, asking questions he could not truthfully answer.

'She's devastated, of course. And most likely in shock.'

'Is that your professional opinion, *Doctor* Melville?'

He ignored her sarcasm.

'What about the funeral?'

'Claire said she'll let me know.'

'That was generous of her.'

The conversation was going round in circles, getting nowhere. 'Claire's a generous person,' he said carefully. But grief was making him reckless and he felt a need to explore Claire's distress. 'I'm worried about her, Lydia. She knocked back my offer of help and refused to talk about it. "Just go," she said, almost pushing me away.'

'Claire was always the strong one.'

'Do you think so? I always thought that under that tough exterior there was a frail vulnerability, as though the bravery were all an act.'

Lydia shrugged. 'To this day, there are things about my sister that remain a mystery to me.'

The image of Claire's stricken face jolted back at him and Alex closed his eyes for a moment, trying to erase the memory. He placed his now-empty glass on the small table in front of him and rubbed his forehead. 'God! I can't believe David's dead! Yesterday we were all talking, making plans. And today ...'

His voice faltered. Lydia sipped her drink, watching him over the rim of her glass.

'It all seems so unreal,' he went on. 'I keep thinking that maybe this is just a bad dream. And in the morning I'll wake up and everything will be as it should be.'

His voice broke and he stopped, feeling disjointed, out of kilter.

'Poor Alex.'

She put her glass on the table, next to his, and slid along the settee towards him, putting her arms around his chest. She was warm, and the subtle scent of perfume, sweet like roses, rose up to meet him.

'Poor David, don't you mean?' he replied, aware of the bitter tone in his voice.

Lydia ignored his words. 'And it was very selfish of Claire to push you away, to think only of herself. She's not the only one affected by this.'

He wondered why she couldn't, or wouldn't, say the words. *David's death*.

Lydia leant forward and kissed him on the cheek, collected the two empty glasses and walked back to the drinks' cabinet. The music swayed out from the gramophone. A woman was singing, a low husky number. Soulful. Sad. He felt like crying.

'Have you spoken to Erica?'

He was taken aback. 'No.'

He should have, of course, but the fact that it hadn't even occurred to him to telephone her was indicative of the state of their marriage.

Lydia came back, carrying the bottle of Scotch. As she leaned forward to refill his glass, the neck of her kimono fell open and he could see the creamy rise of her breasts, and the shadowy cleft between. He was aware of a hardening in his groin, a surge of sexual desire. How long since he and Erica had made love or even touched each other in a sensual way? Months, he thought bitterly. Probably years.

'I should go,' he said thickly, getting to his feet. 'I've got to get back to the hospital, and the last tram for the night will be along any minute.'

'You *could* stay.'

The meaning of her words was implicit, and he frowned, trying to think of a suitable reply. Her face seemed very close and he had trouble focusing. Lips brushed against his and, again, he smelled her perfume.

'No,' he said firmly, stumbling to his feet and pulling away from her touch. 'But thanks for the offer.'

She sat, staring lazily up at him, her mouth curved into a mocking smile. 'Another time, perhaps? When you're not so preoccupied. Just call me. I'll be waiting.'

He let himself out the door and swung onto a passing tram. Cool night air brushed his face, reawakening his senses. He dismissed Lydia easily from his mind. She was shallow and careless, unlike Claire. How two sisters could be so unlike was a source of constant amazement to him. His mind travelled over tomorrow's plans. He'd ring Erica, see how his father was. In the evening's turmoil he'd hardly had time to consider the old man's feelings.

Somehow Claire stumbled through the ensuing days and, despite the worry for her own husband, Kath was a constant source of support. Burial arrangements. Funeral. Mind-numbing realisation that David wasn't coming back. The misery went on and on, never-ending.

Her nights were spent staring at the ceiling, wondering if somehow she were being punished for loving another man. 'You didn't deserve him,' she whispered to herself. 'And now he's gone.' She felt a chill emptiness inside, as though a cold wind were sweeping through her soul.

She felt she was wading through shifting sand, getting nowhere. The war wound around her, endlessly, and there was no escaping the evidence of it. Relentless assaulting reports on the wireless. Newsreels showing burning buildings and columns of soldiers marching past. When things looked their blackest, one thought kept her going: that last weekend she and David had shared had been tender and romantic. Perhaps there was a baby already growing inside her, a tangible legacy of those final days of their marriage. But two weeks later, she felt those tell-tale cramps, watched the bloody discharge in horror, and wept.

Lydia counted the days. A month had passed since that morning in the doctor's rooms when she had learned the awful truth. Thirty days of waiting to talk to Claire, but Christmas and David's homecoming had intervened, then the funeral.

No-one at work had noticed. She was easily able to keep up with the dancing routines, though she crawled into bed each night, exhausted. Finally, in desperation, she arrived on Claire's doorstep one Sunday afternoon.

'Hi, just thought I'd pop around and say hello.'

'Come in.' Claire looked pale and her voice was flat, lacking its usual energy. 'I'd make you coffee, but I'm all out of milk.'

'How's tricks?'

'Bloody awful, if you must know. I hate this war, and all it stands for. And if I never hear "Boogie Woogie Bugle Boy From Company B" again, it'll be too soon.'

They stood, staring at one another. 'I've come to ask you a favour, actually,' said Lydia, deciding to come directly to the point.

Claire seemed instantly wary. 'Yes?'

'I need to borrow some money.'

'Are you asking or telling me?'

'Don't play games. I'm *asking*, all right?'

'How much?'

'Fifty pounds.'

'What for?'

Despite her intentions, she burst into tears. 'Because I'm up the duff, that's why.'

Claire was silent; she crossed her arms across her chest. Not a good sign, thought Lydia.

'You know,' Lydia went on, 'a sprog, a tin lid.'

'I know what you mean.'

'I can't possibly go through with it.'

'Why not?'

'I've my job to think of.'

'Your job!'

'And what everyone will think.'

Claire gave a forced laugh. 'When did you ever worry about what other people thought?'

'I didn't come here for a lecture.'

'You're going to have a baby,' Claire went on regardless, as though she hadn't heard, 'and all you can think of is yourself, as usual. You know, David and I were desperately hoping for a child. God only knows we tried —' Her voice broke and she raised her hands in a wide defeated sweep, blinking back tears. 'After he was killed, I begged God every night: let there be one. But there wasn't.'

'I can't help about David.'

'No.'

'And I'd give anything to change places with you as far as the baby is concerned. For God's sake, Claire! Help me!'

'How far along are you?'

'Just over three months.'

'Three months! You can't have an abortion now. It's way too risky.'

'Well, I can't have it!'

'Of course you can!' Claire snapped. 'There are women who'd do anything to adopt a baby. It would have a good home, two parents who wanted it. It's your child, part of you, and all you can think of is killing it, you selfish little bitch!'

How dare Claire judge her! 'You're a fine one to talk about selfish!' she bit back. 'Other people have feelings, too, and you didn't even stop to think about Alex's.'

'What are you talking about?'

'The night David died. David was his brother, too, and he was upset. Is that what you usually say to a man who tells you he wants to help you — ask him to go?'

Stunned, Claire faced her. 'Who told you that?'

'Alex.'

'You've been talking to Alex?' she asked in a disbelieving voice.

'You're not so perfect yourself, Claire. Not as considerate as you'd like us all to believe. And I suppose now that David's gone, that leaves one less problem.'

'What do you mean by that?'

'You figure it out. Will you lend me the money?'

'No.'

'Very well,' she said, defeated, turning to go. 'I came to you for help and you've turned me away. So much for sisterly support.'

'There's one thing you haven't told me.'

'What's that?'

'Who the father is.'

It was, Lydia thought, a golden opportunity, a chance to pay Claire back for her self-righteous, patronising attitude. A chance to strike back at Alex, too, for his easy dismissal of her on the night of David's death. She paused for a moment, calculating. Waiting to strike the final blow.

'Alex,' she said in a firm voice, trying to suppress a smile. 'Alex is the father of my child.'

CHAPTER 34

It was Easter before Alex managed to get back to Tea-tree Passage, though in hindsight, apart from the anticipation of seeing Josh, he wondered why he had bothered. Erica was usually busy with some task or another, scarcely affording him any time. Punishing him, he supposed, for what she considered to be his desertion of them.

There was a distance between them these days, a marked drawing away that he suspected had little to do with physical separation. Conversation seemed stilted, and sex had become rare and perfunctory, a task he knew she endured. One afternoon, as they took Josh for a walk along the foreshore, he asked her if she wanted a divorce.

She gave a brittle laugh. 'Don't be silly.'

'Well, this doesn't seem to be working.'

'How can it? You're never here.'

Tiredly. 'There's a war on, Erica, in case you hadn't noticed.'

'Don't be facetious. It doesn't suit you,' she hit back. 'Anyway, if we were divorced, how would I provide for myself and Josh? Run back to my parents and ask them for help?'

'I'd always look after you, you know that.'

The weather was cooling, a stiff breeze coming in off the water. Choppy waves slapped at the pylons of the jetties. She wandered away, down to the water's edge, bent down to pick up a shell. The conversation was clearly over.

Josh was almost two years old now, lean and long-legged, with his father's shock of sandy hair. Initially, on Alex's homecoming, the boy had shied away, not remembering his father. But gentle perseverance had won him over. They went for walks together or, if the weather was fine, Alex took him out in the little dinghy.

It was peaceful out there on the water, sunshine beating down on them and the gulls wheeling high overhead. Alex watched as Josh trailed his fingers in the water, and showed him the shadows of the slow-moving fish below. The days passed quickly, melting into each other. Soon he would return to the bedlam that was the hospital and city.

On the last night of his leave, Erica lay stiffly beside him in the bed. 'You can make love to me if you want,' she said in a condescending tone, a well-if-you-must-then-I-won't-complain voice.

He rolled away from her and sat on the edge of the mattress, a hopeless anger welling up inside him. 'Don't bother, Erica! I can do without it!'

He pulled on a pair of shorts and let himself out

the front door. Slowly he walked along the track past Maudie's house, which lay in darkness although it wasn't yet nine o'clock, and on down to the line of jetties. He sat on the edge of one and dangled his feet over the edge. The tide was going out and the water swirled around his ankles, black and surprisingly warm.

His thoughts turned to Claire, as they often did, and he wondered how different his life might have been if events had run a separate course. If Erica hadn't fallen pregnant. If she had lost the baby before the wedding and not after. 'If, if, if!' he said angrily to himself. 'Too many bloody ifs!'

He hadn't seen either of the Carmody sisters since David's funeral, three months earlier, although he had rung Claire, several times. But she had been curt and dismissive, as though she were angry at him. For what reason, he didn't know. '*No, I haven't seen Lydia,*' she'd said the last time he had spoken to her, in a tone that suggested she wanted nothing to do with her sister. Grief, he thought, sometimes had a strange way of manifesting itself.

Just leave me, please! Just go!

He closed his mind to the words — and that remembered anguished expression on her face — and sighed, swinging his thoughts back to the miserable state of his own marriage. If it weren't for Josh, it would be so easy to walk away from the whole damn mess. But he had to make some semblance of an effort, for his son's sake.

There was also another worrying problem, one he could not bring himself to discuss with anyone.

The gossip about Erica had reached his ears. Apparently she had been entertaining American soldiers in the house, going to the pub in town with them. He'd planned to raise the subject with her but, when the time came, he couldn't bring himself to say the words. What did it matter, anyway? Their marriage was all but finished. He lived away from home. What rights did any of them hold over each other?

Lydia smoothed the last of the Cyclax Milk of Roses moisturiser on her face and stepped back, coming to an abrupt standstill. The sight of herself, naked in the mirror, never ceased to shock her. Pendulous dark-veined breasts. Belly hard and swollen, pushed out with the shape of the child. Horrid dark line running from her navel to the triangle of pale hair below. Desperately she hated the silver-blue stretch marks that marred what had once been flawless white skin.

According to the doctor, there were still two months to go until she could rid her body of that heaving, thumping mass. Eight weeks of sleepless nights, and days when it seemed to be lodged high under her ribs, making breathing difficult. Eight weeks of parading a stomach of mountainous proportions. Eight weeks of mothers, pushing prams in the street, stopping her and asking when the baby was due. 'As if I care,' she'd mutter under her breath as she walked away, desperate to have the entire detestable ordeal done with. There was nothing even remotely pleasant about being pregnant.

In the early days she had worn a girdle to flatten her stomach, much to the worry of Ellen, who was always telling her she'd harm the baby.

Lydia had simply shrugged. 'Good.'

'You could cause problems for yourself.'

'I don't care.'

Inevitably she had lost her job at the theatre early in the year. Patrons didn't pay good money to see a pregnant chorus girl and the costume did nothing to hide her condition. 'Come back when you've got rid of the lump, love,' the stage manager had said, eyeing her stomach with amusement.

She found a job in a munitions factory. It was hot horrible work but there was no alternative, not until she had the baby. The other women there were most supportive. Lydia had told them her husband was away at war, the lie helped by the purchase of a plain gold ring which she wore on her left hand.

She hadn't seen Claire since the day she'd asked her for the money for the abortion. She'd been too angry, too incensed, to make further contact. What, parade around there and let her gloat over me? she thought. She preferred to spend her leisure time alone — well, alone except for this lump in her belly that was intent on ruining her life.

She was hurrying towards the train one evening at Roma Street station when she caught sight of a familiar figure striding purposefully ahead. Tall. Fair hair. American uniform.

'Ellis!' she cried, her anger towards him dissolving as she pushed her way through the peak-hour crowd.

He didn't pause in his stride but kept moving forward, the crowd closing around him.

'*Ellis!*' she screamed, louder, fearing she would lose him in the crush.

A train tore alongside the platform with a *whoosh*, lights blazing, piercing shriek announcing its arrival. Desperately she ran at the crowd, frantically pushing, fearing she'd lose sight of him. Heads turned in annoyance. 'Let me through!' she cried, dodging around the dawdlers.

The train doors were flung open and an outpouring of passengers appeared like a tidal wave heaving towards her. There he was, waiting for the last of the departing crowd. She lunged, grasping at his sleeve.

'Ellis! I'm here!'

The man turned towards her, an amused expression on his face, and she realised with a shock that it wasn't Ellis at all, but a stranger.

'Hiya, sweetheart. That's one hell of a pick-up line.'

She gave a small sob and stumbled backwards. The crowd jostled, sidestepping around her. The man waved, smiling. 'Hey! Can I take you some place?' he called as the crowd carried him onto the train.

Lydia shook her head, staring after him. The carriage doors banged shut. She could have sworn it was Ellis, would have staked her life on it. Bastard!

She was dimly aware of sounds: the shriek of the guard's whistle, the clanking of the train as it left the platform, leaving a gaping emptiness and a dank fusty smell. Distractedly she ran her fingers through her hair, separating the strands and letting them fall limply against her shoulders. Her fingers accidentally brushed her cheeks, and she found them wet with tears.

'Oh Christ!' she muttered to herself. A station attendant came along the platform, whistling, to change the name on the destination board. She turned, averting her head, and walked slowly towards the bench to wait for the next train.

Claire had been expecting the phone call for months now.

'It's Maudie, love,' said Nina, her voice unsteady. 'She went in her sleep. I found her this morning. She wouldn't have known a thing, according to Hal.'

'Oh, Mum!'

She didn't know what to say. Stood staring at the yellow-and-black linoleum on the hallway floor, instead, trying not to cry, remembering her great-aunt as she had last seen her, at Claire's own wedding.

Later she telephoned Lydia. 'How are you?' she asked, after she had told her sister the news.

'Fat.'

'When's the baby due?'

'Two weeks, and it can't come quick enough.'

'How are you doing for money?'

'I'm managing. What's with all the questions?'

'I'm concerned, that's all.'

'Well, don't be. I'm a big girl, remember. I can look after myself.'

Somehow Claire wrangled a travel permit and went home for the funeral. It was the first time she had been back for over two years. Nothing had changed, she thought, stepping onto the railway platform. Hal Melville was there to meet her, and gave her a warm hug. 'How are you, Claire?' he said, a tremor of emotion in his voice. He was, she knew, still coming to terms with David's death.

'I'm coping,' she replied quietly. 'How are things around here?'

'Stretched, what with Alex still away. The war's hard on everyone, but we're all making contributions wherever we can. Your Mum, now, she's unstoppable. Comforts' Fund, Red Cross — she's busy organising everyone. Stops her from missing all of you, I expect.'

The funeral brought back memories of David. Inevitable hole in the ground. Pile of damp soil. Lowering the casket. Not much to look forward to eventually, Claire thought.

'Old Maudie's been part of us since we came here,' Nina said. 'I try to imagine what it'll be like without her.'

'Quiet, I suppose.'

'She was a cantankerous old thing in the end, forgetful and rambling, but it wasn't her fault. Oh God!' Nina swept a hand through her own hair. 'Getting old is a terrible thing, Claire.'

Vehemently. 'You're not old!'

Who was she trying to convince, her mother or herself? Nina sported more grey hairs than usual and deep lines had formed at the corners of her mouth. There was a tiredness about her that Claire had never noticed before, an exhaustion that robbed her of her vitality.

'Fifty-four and not getting any younger, however much I might wish otherwise. Some days it's an effort just to get out of bed.'

'It's this wretched war, wearing us down.'

'Maudie's left you the old house, love,' Nina told her later as they sat at the kitchen table, sipping tea. 'Not that it's probably worth much, but it's something. You were always her favourite.'

The next morning Claire wandered around the house that was now hers. It was large, though neglected, and needed a good clean-out. Nina offered to help. 'It won't take long with the two of us, just a few days.'

Claire shook her head. 'Just leave it for now. It'll keep. I don't know what my plans are at the moment.'

She stood in the centre of the smallest bedroom, thinking what a lovely nursery it would make. Yellow walls. Bright mobiles hanging from the ceiling. Nursery! What was she thinking of? But the idea had been festering within her for days now.

The day before she left for the city, she told her mother about Lydia's baby. Nina was quiet for a moment, pensive. 'When's it due?'

'Probably a week or so.'

'And the father?'

'No-one we know,' said Claire, a little too quickly. 'A war-time romance. You know how it is?'

Nina stood, walked to the window and stared out. 'So, I'm to be a grandmother?'

'Lydia doesn't want the poor little scrap, so she plans to give it up for adoption. I've been thinking about offering the baby a home. It seems senseless to give it to strangers, and it might be the only chance I have at being a mother.'

Nina put her arms around her daughter. 'Don't say that, it makes me so sad. There'll be another man for you one day. Babies, too.'

Claire shook her head. 'One thing I've learned is not to expect anything out of life.'

Claire moved in with Lydia for the last week of her confinement. It was July and a cold wind blew through the city, sending dry leaves spinning along the gutters. Lydia was anxious and impatient, lumbering through the rooms, consumed with restless energy.

Daily, the idea of raising Lydia's child seesawed through Claire's mind. They were true, the words she had told her mother. She couldn't see herself marrying again, didn't want the involvement, the complication. But her maternal instincts were stirring, and the prospect of caring for Alex's child held a certain appeal. The initial anger towards him had lessened lately. How could she judge him when she, herself, had felt those same urges, that surge of desire, that sense of losing control?

'I've a proposition for you. How would you feel if I said I wanted to take the baby?' she said to Lydia one afternoon.

Lydia glanced up from the magazine she was reading, frowning. 'Why would you want to raise someone else's child?'

'David's dead and we wanted a family so badly. I know,' she went on hurriedly, 'that this is not *my* child. You can see it whenever you want, and it'll always know you're its mother.'

'I can't give you anything for its upkeep.'

'I'm not asking you to.'

Lydia shrugged. 'I don't care. You might as well take it as someone else.'

'There are two conditions.'

'Such as?'

'Firstly, that you don't interfere in its upbringing.'

'And secondly?'

'That Alex never knows the child is his.'

'There's something —'

Claire raised her hand, cutting short Lydia's words. 'I'll take the child, raise it as I would my own, and we'll never speak of this again.'

Lydia woke her when the pains finally started, two o'clock on the following Sunday morning.

'The baby's coming. I'm scared.'

Briskly Claire slid out of bed and steered Lydia towards the living room. Sat her in a chair. 'Of course you're not.'

'It's all right for you to talk. You're not in pain.' She wrapped her arms around her stomach. 'What if something goes wrong? Women die having babies.'

'Lydia, nothing's going to happen to you. You're not going to die. Childbirth's a natural thing. Just think, this time tomorrow it'll all be over.'

'I bloody well hope so.'

Calmly Claire suppressed a smile and telephoned for a taxi.

* * *

It was bedlam in the jungle camp, with four different sections coming and going and needing meals at odd hours. At midday, desperate to escape, Joe borrowed a bicycle and went into the nearest village, rewarding himself with a haircut.

Afterwards he went to the nearby bar. It was noisy and smoky, and filled with soldiers. He found a corner position, from where he had a good view of the room and the dirt street. There was a grubby cloth on the table, and tarnished silver cutlery. He ordered vegetable soup and an omelette, followed by pork chops, cabbage and potato, with a bottle of local wine.

The meal was better than he had tasted in ages, although the wine was rough. He lingered over it, then ordered another bottle. What the hell! He wasn't expected back in camp for hours. The room was beginning to empty, the other occupants wandering off into the steamy afternoon, but he was not inclined to follow.

Hair cut to a suitable length, belly full — the only thing missing was a bath. It was weeks since he'd had a decent wash and he could feel the lice sucking at his skin. Paying the proprietress for the meal, he enquired as to the possibility.

The woman was very pretty. She was in her early twenties, he supposed, with caramel-coloured skin and dark reddish hair that hung to her waist. Her eyes crinkled when she smiled, revealing two rows of white teeth. Something about her reminded him of Jane — the colour of her hair, perhaps, the long proud line of her neck?

She beckoned him out the back, swinging her hips as she walked in front of him, and pointed to a lopsided building. 'It is in there,' she said.

There was a copper with a fire going underneath. Obligingly she ladled buckets of hot water into a large metal tub while Joe carried several containers of water from the well in the yard. When it was almost full, she brought fresh towels and lye soap. 'Leave your clothes outside,' she offered. 'I will have them cleaned.'

He leant back, savouring the silky warmth of the water against his skin. Studiously he soaped himself, scrubbing vigorously at the raw red lines where the seams of his lice-ridden shirt had rubbed against his skin.

The woman returned as he was wrapping the towel around his waist. 'You are clean now?' she asked.

Joe nodded.

'You Australians come to save us,' she went on in halting English, regarding him from under heavy-lidded eyes. 'I would like to repay you.'

There was no doubt as to the meaning of her words, and Joe tightened his grip on the towel. A sudden thought brought momentary panic. *I can't leave. She's got my bloody clothes.* He was trapped, unless he wanted to ride back to camp wearing only a towel and face the ridicule of his mates.

Then another thought occurred. Perhaps he didn't want to leave?

Swallowing hard, he turned to stare at her. She had a rounded, pretty face and clear skin. Her blouse was low-cut, revealing the swell of her breasts. Funny, he thought, how he had not noticed until now.

'I don't even know your name.'

'It is Velovelo,' she said, taking his hand and pulling him forward.

He had no option but to follow as she led him through the garden, up a flight of rickety stairs at the rear of the house, and into a bedroom. It was sparsely furnished, containing only a bed, a cane chair and a low dresser. Through the window he could look down on the garden and the washhouse.

When he turned, she was undressing. There was something sensual in the way she moved, or was it just that it had been so long since he had seen a woman naked? Dark hair falling across her full breasts. Equally dark triangle of hair below her belly. She moved closer, wrapping her arms around him and laying her cheek against his chest as he breathed in the sweet smell of her.

'The perfume. What is it?' he asked, shocked by the raspiness of his voice.

She shrugged and smiled, suddenly standing on tiptoes and raising her face to meet his. Hungrily she flicked her tongue along his closed lips with quick movements. Her hands moved, warm and capable, at the nape of his neck, massaging practised fingers against the small knot of tension there, moving downwards to explore the length of his spine. Cupping palms around his buttocks, she pulled him closer, igniting urges he'd long since thought dormant. Not unwillingly, Joe felt his body harden in response, and sensed the towel falling to the floor.

He brought a hand down to enclose one breast, and followed the movement with his mouth, taking the brown nipple between his teeth and running his tongue across its hardness. Velovelo stiffened, breathing raggedly. Her back had come up against the wall and she arched herself towards him as his other hand went down, searching.

It had been so long, so long, and the mere touch of her almost brought him to the verge of blessed release. Carefully he steadied himself, dismissing the urge. Not now, not yet, he cautioned, taking a deep breath.

Her hands were kneading him, massaging the engorged skin. The ache in his groin deepened, a physical pain, and he knew he had scant time left before he totally disgraced himself. 'Now,' she commanded, her voice husky with desire, as Joe brought his hands under her buttocks, lifting her easily and bringing her body into direct alignment with his own.

He took her there, roughly, against the wall, driving his body into hers like a man possessed. Each successive thrust, each exquisite movement led to a final shuddering release, followed by the pleasurable sensation of everything blurring, slipping away. Afterwards they lay on the bed and he stroked her hair. He was tired, so tired. His head felt foggy, like cotton wool. He sensed the mist of sleep descending, and was unable to stop it.

It was late when he woke. The bed was empty. His washed and freshly-ironed clothes were folded in a neat pile on a chair under the window. Dressed at last, he left a few coins on the dresser, thankful for what she had given him. And what was that, he wondered. Friendship? Compassion? Satisfaction of the need to be held, if just for a while, by a woman he didn't even know?

Puzzled, he walked back down the stairs, encountering no one, and let himself out the door. His bicycle was where he had left it, propped next to the front entrance. Hoisting himself up on the seat, he rode back to the camp, peddling through the dusk along deserted roads, the golden light shedding its brilliance amongst the leaves.

It had felt good, he thought later. Intercourse, nothing more. No commitment or obligation. No eventual letdowns. No promises made to be broken.

It was only natural, seeing she would raise the child, that Claire stayed with Lydia throughout those long, endless hours. Sterile bland room. Clock on the wall ticking away the minutes. Lydia writhing on the bed as the contractions worsened. As Claire wiped a damp cloth across her sister's forehead, she imagined she could feel her pain.

Lydia crying, tears streaking her face. 'Tell them to fetch the doctor. I can't stand it any more.'

Soothing words. 'Of course you can. It'll be over soon.'

'Not soon enough.'

It wasn't until the following afternoon that Lydia heaved the child from her body, the bloodied slippery mass sliding between her legs and onto the sheet. She lay back against the pillow, her face ashen. 'Thank God that's over.'

The child gave an affronted cry. 'What is it?' Claire called.

'It's a girl.'

The cord was cut and the child handed to Lydia, who shook her head, waving her daughter away. 'You take her,' she said to Claire.

Later they wheeled her back to her room. A nurse bustled in, bearing a tray of medication. Deftly she measured a quantity of milky fluid into a measuring glass.

'Here, this'll help you sleep. It's been a long day.' She turned to Claire. 'And you'll have to go, too, dearie. Visiting hours are over and this young woman needs some rest.'

Lydia squeezed Claire's hand. 'Thanks for being here. I couldn't have done it without you.'

'Nonsense. You're one tough lady, Lydia. Don't let anyone tell you otherwise. Okay?'

It was a truce of sorts, a reconciliation, Lydia thought, after Claire had gone. Everything was falling into place. Claire would take the baby, absolving Lydia of all responsibility. And there was no fear that her sister would ever say anything to Alex about being her child's father, so her lie would never be exposed.

She reached across and turned the bedside light off and lay there in the dark, smiling to herself. Was it only a few hours since she'd given birth? It seemed like days. Already the pain had been forgotten, relegated to some distant corner of her memory. She yawned and stretched. So tired, so tired. She began to feel drowsy — and strangely empty. For nine months, Ellis's child had grown inside her, kicked and squirmed, reminding her constantly of its presence. Now, there was nothing.

She glanced across the room towards the window. Outside, the sky was dark, not even a hint of moonlight. From beyond the door, the sounds of the hospital were a faint murmur in the background. Brisk footsteps along the corridor. Squeak of a trolley. From further away came the muffled cry of a baby.

Was it hers, crying in its crib with no-one to comfort it? Lydia didn't know, didn't care. She was only concerned with her aching breasts.

For Lydia, the days in hospital dragged past, each one interminable. She felt tired and drained. At irregular times, she stopped and put her hands to her belly, half expecting to feel the child still inside her. But her skin, no longer stretched and taut, felt soft and flabby under her fingers. On the third day, she bound her breasts in towels.

There was plenty of time to make plans. The lease was up on the flat and most of her savings had gone. When she got out, she'd look for a cheaper place, go back to the theatre. Ellen had said they were auditioning for a new play. It was time she got on with her life.

On the morning of her discharge, Claire came with a set of baby clothes, and together they dressed Lydia's tiny daughter. Pink gown and bootees. Bonnet. Baby shawl. At the appointed time, the taxi's horn tooted from the roadway below. 'There's your lift,' said Lydia. 'You'd better go.'

Together they clumped down the stairs, Claire carrying the baby while Lydia hoisted the small bag containing bottles, formula and nappies. She watched, amused, as Claire positioned herself on the back seat, clutching the child to her chest, and the driver stowed the bag in the boot.

As the taxi went to pull away, she put her hands on the door sill. 'There's one thing you've forgotten.'

'What's that?'

'Her name. I want you to call her Aurora.'

'Aurora?' Claire muttered, pulling the shawl tighter around the sleeping baby. 'Damn stupid name.'

The last Lydia saw of her child, as the taxi moved away, was a glimpse of fair hair.

PART SIX

Homecomings II

Tea-tree Passage

1943 – 1958

CHAPTER 35

On the way back to the boarding house to collect her belongings, Claire stopped off at work, tendering her resignation. The woman in charge threatened to report her to Manpower. 'You can't just up and leave. I have an office to run.'

'And I have a child to care for.'

'Just whose child is it?'

'My sister's.'

'Then it's her responsibility, not yours. Why can't she look after it?'

Patiently. 'Because she doesn't want to.'

'So you're saddling yourself with the responsibility.'

'I don't see it that way.'

The woman gave a defeated sigh. 'We'll be sorry to lose you, Claire. You've been a great asset to our team here.'

'And I'll be sorry to go. But right now someone else needs me more.'

She said goodbye to Kath, held her in a close embrace. 'Don't lose touch. Come up to the Passage and visit us sometime.'

'Claire, are you sure you're doing the right thing? It's a big commitment, looking after a child. You can't use her to fill the hollows in your life.'

'Don't, Kath. Just know that I need this, okay?'

It was mid-winter. The mullet were coming in to spawn at the top reaches of the creeks. A stiff late-afternoon breeze blew across the water. Even the sand plovers, hunting for pipis along the foreshore, looked cold and ruffled.

Doris O'Reilly, leaning on her front fence talking to Rosie Sharp, glanced down the track towards Maudie's old place. It was a bit of an eyesore these days. The garden was overgrown with weeds. Long shreds of paint were peeling from the walls. Several verandah railings lay where they had fallen on the bleached timber boards. 'Wonder what's to become of the old place,' she mused.

Rosie Sharp shook her head. Nina, who was the only Carmody left in the Passage these days, told them nothing. 'Perhaps it'll get sold, though I don't fancy strangers living there.'

They missed easy-going old Maudie. She had been an institution about the Passage for as long as anyone could remember. Not too fussy about things, just enough to be decent. Nina — now, she was a different kettle of fish. Aloof, in an odd distant way and, though she had grown up there, somehow she didn't seem part of them. She had a bit of class, did Nina, probably from all those years of city living. They'd heard she'd had a fine house and lots of money, but it had all gone during the Depression.

After a while, Erica Melville came towards them, swinging along the track with the boy perched on her hip. *Slut*, thought Doris, eyeing the skirt that came just below her knees and the cardigan that was unbuttoned too far to be decent. 'Erica,' she nodded curtly.

A taxi trundled past, spraying a fine layer of dust in its wake. The three women watched as it came to a stop outside Nina's house. A dark-haired woman carrying a baby got out. Rosie Sharp adjusted her glasses and peered ahead. 'Blow me if it's not young Claire!' She glanced back at Doris. 'Nina's never mentioned anything about a baby.'

'It's not hers,' said Erica in a bored voice. 'According to Alex's dad, it's Lydia's bastard. Claire's going to raise it.'

Doris gave a loud snort. 'If I said it once, then I said it a dozen times. I knew that Lydia would come to nothing.'

She was such a tiny scrap, sleeping most of the way in her wicker carry-cot and waking only for the usual bottles and nappy changes. Luckily the train wasn't crowded, and Claire managed a compartment to herself. She caught herself at odd times staring down at the child — *Alex's daughter!* — trying not to think about the events that had led up to the conception, blotting the image of Lydia and Alex, together, from her mind. Instead, purposefully, she agonised over the name. *Aurora!* What on earth was Lydia thinking of? Couldn't she have come up with something more regular? Like Pauline or Roslyn or Deborah?

As the train rattled over the last bridge into town, the name came to her. *Rory*. It was an abbreviated form of Aurora, concise yet strong, and had a friendly casualness about it. Lydia probably wouldn't approve, but at least Claire had met her sister halfway.

She took a taxi from town. It was dusk as they drove along the track that led to Nina's place. Several swans were flying low over the water and the sun had spread a golden sheen on the waves. The air was heavy with salt spray and she took a deep breath, inhaling the raw almost-forgotten smell.

Nina, hearing the car, came to the door. 'Claire! What a surprise! And the baby, too. Oh, you precious little thing!'

'I've come home. Can we stay for a few days until I clean up Maudie's old house?' Claire asked, giving her mother a hug.

'Of course you can, love. It'll be wonderful having you both here. Though I wish you'd let me know you were coming,' Nina replied, her reproach softened by a smile. 'I would have tidied up a bit, made a bed up for you.'

'Oh, you always fuss too much. Come on, let's have a cuppa, catch up on all the news. And there's Rory to show you —'

'Rory?'

'That's what I call her. She's such a sweet little thing and hardly ever cries. Can you believe it? Lydia insists on naming her Aurora!'

'How will you manage financially?' Nina asked later after Rory had been bathed and fed.

'I've a bit saved, and there's the money from David.' Claire stopped and raised her face towards her mother, eyes brimming. 'I've enough for a year, maybe two. Repairs to Maudie's old place will cost a bit, I expect.'

Nina gave a wry smile. 'That's an understatement.' Then. 'Are you certain you're doing the right thing, coming back? There's bound to be talk.'

'I can handle it. I've been through worse.'

'I know, love. It's just that small-town gossip . . .'

Her voice trailed away and she placed one hand over Claire's. 'No matter. It'll all work out, somehow. I'm so glad you've come home at last, both you and Rory.'

There was both sadness and joy in her voice. Claire watched her mother lift the sleeping child, cradling her in her arms. What was she thinking? she wondered. Was she remembering that other baby, Claire's brother, who had died at birth?

Rory woke at midnight, demanding a feed. Claire cradled the child, felt the solid weight of her in her arms, then sat propped against the pillows, watching as she devoured the contents of a bottle.

It was hard to believe that less than two weeks earlier she had been a kicking lump in Lydia's belly. Claire put her lips to the baby's cheek and Rory's eyelids fluttered open. She lay there, staring up at her with age-old eyes. 'You're just perfect,' she whispered, committing the child's features to memory. Tiny snub nose, rosebud mouth. Fair downy hair.

Lydia and Alex's daughter. *Hers* now. Alex couldn't be part of her own life, but at least Claire had some small part of him.

Nina watched the transformation of Maudie's old place with amazement. She and Claire spent days clearing the rubbish from the rooms. Stacks of old newspapers. Collections of jars and bottles, drawers full of rubber bands and pieces of string, old envelopes. Maudie had certainly been a hoarder. Thankfully, Rory had slept through the bulk of it.

The brown walls and architraves were repainted in neutral sandy tones, reflecting a beach theme. Heavy curtains were ripped from the windows, replaced by sheer ones. Light flooded into what had once been a dark and dreary house. In the living room and bedrooms, the torn linoleum was replaced with beige nubbed carpet. Through the remainder of the house, the timber floors were sanded back, revarnished.

Most of Maudie's old pieces of furniture, Claire told her, were of a surprisingly good quality. She scattered the lounges with lots of cushions in shades of blue and green. On the walls she hung her paintings, sketches of water and fish. New nursery pieces — a cot, change table and matching set of drawers — were sent out by mail-order catalogue from the city.

Under Claire's careful instruction, the exterior of the house came to life. Woodwork was repaired and repainted. Cobwebs were swept from the verandah. A man came to mow the lawns. As the weather warmed, during the late afternoons Claire could usually be found in the garden, wielding a large pair of shears. Music came from the open windows. The baby lay in the pram beside her, a picture of domestic contentment.

All through that summer, Nina felt a contentment she hadn't known for years. Claire's homecoming. Lydia's child. Part of her own self perpetuating into the future. That was what life was all about, wasn't it? Yet overshadowing her happiness was the worry about Joe, serving in the jungles up north. And concern for Lydia, who seemed to be unable to settle. Nina received the occasional phone call from her, hurried, where Rory's name was scarcely mentioned. It was as though her younger daughter had wiped the existence of the child from her mind.

Meanwhile Rory grew, smiled her first smiles and cut teeth, gurgled happily at anyone who came near. She was a dear little girl, placid and undemanding. She crawled, then tottered around the house clinging to the furniture, beaming up at 'Nana Nina'. Said her first words. Daily Claire carried her down to the sea wall, showed her the boats and the waves. Lifted her into the froth so she could feel the silkiness of it on her legs. Told her about the brightly-coloured parrot fish that flitted under the water.

Life was, Nina considered, after the heartbreak of the previous years, as it should be.

Claire loved her newly refurbished house and the bright bold shades of the sea. She felt a contentment there, amongst her books and paintings, the happy company of the child, a welcome substitute for the daughter she and David had never had.

Sometimes she thought back on her marriage, pondered on how unreal those few short months seemed now. There were days when she struggled to recall David's face, his easy smile. Days when she fought to remember that brief time they'd shared, when she had almost been able to forget about Alex. It would have been different, she knew, if they'd shared a home or had a child together. Then there would have been permanent tangible reminders. But all she was left with were the memories, and a handful of leave photos.

The war went on, but she was distanced from it these days, her hours consumed by Rory. Letters arrived from Kath, detailing life in the city that seemed foreign to her now, removed from her own casual existence. She had spent more than she intended on the house, and her finances were low. Carefully she scrimped and saved. Ration coupons were still needed for essentials such as tea, sugar and meat. Sweets and cigarettes became luxuries she couldn't afford.

It wasn't until the following winter that she took up painting again. It was Rory's birthday, her first and, lacking the money to buy a present, which she knew the child was too young to appreciate, Claire decided to decorate the little girl's room.

Firstly she took out Maudie's collection of marine bric-a-brac: the abalone shells, tritons and spindles, cowries and murex, conches, fragile dried remains of a sea horse, the sea sponges and starfish. She lined them up on the kitchen table and sketched them.

Next she transposed the sketches to the walls in Rory's room, interspersed them with whales and dolphins, turtles, bright fish and coral. When she had finished, several weeks later, the mural looked cheerful, colourful, and Rory clapped her hands with delight.

'That looks fantastic,' admired Hal Melville when he called in to see Rory, who had a slight cold. The following weekend he brought out a couple of women from town, wives of acquaintances who had young children. The resulting commissions kept her busy for three months.

'Why don't you start doing your watercolours again, love?' asked Nina when the work ran out. So she did, bold seascapes in bright colours that kept her entranced for hours — and were promptly sold.

Tea-tree Passage had grown during the last year. Sawmills had sprouted up in the hills above, with lorries carting timber down to the boats. Along the road that led to the mills, a new subdivision offered land for sale. Small fibro shacks had begun springing up amongst the tea-trees. Crowds flocked along the foreshore every weekend, poking amongst the rock pools for shells.

Claire knew she had to make a reliable living. The paintings had sold easily and there had been enquiries for more. One Sunday, several women had knocked on her door, asking if she had others for sale. If only she had space, a room where she could set up her paints permanently. Working on the kitchen table was proving increasingly difficult, especially as Rory got older. And packing her equipment away every mealtime was frustrating. Relying on her instinct, she approached the bank manager in town.

He sighed, looked over the top of his glasses at her. 'This is most unusual, lending money to a single woman.'

'A *widowed* woman. Look, I know it's a gamble, but I'm confident I can make it work. I *have* to make it work. It's the only way I can adequately provide for myself and my daughter.'

Grudgingly, he lent her the money.

Claire had a small studio built at the bottom of the garden. It was an airy light-filled room, with the one wall facing the water built entirely of glass. When it was finished, she set up her easel and paints, arranged the brushes and paper. Spread a blanket on the floor and brought a few of Rory's toys down. Then she started painting.

Brisbane was, Lydia thought, a garrison town these days. Streets teemed with soldiers, sailors and airmen. Overflowing troop trains rattled through city stations, and roads were congested with convoys of lorries carrying war supplies.

It seemed that every action, every word, revolved around the war. Railway station walls boasted posters encouraging men to enlist. Children collected Golden Fleece swap cards. War loan bonds, a ban on fireworks on New Year's Eve, rationing — would she ever be able to walk into a store again to buy stockings and chocolates without producing those wretched ration coupons?

Since rejoining the theatre group, Lydia had what Ellen called aspirations. She looked at magazine pictures of Rita Hayworth, who had recently appeared in *Gilda*, and saw herself. Fame, money: the thought of them spurred her on. It wasn't a dream, unachievable. The right opportunity, that was all she needed.

At odd moments she thought of her daughter, Aurora — though Claire insisted on calling her Rory. She hadn't seen the child since that day in Brisbane when she'd handed her to Claire and watched them drive away in the taxi. Hadn't wanted to, either. She felt no attachment to the child, though the anger still welled up when she thought of Ellis's casual dismissal of her and their affair.

She'd given him her heart, and look what he'd done. Broken it, shattered it into tiny pieces. Well, there was no way a man would ever do that again.

'From now on I'm a good-time girl,' she told Ellen. 'Here only for the good times and gone when the going gets tough. Never, ever, will I let someone use me that way again.'

He'd done it subtly, she knew now, wormed his way into her affections, making her respect him in a way she'd never respected a man before. Promised her the world, then disappeared without warning. *Married!* Hank had said that day at Somerville House. Kids, too!

She bought a doll for Rory's first birthday, a delicate porcelain creation. Posted it. *Love from Lydia* she wrote on the bottom of the card. Maybe one day she'd visit, when she got around to it, see for herself how her daughter was progressing. The war was drawing to an end, according to the newspapers, and it was only a matter of time till the whole rotten thing was over.

Sometimes it seemed to Nina that the years had telescoped together and it was like yesterday when she had brought her own children back to Tea-tree Passage, after Frank had died. She had left her dreams in the city, was now content to let each day pass without fuss. She'd done her bit during the early stages of the war: knitting socks, packing Christmas parcels, practising her own economies and letting her children go. Now she was putting her own needs before others, for a change.

But old habits were hard to break and she worried about Claire. Certainly she was doing well. Her paintings were selling and Rory was growing into a bright-eyed toddler. But, in the process, was Claire letting her own life, a chance at further happiness, slip by? She seemed careless of the clothes she wore — Claire, who had loved to wear smart dresses and high-heeled pumps. She hardly went anywhere, except to town for food and art supplies. A couple of the local chaps, Nina knew, had asked her to the pictures, but Claire had refused, citing Rory as her excuse.

'You should buy a new dress,' said Nina, after she'd helped Claire take in the washing from the line one afternoon.

'What would I want a new dress for?'

'It'd be nice, that's all. You should get out more.'

'Mum! I'm happy here!' she said, taking another piece of ironing from the basket. 'Just me and Rory.'

'Happy! Humph!'

'Don't go on so.'

'I'm not going on.'

And so on it went.

Nina tried to be involved, took her granddaughter to the beach while Claire worked, trying to forget how wearying it was looking after a young child. I'm getting old, she thought. Past it all. But when she returned, she often found Claire in the house, not her studio, cleaning out the pantry or sweeping, or some such similar pastime.

What was to become of her? David was dead and Claire seemed disinterested in men, putting all her energies into the child instead. What if Lydia ever wanted her daughter back? How would Claire cope? Then Nina reconsidered, thinking how improbable the idea was. Lydia was too involved in her own affairs. Still, she felt that niggle of doubt.

There seemed a sadness about Claire these days, a grief that welled up inside, sometimes spilling over into her normally happy nature. Was it because of David?

'It's not that,' said Claire.

'What is it, then? A sorrow shared is less of a burden.'

'I don't have any burdens. I have my home. I have my daughter.'

'She's not your daughter,' said Nina gently.

'No,' said Claire bitterly. 'I couldn't even manage that right. No baby.'

'I worry about you.'

'There's no need. I'm fine.'

'I worry that Lydia will want the child. How will you cope then?'

'I'd cope.'

'Please, Claire. I'm a mother. I can sense something's wrong. Tell me.'

'I can't. I don't want to talk about it.'

Nina felt sick at heart. 'Is it too much for you looking after Rory?'

'Really, she's no trouble at all. I love taking care of her.'

It was true, Nina thought, as she watched them later. Anyone watching, not knowing, would think Clare was Rory's real mother. She was so natural, so *involved*. Lydia hadn't even bothered to visit.

The war ended with the Japanese surrender on August 15th, 1945. VP Day — short for Victory in the Pacific — was celebrated the following day. Alex heard 'Land of Hope and Glory' played over the public address system at the hospital at Greenslopes and felt a relief he'd not experienced for years. His job, however, was not finished. It would be months, maybe years, before all the injured were brought back for rehabilitation.

By the time he came off duty, tired yet elated, there were wild celebrations in the streets. Car horns sounded. Tram bells clanged. Tiny pieces of torn-up paper floated into the streets from buildings above, like confetti. Long lines of people ran in and out of buildings, linking arms and laughing, shouting, 'Peace! Peace!'

Somehow he was caught up in their mass, swept along Queen Street. Several women in uniform whisked past. One grabbed his arm. 'Come to the pub and have a drink with us.'

He shook his head, smiling. 'Another time,' he said, knowing there would never be, *could* never be, a day like this again. Six years of tension and fear had dissolved. They were safe. *Safe!*

'Alex!'

Above the din, he heard someone call his name. He turned, staring blankly at the thronging crowd, expecting one of the nurses from the hospital. But it was Lydia running towards him, tears streaming down her face. 'Oh, Alex! Someone I know at last. Isn't it wonderful! It's over! All over!'

There was confetti caught in her hair, tiny flecks glittering oddly in the pale sunlight. He was aware of the noise around him, yet inside his head it was strangely silent. Someone danced past, unbalancing her, and he steadied her with his hand. 'Lydia, it's been a long time.'

'Too long. I suppose now all this is over, you'll be going home.'

Home? He tried to think, tried to focus his mind on the house at Tea-tree Passage, Erica and Josh. Tried to imagine them together again, a family. 'What about you?' he asked, changing the subject. 'What does the future hold in store for Lydia?'

She laughed, swung him around. 'Anything,' she cried, looking upwards, towards the sun, 'as long as I'm rich and famous.'

CHAPTER 36

Claire rang Kath religiously, once a week. She was still living in Brisbane, waiting anxiously for news of her husband Tom, who had been captured by the Japanese a few years earlier. The first of the POWs were beginning to arrive home — gaunt, stricken men — and Kath was hopeful of some news.

The names of released prisoners were published in the newspapers. Claire scanned them daily but his name was never there. Was he alive or dead? Although she tried to keep Kath's spirits buoyed, personally, she was worried. Apart from that solitary letter six months after he had been taken prisoner, Kath had received no further word. Now the full extent of the Japanese atrocities was spilled across the newspaper headlines. Claire read the horrifying accounts, chilled by the details. Decapitation, it seemed, had been the easiest way to die in the death camps there.

It was December before the telegram arrived, notifying Kath of her husband's death. Distraught, she rang Claire. 'He's been dead for two years. All those letters I sent: I was writing to no-one.'

'Come for Christmas,' Claire offered. 'Meet my family, spend some time by the sea. It's very healing.'

There was a bus service from town now, and several local taxis. Weekend tourists spilled into the Passage, eager to soak up the sun and sand. They knocked on Claire's studio door, wanting to look at her paintings, interrupting her.

'I can barely keep up the supply,' she told Kath on the first night of her arrival. 'So I've been thinking about expanding. I could build an art gallery onto this place. It's in a perfect location, close to the beach.'

'And tearooms!' interjected Kath excitedly. 'There's nowhere here to buy a cold drink or a snack. And souvenirs.' She stopped, staring intently at Claire. 'There's only one problem.'

'What's that?' She hadn't counted on obstacles.

'You'd need someone reliable to run it.'

'I already have someone in mind.'

'You do?' A look of disappointment crossed Kath's face.

'It's you, silly,' said Claire, giving her a hug. 'The job's yours, if you want it.'

So Kath moved in with Claire and Rory, and the Passage rang to the sound of hammers and saws as the gallery and tearooms rose, mushroom-like, from the ground.

It was one room, really, very spacious, the two areas linked by a wide doorway. The floors were local hardwood, buffed and polished to a soft sheen.

Claire ordered the walls painted white, to reflect the light. In the tearoom, tables and chairs dotted the area and huge glass windows overlooked the water.

The post-war rationing meant that the project took ten months to complete. However the venture was an instant success. Over a hundred people tramped through the doors that first weekend, buying souvenirs and ice-creams, hot pies and drinks. Claire sold six paintings.

'At least we eat for another month,' she told Kath with a grin.

By the end of 1946, most of the Australian servicemen and women had returned to civilian life, although wartime restrictions on food, clothing and petrol were still in place. The government exercised control over prices. In the tearoom, the cost of a lunchtime meal wasn't allowed to exceed four shillings, while the price of an apple pie was capped at threepence ha'penny and a meat pie at threepence.

Somehow the two women muddled through the annoyances, quickly gaining a reputation for good food and artwork. Tea-tree Passage became the popular meeting place for couples from town. That Christmas, which marked the end of the first year of Kath's residency there, takings exceeded all expectations. The loan had been repaid. For the first time, Claire had a sizeable nest egg in the bank. She was painting well, doing what she loved, and getting paid for it.

During those last exhausting months in the city, whenever Alex let his mind slide back to Tea-tree

Passage — the sandy track leading down to the sea wall, the clumps of tea-trees and casuarinas, the succession of saltwater creeks emptying coffee-coloured water onto the sand after rain — it was the image of Claire's face that superimposed itself onto his thoughts.

She was there, he knew, with Lydia's child: a daughter she was raising as her own. Moved into Maudie's old place, effected lots of repairs. Although Erica, who was usually close-mouthed when it came to Claire, had let a few details slip, it was his father, in those weekly telephone calls, who had provided the information.

What was her motivation for taking the child? He could understand her desire for motherhood. She and David had spoken about having children on that last Christmas Day they had all spent together. Perhaps she'd primed herself mentally for the event, and David's death had put a premature end to her plans. But Lydia's baby? God only knew who the father was!

The news that pleased him most was that she'd started painting again. Bright seascapes, according to his father, that were selling well. Then Erica had told him about the tearoom and gallery.

'I think Claire's trying to civilise us,' she had said into the mouthpiece, her voice slightly mocking. 'I suppose her paintings are passable, at least everyone says they are. They don't appeal to me.'

The bulk of wounded servicemen were discharged and, finally, Alex headed back to Tea-tree Passage. He bought a Hudson Commodore Six to commemorate the occasion, driving it carefully the several hundred miles north. He was playing for time, he knew, spinning out the hours until his eventual arrival home.

His marriage, he conceded, was a muddled nightmare and, during the past eighteen months, his visits home had faded to nothing. He had toyed with the option of staying in the city, not bothering to return; there were dozens of jobs going begging there. Could have set himself up in his own practice, hand-picked his clientele. But he had missed Josh unbearably during those years of city living. Missed seeing him grow, missed those milestones in the boy's life. It was, he admitted to himself, time to go home and be a proper father.

His welcome home was lukewarm, although Erica gave the car an appraising glance. Josh, almost five, shied away from him. He seemed reserved, preferring to follow his mother around. Only his father seemed pleased to see him, asking when he planned to return to work. 'You're badly needed around here,' he told his son, taking him for a celebratory drink at the pub.

It would be, Alex thought, a long hard road back to normalcy, whatever that was.

Although Alex and Erica's house stood alongside Claire's, it was several days before he met up with her. She'd been busy, he knew, the light burning until all hours of the night in that small studio at the rear of the garden. He'd seen only the blurred shape of her as she moved backwards and forwards across the uncurtained window, and watched at a distance as she hung washing on the clothesline.

They were on the beach, she and the child, building a sandcastle. It was an intricate affair, moats and turrets, and a drawbridge edged with tiny shells.

'The tide's coming in,' Alex said, hunkering down beside them. 'What a shame it'll wash away.'

'It's only a pretend castle,' said the child, regarding him gravely.

'Hello, Alex. I was wondering when I'd bump into you.'

He stared directly into Claire's eyes. She blinked, glanced across at the child, and he followed her gaze. 'So this is Lydia's daughter.'

Claire drew the child close, enveloping her in a spontaneous embrace. 'Yes. This is Rory.'

'An unusual name.'

Claire gave an exasperated grimace. 'My sister is an unusual woman. She insisted on calling her Aurora.'

'I see.'

She rose, took a towel from the sand and began to dry the little girl. Alex watched, noting the little gestures — wiping the sand from her face, wrapping the towel around her spindly body. Rory might not be Claire's natural daughter, but he thought her more maternal than a lot of women he knew, including his own wife.

Rory regarded him with large eyes. 'Who are you?'

'I'm Josh's dad.'

'I don't have a father.'

He gave Claire a knowing look over the top of the child's head and she smiled at him, compressing her mouth. 'Would you like to come up to the house?'

On the way back along the path, they talked of Joe, how he'd joined the overseas occupational force. 'He's in Japan,' Claire told him. 'Says he doesn't want to come home yet.'

Alex frowned. 'It gets some blokes like that. Saw it all the time at the hospital. After what they've gone through, it's a wonder any of them ever settle into normal life again.'

'Are you saying Joe won't ever come back?'

'No. I'm just saying that when he does, he might find the going pretty difficult.'

Nina was waiting for her granddaughter, and she whisked her away in the direction of the bath, clucking like an old chook. Meanwhile, Claire took him on a tour of the gallery. 'Kath manages this part of the business. Her husband didn't make it back from the war and she was at a bit of a loose end. So I asked her to stay with us.'

'Rory and Kath,' he said with a smile. 'So you're taking in strays these days.'

'Sometimes I think I'm the stray and they look after *me*,' she chuckled. 'I corner myself away in my studio and let the world go by. Couldn't do it without Kath helping with Rory. Mother, too.'

'Rory seems a nice kid.'

Claire nodded. 'She's almost four now. Growing up so fast. Do you know Lydia has never been to see her?'

Alex made a pretence of studying the artwork, watching out of the corner of his eye as she wandered around the room, straightening the occasional painting, arranging a collection of pottery on consignment. She had filled out a little, was no longer coltish or angular, but shapely in all the right places. There was a new sense of maturity about her, a competence that had come, he supposed, from looking after the child. She was more purposeful, more centred. He was delighted she'd made a career of her art, and told her so.

'I'm impressed with your work. It's matured, strengthened. You've come a long way since that day I first met you.'

'You're to blame for my new career,' she told him with a smile. 'Remember how you encouraged me, bought me the paints?'

He nodded. It seemed a lifetime ago — *was* a lifetime ago — since he'd come across her drawing down by the water. He still had that sketch somewhere, packed away with his personal papers. He'd taken it out over the years, studied it, wondered how different his life would have been if —

'Would you like a coffee? Kath has a new machine that pours lots of froth on top. It's called cappuccino. Very Italian, if I can work the wretched thing.'

Erica was waiting in the living room when he got home, hands on her hips.

'I saw you down there with her.'

'Claire or Rory?' he asked amicably.

'Both of them. Do you think I'm stupid?'

Patiently he replied, 'No.' Jealous and argumentative perhaps, but never stupid.

Suddenly she moved closer, wound her arms around his neck. Pressed herself against his chest until he could feel her small pointed breasts. 'Alex, I've been thinking. I'm tired of living in this dump. Let's move into town. There's no reason why you couldn't have a nice bungalow built, something with a few enclosed verandahs for entertaining and a modern kitchen with a new electric stove, instead of the old monstrosity of an Aga.'

During the following weeks she brought up the idea at odd times, reinforcing it with further argument. Josh would spend less time travelling to school and there would be other boys nearby his own age. Alex would be closer to work. As a local doctor, he needed to maintain a public image. It wasn't good for Josh to play with Rory, Lydia's bastard daughter. She wanted her son to mix with children from normal families.

What's normal? he thought, irritated. His and Erica's relationship? The way they warily circled each other?

However there was one point his wife had failed to raise, Alex realised with certainty, knowing it was the unspoken driving force behind her plans. If they moved to town, Claire would be more distant from their lives.

By the end of the war, Joe was exhausted. He'd seen enough bloodshed to last a thousand years, witnessed every possible depraved and disgusting sight imaginable. Or so he thought. Liberating the skeletal remains of prisoners from the Japanese camps. Listening to the horror stories of Japanese brutality. Holding one soldier in his arms as he died from the effects of gangrene, hours after the war had officially ended.

Yet the prospect of going home, back to that normal *conventional* life, became increasingly unthinkable. After years of sleeping on the ground or, at best, rough straw mattresses, how could he sleep in a bed? How could he eat a decent meal and not remember the weevil-infested food in Milne Bay and Kokoda? Home, he knew with certainty, was a place of the past, not the future.

He joined the Australian component of the British Commonwealth Occupational Force, landing in Kure, near Hiroshima, aboard the *Pachaug Victory*, a US-registered cargo ship. He saw the desolation there, and at Nagasaki. Grey weeping countryside, the splintered remains of trees. Whole city blocks reduced to small piles of rubble. Children wandering blank-eyed amongst the debris.

By the end of '47, over two years after the end of the war, Joe had had enough. He thought of Nina's home by the sea, bare verandah boards bleached silver by the sun, and the sandy path that led through the tussocky grass to the water's edge. Remembered the sickly smell of the jasmine climbing up the latticework at the end of the verandah and the native bees hovering around the tiny flowers; the way the paint peeled from the front steps into long flaky shards. Thought of Claire and Nina, Lydia, and Rory, whom he had never seen. His niece, now four years old. Time was passing him by, thrusting him into the future. The following day, he applied for demobilisation.

*　*　*

It was a typical summer's afternoon, hot and still
with grey skies threatening rain, when Joe's letter
arrived. Nina was pensive — was it something to do
with the weather? she wondered — as she read the
words, thinking of the son she hadn't seen for over
five years. He would have changed, she knew that;
no longer her 'boy', but a grown man, hardened and
toughened by the experiences of war. Would she see
hate in his eyes?

Flies buzzed at the screen door. As she refolded
the page, thunder rolled and the first drops began to
fall. She ran all the way to Claire's studio, heedless of
the rain, and threw open the door without bothering
to knock. Claire swung towards her, surprised,
paintbrush in her hand and tiny splatters of paint on
her cheek. 'Joe's coming home!' she cried, waving the
letter. 'It'll be a few weeks. There's the boat journey,
then he has to be discharged.'

Claire was smiling, a broad grin creasing her face.
'That's the best news we've had for a long while,' she
said, kissing Nina on both cheeks and waltzing her
around the floor, dodging the piles of canvases and
picture frames.

'Stop!' Nina called, breathless. Claire released her,
laughing, and she collapsed into the chair next to the
window. She laid her face against the cool glass of
the window, closed her eyes and felt them fill
unexpectedly with tears. 'Thank God!' she
whispered, her voice barely audible. 'Oh, thank
God!'

The weeks passed interminably, waiting for him. Each day Nina wondered if a letter, or a phone call, might tell her he was on the final leg of his journey. But, like his father after that last war, he arrived unannounced, a knock heralding his arrival, his face fuzzy behind the screen door.

'Hello, Mum.'

He stood there, smiling uncertainly. At first glance he seemed shrivelled, emaciated, his clothes hanging in loose folds and his boots looking too big for his feet.

'Oh, Joe!' she cried, shocked at his thinness. 'Look at you!'

'This is good,' he said with a grin. 'You should have seen me before.' He dumped his kitbag on the floor and hugged her in a clumsy, self-conscious way. 'It's good to be home.'

'It's wonderful to have you here. I've made up the bed in your old room.'

He shook his head. 'Mum,' he began tentatively. 'I'm not planning to stay.'

The words ticked slowly through her consciousness. He was barely home, yet already he was talking about leaving. 'Where are you going?'

'I'm going to live on the boat.'

She frowned, trying to make sense of his words.

'I've been thinking about it for a while,' he went on. 'I'll do a bit of work to the cabin underneath, put in a bed and a cupboard. There's already a small kitchen. Big enough for one. Don't get upset. It's not you. It's me. Don't think I can live in a house again, least not for a while. You know how it is?'

She nodded and took his arm. 'Come and sit down and I'll put the kettle on. We'll have a nice cup of tea.'

'No, I have to go out for a bit. There's someone I want to see.'

'Where are you going?'

'Just out.'

'To see Jane?' she asked warily.

Nina wasn't exactly sure what had happened between Jane and Joe, and no explanation had ever been forthcoming. The collapse of their relationship was probably another casualty of the war. The girl was married now and had a young family of her own. Nina occasionally ran into her in town and she was always pleasant enough, asking after Nina's health.

'I might be.'

'Joe, I don't think —'

'It's something I have to do.'

'What about a bath first? A change of clothes?'

'No.'

'You don't know where she lives.'

'How difficult can it be to find?'

'Don't torture yourself, Joe. These are different times now. Let it go.'

'Just leave it, okay?' He gave her a quick kiss on the cheek. 'I really missed you, you know that.' And he was gone.

She closed her eyes to his retreating form, heard the screen door slam and the tramp of his boots down the path. She put her hands to her cheeks, trying to stem the pain. 'Oh, please God,' she sighed.

* * *

Joe knocked on the door, listening for any sound that meant someone was at home. Waited until the door was flung open and she stood there. All those years had passed, yet Jane had changed little. Red hair cut short, smattering of freckles across her nose. Mouth that curved up at the corners into a smile.

'Joe!'

She moved forward, onto the top step. A small girl wrapped her arms around one of her legs, thumb in mouth. Same red hair and freckles. Obviously a miniature version of her mother. Jane smoothed her hand across her apron. Joe could tell by the way the fabric pushed out with the shape of it, that she was heavily pregnant.

Someone had told him she'd married, had a kid. But he'd wanted to see for himself. Why, he didn't know. Some form of self-punishment, he supposed. Or was he seeking a sense of closure, a finalisation to the unresolved feelings that had gathered momentum, now he was home?

'Hello, Jane.'

'You're looking good.'

'Yair,' he grinned. 'Skinny as a rabbit.'

'At least you got back safe.'

Safe: what was that? Having all your body parts intact? No scars. He thought about Hiroshima and a surge of nausea made him catch his breath. 'Yair, safe,' he agreed.

Unconsciously she brought her hand to her belly, holding it there as pregnant women are wont to do.

For a few seconds he was unable to take his eyes from it, and when he glanced up, found her staring at him, an odd expression on her face.

'I'm sorry, Joe, about what happened between you and me.'

'Nothing to be sorry about.'

From inside he heard the wail of a small child and she visibly started. 'Is that yours, too?' he asked.

'Yes.'

Abruptly he turned and walked away, leaving her standing in the doorway. He didn't look back, simply kept walking, placing one foot after the other in a mechanical way. Halfway between town and Teatree Passage, he strode into the bush. When he could walk no more, his breath coming in ragged sweeps, he hunkered down on the damp leaf-littered soil, his back against the trunk of a tree, aware of the rough bark beneath the fabric of his shirt.

What had he expected, seeing Jane? That somehow he had got it wrong? Or that she had changed her mind, was waiting for him after all these years? But she wasn't. She'd gotten on with her life. Two children already, another on the way. In another life they could have been his. Oh, God!

He leaned back and closed his eyes, felt the tears begin to form. Why was he crying? For Jane and the relationship he had lost? For his own disenchantment, or for those awful bloody sights he'd seen during the past few years?

Blankly he stared upwards, not knowing. A throbbing had started deep inside his head. His brain seemed at bursting point, a pressure building there that made him bring his palms to his temples, as though to stop them from exploding. Perhaps, he thought wildly, he was going insane.

Images, dozens of them, coursed through his consciousness. Jane sunbaking on the deck of the *Sea-spray*, or leading him down the stairs to that tiny cabin below. Sitting in the jungle, holding that *fucking* letter. Dead men and the rotten stench of decaying vegetation. The flat plains of Hiroshima, where a shadow on a footpath was the only reminder that a person had once stood there, had breathed air and spoken and loved. Oh, God, and how he had loved her! And now Jane standing big-bellied in some other man's doorway, carrying another man's child. *You're looking good. At least you got back safe.*

Platitudes. Useless fucking words that meant nothing, said nothing. He felt a hatred surge up inside him. When would the nightmare end? What were the limits of human endurance? And at what point would his mind and body simply refuse to work?

CHAPTER 37

It seemed to Erica that her hatred of Tea-tree Passage grew daily. The place was like a prison, miles from anywhere. And the house was old — draughty in winter and like a furnace in summer. All the women there were much older, almost Nina's age, except for Claire. And there was no way she'd spend time with *her*.

She was, she admitted to herself, dissatisfied. At least during the war, she'd lived her own life. There had been no-one else to answer to except Josh, and she'd done her patriotic duty, entertaining the troops. Keeping the boys, and herself, happy. There had been talk, she knew, amongst the locals — they were more loyal to Alex than herself. But she'd tossed her head and ignored them. How she conducted herself was none of their business, and if her husband had gone to the city, well ... she was a normal healthy woman, after all.

Now Alex was home, life had reverted back to that same mundane, predictable existence. The war years had changed nothing. He was still tied to his job, allowing himself to be called out at all hours. When she complained, an argument developed.

'We never spend any time together. Why can't we go to dinner sometimes? I'll tell you why,' she went on in a rush, not giving him time to answer. 'Because when you do grace us with your presence, you're too bloody tired!'

'My father's slowing down these days, taking less patients. I've got to take up the extra.'

'I don't know why you don't advertise for another doctor.'

Eventually he did, and a young woman came from the city for an interview. She was too young and much too pretty, and Erica had reconsidered. 'Perhaps it wasn't such a good idea,' she told him. 'The locals are a bit set in their ways. I don't think they'd go to a woman doctor.'

Had she imagined it, or had Alex smiled as he turned away?

She found him too complacent, too accepting of his life. Dull even, absorbed in his books, his music. Going for long walks along the beach, either with Josh or by himself. For her own part, she couldn't see the sense in simply *walking*. If you were going to exert yourself, then it had to be for some worthwhile purpose.

Then there was the problem of Claire. Well, she wasn't so much a problem as a general annoyance. Since the younger woman had returned home with Lydia's bastard daughter, Erica had found living in Tea-tree Passage even more unpalatable. She hated seeing Claire on the beach with the child, pretending to be her mother when everyone knew the truth. It was pathetic, really. And all those paintings she churned out of that small room that she optimistically called her studio ... *Studio!* How pretentious!

Personally, Erica couldn't see much merit in the paintings. Turtles and fish, coral and water: they were too bright and gaudy for her own taste. But obviously others found them attractive. There was a constant stream of visitors to the gallery and tearoom, especially on the weekends.

'You're just jealous,' Alex had told her once, bluntly, when she had voiced her opinion.

'Jealous? Of Claire and those amateurish sketches? I hardly think so.' And she had run her fingers along the side of his neck, teasing him in the best way she knew how.

Alex and Claire. Teddy's wife Harry had told her, years earlier, that there had been something going on between them during that summer before he and Erica had married. Was the attraction still there? Erica had seen no evidence of it, yet sometimes Alex was a dark horse, keeping his thoughts and emotions to himself.

There were days when she wondered what she had ever seen in Alex. Certainly he was a doctor, and that guaranteed some prestige and financial advantages, but what was the use of it all if she was dying of boredom? She sighed, thinking back. 'Face it,' she told herself. 'If you hadn't been pregnant, you never would have married him.'

She was forced to admit that Alex had tried to make the best of it over the years, but the relationship had never really gotten off the ground. There was an underlying tension between them, a forced joviality. They were two people going in different directions. In the early days she'd pretended, fooled most of the others into thinking what a lovely couple she and Alex made. But it was all a charade, a sham. And now, as the cracks in their marriage widened, she could scarcely be bothered. It seemed the only common ground they shared was Josh.

Josh: her thoughts turned to her son. He was a funny little boy, all wide-eyed and serious. He was at school now which, thank God, freed up her days. She'd despised those years of his babyhood, the endless nappies and daytime naps, the having to organise her own life around his needs. Babies! Thank God there had never been another!

Alex idolised the boy, taking him on those long useless walks along the beach, and out fishing in the little dinghy. Patiently he'd taught him how to bait the hook and cast the line, showed him the slugs and tiny fish, the broken fragments of coral in the shallow rock pools at the end of the point. For her own part, Erica couldn't be bothered. She treated Josh casually, never making a fuss, yet some days it seemed he never left her side, trotting along beside her, not wanting to let her out of his sight.

'Come on now,' she'd say. 'You don't want to be a mummy's boy.'

And he'd look at her, soulfully, with big brown eyes, making her feel strangely guilty.

At least Alex had given in and bought her a car. She went into town several times a week, using any small excuse to escape. She had joined the newly constructed golf club, met a few women and had regular lunches.

She started drinking. Just socially at first, a sherry with lunch or dinner, followed by a few wines. They dulled her senses, made life bearable — blotted out her repetitious boring life, the endless round of arguments. Why couldn't Alex see things her way, pander to her more? Why couldn't they be like normal couples? Frustrated, she used words to goad him, to provoke a response of some kind. She wanted to see him angry, like herself.

One Saturday evening Erica invited several of her friends out from town. They were arty types mostly, newcomers to the area, trendy and stuck-up, and full of their own importance.

Alex went along with Erica's plans, making sure he was home early from the surgery and playing the congenial host. He watched as they drank his wine — Erica had insisted they needn't bring a thing — and ate the food she had prepared. Afterwards, someone put a few records on the gramophone and turned the volume up, and they'd sat around and smoked, or danced on the verandah. When most of the grog had been consumed, they climbed back into their sporty cars and drove away, leaving her restless and argumentative.

'I don't see why we can't move,' she complained, puffing furiously on a Capstan. 'I'd see more of my friends if I lived in town. No one wants to drive all the way out here. And tonight, I could sense them looking the place over and finding it wanting.'

'You shouldn't be so influenced by other people.'

'I'm not. I hate it here. I've *always* hated it here.'

'You'd like it if you let yourself.'

'Never. It's a dull little backwater.'

She walked over to the drinks' cabinet, poured herself the last of the Scotch from the bottle. She swayed slightly as she did so, sloshed a few drops onto the timber veneer surface. Then she giggled and raised the glass to her mouth, consuming it with one swallow.

'Don't you think you've had enough?'

She put the glass down slowly, stood there glaring at him. 'Are you trying to be my moral guardian, Alex?'

'Hardly.'

'I'm a big girl, remember? I can drink whatever I want and you won't tell me otherwise.'

'You're drunk and I refuse to argue with you.'

'That's right,' she threw back at him. 'Don't even begin to confront the issues!'

Patiently. 'What issues, Erica?'

'And don't patronise me by talking to me as though I were a child! The issues of our marriage, moving away from here.'

He was tired of the endless arguments, the petulance, the anger. 'I'm not moving, full stop! And as for our marriage, we can finish it any time you like!'

'If I go, I'll take Josh.'

It was a threat, he knew that. He knew also that he couldn't bear losing the boy. His son was the one solid consistency in his life and, if he believed she would make good her promise, he'd have to put up with things the way they were.

Dispirited, he let himself out the front door and walked down the track towards the sea wall. Past Claire's house he went, seeing movements behind the drawn curtains, dark shapes that came and went. Kath probably, he thought, noting that the light was on in Claire's studio at the back of the garden. She would be down there, working hard, spreading the paint meticulously on the paper or canvas, depending on what medium she was working with.

Alex fought back the urge to knock on her door, take refuge in that calm quiet place and unburden his soul. But what good would that do? He had made his choice years earlier, and he had to live with that.

He sat on the sea wall instead, staring out towards Turtle Island. The moon had come up, turning the water a dark silver. In that pale light, he could see the rhythmic flow of it, imagined the tiny grains of sand being pulled along by its quiet strength, and the fish fighting against the current.

That's what I'm like, he thought, surprised. A fish, or a minute sand particle, being pulled this way and that by Erica's whims. He could fight it, he supposed, or, like the fish, let himself go with the tide. Somehow, it might be easier that way. Give in to her demands. Build her a house in town. Restore some peace, some sanity, to their lives. He could still come back here on weekends, bring Josh. Row the dinghy through the mangroves along the creek or dig for pipis in the sand. If he were lucky, he might catch a fleeting glimpse of Claire.

What had they become, he and Erica? Not really a couple, just two people tugging alternately at the boy. Or rather Erica pushing both of them away, then teasing Josh back again, promising him affection then withdrawing. Was she capable of loving anyone but herself?

He had never asked much of her — had that been a mistake? — or made demands. Instead they had shambled along, meeting irregularly, each in a separate void. There was a coldness about her sometimes, an unapproachability that confused him. Her moods were as changeable as the wind and, once she started drinking, her words became nasty. They were both entitled to more, after all these years together. Companionship. Some semblance of friendship. Even the sex was almost non-existent.

She was drinking, he knew, but not enough to arouse suspicion. A glass here and there, strange bottles appearing in the cupboard under the sink. He'd tried to make a joke of it but she'd snatched them away. 'It's nothing,' she'd said, whisking them from his sight.

Teddy — his old mate — had been up for a few days, leaving Harry, who was expecting their third child, in Brisbane. Teddy had changed in the past few years, had become overweight and smoked like a chimney. For a doctor, he seemed to care little about his own health.

'What's with Erica?' he'd said after he'd been with them a few days. 'She seems damn pissed off all the time.'

Alex had shrugged. 'You were wrong, all those years ago.'

'Wrong about what?'

'Love. You need it to sustain you, keep you going. Life's pretty empty without it.'

Rory sat at one end of the table in Claire's kitchen with her colouring books and pencils. She moved the pencil carefully over the page, keeping the colour inside the lines, as Claire had taught her. Her aunt stood at the other end of the table, kneading dough, her face furrowed with concentration. Outside, a cold wind howled around the corners of the house. However it was warm in the kitchen, the old Aga pumping heat into the room and, presently, she smelt the aroma of baking bread.

From time to time, Rory glanced up at her aunt and examined her features: pretty face, dark hair cut into a short bob. She saw Claire's hands working at the dough. Rolling and folding, rhythmic: like down in her studio when she dipped her brush in the paint and spread it over the paper with smooth, even strokes.

Aunt Claire. How stern she had once thought that name sounded, not at all pretty and feminine. But her aunt was all those things. Rory loved to tiptoe into her bedroom when Claire was down in her studio and Kath busy with the tearoom: she would pat Claire's perfume on her wrist and dab lipstick on her mouth, staring at her reflection in the mirror, wondering where she had come from, and why.

She knew Claire wasn't her mother; that had been made clear from the start. Mother was a lady named

Lydia, whom she had never met, but who sent her presents on her birthdays, pretty feminine things that made Claire click her tongue with annoyance.

'Useless damn trinkets,' she had once heard Claire say to her own mother — Rory's grandmother. 'A few quid towards the food bill would be better.'

But Rory loved the things Lydia sent. Bright baubles, pretty photo frames and trinket boxes, and one time a porcelain doll that sat on the end of her dressing table and couldn't possibly be played with because Rory might break it.

She showed these things to the other girls at school. 'Look what my mother brought me,' she would say, passing them over for inspection, seeing the envious eyes.

Kath was keeping company with one of the local chaps in town. A romance had blossomed, with her friend confiding to Claire only the previous week that she thought a marriage proposal was imminent. 'I don't think I'll accept, though,' she had added.

'Why ever not? You like him, don't you?'

Kath's eyes had welled with tears. 'I feel so guilty, that's all. Tom's dead, and I'm letting someone take his place.'

'No-one can ever take his place,' Claire had replied fiercely. 'You'll always love Tom, whatever happens. But you deserve some happiness, too.'

What about her own happiness? Claire wondered later. Over the past few years she'd had a few male friends. A new solicitor in town, a local bank manager. Trips to the picture theatre or dinner in town. They had been nice men, sensible and hardworking, but unconsciously she had compared them all with Alex and found them lacking.

Instead, she arranged her working life around Rory, seeing her off on the school bus each morning, waiting for her return with home-made biscuits or cake. In the early evenings after the child had gone to bed, she went back to the studio, working until late to fill those missing gaps in her life, deliberately pushing herself towards exhaustion, so there was no time left to care.

She organised a party for Rory's sixth birthday and invited several of her school friends. Lydia had promised to arrive for the occasion. It was the first time she would see her daughter since she had handed her to her sister all those years ago.

Claire showed Rory a photo of Lydia. 'This is your mummy,' she told the little girl. 'She's coming to see you next week.'

The photo was years old, tattered around the edges, yet it was all she had. Rory took it, peered at the image of the woman who had borne her. Then she handed it back, shaking her head. 'You're my mummy,' she pronounced. 'No-one has two mummies.'

'Remember I told you how your Mummy couldn't look after you, so I brought you here. You were just a few days old. Tiny, like this.' Claire held out her hands, thinking she was like Joe when describing the size of a fish.

Rory climbed up on her lap and put her head on Claire's shoulder. 'Tell me again. All of it.'

Claire had tried, over the years, to tell Rory the truth, gradually dropping bits of information when she thought the child was old enough to understand. She'd never tried to hide the fact that she wasn't Rory's real mother and stressed the fact that Lydia had been unable to take care of her.

'Why couldn't she?'

'Because she has a very demanding job.'

'What is she again?'

'An actress.'

'An ac-tress.' Rory sounded the name, breaking it into syllables. 'What's an ac-tress?'

'A lady who performs in a play. Remember when you had your Christmas pageant at school and you were one of the Three Wise Men?'

'Ye-es.'

'Well that's what your Mummy does, stands on a stage and reads her lines.'

'And people come and watch?'

'Yes. She's had some quite good reviews.'

'What's a review?'

'When someone writes an article for a newspaper, to say why they did or didn't like something.'

'Did they like my Mummy?'

'Of course.'

Lydia had enjoyed some moderate acting success over the years and, although she was based in Brisbane, her work had taken her across the country. Occasionally, a postcard from her had arrived unexpectedly at the Passage, bearing a few scribbled words. And when Claire had seen an article on some play her sister was appearing in, she had cut it out and pasted it into a scrapbook. She was planning on giving Rory the clippings for her birthday.

The day of the party arrived, and one by one the children arrived, bearing gifts. 'My other mummy's coming,' Claire heard Rory tell the other girls as she was opening the last of the presents.

However there was no sign of Lydia. No car pulling up at the gate. No telephone call explaining her absence. From time to time, she saw Rory run to the front door and glance up the track, in the direction from which her mother would arrive. Saw her walk back dejectedly.

The day went smoothly, the children finally leaving mid-afternoon. As Claire was cleaning up, the telephone rang. It was Lydia. 'Claire, there's a bit of a problem, I'm afraid. Something's come up.'

'Where are you?'

'Brisbane.'

Incredulously. 'You haven't even left yet?'

'Well, I told you, something's come up. Bit of a do, and I have to be there. I'll be on my way in a few days.'

Claire slammed the telephone down, seething. How dare Lydia make promises and then break them! Rory had been waiting anxiously for her mother to arrive. Now she, Claire, would have to break the news.

'There's been an unexpected problem. Mummy has to work a few extra days,' she told Rory, hating herself for lying. Why couldn't she just come out and say it, as she had already told Nina. 'Your mother simply doesn't care.'

It was a week before Lydia pulled up, unannounced, at the front door and driving a fancy car. 'It's Gerald's,' she said, stepping gingerly out onto the dirt. 'God, this place hasn't changed.'

Gerald, it turned out, was her latest boyfriend. His parents owned a factory and employed sixty people, a fact which seemed to impress Lydia more than any of Gerald's qualities. Claire heard all this before she and Lydia had made it to the front door.

'Come and say hello to Mummy,' said Claire to Rory, noticing the child hanging back, reluctant to intrude. Rory looked up at Lydia with wide eyes, moved beside Claire and took her hand.

'Mummy's come all this way to see you.'

'Leave her,' said Lydia. 'She'll come around when she's ready.'

Stung, Claire compressed her lips and bit back a reply.

Lydia prowled about the house, taking scant interest in Rory, although she talked constantly about Gerald. Gerald this, Gerald that, until Claire was heartily sick of the man she had never met. 'Who'd have thought, Maudie leaving this old place to you,' she said suddenly, changing the subject.

'Would you have liked to come back here?'

'God, no! Sorry, I know it's your home but you have to admit there's nothing here. By the way,' she added, as though the thought had only now occurred to her. 'Do Alex and Erica still live next door?'

'Not for long. They're building a house in town, so I suppose they'll be gone soon.'

'How's Joe?'

'Keeps to himself these days. He'll probably come up later and say hello, when he sees the car.'

'And Mum?'

'You should have gone there first, said hello.' Nina, seeing the car pull up at Claire's and her younger daughter emerge, would be hurt.

'Later,' Lydia shrugged. 'There's plenty of time.'

'How long are you planning on staying?'

'At least until the morning.'

'You'll get to meet Kath, then. She's gone into town to pick up some supplies and won't be back until the last bus.'

Claire closed her eyes momentarily against the sight of her sister, her nonchalance. Lydia regarded the trip as a duty visit, she knew that now. Magnanimously she had allocated a few precious hours from her busy schedule to visit her family, her daughter.

'This is Rory's room,' Claire said as they came to the last doorway along the hall. Lydia glanced inside, not commenting on the sea-blue walls and the bright mural, the venture that had taken Claire back into the world of painting years earlier. 'Oh, blast!' she said instead, examining a small chip in one of her fingernails, not even commenting on the rows of shelves containing the toys she'd sent during the past few years. They were expensive dolls mostly, good collector's items, but scarcely suitable play toys.

After she had spent a few hours at Nina's, and Rory had gone to bed, Lydia took a bottle of Scotch from Claire's drinks' cabinet.

'At least you've a decent taste in whisky.'

'As opposed to a lousy taste in . . . ?'

Claire let the question hang between them and Lydia raised her eyebrows. 'Still the touchy one, Claire. Lighten up. I wasn't being critical. I was complimenting you,' she said, pouring a glassful. 'Would you like one?'

'No thanks. Nice of you to ask though.'

Lydia ignored her, lit a cigarette and took a swig of the drink. 'You've done a reasonable job of doing up this old place,' she admitted, a grudging tone to her voice. 'It used to be a bit of a dump.'

'Depends on your perspective.'

'You have to admit Maudie was pretty hopeless in the housekeeping department. A coat of paint and a good clean-out makes all the difference.'

'We wouldn't mind a new stove, and a fancy car would be nice, but there isn't money enough for more.'

Immediately she regretted the words.

Lydia shot her a look. 'I can't afford to send any, if that's what you're hinting.'

'No, but you waste your money on all those silly dolls that Rory never touches.'

Lydia's visit, Claire admitted to herself after her sister left the following morning, had not been a success. She seemed disinterested in her daughter, disinclined to involve herself in her life. But had Claire really expected more? Heartsick, she watched Rory as she stood by the side of the road, waving goodbye. What was the child thinking? Lydia was her mother, after all, and she was leaving.

CHAPTER 38

Claire's paintings were selling well and, between the gallery and the tearoom, she managed to pay the bills and survive. She and Rory were comfortable, she supposed, had an annual holiday and, although Rory saw little of her mother, she had grown into a self-possessed young girl, mostly happy and outgoing.

She was at the age when she had begun to ask questions and expected rational answers. Increasingly, Claire found herself unable to fob her off. 'If Lydia's my real mother, then why can't I go and live with her?'

'Because she travels a lot with her work, you know that. It's easier for you to stay here with me.'

'Why did she have me if she couldn't look after me?'

Why, indeed? How could Claire tell her that Lydia would have happily aborted her child if she'd had the money? — money Claire had refused to lend. 'Not everything we do in life is planned.'

'Do you know who my father is?'

Claire shook her head. May God forgive her for lying! There was no way she was going to open that can of worms. Rory would have to tackle her mother on that issue.

'Doesn't she love me?'

Claire stared at her niece's upturned face and thought she might cry. Swallowing back tears, she said, 'No, darling, she loves you very much. She comes to visit, doesn't she?'

'Sometimes,' Rory said in a small voice.

There were times when Claire sensed something lacking in her personal life. Male affection. The touching and hugging. Sex. One part of her wanted to provide a normal environment for Rory. Mother. Father. Other siblings. Then she'd stop, reminding herself that Rory wasn't her daughter. And if David had lived, how different would her life be now? In many ways, she wished she'd been able to love him more.

Her memories of the past few years were hazy. She had become like a mechanical being, moving in an automated way. Sometimes she felt detached, disjointed, as though her body were performing routine functions while her mind was far away. There were great stretches of time she had no memory of, few days standing out as distinct from the rest. Alex and Erica's move into town and the house next door standing empty and desolate. Kath's marriage and the birth of her two children. The purchase of her little car. What about the other days? she thought, wondering if she really wanted to remember. Sometimes, despite Rory and the busy demands on her life, she had never felt so alone.

Kath and her family lived in the old Melville place next door now, and the happy laughter of children emanated from its interior. Rosie Sharp's eldest daughter ran the tearoom and gallery, helped out on the weekends by Nina, who was slowing these days, her hands swollen and made clumsy by arthritis.

Lydia arrived at odd intervals, usually unannounced. 'Aurora!' she'd call, flinging open the front door. 'Mummy's here.'

And Rory would look up with a frown from the kitchen table where she'd been doing her homework. 'My name's Rory!' she'd reply stubbornly.

'Come and give Mummy a hug.'

'You're not my mother. Claire is.'

'Rory!' Claire would admonish gently, mindful of the unusual situation, but Lydia would simply laugh.

'You're too hard on her,' said Lydia on one occasion. Uninvited, she had followed Claire down to her studio. Casually she wandered around the room, idly picking up the carefully arranged tubes of paints and putting them down in a different order.

'Oh, for goodness sake, stop that!' Claire exploded, taking a tube from Lydia's hand. 'And while we're on the subject, you needn't walk in here whenever you feel like it, offering ideas on the way Rory should be raised.'

'She's only a child!'

Patiently Claire replied, 'I have to set boundaries.'

'*Boundaries*! You sound as though you're trying to fence her in. She's a free spirit.'

'She's *not* a free spirit, Lydia. She's a thirteen-year-old-girl and she needs to be taught right from wrong. I'm the one looking after her, providing for her, so back off!'

'I send money.'

'Lydia, have you any idea how much it costs?'

'So you want more?'

'No. I just want to be able to raise her my way.' She walked towards her sister, arms folded. 'There's something else you should know.'

Lydia grimaced. 'There's more?'

'Rory's been asking about her father.'

'You didn't say anything?'

'About Alex? Of course not. But she's curious.'

'Just ignore it. She'll forget all about it eventually.'

Dismissed. Just like that. As though Rory were of no consequence, a mere irritation that would eventually resolve itself. And the next day Lydia was gone, leaving the problems of raising a teenager behind and, as usual, there was no word for weeks or months.

The other dilemma was Joe. After all those years abroad, he'd found it hard settling back into civilian life. Claire was constantly finding him drunk in town, bringing him home and sobering him up. Hiding the worst of it from Nina. He drifted along, lost and lonely, unable to form any long-lasting relationship. There had been a few women, barmaids from the local pub mostly, but they had come and gone like a summer breeze. He was sliding out of control, unable to point himself in a sensible direction, and her heart went out to him.

Something about him reminded her of her father: a coarse belligerence offset by a child-like vulnerability; a sense of inadequacy, of not belonging. He was back behind the wheel of the *Sea-spray*, gone for days at a time, happy only when he could lose himself in that wide expanse of ocean.

Occasionally he came to her studio late at night, made a pot of tea and watched from the settee under the window while she worked. Sometimes there was a comfortable silence between them, no sound except the scrape of the brush against her palette and the whirr of the ceiling fan. At other times, he was inclined to talk.

'Do you think Mum's lonely, living by herself?'

'You could move back in with her.'

'No way! After all those years away, I couldn't live in a house doing ordinary things. I need to be by myself.'

'Was it so awful, then?' she asked softly. 'You never talk about it.'

He shook his head, glanced away. Claire could see his throat working, swallowing hard. 'What's to talk about?' he said after a long silence. 'Won't change anything. It's all still there in my head, day and night.'

She put the brush down and walked across the room towards him. Gently she wrapped her arms around his bony frame. He was drinking too much, not eating properly, as though he had ceased to care. 'I love you, Joe. Just remember that.'

The other subject he never brought up was Jane. Before the war they had been so happy together, according to her mother, and Claire had often wondered what had gone wrong with their relationship.

'Do you ever bump into Jane in town?' she'd asked once.

'No!' he'd replied abruptly, then changed the subject. 'You've done well for yourself, Claire. Remember those drawings you did when you were a kid? I can still picture you in the garden in that big house in Sydney, pencil flying, face screwed up with concentration. How old were you? Seven? Eight?'

She nodded, dabbing a layer of sepia on the underbelly of a turtle. 'About that.'

'After we lost that house, I thought we'd never be able to get on top again. But look at you now. Smart businesswoman. Mother to Rory. You've managed to pull your life together.'

'You've forgotten one thing,' she replied light-heartedly. 'My definite lack of romance.'

'Nothing lost there. Love's not all it's cracked up to be.'

'Lydia's doing well for herself, too. Did Mum tell you she's just landed the role of Ophelia in a new production they're doing down in Melbourne? And she's ditched Gerald. Apparently she's having a fling with her new stage manager.'

Joe smiled and shook his head. 'Who would have thought that Lydia would make a reasonable name for herself in the world of theatre? Seems like I'm the odd one out.'

Later, out of the blue, he said, 'Did you know I asked Jane to marry me before I went away?'

'And she said no?'

He nodded. 'She also said words to the effect that nothing would ever be the same again. That I'd come home a different man. Remember Dad? Obviously we didn't know him when he went away to war, but he must have changed, too.'

Claire paused, wiping a stray strand of hair from her face with the tip of her brush. She thought about her father and all those times he had come home drunk.

Take Daddy his dinner, Claire.

There's a good girl.

Claire: Mummy's best helper.

Claire: the sensible one.

'Why didn't you come home right away after the end of the war?' she said at last, softly.

He shrugged. 'I was afraid.'

'Afraid?' She couldn't imagine him scared. 'You spend months, years, being shot at, bombed and deprived, then you were afraid to come home?' Her voice had taken on a touch of incredulousness. 'What were you afraid of?'

He looked away, towards the sea where the waves crashed, invisible in the dark. 'Myself.'

She closed her eyes, blocking the sight of him. What have we become? she thought. A dysfunctional ragged family, with Nina the only common thread.

Joe laughed, breaking her train of thought. 'We've all changed, I suppose. You. Me. Lydia. Even Mum.' He levered himself to his feet, rinsed his cup in the sink. 'Anyway, I'm off. Might as well get a few hours' fishing in before dawn.'

She sat the brush down and studied his weary face. 'Don't you think you should get some sleep first?'

'Sleep? What's that? You know me. No ties, remember. I work when I want.'

And he went out the door, whistling.

Joe walked back along the track that led down to the jetties. The Passage had changed during those last few years. There was a pub now — The Plaza — which sported a fancy beer garden. A few guesthouses had sprung up in the hills overlooking the beach, spindly timber structures that looked as though a stiff breeze would send them falling like matchsticks and, during the summer, there were tents pitched along the foreshore.

Town had grown, spread towards Tea-tree Passage until there was no definite line of demarcation. Fibro houses, parched lawns, cars parked on the streets and children crying: it wasn't the quiet little backwater he remembered from his boyhood.

The thought swirled laboriously in his mind as he uncoiled the ropes that bound the *Sea-spray* to the wharf; why had he opened up like that to Claire about Jane? He'd never told anyone those things he'd told his sister tonight. Christ! he was getting soft!

Starting up the engine, he let the boat chug across the calm water towards the bar. He thought of the woman he had met the night before. Gloria. Brassy blonde wearing a low-cut blouse. Waitress at the cafe in town where he'd gone for steak and chips.

'What's a good-looking fellow doing alone in a place like this?' she'd asked, giving him a wink as she took his order.

Later she'd sat down next to him, watched over the rim of a coffee cup as he ate the last of his meal. 'Doing anything later?'

'I might be.'

'I get off at ten, if you'd like to wait.'

He had, drinking several cups of coffee in the meantime. He guessed Gloria was a good ten years older than himself, a bit tattered around the edges. She'd been married, she told him later, but that had broken up after the war. She was compliant and passive, and when he'd left her flat, hours later, the sun had just crept over the horizon.

She'd probably be looking out for him again tonight, eager to put down roots, form an attachment, but he wasn't interested. Not since Jane. Not since the war. There were too many memories and images blocking him.

Now he crossed the bar, aiming the *Sea-spray* towards the deeper water, further out. Thank God for the boat, he thought, grinning to himself in the dark. It didn't ask questions of him, like Claire and Nina. Didn't expect answers.

His mother and sister had both wanted to know the details of the war, had hinted in a subtle kind of way. But how could he possibly make them understand? You had to have been there, in the midst of it. Words, years later, were a useless bloody substitute. And in an odd obtuse way, he didn't want them to understand. This was his own private kind of hell.

So it was, he knew, the *Sea-spray* that kept him sane, led him along alternative paths when he felt the world toppling in on him. And even cleaning the hull down or painting on the two or three coats of anti-fouling red, feeling the sun hot on his back and listening to the cry of the gulls, he could have been anywhere, anyone. Not Joe the alcoholic. And definitely not Joe the loser.

For years now, Alex had been urging Claire to hold an exhibition of her art in the city. He knew someone, who in turn knew someone, who owned a gallery off Wickham Terrace.

'This is good work, Claire,' he told her earnestly. 'Equal to anything I've ever seen. You should broaden your horizons a little. Step out of what you see as a comfortable existence. There's a better market for this stuff in the city. People will pay more.'

He'd come out from town for the day, bringing Josh. They'd bought a puppy, a Golden Labrador that Josh had named Jess, and were planning to take it for a walk along the beach. Alex had ordered a coffee in the tearoom before setting off. Josh — with Jess under one arm — had wandered off in the direction of the sea wall.

'Rubbish,' Claire countered. 'I already charge more than I think they're worth.'

Alex put the palm of one hand to his forehead, feigning annoyance. 'God, Claire, you're still at it, even after all these years. Stop underrating yourself.'

'Look, you're the one with all the confidence. You organise it and if it pans out, then I'll go along with whatever happens, okay?'

'Done. Now where's Josh? We really should be going.'

Claire walked down the front steps with Alex, into the sunshine. The boy was lounging against one of the automobiles, talking to Rory who was cuddling the puppy. She stood for a moment, watching them. Didn't Alex ever wonder, looking at Rory, if she were his daughter? Certainly there was no resemblance, Rory favouring Lydia's colouring with her blonde hair, blue eyes and fair skin. But Alex was a doctor. Surely he must have suspected she could have been his daughter, given Rory's birth date.

There had been times when she had almost brought up the subject, checking herself at the last moment, remembering. At her own insistence it had been one of the conditions on which she had taken the child: that Alex wasn't to be told.

A week later, a tall attractive man knocked on her studio door and introduced himself as Paul. He was a partner in the gallery Alex had told her about and, given the lead from Alex's friend, he had come to look at her work.

Over coffee and a sandwich, Claire told him a little of her life — just as much as she thought he needed to know. Her marriage to David and his death just over a year later. Her bringing Rory, her niece, back to Tea-tree Passage days after her birth. The way her art career had blossomed, almost by accident. 'So, you see, we're an odd little family, just Rory and me. She's a good kid, mostly. Typical teenager, I suppose.'

Paul loved her work and told her so. He was wearing a pair of camel-coloured trousers and a long-sleeved shirt, the sleeves of which were rolled to just above the elbows. Over six feet in height, he had a lean body and sandy-coloured hair that framed an interesting-looking face. Probably around her own age, she decided, glancing at his hands as he stirred a spoonful of sugar into the hot liquid. Long tapering fingers, neat nails.

'So I'd like to offer you an exhibition date. Say October. We'd need about fifty pieces. Do you think you could manage that?' He stared unblinking into her eyes, smiling, forcing her attention back to the conversation. Making her glance away.

Something about him reminded her of Alex. Was it the hair or the way he spoke, the way he moved his hands? For one brief moment she imagined those same hands cupping her face, his mouth kissing hers. Oh, Lord! How long had it been?

'Claire?'

She blinked, colouring under his gaze. Did a quick calculation. Working six days a week, not to mention nights, she would probably make it. 'Fifty pieces? I'm certain I could.'

He helped her to her feet, his hand lingering on her arm a fraction longer than necessary, his eyes holding her own. Had he somehow read her mind?

'It's a long drive back to the city, so I was planning to stay the night. I've a room booked at the

Pacific. How about joining me there later for a meal? Say seven-ish?'

'Lovely. I'll look forward to it.'

Claire knew, even before she left the house, that she and Paul would end up in his hotel room later. There had been an attraction between them, a mutual frisson of desire that had left her feeling reckless and impulsive. Yet that inner voice of sensibility intruded. Be careful. Don't get involved. You've been too long without a man in your life and you're vulnerable.

'Nonsense,' she said to herself, dabbing perfume on her wrists and behind her ears. 'I'm a grown woman and I can do what I like.'

He was waiting in the hotel foyer when she arrived, looking infuriatingly handsome in a pale shirt and tie, dark trousers. 'Ah' he said, glancing at his watch with a grin. 'What a rarity! A woman who's on time.'

She laughed, nervous, unsure of what to say next.

'So you're going on a date?' Rory had asked earlier. 'What's he like?'

'Rory!' she'd replied, trying to sound shocked, but secretly pleased. Then. 'In answer to your question, he's tall and quite good-looking.'

Very good-looking, she thought now, as he took her arm and led her towards the dining room, pulling out the chair for her. 'I've arranged for the best table in the house.'

'I didn't know there was a *best table* in here.'

'There is now.'

She laughed again, accepting a glass of wine. The waitress came to take their orders. 'You look very sophisticated with your hair pulled up like that,' he whispered when she had gone.

'I bet you say that to all the girls.'

She was flirting, she realised, momentarily surprised by the fact. Very Lydia-ish. Very daring. She took another sip of wine, thinking she was becoming more assertive lately, more self-assured. That was how men seemed to like women these days.

They chatted, Claire telling him a little about the town and how it had grown over the past few years. Paul touched on the war. 'Like you, I was married,' he explained. 'I was up in Darwin, about the time of the bombing raids up there. When I got back, I discovered my wife had run off with a Yank.'

'So you're divorced?'

He nodded. 'Thank God there were no children to complicate things. She lives in America now.'

Several times through dinner Claire glanced up to find him watching her and, lowering her eyes towards her plate once more, she felt herself blush. She tried to make conversation but it was difficult, thinking only of later, wondering if her words and actions were so transparent that all the other diners knew her intentions. She projected her mind forward, wondering about the inevitable sequence of events. Walking up the stairs. Entering his room. The process that would take her into his bed. And how should she act? Hesitant? Coy? Or as though this were a normal everyday event?

She could scarcely eat, instead pushed the food around on her plate, mostly, rearranging it with her fork. Finally the waitress came and removed it. 'Sorry, not very hungry,' she said to Paul's enquiring glance. 'Truly, the food's fine, it's just that —'

She stopped, unable to say the words.

'That's okay. I'm not very practised at this, either,' he smiled uncertainly. 'Silly, really, when you think about it. But when I got married I expected it to be for keeps. Never thought I'd ever be going through this again. More wine?'

'Thanks, lovely.'

His mouth was mere inches away. Claire's breath caught in her throat and she resisted the urge to put her fingers there, along the line of his lips. She glanced away instead, inordinately aware of him, not simply as a business colleague, but as something more.

A band had started up in the room next door, the strident notes of a saxophone merging with the beat of a drum. He reached forwards and touched a finger lightly to the back of her hand. 'Claire?'

Would her voice work? 'Yes.'

It was as though her whole being were rushing towards him, uncontrollably. Her legs felt like jelly and she was thankful she was sitting.

'It's a bit noisy down here. Would you like to come up to my room for a nightcap?' He paused for a moment, smiling at her. 'I'm not making any promises, Claire. But there are no obligations, either.'

There, that was the first dreaded part of the evening dispensed with. That initial invitation, with

Paul waiting, not knowing whether she'd say yes. Of course she would, but she hesitated, not wanting him to suspect, to know, how badly she needed this.

Then she glanced up at him, smiled, and he held her gaze. 'Yes,' she said. 'I think I'd like that.'

Paul paid the bill and they walked up the stairs. He took her hand and led her along the hallway, his fingers warm around hers. Inserting the key in the lock, he swung the door open and propelled her through.

He walked on ahead, towards the window, flung it open.

'Can I use your bathroom?'

He inclined his head towards the closed door. 'It's through there.'

She closed the door firmly behind her. Impatiently she pulled her dress over her head, folded it and laid it on the edge of the bath. Kicked off her shoes. Brassiere and stockings followed, suspenders and knickers, until she stood naked.

She leant against the basin, her breath coming in ragged waves, and stared at herself in the mirror. Eyes dark and wide. Pulse throbbing at the base of her throat. Still-flat stomach. Firm breasts. Tentatively she cupped her hands under them, lifting. Then she moved her fingers down to that dark triangle of hair, fighting back a stab of panic.

Determinedly she closed her eyes, inhaling deeply. I can still leave, she told herself. Extricate myself from this situation as neatly and cleanly as possible. But she knew she had come too far mentally, and the wanting, the intense need for him, had become an ache in her belly.

Slowly she opened the door. Paul was facing away from her, fiddling with the radio knob, trying to locate a station. She studied the broad sweep of his shoulders, the way the collar of his shirt hugged the nape of his neck. When he was successful at last, the strains of a melody swayed towards her, soft and soothing.

She leant against the open door frame, unable to go on for a moment. A dozen steps and she would be beside him, and the night would progress to its inevitable conclusion. But her feet refused to move and, for some inexplicable reason, her hands had begun to shake. She folded them across her chest, tucking them under her forearms.

As though sensing her uncertainty, he turned back towards her and held out his hand. 'Claire.'

A breeze billowed the curtain inwards. A jangle of noise rose up from the street below: laughter, a car horn, a faint strain of the music they had sought to escape. Somehow she responded. Closed the bathroom door and walked towards him. One step. Two. Each one taking her closer, towards a planned yet vague destination. She laid her face against the soft fabric of his shirt and his arms enclosed her, crushing her to his chest. The faint aroma of aftershave rose up to meet her as he pressed his mouth against her hair. Then, with a sudden desperate longing, she raised her mouth to his.

It had been so long since she'd been held, kissed, that, at first, she felt tense. 'It's okay,' he said, tracing his mouth along the length of her neck, sending tiny shivers down her back.

'Sshh.'

Impatiently she worked her fingers at his belt, then the buckle. Pushed buttons through buttonholes. Slid the shirt from his back. Felt smooth skin beneath her hands. Somehow they were on the bed — how had she gotten there? — and his hands were sliding along her breast, sliding down. His mouth followed, his tongue taking her to somewhere she hadn't been for such a long time. Oh, God! Don't stop!

Later she propped herself on her elbows, watching him, running one lazy finger along the length of his ribs. 'Isn't this the part where you're supposed to say cheerio and goodbye, that this was all a bit of a mistake?'

'Never!' he protested with a grin, pulling her head towards his and kissing her soundly. 'Although I do have a confession to make. I hadn't wanted to come up here, to Tea-tree Passage.'

'Why not?'

'The usual reasons. Not enough time, and tired of thinking up creative comments to describe fairly ordinary artwork.'

'Oh.' She was taken aback. Did he mean hers?

'Not that I had to look twice to see you had talent,' he assured her quickly, as though he had read her mind. 'I do know good work when I see it.'

'So,' she asked boldly, 'are you glad you came?'

'What do you think?'

He hadn't answered her, not directly, but the inference was clear. 'And if you doubt that,' he went on, 'then come back to bed and I'll prove it to you again.'

Later she dressed, kissed him again. 'I wish I didn't have to go, but there's Rory to consider.'

'Till next time. You'll be down, for the exhibition.'

She'd temporarily forgotten the reason for his visit. 'Yes, the exhibition. I've a lot of work to do between then and now.'

He nodded, smiled. 'Thanks for tonight.'

Unexpectedly her eyes filled with tears. 'So it's goodbye, then,' she said, trying to keep her voice even.

'Oh God!' he said, springing to her side. 'Have I done something, said something? Have I hurt you?'

'No, you haven't hurt me, Paul.' She pressed a finger against his mouth, silencing his words. 'For the first time in ages, I feel alive! Oh, Lord! So alive ...'

CHAPTER 39

Guesthouses kept springing up further along the Passage, tiny fibro shacks — holiday homes mostly — on small allotments. Couch lawns ran across what had once been tea-tree swamp. Pub, general store, chemist and newsagent — Nina watched them all appear in amused silence, watched the community that was her home spread out in a haphazard rambling way, without structure or planning. The houses, in particular, brought back memories of that long-ago time after the first war: she and Frank living in the city, building those same little box-like structures.

The increase in weekend tourists had been a boon for Claire's business, though Joe complained about the motor launches that roared around the island, towing skiers by thin ropes. 'Scare the bloody fish away,' he'd say. 'No use putting out the nets today.' And he'd go to the pub, instead, coming home hours later.

What did they think she was — senile, like Maudie had been before she'd died? Did they think she didn't notice her son staggering back along the track towards the wharf where the *Sea-spray* was moored? But no-one mentioned it. Neither Claire nor Kath. Nor Alex, when she had cause to see him.

It was everything she had feared. Like father, like son. The past had become the present. Frank's drinking had somehow manifested itself in Joe, and Nina was at a loss what to do.

She scarcely saw Lydia. Her younger daughter came home occasionally, breezing in and out, pleading work commitments. She was hard and demanding these days and filled, Nina thought privately, with her own self-importance.

Rory, though, was Nina's delight. She'd had reservations at first about Claire bringing the child home, raising her as her own, but those fears had long since vanished. In some ways Rory had tempered Nina's older daughter, giving her purpose after those dreadful years of the war. Rory was a bright girl, excelling at school, yet she was wilful and strong.

'Tell me about my father,' she'd demanded of Nina, weeks earlier.

'I don't know anything about him,' she'd answered honestly. 'Why do you want to know?'

'Because I hate being different! All the other girls at school know their fathers.'

'You'll have to take the matter up with your mother.'

'I've asked, but Lydia won't tell me. Why do you think that is?'

Nina shrugged. 'I have no idea. Maybe the not-knowing is something you'll just have to accept.'

'She didn't want me. That's why she gave me to Claire.'

'Claire loves you as though you were her own daughter.'

'But she's not my mother.'

Rory was a confused mass of contradictions. She had a scrapbook that Claire had given her years earlier, which contained newspaper clippings about Lydia. At the time, Nina had thought it a good idea. The child should know about Lydia, and Claire had never made a secret of Rory's past. But now she wasn't so sure. Rory seemed to spend hours poring over it, unnaturally absorbed and, lately, she seemed obsessed by her own mother and lack of knowledge about her father.

Her thoughts were interrupted by a knock on the door. It would be Alex, she knew. She'd been feeling unwell all week and he'd promised to call by.

Claire arrived a few minutes later. 'I saw Alex's car. What's wrong?'

'Nothing,' said Alex, shutting his bag with a snap, 'that a bit of rest won't cure. Actually, I'm glad I've caught you. Erica's throwing a party for Josh's sixteenth birthday on the weekend. I hope you're bringing Rory?'

'She hasn't been invited.'

'Then I'm inviting her.'

She looked at him doubtfully. 'I don't think Erica —'

But he cut her short. 'No excuses. I'll expect you on Saturday at two.'

They left together. From her front window, Nina watched as they stood on the dirt track beside Alex's car, talking. Claire: hands on hips, head cocked to one side. Alex leaning forward slightly, as though trying to make a point.

It was no secret that Erica disliked Claire and had, over the years, tried to steer Josh away from Rory. Despite that, the two teenagers were friends, had grown up in adjoining houses until Erica had insisted that Alex build her a new house in town. Nina sighed. 'What if?' she said to herself. What if, indeed? There had been something between Claire and Alex that summer before the war, yet they had both gone on to marry others. Why?

She shook her head, not knowing, and drew the curtain against the sight of them.

Claire took Rory into town and they scoured the shops, hunting for a suitable gift for Josh. On Saturday afternoon she delivered Rory to the Melville house at the allotted time. Alex's car was in the driveway, as well as Erica's: a red sporty number in which Claire had seen her about town.

The house was fairly imposing, compared to its neighbours. Red brick. Rambling Federation style built across a double block. Neatly manicured lawns and gardens. Erica, Claire knew, professed to have no interest in its external upkeep, and Alex employed a gardener who was obviously earning his salary.

Claire rang the doorbell and waited for the sound of footsteps, hoping Alex would answer. But it was Erica who threw open the door. 'Alex said you were coming,' she said in a bored voice. 'You can come back at five to collect Rory.'

She was dismissed. At a loose end, she wandered about town, peering in shop windows, thinking she should go back home, spend a few hours in the studio. The weeks were passing and the deadline drawing closer for the exhibition. But those four walls were all she had seen for weeks. Several letters had arrived from Paul — which she had promptly answered — friendly missives that detailed the routine of his life, how he wanted to see her again. She smiled, thinking of what he had written, unsure how she felt about him. He was fun and friendly, and the sex had been great. But a permanent relationship?

It was late when she went back to collect Rory, half an hour after the designated time. Alex was out on the driveway, waving goodbye to one of the last guests.

'At least that's over,' he said to Claire, steering her towards the front steps. 'I don't know what's worse. A house full of five-year-olds or teenagers. Look, I can't stay. They've just phoned from the hospital and I have to rush over. Rory's out the back with Josh.'

He looked tired, she thought, a few grey hairs starting to show at his temples. The medical practice was frantic these days. Hal wasn't getting any younger and had been forced to cut back his hours. What they needed was another local doctor, someone to help carry the load.

She knocked on the front door but there was no answer. Erica's car was still parked in the driveway, but of the woman there was no sign. Tentatively Claire let herself in the front door and walked through to the kitchen. 'Where's your mum?' she called to Josh through the window. He and Rory were sitting on the swings at the bottom of the garden, the dog Jess at their feet.

The reply came floating back. 'She's in bed. Not feeling well.'

There was a mess everywhere in the kitchen, the benches covered with the evidence of food preparation. Methodically Claire began stacking plates and bowls in the sink, wiping the surfaces clean with a cloth as she went. It took her almost an hour to wash up and straighten the room. Then, pouring a glass of water from the tap, she walked along the hallway, guessing the direction of the bedroom Alex and Erica shared.

Erica lay slumped in a chair on the opposite side of the bedroom. Her face was pale and her eyes were closed. For one brief moment, Claire thought she was asleep.

'What do you want?'

'I've brought you some water.'

'Bullshit! You've come to gloat. Claire with her perfect, perfect life.'

'Hardly perfect.'

'No.'

'What do you mean by that?'

'They say motherhood's the ultimate experience. Don't you ever wonder what it would have been like to have your own child instead of raising someone else's bastard kid?'

Stiffly, not knowing how to answer. 'Rory's like a daughter to me.'

'But she's not, is she? There's a world of difference.' Erica levered herself to her feet and lurched across the room. 'Don't think I don't know,' she slurred, bending down so her face was level with Claire's. 'I've seen the way you look at my husband.'

'Don't talk nonsense.'

'You'll never have him. He's not interested in you. It's me he married.'

Patiently. 'Alex isn't some possession to be fought over, Erica.'

'I'm glad you realise that.'

She turned, mentally biting back a retaliation, and retraced her steps along the hallway, heart pounding. Although Erica obviously had some insecurities where Claire was concerned, she'd had no right to say those things. Claire had never intruded into their lives, had often gone out of the way to avoid contact with Alex.

Alex was propped against the sink, staring out towards the back lawn. Josh and Rory were still sitting on the swings, talking. He didn't turn, and she stared miserably at his slumped shoulders and the defeated curve of his back. 'So now you know,' he said.

'Alex, how awful! How long has —'

'How long's she been an alcoholic?'

'Yes.'

'Years. All through the war, probably. But it's getting worse.'

'She needs help.'

581

He gave a scornful laugh. 'Help? I've tried every damn way I know. But until she admits she needs it, then I'm wasting my time.'

He stopped, indicated his son through the lacy curtain. 'It's Josh I'm worried about. This business with his mother is affecting him badly. He won't talk about it, won't open up. In a bizarre way, I think he blames me.'

'No!' She grabbed his hand, forcing him to face her. 'Alex, you are not to blame for this!'

'Maybe he's right. I'm not perfect. I've made mistakes.'

She shot him a hard look. 'Mistakes?'

'Marrying Erica.'

The implication was obvious and she gave a laugh, which sounded slightly hysterical to her own ears. 'Don't let's go down this road again, Alex. It isn't helping anyone.'

He was facing her, his mouth mere inches away. 'Tell me you don't care.'

His words lay like unravelled threads inside her. Unbearable. An odd burning sensation welled up behind her eyes. 'Don't do this,' she replied angrily, close to tears.

In that brief unexpected moment, he kissed her. She felt the warmth of his mouth, that sudden urgency, the quick flare of desire. Was aware of her own hands moving to the nape of his neck, pulling him closer. Opening her eyes, she glanced past his shoulders, saw Josh and Rory moving towards the house from the swings. 'Alex — no!'

She threw herself backwards, releasing herself

from his grasp. The air was cold against her skin where his hand had lain, the movement almost like a physical blow. 'I've got to go,' she whispered.

Rory and Josh flung themselves into the room, followed by the dog, which Alex promptly shooed outside again. Claire used the interruption to catch her breath. 'Rory, time we were leaving,' she said abruptly, striding towards the front door.

She drove back to the Passage faster than usual, quite recklessly, in fact. Claire, the sensible one, she thought. If only they could see her now. Maudie. Nina. Even her father, long dead. Rory said nothing, staring directly ahead as though sensing some irregularity.

In Tea-tree Passage, Claire parked her car outside the tearoom. She sat there for a long time behind the steering wheel, long after Rory had gone inside, waiting for her hands to stop shaking and her breathing to return to normal.

Something woke Alex. He sat up in bed, not knowing for a moment where he was. Moonlight slanted through the uncurtained window. Outside, he could see the bare branches of a tree thrashing about in the wind.

He was in the spare room, he realised at last, remembering the awful events of the previous afternoon. Josh's party. Erica getting herself sloshed during the course of it, and her argument with Claire. His own rambling conversation with Claire. *Tell me you don't care.*

He'd had no right to say that. No right to compromise her, put her in that awkward position.

He flung his legs over the side of the bed. Cold bit at his feet as he lowered his head into his hands. He and Erica battering against each other, saying hateful words. When would the nightmare ever end?

There was a movement at the end of his bed, a quiet shuffle of feet. Alex glanced up, seeing the outline of his son. He was sitting in the chair beyond the window, motionless, facing him. His features were lost in the dark.

'Josh?'

There was no reply. Alex could hear the ticking of the bedside clock and imagined his own steady breathing.

'Come on, mate. Back to bed. It's too cold to be out.'

'Why are you sleeping in here?'

'Your mother wasn't well —'

'Don't bullshit to me! I'm not a child!'

'Josh!'

'Why can't you do something?'

His voice was hard and small, barely audible, as though said through gritted teeth. Alex searched his mind for an explanation. 'She's an alcoholic, Josh. She can't help herself. It's a sickness.'

'So, you're a doctor. Make her better.'

He shook his head. 'It's not as easy as that. She has to want to help herself.'

Josh stood. He was tall these days, almost six feet in height, and he towered over Alex where he sat on the edge of the bed.

'I *hate* you!' he said.

* * *

Somehow Claire managed the fifty paintings, with a week to spare. She packaged them carefully and sent them on ahead by train, planning to follow in a few days. Rory elected not to come, bunking in with Nina, instead. Claire was secretly grateful. Paul had asked her to stay at his flat and she wanted to spend a few extra days treating herself to some shopping.

The exhibition opened on a Friday night. Drinks and canapés were offered by two waiters. A string quartet played subtle music in one corner. 'Who's paying for all this?' Claire asked, taking a glass of champagne from a tray.

'You are.'

'*Me?* Paul, I can't afford this!'

'Of course you can. Have you seen the price tags on your paintings? We've sold four already.'

Lydia wandered in an hour later, one of her men friends in tow. She was wearing a low-cut strapless gown, which Claire thought quite inappropriate for the occasion. 'How's Rory?' she asked in a bored voice.

'Fine. She staying with Nina while I'm away.'

Lydia wandered off, making a pretence of looking at the paintings while getting pissed on Claire's champagne.

The exhibition, which lasted a week, was a sell-out. In his spare time Paul showed her around Brisbane, which was much changed since the war. New buildings. Suburbs springing up where once there had been farms. They went to the theatre, dined out in several restaurants. Walked alongside the river at dawn, the city lights reflecting back from the still-inky water. She woke in the mornings to a warm tangle of arms and legs, loath to extricate herself. The sex, after such a long abstinence, was breathtaking.

'You know,' said Paul at the end of the week, 'it hasn't seemed like work with you here. Just knowing you'll be here at the end of the day makes it seem like a holiday.' He cupped his palms around her chin and raised her face towards his, kissing her.

'I've enjoyed it, too.'

'We could make it permanent.'

She held her breath, waiting for the words she knew would follow. 'Permanent?' she answered lightly.

'My work's here, but yours is portable. There's plenty of room in the flat. We could turn one of the spare rooms into a studio.'

'What about Rory? We're a package, she and I.'

'I'm sure she's a great kid. I'd enjoy having her here, you know that.'

'That's true,' she admitted.

He stared directly into her eyes. Smiled at her in a slow and conspiratorial way. 'I'm asking you to marry me, Claire.'

She exhaled, studying his face. He was warm and generous and, she suspected, she'd go far to find a better man. 'Paul,' she said gently, 'we scarcely know each other.'

'Time won't make a difference to the way I feel about you. We're comfortable in each other's company. We complement each other. It's a miserable existence, being alone.'

While the offer was tempting, there were other considerations. Leave Tea-tree Passage? Nina and

Joe: who would look after them? It would mean uprooting Rory, taking her away from her school friends. True, the girl would probably see more of Lydia, but that wasn't necessarily a good thing.

It wasn't until later, until she lay next to Paul in bed, listening to his even breathing, that she allowed herself other reflections. Not once had Paul said he loved her. No magical three words, no declarations. She had the impression that, to Paul, marriage would be more of a convenience, an end to the lonely nights. And there was another point, one she had not allowed herself to contemplate: moving to the city also meant leaving Alex, and she wasn't ready to do that.

Alex was quiet during the drive home. He gripped the wheel and stared straight ahead, white-hot anger consuming him. Erica lay slumped in the seat beside him, eyes closed. Whether she was sleeping or not, he wasn't sure. He was thankful, though, for her silence, knowing that if she forced him to utter one syllable, he'd explode.

What had possessed her? he wondered. Getting pissed at home was one thing, but rendering yourself almost legless at the annual golf club ball was another. Through the course of the evening she had flirted shamelessly with almost every man there, much to Alex's embarrassment. Then she'd thrown up on the outside patio. This time, he thought grimly, she'd gone too far.

He pulled up in the driveway with a screech and she sat upright. 'Where are we?'

Her voice was slurred and he resisted the urge to shake her. 'Home,' he said instead, his voice terse.

'What about the party? I want to go back.'

'I think the party came to an abrupt end when you vomited all down the front of the local councillor.'

'I did not!'

He couldn't be bothered arguing, knowing from experience that the conversation would wind itself round and round in circles, getting nowhere.

He opened the front door and propelled her through. She resisted for a moment, pulling her arm away from his. 'Don't touch me!' she hissed as she staggered across the living room to the cupboard where the drinks were kept. 'I'm having a vodka. Want one?'

'Don't you think you've had enough?'

She ignored him, instead wrenching open the bottle and unsteadily pouring herself a glassful. Several drops spilt on the polished timber cabinet and she dabbed at them, licking them off her finger. 'You're in a foul mood. Didn't you enjoy the party?'

'Not particularly.'

'Any definite reason?'

'It was embarrassing, you falling all over half the men there.'

She offered him a slow secretive smile over the rim of her glass. 'Alex! I do believe you're jealous!'

He was exhausted, rendered almost speechless by her words. 'Whatever you say, Erica. I'm going to bed.'

'Go on, then. Walk away! Avoid the important issues!'

She threw her hands in the air, slopping her drink down the side of the glass. Alex watched the droplets spraying through the air. Thank God it was vodka and not red wine, he thought, glancing past it to the cream-coloured carpet. 'I'm not averse to confronting issues, Erica. It's another senseless argument that I don't need.'

'You know the problem with you, Alex?'

'No, but I suspect you're about to tell me.'

'Don't be so pompous! You're boring, that's your problem. And predictable. Why don't you go down to the pub more, like other men? Get drunk, for once in your life.'

'That's your answer to everything, isn't it? To get drunk!'

She shrugged. 'It makes for a change. We're bogged down, stagnant. We never even have sex any more.' He regarded her steadily, until she glanced away. 'Oh, don't look at me like that. I'm going to get another drink. Go to bed, then. See if I care.'

There was a movement at the doorway and he glanced up to see Josh standing there. 'What's going on?' the boy asked. He'd obviously been asleep and his eyes were screwed up against the light.

'It's just your father, being a wowser. He's no fun any more. He used to be, Josh, before we were married.'

What was she about to tell the boy? 'Stop it, Erica!'

'*Oh, stop it, Erica!*' she mimicked, dancing towards her son.

'She's been drinking again!' Josh yelled at Alex. 'Why didn't you stop her?'

Alex turned and walked away. 'That's right!' Erica screamed after him, picking up an empty vase from the sideboard and flinging it in his wake. 'Go! Just go!'

Her aim was wide and the vase hit the wall, shattering into tiny slivers. He stared at it — the smashed flowers, water spreading in a damp stain over the carpet — then glanced wearily at his wife. Her hair was lank, her mouth twisted. 'Don't tempt me.'

He walked from the room, down the hallway towards the spare room. She ran after him, battering his back, but he shrugged her off, quickening his pace. There was a sharp cry and he heard her fall.

'Now look what you've done! Alex! You bastard!'

But he kept walking, leaving Josh to pick her up.

The next day at the surgery, Alex met his father in the corridor.

'What happened to Erica?'

'What do you mean?'

'The bruises.'

'She fell. Why the inquisition?'

'She was in here earlier. She told me you did it.'

Wearily. 'I told you. She fell, chasing me down the hallway in a drunken rage, if you must know. How could you believe her word against mine?'

'I'm sorry, Alex. I just had to ask. Have you thought about getting help for her?'

He gave a bitter laugh. 'Help! Erica doesn't think she needs help. She thinks she needs a more understanding husband.'

'Would you like me to have a word to her?'

He raised his hands in a resigned way, then let them fall. 'Try if you want, but you won't get anywhere.'

How could she lie like that? he wondered as he let himself into his own office. Especially to his own father.

CHAPTER 40

During the summer of '57, Rory managed to land a part-time weekend job at the new motel further along the beach. The Eldorado was a low sprawling building with a small concrete pool at the front of the reception area, and flags flapping from a series of small poles that fronted the road. She had told the manager she was fifteen, which was only a half-lie: she would be — in six months' time.

She worked Saturdays and Sundays, four hours each morning. It meant getting up before the sun, carrying the breakfast trays to the rooms, stripping beds and cleaning bathrooms — none of which she especially enjoyed. But it gave her a measure of independence and her own money. She was saving for a bikini, though she hadn't told Claire. The small two-piece swimming costumes were the latest rage and most of the girls at school had one. And the job, which finished at ten in the mornings, afforded her plenty of time for the usual weekend activities.

Rory loved summers at Tea-tree Passage. The place was full of holiday-makers, and loudspeakers blared music onto the sand. There were concerts and Hawaiian nights. Everyone played 'Hokey Pokey' on the beach on Sunday afternoons, and there were prizes and competitions. On the busy days a photographer roamed the beach, looking for willing subjects.

The Flamingo Cabaret and Cocktail Bar opened in a downstairs area of the Plaza Hotel. At night there were dances on the sand, with large bonfires turning everyone's face orange, and fireworks outside the kiosk.

On the foreshore, the local council had built a pier for the motor launches, and an enclosure for swimming. The pier was a ramshackle wooden affair that straggled aimlessly out into the water, suspended by huge pylons which somehow managed to stop it from tumbling into the water. At the end of the pier was the theatre, an equally ramshackle lopsided building that somehow defied the laws of gravity. Rory's favourite outing was the matinee there on Saturday afternoons, the smell of the ocean mingling with the choc-orange aroma of Jaffas, and the sound of the waves washing endlessly against the pylons below.

It was, she had to concede, an eventful time. Josh came out regularly from town, riding his bicycle, with Jess running along behind. Soon he'd have his licence and he was hoping his father would buy him a small car. They swam and fished, and walked along the beach, past the bathing boxes and multi-coloured umbrellas, to the headland where the water was crystal clear and, when you waded out, you could see the sand between your toes. Jess loved the water, too. She was always running at the waves, barking like a mad thing.

At Rory's insistence, they had hidden their blossoming friendship from their parents as much as possible. 'They'll only try to keep us apart if they know,' she explained. 'And I know your mother doesn't want you hanging around with me — the town bastard.'

'*Rory!*'

It was one of her worst traits — speaking her thoughts out loud. She gave Josh an apologetic grin. 'Well, it's true,' she went on, 'so there's no use denying it.'

Josh shook his head. 'I'm not so sure. It might have something to do with Claire.'

'Claire? In what way?'

'Apparently she and my Dad were friendly, years ago, before he married Mum. I overheard my parents arguing about it one day.'

Rory shrugged. 'Whatever the reason, they don't need to know about us, okay?'

Claire was such a worrywart. Already she and Rory had had what Claire termed 'a little talk' about that 'sex' subject, with Claire emphasising words such as love and commitment, and how she didn't want Rory to end up 'in a certain situation'.

'Like my mother?' Rory had asked. 'Pregnant and unmarried?'

Claire had swallowed hard and frowned. 'Yes. Exactly.'

'They want me to go to university when I finish school next year,' Josh told Rory now, dipping his hand into a large rock pool and bringing up a handful of seaweed. 'Dad says, with my grades, I could be a doctor or a lawyer. But I think they just want me out of the way.'

'Why's that?'

'So they don't have to worry about me listening to their fights. They're at it day and night. It's bloody unbearable.'

'Poor Josh.'

She took his hand and led him along the sand, and Jess followed. 'Do you think they'll get a divorce?'

'No. I think they like making each other miserable.'

'Why do people get married if they don't like each other?'

'Perhaps they did, a long time ago.'

'So I wonder what changed all that? What makes you love someone one day and hate them the next?'

'Pooh! There's no such thing as love.'

'There is, too.'

'You're only saying that because you're a girl.'

Rory dug him in the ribs. 'You're a sexist pig, Josh Melville.'

Josh laughed, revealing a set of white teeth. 'And you're going to end up a prize fighter with a jab like that.'

'At least you live with your parents and you know who your father is. My mother visits once a year, if I'm lucky, and I've never even seen a photograph of my dad. What does he look like, do you think?'

'Tall, dark and handsome. Isn't that how women like their men?'

'Silly!' Rory stared out towards Turtle Island. 'Hey!' she said, shielding her eyes against the glare. 'That looks like your mum out there in that little runabout.'

Josh hunkered down on the sand, one arm around the dog's neck, and watched the dinghy weaving in and out of the waves. Rory was right. It *was* his mother; he would have known her blonde hair and bright blouse anywhere.

Rory plopped herself on the sand beside him, hugging her knees. 'Where do you suppose she's going?'

He shrugged. 'Beats me.'

Erica ran the little boat aground on the island, tugged it higher up the sand, past the tide mark, and wandered off into the scrub.

'Come on,' challenged Rory, scrambling to her feet. 'Let's go back. Last one to the pier's a rotten egg.'

Erica hadn't been out to Tea-tree Passage for years, not since the day they'd moved into the new house in town. She was surprised how much the place had grown: clumps of new houses dotted amongst the tea-trees, land sales offices, motel. Even a store and a pub.

She wandered into the bar, idled over a few vodkas, then, on an impulse, ambled down to the boat hire shed. One of the O'Reilly boys had opened the business, she saw on the sign above the doorway. Taking possession of the dinghy, she started the motor and headed towards Turtle Island.

It felt good out on the water, the sun on her skin and the wind whipping her hair about her face. The boat crested the small waves then slid into the intervening troughs and, for the first time in ages, she felt a sense of freedom. I could keep going, she thought, scanning the horizon. Until the boat runs out of fuel. The idea was not repugnant, merely interesting. How long would it take them to find her?

The island loomed closer until finally the gravelly beach slid under the boat. She levered herself over the side into ankle-deep water and hauled the hull up the beach, past the high tide mark, gathered her book, bag and towel and headed over the first ridge of sand dunes into the scrub. She stowed her bag in the shade of a casuarina and spread her towel in the sun. Pulled the blouse over her head. Unhooked her bra, then stepped from her shorts and knickers.

There was an illicit thrill in removing her clothes, exposing her body to the sun. Carefully she coated herself in coconut oil and lay face down on the towel. For a few minutes she tried to read her book, but the words danced blackly in the heat and she couldn't concentrate.

She rolled onto her back and stared upwards. A lone gull hovered high on an updraft of wind, a white smudge against the interminable blue of the sky. A bank of dark clouds was building, low on the eastern horizon, promising a late-afternoon storm. From the mainland came the shriek of a car horn.

Her thoughts kept turning to Alex and the fight they'd had the previous night. There had been yelling and accusations. She'd slapped him, hard, across the face and he'd stood facing her, not moving, not saying a word. In some ways she'd wished he'd retaliate. Had expected it, even. But he'd turned and walked towards the spare bedroom next to her own, where he spent his nights now.

How much longer could they go on? At what point should she walk away, call it quits, no matter what the consequences? There had been a time when she'd delighted in baiting him, trying to provoke some reaction. But no longer. Lately the enjoyment had palled and the resulting arguments seemed childish and pointless.

Thoughts and probabilities churned in Erica's mind. What had gone wrong? At what point in their lives had she and Alex begun heading in opposite directions? There had been times, early in their relationship, when just the touch of his hand against her neck had been enough to send her all goose-bumpy. But now? Too many things had conspired to reduce the romance in their lives. Josh. Her own dissatisfaction. Alex's work absences. She couldn't get excited about anything to do with her husband these days, especially when it came to sex.

'I'm a red-blooded woman and I need more,' she shouted to the sky. 'I need to be noticed. I need to be loved.'

If her marriage were grinding inexorably towards its final death throes then, perhaps, it would be prudent to plan ahead. There were several men in town she had admired, from a distance, since Alex had returned after the war. Maybe it was time she made a move, expanded her horizons. Perhaps she'd have a fling or two on the side, discreetly, of course. You never knew what might eventuate. What a coup it would be to tell Alex she was leaving, that she had found someone else!

That decision made, she closed her eyes and felt the sun on her face. She could have slept. Certainly, when she became aware of her surroundings again — the wind and the crashing sound of the surf — the sun was heading towards the west.

Back at Tea-tree Passage, Erica moored the dinghy as instructed, then wandered back inside the pub. She was thirsty after her trip to the island, hadn't thought to take a bottle of water with her. But it wasn't water she needed now. Her hands had started shaking slightly. Not that anyone else would notice, but *she* was aware of it. A few drinks would calm her, enable her to drive home again.

Afterwards she wandered, bored, down towards the jetties where the fishing boats were docked. Alex and Josh would be home in a few hours, expecting their tea. Perhaps she'd manage to pick up some fresh fish.

Joe Carmody was sitting in the sun on a turned-up crate beside the *Sea-spray*, mending his fishing nets. He was naked from the waist up, his checked shirt tossed carelessly on the ground beside him. His skin was tanned to a deep bronze from the hours spent in the sun, his chest and arm muscles taut and sinewy, she noticed, as she watched him push the hook-like needle through the webbed rope. Suddenly realising her presence, he looked up and smiled, revealing two rows of white teeth.

Her heart seemed to thud to a standstill. *Joe Carmody*! Why was it she'd never really noticed him before? He'd been in his late teens — just a kid, really — when she had come to The Passage as a young bride. And over the years she'd scarcely said more than two words to him.

'Erica,' he said now, placing the net on the ground beside him. 'What brings you down here?'

She had a sudden impulse to bend down and pick up the shirt, hold it to her face and inhale the raw scent of it. Male sweat and lust. The thought of it became an aphrodisiac. Secreted away in his air-conditioned office, Alex never perspired, and it had been a long time since he had desired her. Joe, she sensed as she suppressed a smile, would be more in tune with those baser male instincts.

Joe glanced up to see, beyond the haze of the sun, the silhouette of a woman. He blinked, shielding his eyes with his hand, suddenly realising the identity of his visitor. Erica Melville: Alex's wife.

She was wearing a pair of shorts and a sleeveless blouse, the bottom of which was tied in a knot at her waist, revealing her navel. Her blonde hair was swept to the back of her head, escaping tendrils fanning about her face in the breeze. He let his eyes travel appraisingly down the pair of brown shapely legs to her bare feet.

He still remembered the day she had come to Tea-tree Passage as Alex's surprise bride. They'd all been dumbfounded at first, especially Claire, who'd had some sort of a romance going with Alex the previous summer. But that was long ago, all in the past and, over the years, he'd had little to do with either of them — Erica or Alex — the war years having separated them in more ways than distance.

What age had Erica been when she'd come here? Twenty-one or two, he supposed, and he'd been seventeen. As a teenager, that four-or-five year age difference had seemed like a chasm. Now, almost twenty years later, the gap was negligible.

'Erica,' he said, throwing the net on the ground beside him. 'What brings you down here?'

She hesitated, stared at him for one long moment over the top of her sunglasses. 'Nothing much. Bored, I guess.'

'Bored? With all the wealth and prestige a doctor's salary brings?' he teased, unable to disguise the slightly mocking tenor in his voice.

'Bloody doctors,' she replied, plonking herself on the top step of the wharf. 'They're not all they're cracked up to be.'

She'd been drinking, he could tell. There was a slight slurring to her voice, a slowness of movement and a vacant glassy look about her eyes. A few spirits knocked back at the pub, he supposed. Not enough to leave her legless, though. Just sufficient to blur the edges and dull the sharper pains, as it did for him.

But what was it that Erica found unbearable in her life? She had it all. Good looks and money, although he had the impression she was lacking somewhat in the brains department. She'd never had to work, not since her marriage. By all accounts she spent her days swanning around the golf course in town with her fancy friends, or lunching at the few local restaurants. Josh was a bright kid, doing well at school — hadn't someone told him he'd been top of his class last year? — and Alex would be a good catch in any woman's eyes.

'How's Alex these days? I haven't seen him around in a while.'

She regarded him lazily, awarding him a slow smile. Then she put her arms around her legs, hugging them close in a suggestive, erotic kind of way, rocking backwards and forwards. 'I wouldn't know. I scarcely see him, either.'

'Must be busy work, being a doctor.'

'It leaves me plenty of spare time, if that's what you mean.'

Did he? Joe wasn't sure. The one thing he was certain of, however, was that Erica was telling him she was definitely available, if he were interested.

He felt momentarily uncomfortable. He'd known Alex for years, and Claire had been married to his brother David. The Melvilles were like family. Almost.

She placed her hands on the bleached decking of the wharf and levered herself into a standing position. 'Actually, I was hoping for some fresh fish.'

Joe indicated the wooden boxes sitting in the shade, draped with wet hessian sacks and waiting for collection. 'I've got whiting, if that's okay.'

He ambled across to the box. Erica followed, peering inside. Her arm brushed against his. 'Lovely. Can I have three?'

Joe took the fish, wrapped them in a piece of newspaper. 'There. Enjoy your tea.'

Erica fumbled in her purse. 'How much do I owe you?'

'Nothing. Call it a gift, on the house.'

'I can't possibly accept that. I'll feel terrible coming back, asking for more.'

'No you won't. And you can come back any time you like,' he added, giving her a wink.

She glanced at her watch. 'I should go,' she said, turning as though intending to walk away. At the last moment she swung back. 'Will you be here tomorrow? I may need some more.'

'So soon?'

'I like fish.'

'Obviously.'

Joe was enjoying this, the easy bantering, the playing with words. And he could tell by the slight wrinkling of her forehead that Erica wasn't sure how to take his comments. Perhaps she was used to a more direct approach.

'So, will you be here?'

'I might.'

'I could come earlier, so we'd have more time.'

'Whatever.' He shrugged, feigning nonchalance. He knew from experience where women were concerned, it didn't help to appear too keen. Back away, and it kept them interested, on their toes.

Joe pursed his mouth as he watched her walk away. He noted the subtle swing to her hips, her shapely arse and those long, long legs that went all the way up to her ...

'Bloody hell,' he said, wiping a hand across his forehead. The thought occurred to him that she was probably teasing him, laughing at his expense. Likely he'd not see her again. And if he did? He shrugged and grinned to himself. Lucky Alex coming home to that every night! And, if he'd read the signs correctly and played his cards right, lucky Joe! The future suddenly looked very promising, indeed. There were worse afternoon diversions, he supposed, than entertaining Erica Melville.

Erica began coming down every second afternoon, sitting in the shade on the deck of the *Sea-spray*, sipping a drink while he repaired the nets. He found himself watching for her car, alert to that telltale cloud of dust that meant someone was driving along the track between town and Tea-tree Passage.

The first few times she used the pretence of wanting fish. He obliged, playing along with her game, curious to see what turn the events would take, and when. Conversation was haphazard, darting between various subjects. Family. Work. Erica's amazement over the growth of the Passage in the years since she'd left.

'Tell me about the war,' she said one afternoon.

'No.'

'Why not?'

'It's not something I want to discuss.'

After she had taken possession of the fish, she asked Joe if he would show her the below-deck area of the boat.

'There's not much to see.'

He was playing that game again, stringing her out. He'd met women like this before. The chase was like an aphrodisiac and, by the time he got her into bed, she'd be so damn horny, begging for it.

'But I want to!' The corners of her mouth came down, purposefully, into a pout. Teasing. Flirting. 'I want to see so I can imagine you there, when I'm not here.'

'Sure. Come on, then.'

He showed her the small galley kitchen, the bedroom and minuscule bathroom tucked away in the bow of the boat. 'Oh, how cosy,' she said, bouncing on the edge of the mattress, 'I could just imagine myself lying here, feeling the waves rocking underneath. You could set off in this, go away, forget all your worries.'

'You can never forget.'

'You can have a damn good time trying.' She sat, staring up at him, silent for a while. 'Don't you like me?' she asked, after what seemed like a long time.

'I find you a very attractive woman.'

'But?'

'You *are* married.'

She gave a bitter laugh. 'Married! That's a joke! Besides, from the stories I've heard, that's never stopped *you* before.'

Joe suppressed a smile. 'Now where would you get an idea like that?'

She sat on the edge of the bed, nursing her drink and telling him about her relationship with Alex. 'All he ever thinks about is his patients. Josh and I come a poor second.'

'Doctors are like that,' he offered, feeling a fleeting sense of disloyalty towards Alex. Why was it that he wanted to defend the man, offer some excuse? 'It's part of their job.'

'I hate what we've become.'

'You could try to fix whatever's wrong.'

'If we could stop arguing long enough to try.' Her voice held a note of sarcasm and she paused, inspecting a fingernail. 'Anyway, it's too late for that.'

He thought of Jane, and that one abortive effort he'd made to see her when he'd come back from the war. 'It's never too late. One lucky chance, that's all it takes. And a little bit of compromise.'

'I don't love Alex.'

'Why do you stay then?'

'Habit. Convenience. There's Josh to consider, and Alex's position in town. Divorces are damn hard to get, and pretty messy.'

'So you just put up with it? That's not living, Erica.'

She took a sip of her drink. 'I have my own life.'

'Meaning?'

'There are other ways of providing excitement.' She gave him an appreciative glance over the rim of her glass. 'I could show you if you like.'

It was inevitable, he thought later. The setting was right — the bed, the water washing against the hull and setting up a slow rocking motion below, the privacy. Erica getting to her feet and walking towards him, the taste of her mouth on his. Hurried, demanding kisses. Frantic tearing at clothes. As though they had been waiting, marking time, all their lives for that one moment.

CHAPTER 41

Leaving Rory in Nina's capable care, Claire drove down to Brisbane, taking time to stop in little towns along the way. It was ages since she'd been away, not since the art exhibition a few years earlier. Goodness, she thought with surprise as the scenery flew past, have I known Paul that long?

He was waiting at his flat when she arrived. 'I've missed you,' he murmured into her ear.

Later, lying in his arms, she admitted to herself that it was enjoyable having a man in her life. Their meetings, though irregular, gave her something to look forward to and kept her from being totally occupied with work and Rory. Paul was a nice man and they shared many common interests. The sex was great, but she knew she wasn't in love with him. He was a release, an outlet for all those pent-up needs and desires.

The following afternoon she went to see Lydia. Her flat was in a quiet leafy street, five minutes' walk from the nearest railway station. It was small and compact, very modern, with a cosy breakfast room off the kitchen. 'There's only one bedroom,' said Lydia, 'or I'd ask you to stay.'

She was simply being polite, Claire knew, which was a pleasant change. 'How's work?' she asked. 'Where are you playing now?'

Lydia went to great lengths to tell Claire about her latest achievements. Rory's name, she noticed, hadn't been mentioned.

'You haven't been to see Rory in a while,' she said later in the kitchen as Lydia made a pot of tea.

'I've been busy.'

'She *is* your daughter. You owe her something!'

'I owe her nothing. You agreed to take her, to bring her up. It was your idea to tell her the truth about me. You could have lied to her, told her you were her mother.'

Claire laughed. 'As if she'd fall for that. She looks nothing like me. And as for telling her the truth, only you can do that.'

'What do you mean?'

'She's desperate to know about her father. She's been asking me for ages now. It's become an obsession.'

'Back off, Claire. Leave it. I don't want to talk about it, *ever*!'

After Claire had gone, Lydia sat by the window, staring into the leafy yard below. Oh what tangled webs we weave, she thought, regretting the day she had lied to Claire, telling her Rory was Alex's daughter. Why had she done that? Spite? Anger?

Targeting Claire instead of the absent Ellis? Childhood resentments spilling over into adulthood? How could she say now that she'd been untruthful all those years ago?

There were times when she regretted allowing Claire to take Rory. In hindsight, adoption would have been a better option. Lydia would never have had contact with the child again, could have gotten on with her own life without the reminders. But she only had to see Rory, for the whole episode with Ellis to come rushing back at her. It hurt, even after all this time.

Memories, long repressed, wafted back. Ellis pinning the orchid on her dress on their first date. Dinners and dancing, the first time they had made love. The night before his leaving: sitting on the bed wearing one of his shirts, watching as he meticulously laid his clothes in the suitcase. Him handing her the photographs — the ones he'd had taken that afternoon up in the mountains, the first day they'd made love. *Look after these until I get back.*

She remembered the pain of knowing he'd lied to her, knowing she would never see him again. The unspeakable agony of Rory's birth. Handing her daughter to Claire days later. Everything important in her life gone.

Rory: Ellis's daughter — not Alex's — yet she couldn't allow herself to love the child, couldn't give herself wholly to anyone again. All she had was the photos.

Over the years she'd purposefully distanced herself from the child. Don't ask questions and don't get involved: those had been her maxims. And it had worked. Mostly.

There had been a scene years earlier, though, which she'd never forgotten.

'Here's Mummy,' Claire had said, propelling Rory forward on one of Lydia's rare visits.

'Lydia's not my mother, Claire! You are!' Eyes blazing, tight, obstinate set of mouth.

'Hello, Aurora.' She'd tried to put her arm around her daughter's stiff little body, but the child had pushed her away with such force that Lydia had almost fallen.

'My name's not Aurora. It's Rory!'

'Rory! Don't speak like that!' Claire had remonstrated.

'She doesn't want me.'

They'd been talking as though she, Lydia, were invisible. She'd waited, not knowing what to do, fighting back tears. *Don't let them see me cry. Be strong.*

'Your mother loves you.'

'Lydia hates me!'

'Never! Lydia's just . . .'

'Lydia,' Rory had said as she'd run from the room.

Claire had looked apologetic. 'I'm sorry.'

'For what?'

'She doesn't mean it. She's just a child.'

'Without a mother.'

'You're her mother, Lydia,' Claire had replied wearily.

'I'm the woman who gave birth to her, but you're

the person who loves and nurtures her. I failed at the most basic part of being a woman: motherhood. She hates me.'

'She doesn't know the meaning of hate.'

'Perhaps.'

The words had stood between them for the remainder of Lydia's visit, the veiled antagonism entangled oddly in the warm days and the way Rory and Claire had both avoided her.

Over the years there had been other men, but she'd used them to forget that first painful love. She'd built walls around herself, purposely, not allowing herself to get emotionally involved. Money and prestige: that was all that interested her these days. Rory could go whistle at the moon, for all she cared. Reveal to Claire she'd lied about Alex? Tell Rory about Ellis? Dredge up the whole sorry mess and relive the pain? No way! Her lips were sealed, and nothing, or no-one, could change her mind.

There were times when Claire felt she was being punished, though for what she wasn't sure. Arguments with Lydia. Worrying about Nina's health and Joe's solitude. Demands from Rory.

'Why won't you tell me about my father? I need to know.'

'You'll have to ask your mother.'

'I never see her. She doesn't come here any more.'

'Rory, it's none of my business.'

Why couldn't Rory leave it alone?

In the train, heading back to Paul's, she thought about Rory and the scrapbook she'd given her on her sixth birthday. Over the years the girl had added to it, carefully cutting out every news clipping she'd seen of the mother she scarcely knew. Now the pages were almost full of photos and news articles. Lydia as Titania. Lydia at the Lyric or Lyceum or Capitol theatres. Bit parts or main roles. Lydia in a skimpy dress or clad in Elizabethan costume.

It was a pathetic link, really, and there were days when Claire regretted giving Rory the book. Perhaps it was better not to know, she considered now, than cling to something just out of one's reach. And it was time also, she thought with determination, to curb the friendship between Rory and Josh when she returned to Tea-tree Passage. The pair were becoming far too close these days.

Josh and Rory, away from the wary eyes of both Claire and his mother, spent most of their communal free time at the beach. A local surf club had started up the previous summer and there were several carnivals planned, with board-riding events. Josh had a surfboard, a new Chappell fourteen-footer which had been freighted to the railway station in town. Made from varnished plywood, it looked more like a small boat, he thought.

He couldn't believe how quickly the last year had disappeared. His final exams had come and gone, and the results would be released after Christmas. Then he'd head off to uni, he was sure.

In many ways, his going away would be a blessing. It would remove him from all the shit that went with family life at the Melvilles. Arguments and threats. Protracted silences. He'd long since closed his mind to them, hating the constant friction and upheaval. Yet he worried about his parents and had reservations about leaving. What would happen if he weren't there?

He worried also about Rory. She was mercurial these days, her moods swinging. Sitting staring at that bloody scrapbook, preoccupied by things she couldn't change, and events that had happened in the past. It must be a girl trait, he thought, this needing to know everything about how you came to be, and why. Personally, he didn't give a toss about his own family. That was a mess and, unlike Rory, he preferred not to know.

Paul spent a week at Tea-tree Passage over Christmas, staying at the pub. The visit, Claire thought, was not a success. Rory was fractious and the weather was suddenly humid and unbearably hot. She, herself, was short-tempered.

Paul made an effort to spend time with Rory, getting to know her. 'She's a mixed-up kid,' he told Claire after a few days. 'And she and Josh seem to be spending a lot of time together. Is that wise? She's only fifteen.'

Was he criticising her? 'They're only friends,' she snapped back, feeling guilty because she'd had so little time or opportunity to steer Rory away from Alex's son. And Paul was right; the pair *were* constantly in each other's company. Rory might only be fifteen, but she was mature for her age. What if something further developed? A romance. Or, God

613

forbid, a sexual relationship! Blast Lydia! She would be glad when Josh went off to uni in another two months.

Paul raised his hands in surrender. 'It's okay. I was only making a suggestion.'

Claire surprised herself by bursting into tears.

'Hey,' he said, lifting her chin with one finger. 'What's up?'

'Oh, I don't know. I'm acting like a shrew.'

'You're acting like a mother.'

Unexpectedly they ran into Alex. Claire introduced Paul as a partner in the art gallery where she had held her first exhibition. The two men shared a reserved handshake and chatted awkwardly about their mutual friend.

Alex seemed uncharacteristically abrasive, his voice tense and he rushed away as soon as he could.

On the last night of his holiday, Paul asked her again to move to the city. 'I've been patient, Claire, and I've tried not to pressure you.'

'I can't. My life's here. Rory. My mother. She's getting on and I can't leave her. She'd have no-one.'

'There's Joe,' he reminded her gently.

She gave a laugh. 'Joe's flat out taking care of Joe.'

'This isn't going to work, Claire. I'm getting older and I need someone long-term in my life. I want children, a permanent relationship. I'd rather it be with you but, if you're not willing to make the commitment, then we both need to move on.'

So this was the end. Claire couldn't blame him, not really. He had a future to consider also, and maybe there was someone out there who could be all the things to him that she couldn't. Paul was right. It was time to finalise their relationship, admit its failure.

'It's been lovely, Paul, but you're right. It *is* time to move on. Still friends?'

'Friends.'

He kissed her lingeringly on the mouth and for one agonising moment she wondered if she had made the right choice. 'Make love to me,' she whispered. 'One last time.'

He was gentle and tender, and it was a goodbye of sorts. He'd never come up here again, she knew that. And on her occasional trips to the city she might call him and they'd have dinner, remember the good times they'd shared, perhaps fall conveniently into bed, but that was all it could ever be.

The following day she couldn't settle. It was hot and she tried to work, slapping the paint dispiritedly across a fresh canvas. After a while she threw down her brush and wandered outside for some fresh air.

It was midday, and a warm breeze came from the hills. Beyond the dunes she could hear the boom and crash of the waves, and the occasional voice over the loudspeaker. A surf carnival was in progress. At breakfast Rory had announced her intention to watch.

Claire wandered down the track that led to the jetties. Under the tea-tree she spotted a flower. Pale mauve. Unusual. Carefully she broke off the small stem, keeping the flower intact. When she got back to the studio, perhaps she'd paint it.

It was as she was straightening, coming once more into an upright position, that she saw the woman climbing onto the deck of the *Sea-spray*. Blonde and willowy, wearing a pair of shorts and a skimpy top. Joe came up to meet her and they kissed, mouths fused for what seemed like a very long time. Joe's hands moved down, cupping the woman's buttocks, pulling her suddenly against his groin. The movement was so explicit, so ... erotic, that it left no doubt as to the meaning.

The couple moved away, walking arm in arm down the narrow stairway until they disappeared from view. The sun beat down, pouring its heat on her. Nothing moved, except for the flow of the outgoing tide and a lone gull that pecked along the decking of the wharf.

'What was Erica doing down at the jetty this afternoon?' she asked Joe later, when he called into her studio for his customary late-night drink.

'Nothing,' he replied casually. 'She was just after some fish.'

Alex called to see Nina, who had a bad summer cold. 'I'm worried about her,' Claire told him as they stood outside in the shade beside Alex's car, after he had examined her mother. 'She's not getting any younger.'

'None of us are. She's in fairly good shape for her age. It's just a cold.'

'You'd tell me, wouldn't you, if there *were* something?'

'You know I would.' He put one hand on the car,

as though to open the door, then turned his attention back to Claire. 'Actually, you're the one I'm concerned about.'

'Me? I'm not sick!'

'It's to do with Paul.'

'And . . .' she prompted.

'I'm concerned, that's all. Rory needs a stable male figure in her life, not someone who comes and goes.'

Anger flared inside her and she rounded on him, furious. 'For your information, Paul asked me to marry him, to move to the city.'

'So you're leaving?'

His eyes met hers and she glanced away, unable to hold his gaze. 'No. I told him I couldn't leave here. There's Rory to consider, and Mum and Joe. I simply can't walk away. So the relationship's off. Happy?'

'Claire, I've only got your welfare at heart.'

'Bullshit!'

She turned her back on him and began to walk away. How dare he! Alex hadn't been a part of her life for a long time. He had no right to dictate to her.

'Claire, I'm sorry.'

She swung back, faced him squarely. 'Don't come here preaching about what's good for me; I can't bloody-well bear it! Just go, Alex! Butt out! Concentrate on putting your own marriage in order.'

Nina stood at the kitchen table, kneading a lump of dough. Claire was always at her to give up. 'No one makes their own bread any more,' she had said, only the previous week.

The baker called every day from town, the wicker basket over his arm filled with warm loaves. It would be convenient, Nina supposed, to have him deliver one to her door, but she liked being there, in her kitchen.

It was part of her routine, standing at the table, measuring the ingredients. Flour. Water. Yeast. A pinch of salt. She enjoyed the feel of the dough beneath her hands, the way it squished through her fingers. She took pleasure in the repetitive pummelling movement, the flick of the wrist.

Push. Roll. Push. Roll.

With a sigh she placed the dough in a bowl, and set it aside to rise, on the window sill. It was warm there and the dough would soon expand, doubling in size. In the background, above the warble of a magpie, she heard the muted roar of the bulldozers. A new subdivision was being prepared behind the motel. Acres of tea-trees were being ground into the sand and new little box-like houses would soon spring up.

Nina's thoughts turned to her family, as they so often did these days. Claire and Lydia: her daughters were successful in their professional lives although, in a personal sense, she found each wanting. Lydia was brittle and cold, qualities she found puzzling and unattractive. Claire, since David's death, seemed to be marking time, though for what Nina wasn't sure. Whatever had happened to that nice young man from the gallery, Paul? He and Claire had seemed comfortable with each other, and she was certain something could have come of the friendship.

Marriage. Babies. Oh, how she'd love to see Claire with her own child. It wasn't too late. Late thirties. She had been that age when —

She stopped, remembering the death of her tiny son, pushing her grief back into the past.

Thinking of her daughters, she sighed. Not that she would ever say anything. Being part of a couple was an individual choice, after all, and Nina herself had been without the intimate company of a man for a long time now.

'Have you ever thought about marrying again?' Hal had once asked her.

Nina had shaken her head. 'I made a bit of a mess of it, the first time!'

'That was a long time ago.'

'Longer than I care to think. No,' she'd continued, after some consideration. 'I like being by myself, always have done. To consider changing all that now . . .'

Had Hal been working towards a marriage proposal, or had he been simply curious about her own solitary state? Nina hadn't known. She'd put her hand in his, instead, saying, 'But it's nice to know I have friends who care about me.'

Unwillingly, now, she let her mind slide sideways. Joe: her only surviving son was caught in his own private hell. He'd never be anything other than a fisherman, never let himself close to anyone now, not even Nina. He'd drawn away, markedly so, since the war. Closed himself off in that boat, preferring the company of a bottle of grog. Although she'd noticed, during the past few weeks, Erica Melville's car parked down near the jetties for hours at a time, and had seen the woman following Joe across the deck of the *Sea-spray*.

She closed her eyes, letting the implication push past her. Some days she felt too old for such intricacies, such complicated interweaving of lives. Whatever had happened to fidelity and trust? But then Frank had never subscribed to those attributes either. Her tolerance these days was for the small comforting routines, kneading the bread dough, watching Rory as she walked past on her way to the school bus, the soothing regularity of the tides.

Alex crushed the letter and threw it in the bin. It had been the last of several. Unsigned. Cut-out alphabet from newspaper articles, glued together in a haphazard way. Even the spelling was crude.

Concerned, he'd shown the first one to Claire. She'd read it, folded the paper and handed it back to him, saying nothing.

'I suppose I'm the last one to know?'

'It's none of my business, Alex, and certainly not my place to tell you. But this . . . .' She'd fingered the letter, a frown crossing her forehead. 'Who do you think sent it?'

'I have no idea. It's not only letters. There are the late-night phone calls, too. Look, I'm not naive enough to think that Joe's the first. But at least, up until now, she's been discreet.'

'Until now?'

The words had hung between them and he'd been

unable to form a reply. And now, here was another letter, same as all the others. He'd have to say something.

He found Erica standing by the sink, staring into the rear yard. In her hand she held a glass filled with amber liquid. What was it? Alex wondered. Rum? Scotch?

She was unaware of him and he waited by the kitchen door, seeing her with a kind of detached pity. At forty she was still an attractive woman, lean and supple, tanned. He ran his eyes along the proud line of her neck, the sweep of her shoulders. In another part of his lifetime he had grazed his mouth along those same contours. But that time was long gone. Somewhere along the way, at some undefined point, they had ceased to touch each other.

In one sense he thought they belonged together: Erica and Joe. They were both wounded souls, needy of others, yet not needing others at all, if that made sense. Independent. Proud. Self-sufficient.

'Erica.'

She turned to face him, her face blank. How many glasses had she already consumed? Alex wondered, not for the first time, how well he'd known this woman he had married and who had borne him a son. How much do we ever know about someone? he thought. Certainly, he had his own secrets.

'At the risk of causing an argument, there's something we need to discuss.'

'What could that possibly be, Alex?' she said in a sugar-sweet voice, humouring him.

How to phrase the problem without causing too much disruption? Whatever he said, whichever way he arranged the words, she was certain to retaliate.

'As the wife of a local doctor, you're expected to have a certain standing in the community, to live by an unquestionable code of behaviour.'

'Who expects that?'

'The people who send me obscene letters and ring me at night to whisper stories about you down the telephone.'

She stared at him, unflinching. 'What do they say, these anonymous busybodies?'

There was a slight inflection in her voice. Tell me, Alex, her tone dared. Bring it out into the open, lay it naked so we can both see.

'Erica, if you feel the need to have an affair, you could at least be discreet about it.'

She laughed, a high-pitched hysterical sound, and wobbled across the kitchen towards him. 'Oh, I get it. You're more worried what people will say about you than me. At all costs we must protect your reputation, *Doctor* Melville.'

She thrust herself towards him and he wanted to hit her. Badly. Wanted to slap that smug self-centred look from her face.

'And what do they say, Erica?' he yelled instead, all restraint gone. 'There goes that silly fool, Melville. Turns a blind eye while his wife fucks every bloke in town!'

She reared back as though stung. 'You bastard!' she screamed, flying at him and pummelling his chest, his face.

He pushed her away, easily. 'Our marriage is over. I know that. Has been for years. Why we're still together, I have no idea.'

'It's probably got something to do with that sense of propriety you mentioned earlier.'

She stared sullenly at him, then turned to walk away, tossing her head. Alex grabbed her arm, bringing her to a halt.

'Let go. You're hurting me.'

'Where are you going?'

'Out.'

She tried to wrench her arm away but he simply tightened his grip.

'Out where?'

'I'm going to Tea-tree Passage. Satisfied?'

Dully. 'You're going to Joe?'

She nodded.

Exhaustion swamped him. He was tired of the pretence, and the constant arguments were badly affecting Josh. 'Our farce of a marriage is over. I want a divorce.'

'Fine. I'll move in with Joe.'

Wearily he nodded. 'Do what you want, Erica. You always have.'

'I'll be back in the morning to get my things.'

He walked to the window, to the place where Erica had been standing. It was dark outside and the window had become mirror-like. He closed his eyes against his reflection. So the moment had finally come. Erica was leaving. He heard her grab her bag, her car keys. Heard footsteps down the hallway — brisk staccato sounds of stiletto against the polished floorboards. *Clickety-clack*. Heard the motor on her car turn over, catch, and she roared away with a spray of gravel.

There was loud music coming from Josh's room. He'd have heard it all, turned the volume up to cover their voices, Alex knew. With a sigh he made his way along the hallway. Josh was lying on his bed, his back to the door.

'Josh!' he yelled, trying to make himself heard above the noise.

Josh turned, awarding him a reproachful look, slid from the bed and turned the music down with one flick of his fingers. He was noticeably agitated, upset. Obviously he'd heard everything.

'What do you want?'

The tone was belligerent, challenging. And what exactly did he expect to achieve by coming to the boy's room? To explain what had gone wrong? To tell him that there were no happy-ever-afters, as far as the Melvilles were concerned? To say I love you? But the words wouldn't come.

'Why didn't you stop her?'

Patiently Alex replied, 'Because it's time we put an end to all of this, got on with our lives.'

'What about me? What am I supposed to do?'

'We'll stay here, mate, for the time being, and you'll go off to uni as planned.'

'What if I don't want to stay?'

Alex ignored the question. 'I'm thinking about taking the boat out tomorrow,' he said instead. 'Want to come?'

Josh shot him a look of distain. 'No thanks. I've more important things to do.'

Erica drove towards Tea-tree Passage. She was going too fast, she knew. The car tyres squealed as she rounded the corners, headlights illuminating the road ahead. The speed caused a bubble of exhilaration in her chest. She'd left Alex, finally, and was on her way to Joe.

She slowed as she came down the dark track that led to the jetties, swung the car off the road and parked, switching off the headlights. Joe was coiling ropes on the deck of the *Sea-spray*. He seemed surprised to see her, swinging towards the sound of her approach. 'Erica,' he said. 'What are you doing here this late?'

'I've left Alex.'

He stood on the deck, facing her, the outline of his body dark against the wheelhouse. 'What do you mean you've *left Alex*?'

'The marriage is over! Finished! I'm coming to live with you.'

He laughed. 'Come on, Erica. You know that's not possible. There's no room.'

'I won't take up much space.'

'Sometimes I spend days at sea.'

'I could help. I can cook, in case you haven't noticed.'

'It won't work.'

'Okay. Forget the boat. We could get a little place in town —'

'No!'

'Joe —'

'You're changing the rules, Erica. "Don't get too involved", you said. "Nothing too serious. It's just for fun".'

'I love you,' she replied tearfully.

'Rubbish! I'm an escape from your boring, tedious life.'

'You're ashamed of me.'

'I am not. Seriously, how could this ever work? This is a small place and you're someone else's wife.'

'I wouldn't be if you married me.'

He stared at her incredulously. 'What?'

'You're no different from Alex,' she countered. 'Bloody protocol, that's all you're worried about. I don't give a damn what anyone says.'

'I don't gave a shit about protocol, either. I don't want commitment, that's all. I like living by myself.'

'Bastard! It's all right for you to fuck me, though,' she yelled vehemently.

He turned his face and she could see, in the light that splayed out from the window of the wheelhouse, the fine chiselled nose, deep-set eyes, strong mouth. A few strains of music tumbled from the direction of the pub and further back, a shout of laughter. A car started up, backfired several times, then roared away.

'Joe,' she said tentatively.

'Look, this isn't a good time. I'm really busy.'

He ran down the stairs to the cabin below and Erica followed. In the cabin, he threw a few clothes into a bag. Jumper and all-weather coat.

'Where are you going?'

'One of the O'Reilly boys needs a crew for the night. He'll be here any minute.'

'But I need you,' she wailed. 'Please don't go.'

'Erica, I can't sit and hold your hand. Besides, I think it'd be best if you're gone when I get back in the morning.'

'Where am I supposed to go?'

'You'll think of somewhere.'

She could hear the wash of an approaching boat and the slow chug of the engine. 'Joe?' someone called as a boat's hull ground against the wharf.

'Coming.'

'Joe! Please!'

'I've got to go. Look, Erica, you go home and sort out your marital problems. If you want to leave Alex, then fine, but don't involve me in all this.'

She waited until the noise of the boat faded, and the only sound left was the slap of water against the pylons and the cry of a night bird. Dejectedly she sat at the table in the cabin and poured herself a generous measure of Joe's whisky.

'*Bastard!*' she said again. Leaving her high and dry! What was she going to do? She couldn't go back to Alex. Things had gone too far for that. Besides, Alex had told her he wanted a divorce. She'd been counting on Joe, expecting some support. Obviously she couldn't have been more mistaken.

Quickly she drained the glass and poured another. Her hands were shaking and she rummaged on the shelf for Joe's tablets: little white spheres that calmed him, or so he'd said when she'd asked. She opened the lid, tipped four into her palm. Rolled them onto her tongue and washed them down with a large swig of scotch. The night promised to be a long one, and she'd be damned if she'd leave before emptying the bottle.

She raised the glass in absent salute.

'Up yours,' she said.

CHAPTER 42

Rory picked up the telephone on the fourth ring. 'Hello.'

'Thank God! I was hoping Claire wouldn't answer.'

'She's working in her studio. I'm the only one here.' Then. 'What's wrong? You sound upset.'

'They've been at it again! Fighting! I can't stand much more of this.'

'Oh, Josh! I wish I could help.'

'It's worse this time. Mum's gone!'

'Gone! Why? Where?'

'She says she's going to live with your uncle Joe!'

Rory was silent for a moment, not knowing what to say. Josh's mum and her uncle? Together? That would take some getting used to.

'I hate my father! He's not being fair!'

'Where is he now?'

'Don't know.'

'I'm coming over. No! Don't argue. You need to be with someone. Claire won't even know I'm gone. She thinks I'm in bed.'

She took her bicycle from the shed at the side of the house, careful not to alert her aunt, and set off down the dark road. On the outskirts of town, she passed someone walking. It was Josh's dad, she knew, the dog Jess straining at the lead. Head down, she pedalled past furiously, hoping he wouldn't recognise her.

'I passed your father on the way in,' she said to Josh when he answered the door.

'What was he doing?'

'Walking. He had the dog. He was heading in the direction of Tea-tree Passage.'

'So he's going to her, then,' Josh replied dully.

'Her?'

'To Claire. Mother always said he loved her.'

Rory's mind slammed to a halt, stunned by Josh's words. 'My aunt? *Claire*? He's going to her *now*?'

But Josh's thoughts were already heading in a different direction. 'You might as well know that I'm leaving. I can't bear to stay here another two months until uni starts.'

'Where will you go?'

Josh shrugged, his shoulders falling in a despondent way. 'I don't know. Brisbane, I suppose. I could get a job.'

'I'll come, too.'

'You can't. You'd get into a heap of trouble.'

'I can and I will. I want to see my mother. There's a pile of questions that I want answers to, and this time she's going to cough up.'

Alex had walked out on the back step, staring up at the night sky, the wind fanning towards him in hot gusts. Clouds were rolling across the moon and thunder rumbled in the distance. Summer storm, he'd thought, hoping a shower would cool the temperature.

Jess had been waiting, wagging her tail in anticipation; he often took her for a short walk before going to bed. Mechanically he'd taken the lead and fastened it to her collar. Then he'd started walking, the dog pulling him forward.

The town had been quiet. Lights shone behind closed curtains. In the distance he'd heard the barking of a dog. Pools of luminescence, from the street lamps above, had glistened on the roadway. He stepped through them, scarcely aware, his mind churning over the events of the evening. Someone had ridden past on a bicycle, head down, but he'd barely glanced in their direction. It wasn't until long minutes had passed and his surroundings had become dark that he realised he was walking along the road to Tea-tree Passage.

He was coming home, he knew, although twenty years too late, to Claire and the rambling collection of houses that sprawled along the waterfront. Past the Sharps' and the O'Reillys' he went. Past Nina's house and the old Melville place where Kath, her husband and kiddies now lived.

Finally Claire's home: his subconscious destination. Everything lay in darkness — tearoom, gallery and main house — except for her studio at the end of the garden, well away from the house. He waited by the front fence, wondering momentarily if he had done the right thing by coming here. What to say to her? How to explain how he felt, how he'd *always* felt? Would she even want to listen?

The clouds shifted. Along the track that ran down to the jetties through the tea-tree, he caught a glimpse of Erica's little car in the moonlight, parked haphazardly, nose-in to the scrub. The sight of it strengthened his resolve. Joe was welcome to her, he thought, feeling that a great weight had been lifted from his shoulders.

He picked his way along the path that led to the studio door, past fragrant honeysuckle and jasmine. He took a deep breath, inhaling the perfume. Then he paused by the front door, looping the dog's lead around the stair post, and knocked.

Claire answered the door, paintbrush in her hand, wearing a man's shirt. It was paint-splattered and several sizes too big for her, coming almost to her knees. 'Hello, Alex,' she said, almost casually, as though his night-time arrival on her doorstep was a regular occurrence.

'May I come in?'

'Of course.'

As she turned to walk back into the room, beckoning him to follow, he was aware of shapely tanned legs and bare feet padding across the floor.

Although it was the first time Alex had been inside her studio, he felt immediately at home amongst the clutter. A large easel sat against the opposite wall, next to dozens of canvasses in varying stages of completion. Pots of paint, jars containing several different-sized brushes, and palettes were scattered around the room in an untidy yet comfortable array. A worn sofa sat under the window. In the corner was a small kitchen, complete with sink and fridge.

One painting in particular stunned him, and Alex walked towards it, studying the details. On the rippling water sat an old dinghy, grey and peeling. He could almost see each flake of paint, long dangling strands, could imagine them brushing against the damp and rotting timber boards in the breeze. At the end of the boat sat a pelican, feathers ruffled. The bird was watching the water, head cocked at the opposite angle to his own. Was it waiting for a fish to jump skywards from the silent ripples? The painting was so real, so lifelike, that he felt he could reach forward and touch the feathers, could immerse his hand in the water.

'Do you like it?'

Her words startled him and he swung back to her. 'Sorry. I was miles away. It's stunning. Really.'

Claire offered to make a pot of tea. 'Unless you'd like something stronger?'

He shook his head, thinking of Erica wobbling across the kitchen earlier. 'Tea's fine.'

She filled the kettle at the tiny sink and put it on the gas ring to boil. 'Have a seat,' she said, indicating the settee under the window. Then asked, 'Have you eaten?'

Had he? Alex wasn't sure. He let his mind wander back through the night's painful events. 'No,' he said at last. 'But, please, don't —'

'It's no bother at all.'

She prepared a plate of sandwiches, taking sliced ham and butter from the fridge. 'I keep all sorts of supplies down here,' she explained. 'Saves me from going up to the house when I'm starving while in the throes of creativity.'

He laid his head back against the settee and closed his eyes, listening to the sounds of her domesticity. Clink of cups and plates. Click of the door. Heard her talking to the dog.

Over the sandwiches and tea he told her. 'My farce of a marriage is finally over. I wanted to tell you first.'

'What about Josh?'

'He was there, heard the argument. He knows she's gone, where she's gone. I tried to talk to him, tried to explain, but it's like hitting your head against a wall. He's so full of anger.'

'Where is he now?'

'Home. He's locked himself in his bedroom.'

'He'll come through. Kids are pretty resilient.'

'Like Rory?'

Claire nodded and bit her bottom lip. 'Erica's gone to Joe.'

It was a statement, not a question, and he nodded. 'Perhaps he's the right person for her. I certainly wasn't.'

'Joe!' Claire gave an incredulous laugh. 'I don't know what sort of a future Erica thinks he'll provide. Joe's not the sort to let himself get tied down with a woman. He's a free spirit. At least, that's what he tells me.'

Wearily Alex placed the empty cup on the low table in front of the settee. 'The truth is, Claire, I don't care any more. I just want my life back.'

A low rumble of thunder echoed, and the first drops of rain began to fall. He could hear them, thudding on Claire's roof. The breeze, cooler now, brought the sweet scent of damp earth.

Claire inhaled deeply. 'I always love the rain, don't you?'

A sudden thought occurred to him. 'Oh, Christ, Jess! I forgot about the dog. She'll be soaked.'

Claire was at the sink, rinsing the plates. She gave an amused chuckle. 'Jess? I gave her a drink and let her go ages ago.'

She turned and leaned back against the sink, staring at him. Her eyes were dark and mysterious against her unusually pale face. Her lips were parted, and it was as though he were seeing her for the first time.

'I'm glad you came here tonight, Alex.'

The rain beat down, a steady rhythm. It was a comforting sound, welcoming.

Alex levered himself to his feet. 'I know it's twenty years too late, but —'

'Sshhh.'

Slowly Claire came across the room. She stared upwards, for what seemed like a very long time, into his face, then wrapped her arms around him. He felt the warmth of her, the substance, as she laid her head against his chest.

'You're here now,' she whispered, raising her mouth to his. 'And that's all that matters.'

Erica woke to find herself sprawled on Joe's bed, an almost-empty bottle of scotch beside her. There was a damp patch on the bedspread where the bottle had tipped on its side and some of the contents dribbled out. Confused, she pressed her hand against the wetness, trying to focus her mind. Where was Joe? And what was she doing here?

Her head fell back onto the pillow and she closed her eyes, wishing away the pain that throbbed at the base of her skull. Her limbs seemed detached from her body. Her hands, however, had stopped shaking. Joe's little magic tablets were obviously working.

Bit by bit, the memories slunk back. The fight with Alex and her announcement that she was leaving. *Our farce of a marriage is over. I want a divorce.* Had Alex really said that? He must have, she reasoned, or the words would not have come so readily to mind. She remembered Joe's surprised reaction at her arrival on the boat, his insistence that she couldn't stay. He'd even gone out fishing, *prawning*, and left her. Tonight, of all nights!

She struggled to her feet and wove her way across the cabin. The room swam in and out of focus and the floor appeared to buckle beneath her feet, rising and falling with each successive step. She'd never experienced these sensations before; it must be Joe's tablets. Perhaps, she thought too late, she should have only taken one. Carefully she retrieved her shoes from the floor, where she had kicked them from her feet earlier. 'Bloody men!' she swore, wriggling her feet into them. 'Stuff the lot of them!'

What to do now? Joe said he wanted her gone by morning, but what if she simply stayed? Would he evict her, carry her bodily from the boat? Or perhaps she should get in her car and leave. Go away, miles from this bloody place, so no-one would find her. Neither Alex nor Josh nor Joe. Serve them right! Let them worry.

But first she'd make Joe pay for his abandonment of her. She scrambled up onto the deck, casting her eyes around. The light from a nearby channel buoy shed a glow across the piles of ropes and nets. She stood, surveying them. What if she untied the boat? From the suck and flow of the water, she knew the tide was going out. Perhaps the *Sea-spray* would be pulled across the bar. The occasional boat had been known to capsize out there, when the conditions were right.

Thunder rumbled out to sea. A sheet of lightning lit the horizon, then was gone. The first of the rain began to fall: hot drops that seemed to sizzle against the deck. She raised her face to them and closed her eyes. Felt them wet against her cheeks.

Within seconds, Erica was drenched. She leant out from the boat's deck, over the water, struggling to unhook the mooring line from the bollard. The rope was thick and her fingers clumsy, so she stretched herself further, tugging furiously. Slowly it came, easing up towards the top of the post.

Suddenly the boat shifted. The deck was slippery from the rain and Erica, leaning out too far, felt herself falling effortlessly through the air. Her head hit something — the side of the boat? — and dark pain flowed behind her eyes.

Water swirled soft and warm about her. She spread her arms wide, feeling it encompass her body.

Her limbs felt heavy, weighted down, her eyelids barely able to remain open. She was tired, so tired. Perhaps she'd just rest here a while, keep warm in the water until Joe got back. Perhaps he'd tell her it was all a joke, or a misunderstanding, that she could come and live with him on the boat and they'd be together always.

She took a deep expectant breath, and it felt like cotton wool in her nose, her mouth. Reluctantly she opened her eyes. The light from the channel marker buoy wafted down, refracted, and swirled away. A dark shape loomed before her. Was it the hull of the boat? She tried to swim towards it, but her movements were sluggish now. Tired. So tired, she thought, closing her eyes again, waiting for sleep to overtake her.

It was late when Alex left. 'Must you?' asked Claire, stretching lazily.

'I want to be there for Josh when he wakes up. He's been through a lot. Well, we all have, but he's just a kid and going through a rough patch. You do understand?'

'Of course I do,' she replied, and he felt that same old blend of desire and love well up within him.

He kissed her. 'I'll be back tonight and we'll make plans.'

'Plans?' she asked drowsily.

'We've been apart too long. I'm not waiting forever, Claire.'

He walked outside. The night was clear, stars shining brilliantly above. The storm had moved out to sea, tiny flickers of lightning dancing on the eastern horizon. Back along the track toward the jetties, he could see Erica's car still parked in front of the scrub. Good! She was obviously intending to stay with Joe, as promised, so there would be no more arguments tonight. There would be time enough for those tomorrow. He walked home whistling.

Every light in the house was blazing when he arrived home. Josh was waiting in the living room, pacing across the carpet. 'Where have you been?' he demanded.

What to say? He could hardly tell the lad he'd been with Claire.

'There was a bit of a medical emergency —'

'Mum's right! You're never here when we need you!'

'I'm here now.'

Josh wanted to know what was going on. 'If Mum's gone, then where am I going to live?'

'You'll stay here, until uni. This is your home.'

'What if I want to live with Mum?'

'I don't think that's going to be possible.'

'Why?'

'Just leave it, Josh. I don't want to talk about it tonight. We'll discuss it in the morning, when we've slept.'

It was mid-morning when Joe, behind the wheel of Bert O'Reilly's boat, came back across the bar. It was hot already, the storm of the previous night having done nothing to dispel the heat. As he motored down Tea-tree Passage, he could see a throng gathered at the jetty near the *Sea-spray*.

He brought the boat up expertly alongside the wharf and, handing the wheel to Bert, leapt from the deck to the bare planking.

'What's up?'

One of the policemen from town was there. He detached himself from the crowd and came towards Joe.

'Joseph Carmody?'

'Yes.'

'Where were you last night?'

Joe indicated the boat which he'd just left. 'Out in that. Prawning. Why?'

The policeman ignored the question. 'From what time?'

'About ten o'clock.'

'Can someone vouch for that?'

'Yes. Look! What's going on? I'm not going to answer any more damn questions until you tell me.'

'Erica Melville: is she a friend of yours?'

'Yes.'

Fear lurched in his belly. At that instant his eyes were drawn to something unfamiliar on the wharf, further along: a yellow tarpaulin-wrapped shape. He took one step towards it, but the policeman was there, holding him back.

'I'm sorry. She was found dead in the water next to your boat half an hour ago.'

'You're missing all the excitement, sleeping in,' said Rory, coming into Claire's room. 'Something's happened down at the wharves. There's been a heap of cars go past, and an ambulance.'

Claire was instantly awake. Joe! she thought at once. Something had happened to Joe!

She scrambled from her bed. Quickly she threw on a dress and ran a comb through her hair. Slipped a pair of shoes on her feet and ran down the track. Several cars were parked in the shade, Erica's amongst them. A knot of people had gathered at the end of the wharf, waiting. Thank God! She could see her brother there, talking to a policeman.

'What's happened?' she asked a man walking back to his car.

The man shook his head. 'Terrible business. The doc's wife. They found her down there in the water.'

Alex slept late, woken at last by insistent banging. By the time he'd stumbled from his bed and walked down the hallway, Josh had already opened the front door.

A policeman stood there, hat in hand. Although he was fairly new in town, Alex had seen him once or twice in the surgery, but couldn't, for the life of him, remember the man's name.

'Doctor Melville,' he said now, taking a step towards him. 'I'm afraid I have some bad news.'

It was Erica, he knew instantly. 'My wife?' he asked, instinctively moving closer to Josh.

'She fell from one of the boats out at Tea-tree Passage. She'd been dead for hours by the time someone found her this morning and raised the alarm.'

'*Dead?*'

His mind stalled, refusing to form thoughts. Erica dead? Couldn't be. Only hours earlier she had stood in this same house, issuing threats. But Josh was backing away from him, disgust etched plainly on his face.

'It's all your fault!' he yelled. 'If you hadn't argued with her last night, she wouldn't have gone!'

Someone came up behind the policeman, pushed past. It was Claire. She stood, arms folded, eyes filled with unshed tears. 'Oh, Alex, I'm so sorry. I just heard.'

Josh gave a visible start, started to say something, then stopped. 'And you are?' the policeman asked Claire.

'Claire Melville, Alex's sister-in-law. I live at Teatree Passage.'

Josh threw Alex another look of disgust, turned and walked from the room. Alex made to go after him but Claire was blocking his path.

'Leave him,' she said simply, folding him in her arms. 'Let him alone for a while. He has his own grieving to do and you'll simply make things worse.'

CHAPTER 43

The coroner placed Erica's time of death at around midnight.

'Accidental,' the police told Alex later. 'She was full of sedatives, and there's evidence she hit her head on the side of the boat as she fell. Along with the alcohol, she didn't stand a chance.'

Everyone seemed to be carrying their own private guilt. Joe. Alex. Even Josh seemed subdued. He and Rory were spending inordinately long periods of time on the telephone, Rory conspicuously clamming up whenever Claire came near. 'Do you mind?' she'd say, holding her hand over the mouthpiece. 'This is private.'

Claire felt shut out, unwanted. Rory, it seemed, no longer needed her. Joe was firmly ensconced in his own private hell, and Nina was self-absorbed. Kath had her own growing family.

Alex had told her that he'd attempted to talk to Josh, to resolve the whole sorry affair. Tried to explain how Erica had been pregnant when they'd married, how she'd lost the child. Described his love for Claire.

'I don't want to hear,' Josh had said, turning his head to the wall and refusing to pay attention.

Eventually Alex had given up. 'I can't force him to listen,' he'd told Claire.

The funeral was a sad affair. Rain poured down, washing the landscape into monotone grey. Grey skies and grey dripping trees. Grey gushing water and grey mud around the grave site. Most of the townsfolk attended. Alex and his father had been the only local doctors for years now, and were known by everyone. Erica's flighty friends, Claire noticed, her lunch and golf companions, were conspicuous by their absence.

After the funeral, Claire stayed behind to help Alex clean up. 'I'd better be going,' she said when the last of the dishes were dried and put away. 'Rory's had a few late nights.'

'Speaking of Rory,' said Alex, 'I haven't seen her or Josh for ages. They must be up in his room.'

They walked up the hallway together. Josh's door was closed and Alex knocked. 'Josh. Claire's leaving.'

There was no answer.

Slowly Alex pushed open the door. The bed was neatly made, the dresser bare. There was a palpable emptiness about the room that was hard to define. Alex glanced towards her, a puzzled expression on his face. 'Something's wrong.'

He strode to the cupboard and flung open the door. A gaping space sat where, Claire guessed, if

Josh was anything like Rory, there was usually a tumbled assortment of clothes.

'His bag's gone,' said Alex tersely.

'And he's taken Rory!' Her mind was scrambling in a dozen different directions. 'Think! Think! Where could they have gone?'

Alex faced her, looking puzzled. 'How do you know Rory's with Josh?'

'I'm only guessing.' *Oh, God, please don't let them be together*. 'I should go home and check. See if any of her clothes are missing too.'

Alex said he'd try the railway station, ask if anyone had seen them earlier. 'Phone me,' he told her, 'if you find anything. I'll wait at home for your call.'

Claire drove out to Tea-tree Passage, too fast for the road, the tyres squealing around corners. Her house lay in darkness. Rory was nowhere to be found and some of her clothes were missing as well. She sat for a moment on the edge of Rory's bed, in that room with the bright murals painted a lifetime ago, trying to catch her breath.

Calming herself she walked back into the kitchen and rang Kath. 'It's Claire.'

'Something's wrong. I can tell.'

'You haven't seen Rory, have you?'

'Not since the funeral.'

'Are you certain she didn't come home afterwards, take a bag maybe?'

'I've been busy with the children since I came back, getting dinner, cleaning up, the usual things. Why?'

'I think she and Josh have run away,' Claire replied, her voice dull.

The phone line went dead and Kath burst into the room half a minute later. 'What do you mean, *run away*?'

Despite Claire's resolve, the tears came, coursing down her cheeks. Kath put her arms around her shoulders, hugging her close. 'Hey! They won't go far. It's probably just a childish prank. Like as not, they'll be back by morning.'

Morning? That was hours away. Oh, God! The secrets and lies! 'You don't understand,' she sobbed. 'There are reasons I have to find them.'

'Claire?' Kath stepped back, holding her at arm's length. 'What reasons?'

'Alex is Rory's father. Josh and Rory are brother and sister.'

Kath brought her hand to her mouth and her eyes were wide and dark in her face. 'Oh, my God! You don't think ... ?'

The words died away, unspoken, though the implication was clear.

Kath paced the linoleum beside the kitchen cupboards, drumming her fingers against her mouth. 'What about Alex? He must be frantic with worry that they're together.'

Claire shook her head. 'He doesn't know.'

She came to a halt, staring at Claire. 'I can't believe you're telling me this! You can't keep something like this from Alex! He has a right to know. Josh and Rory too.'

'I can't even begin to think about that now. I have to find them first, make sure they're all right.'

'Come on. Back to Rory's room. Maybe there's a clue there, some indication of where they've gone.'

It was Kath who noticed Rory's address book on the bedside table, open at her mother's name. 'Lydia!' she cried. 'They've gone to Lydia's.'

'Oh, Lord!' said Claire. 'That's all we need.'

Josh and Rory made the six o'clock train with five minutes to spare. They threw themselves down in an empty compartment and kept their heads lowered, thinking any minute they'd be discovered and hauled off home. But the guard came past the window blowing his whistle, and the carriages pulled effortlessly from the station.

They looked at each other, smiled. 'Well, that's that,' said Rory as the train gathered speed, racing through the dusk. 'Brisbane, here we come.'

The journey seemed to go on forever, the train wheezing to a stop at the small towns and sidings along the way. Rory and Josh huddled together in the dark. Although it was summer, the night was cold. They ate lukewarm pies at midnight in a station cafeteria and sipped scalding coffee.

Josh seemed distracted, preoccupied with thoughts Rory was not privy to. He'd been through a lot these past days and the stress, she suspected, was beginning to take its toll.

'Hey,' she said as they ran back to the waiting carriage, carrying the disposable coffee cups. 'Cheer up! Nothing's as bad as it seems.'

'You haven't lost your mother,' replied Josh morosely. 'It feels weird.'

'You're wrong there. I've never really even known my mother.' Then she asked, 'You're not having second thoughts about leaving, are you?'

'No.'

The train moved, pulling slowly away from yet another platform. Rory pressed her nose against the glass, watching the lights fade into the distance. 'Me either,' she said at last. 'And the sooner we get to Brisbane the better.'

'Rory, about your father.'

'Yes.'

'Don't you think sometimes it's better not to know? What if you discover something terrible?'

'Such as?'

She saw Josh shrug in the semi-dark, and she put her head against his shoulder. 'I don't know. He might have been a bad person. A murderer.'

'Oh, silly.'

She gave him a playful punch, staring up at him. There was a sadness to his face, a despondency that had settled over him like a cloak. 'What are you thinking?'

'About the night my mother died.'

She waited, silent, for him to continue. He seemed to be struggling to find the words, embarrassed perhaps by his thoughts and emotions. 'While she was in the water, drowning, my father and Claire were . . .'

His voice trailed away and she squeezed his arm. 'You don't know that.'

'No. Maybe not.'

'They do love each other. I've never seen Claire

look at anyone like she looks at your dad. Do you suppose they'll get married?'

'Would that make us brother and sister?'

'Sort of. By marriage. I've always wanted a brother.'

He laughed, a choking sort of sound, and buried his face in her hair. She stared out the window, watching the miles flash by. Saw the lights of an occasional farmhouse and the moon reflected in a dam or creek: silver ribbons streaming away, quickly glimpsed then lost to view. After a while she dozed, head firmly against Josh's shoulder and, when she woke, the first rays of sunlight were pink-tipped in the sky.

It was late before Claire set off in the car. There had been the tearoom and gallery to organise, Nina to be told. She played down the urgency of the situation with her mother, saying only that she wanted to find the couple, bring them safely home. At the last minute she had thrown a few clothes into a bag. Goodness knows how long she'd be gone! If Rory and Josh had left on the six o'clock train, as she suspected, then they had several hours start. But the train was slow, Claire knew, and there was every chance she would arrive in the city at a similar time.

The phone was ringing when she left, the shrill tone following her down the path. It would be Alex, she knew. 'Phone me,' he'd said and she hadn't. She needed to find Rory and Josh first, sort out that problem. But Kath was right. They'd all have to be told eventually.

She sat in the car staring straight ahead. The wide sweep of the headlights lit her surroundings. 'Keep an eye out for kangaroos,' she told herself, her eyes raking the shadowy sides of the road. From time to time, she glanced at the dashboard, amazed at the speed she was travelling and forcing herself to slow down. It was late and she was tired.

She stopped at the first town, a collection of houses along the highway, and rang Alex's number. 'Thank God,' he said, relief flooding his voice as the long-distance pips faded. 'I tried to phone you but there was no answer. I've been imagining all sorts of things. Where are you?'

'Alex, I know where they've gone.'

There was a momentary silence on the other end of the line. 'Well,' he said after what seemed like a long time. 'Aren't you going to tell me?'

'Just let me handle this, okay?'

'Claire! I'm worried sick!'

She could almost see the worn expression on his face, the resolute set to his mouth, and she hated herself for not having the courage to tell him. 'Trust me. I'll find them, bring them home,' she said. 'Think positive, that's what Nina always says.'

'I hope you're right.'

Several hours into her journey, Claire pulled into a parking bay at the side of the road. She was exhausted, and to continue was madness. The journey ahead was long and she needed a few hours' sleep.

* * *

It wasn't until late afternoon that the countryside gave way to sprawling suburbia and chimney stacks. The train trundled past city stations, where passengers waited with bored expressions on their faces. Rory and Josh piled onto the platform at Roma Street Station and joined the thronging crowds. In her pocket, Rory carried a crumpled piece of paper with her mother's address.

They had five pounds between them, enough for a couple of days. By the time Josh hailed a taxi and gave the driver Lydia's address, it was dusk. Streetlights flickered on as they wound through the suburbs, finally coming to a halt in front of a smart apartment building.

They struggled up the stairs, carrying their bags. Found the right flat and knocked on the door. It seemed an age before Lydia answered, and they were almost ready to turn away when the door clicked open. She was tousle-haired and yawning, as though she had just woken. 'Who is it?'

'Me,' said Rory brightly, pulling Josh into Lydia's line of vision. 'And you remember Josh Melville?'

Lydia blinked and ran a hand through her hair. 'Alex Melville's son? Oh, God! What time is it?'

'Seven o'clock.'

'You'd better come in,' Lydia suggested in a tone that said she'd rather they didn't. 'Can't stand here in the door talking all night.'

Rory and Josh followed her down the narrow hallway into a spacious living room. 'We've come to stay,' said Rory, letting her bag fall on the floor.

Lydia's voice was hard, promising little hope for debate. 'That's not possible.'

'Just for a few nights,' continued Rory hopefully.

'You'll have to go. It's rather inconvenient, you being here.'

'We haven't much money. We were counting on a bed here until Josh finds a job.'

So far, Lydia's reaction to their arrival had been anything but welcoming and, Rory realised with sudden certainty, it had been a mistake to count on her mother for anything. But that shouldn't have come as a surprise, she thought bitterly, judging by Lydia's past actions.

Lydia walked over to the mantelpiece and rummaged in her purse. She handed Rory several pound notes. 'There. That should be enough for your fares home and something left over for food.'

Fares home? Rory stared at her mother. She and Josh hadn't come all this way only to turn tail and run back to Tea-tree Passage.

Lydia picked up Rory's bag from the floor where she had dropped it, handed it to her. 'Be sensible, Rory. Go home to Claire.'

She ushered her along the hallway, towards the front door. Josh followed along behind, not saying a word. What was he thinking? Rory wondered. What an undependable fruitcake she had for a mother?

Rory came to a halt in front of the closed door and crossed her arms. 'Okay, I'll go. But there's something I need to know first.'

Lydia's mouth flattened into a tight line, which Rory found most unattractive. 'And what's that?'

'I need to know about my father.'

'No! I don't want to discuss it.'

'Why not?'

'Because I don't, that's why! Not now! Not ever!'

The door opened and they found themselves standing outside. It was dark now. Moths hovered around streetlights and the occasional car rolled past. Rory didn't have a clue where they were, in relation to the centre of the city. She'd been so excited in the taxi that she'd failed to take notice of the direction in which they had headed.

Lydia pointed towards the end of the road. 'There's a bus stop down there. The Roma Street buses come every hour. Look, I'm sorry, Rory. But there are certain parts of my life I don't want to remember, and your father is one of those. You'll have to respect that.'

Rory turned and walked towards the bus stop at the far end of the road. Her bag bumped against her legs. A headache threatened. She was tired, exhaustingly so. It had been a long fruitless journey, as far as her mother was concerned, and she and Josh had some decisions to make.

It was after eight when Claire arrived at Lydia's. She had gotten lost several times in the city traffic, and exhaustion wasn't far away. She slid her car into a handy parking space, raced up the stairs to Lydia's flat and banged on the door. 'Dear God! Please be home,' she prayed.

Lydia answered on the sixth knock. 'There's no need to break the blessed door down,' she said crossly, flinging it open. 'Oh, it's you.'

'Where is she?'

'I take it you mean Rory.'

'Of course I do. For God's sake, Lydia! This is serious.'

'She's not here.'

Claire sagged against the door frame. She hadn't realised, until now, how certain she had been of finding Rory here. Lydia beckoned her inside and closed the door behind her. Claire followed her down the hallway to the living room.

'But she was,' Lydia went on, settling herself on a comfortable lounge. 'She wanted to stay.'

'And?'

'Well, it's not convenient at the moment and —'

'So you turned her away? Your own daughter!'

'I didn't have a choice. I'm expecting company later —'

'You've always had choices, Lydia! You've just always taken the easy way out. Was Josh with her?'

'Josh Melville? Yes. Seems like a nice kid. I heard about Erica.'

'Lydia!'

'What's wrong?'

She stared at her sister, dumbfounded. 'Hasn't it occurred to you? They're brother and sister! We have to find them quickly before —'

Lydia held out her hand, silencing her. 'Claire, there's been something I've been meaning to tell you for a long time. Rory isn't Alex's child.'

Claire froze, shocked. She stared at Lydia, not believing what she had heard. 'What did you say?' she said slowly.

'I was wrong, all those years ago, when I told you that Alex and I —'

'So you never ...'

'Never.'

Fury rendered her speechless, but only for a moment. 'All these years I've gone along believing that you and Alex had some sort of a sordid affair. Why, Lydia? Why on earth did you lie to me?'

She had the grace to look contrite. 'Jealousy, I suppose.'

'You were jealous, of *me*?'

'You were always Mother's favourite.'

'I was not!'

'And smarter than me. Talented. You had a good job in an office. I had a good job too, a start in the theatre. But Ellis had gone off and left me, and I'd just found out I was pregnant. I was about to lose everything. Then when you wouldn't lend me the money for the abortion, I was so angry. I knew you loved Alex —'

'Who's Ellis?'

'Oh, don't look at me like that! Ellis —' Lydia's voice broke and she brought her hands up for a moment, covering her face. When she lowered them, Claire saw her eyes were brimming. 'Ellis is Rory's father.'

There was a pounding at the front door and Lydia went down the hallway. Two sets of footsteps came back. Claire glanced up to see Alex. His face was grey with exhaustion, his brow creased. 'Thank God,' he said, reaching for her.

'How did you know where I was?'

'I tried to sleep after you rang, but I couldn't. So I went out to the Passage, spoke with Kath. She gave me Lydia's address.'

'Josh and Rory aren't here,' said Claire in a small voice.

Lydia took a deep breath and pointed towards the roadway. 'They went to the bus stop at the end of the road. I gave them money for the fare home.'

'How long ago?' broke in Alex.

Lydia shrugged. 'Half an hour, I suppose. They could still be there.'

'I'll go.' Alex raced off down the hallway.

'You told her to go home? Back to Tea-tree Passage?'

'Look, Claire. You're more of a mother to Rory than I can ever be. I know nothing about children.'

'She's nearly sixteen. Hardly a child,' Claire replied dryly. 'Rory's a great kid. I love her like she's my daughter. But that's the problem — she isn't. And she's dealing with lots of unresolved issues.'

'What do you want me to do?'

'Talk to her. Tell her the truth about her father. You owe her that much.'

Alex found Josh and Rory huddled in the bus stop. Their faces, turning towards him as he approached out of the darkness, were pale orbs in the glow of an overhead streetlight. 'What are you doing here?' asked Josh, looking surprised.

Alex sat down beside his son. 'I've come to take you home, mate.'

'What if I don't want to go?'

Alex shrugged. 'It's up to you. If you want to stay here, there's not much I can do about it. You're a bit big to throw over my shoulder.'

Josh managed a weak smile and glanced across at Rory. 'Where's my mother?' she asked Alex.

'Lydia's back up at her flat.'

'I meant Claire.'

'She's up there, too, waiting for you.'

Rory picked up her bag and walked back along the darkened street. Josh watched her go, then turned to his father.

'It's not going to be the same at home, with Mum gone.'

'No. I don't imagine it is. But you'll be off to uni soon, making a new life. Come home for a few weeks first.'

'Maybe.'

Rory let herself through Lydia's front door and walked back down the hallway to the living room. Lydia sat on a chair under the window.

'Where's Claire?'

'In the bathroom.' She patted the chair beside her, indicating that Rory should sit there. 'We need to talk.'

Warily Rory sat, facing her mother. Lydia was holding a small collection of photographs. She passed one to Rory.

'Who's this?'

'Your father.'

Rory peered closer, taking in the short fair hair and wide mouth, the American uniform. The woman with him was obviously Lydia. Much younger than the man, more youthful-looking, but the facial features were the same. They were both laughing into the lens of the camera, a moment frozen in time.

'His name was Ellis. I was four weeks pregnant with you when he went away,' Lydia said quietly, 'although I didn't know it at the time. When I did find out, he was already back in the States with his wife and children. At the time I didn't know about them either.'

Rory stared at the black-and-white image. 'So he never knew about me?'

'No.'

'Do you suppose he'd want to, after all this time?'

'Is that what you want?'

Rory shrugged, not knowing. 'No, not really. I just wanted to know who he was, that's all.'

She handed the photo back, but Lydia waved it away. 'Keep it,' she said, handing over the others she held in her hand. 'I'm sorry, Rory. Perhaps I should have told you ages ago. But the memories are terribly painful, even now.'

Rory glanced up to see Claire waiting in the doorway. She'd been so absorbed by the photograph that she'd failed to see her come into the room.

Claire gave her a tremulous smile. 'Hello, Rory.'

Somehow Rory got to her feet and walked across the room, tears streaming down her face. She wound her arms around Claire's neck and buried her face in that small hollow at the base of her throat.

Claire held her, awkwardly, her arms stiff. 'I'm sorry, Rory.'

Rory pulled away, staring at that familiar face. Unselfish, self-sacrificing Claire. Claire who had taken her as a child, her sister's baby, brought her up and lavished as much care and attention on her as though she'd been her own.

'*You're* sorry!' she sobbed. 'I'm the one who's been an absolute bitch. I wouldn't blame you if you never wanted to see me again.'

'Hey!' Claire raised Rory's face to her own. 'I think we've had enough excitement and tears during the last couple of days to last a lifetime. Let's go and find Alex and Josh.'

A bus screeched to a halt at the bus stop. Several passengers came down the stairs and wandered away into the dark, briefcases in hand. Alex stared at Josh, seeing a man in the shadows, not a boy. It was time he listened to the truth, accepted it.

In halting words he told him all the details about that first summer he'd met Claire, the promises he'd made. 'I loved her, from that first moment,' he said, his mind sliding back through the years, remembering how he'd first found her, sketching, down by the water.

He recalled Erica's pregnancy changing all his plans, the wedding and the miscarriage. 'We had no choice, Josh, your mother and I, though we tried to make the best of it. Later we had you and we were a family. I suppose we were happy for a time.'

'I can't remember my mother ever being happy.'

'We each have within ourselves the power of contentment. Some people are just restless souls, seeking more.'

'Do you think Mum was trying to find her own happiness?'

'Maybe.' Then he added, 'Contrary to what you might think, her death gave me no satisfaction. I'm a doctor, Josh. My job is to save lives.'

'How would you feel about me going to med school?' his son asked, changing the subject. 'I could come back to Tea-tree Passage later and join the practice.'

'I'd like that,' Alex replied simply.

'Me, too.'

'What about Rory? Do you plan to come back to her, too?'

'At least you didn't call her a kid. She's more grown-up than a lot of adults I know. But, as for the future, who knows? We're friends, that's all. Mates.'

Alex took a deep breath. He might as well tell Josh everything, seeing he was in a confessing mood. 'I want you to know that Claire and I plan to marry. Neither of us is getting any younger and she'd like children of her own. How would you feel about a brother or sister?'

Josh shrugged, grinned. 'Think you can handle the sleepless nights?'

Alex took a playful swipe at his son, and then said, 'Come on, let's go back to Claire and Rory.'

They both rose and Alex picked up Josh's bag. He slung one arm companionably over his son's shoulder as they headed along the road. Their shadows loomed out in front of them, long and angular, blurred edges melting into the dark. The bag bumped against his leg, a heavy weight.

He could see Claire, Rory and Lydia waiting ahead on the footpath outside Lydia's apartment building. Claire had her arm around Rory, in much the same fashion as he had his arm around his son, and a burst of laughter echoed towards him.

He had a sense, then, that everything would be all right. Josh was coming around, seeing things as they were, had been. Accepting the truth, and his own responsibilities.

And Rory?

As he and Josh came up to them, Claire gave him a smile and took his hand. 'We're ready to go home, Alex,' she said quietly. 'Back to Tea-tree Passage.'

WHEN

Wattles

Bloom

Robyn Lee Burrows

WHEN WATTLES BLOOM
ROBYN LEE BURROWS

Michael's thoughts went back to the Corduke house at 27 Brunswick Street — and to Bonnie and Freya, and Callie with the grey eyes. Why did Michael's father have a keepsake with Hannah Corduke's name engraved on the back? And just who was Ben?

Callie's family home — a symbol of security and love — is to be sold and she is trying hard to shake off the feelings of sadness and loss. When a sandy-haired stranger named Michael knocks at her mother's door asking questions about the family and great-aunt Hannah, Callie finds herself delving into secrets that have been long kept hidden. Together Michael and Callie start to unravel a love story between Hannah Corduke and a young blacksmith, Ben Galbraith. It's a story of true love, heartache and indomitable spirit that resonates through Callie's and Michael's own lives. What was Ben and Hannah's fate? And will the answer bring Michael and Callie together or pull them apart?

A poignant, romantic and moving story about love, loss and the circles of time.

ISBN 0 7322 6658 0